The Ides

PETER TONKIN

First published 2016 by Endeavour Press Ltd.

This edition published by Sharpe Books 2018.

ISBN: 9781790410774

TABLE OF CONTENTS

For Cham, Guy and Mark, as always. And with special thanks to Nick Slater.

I

The woman wriggled out of the window and her lively weight pulled at his arms like fish on a line. Artemidorus slipped forward until his head and shoulders also went through the gaping frame. The edge of the sill slid beneath his chest but it was wet and slimy. Like the tabletop he was lying on. The all too active burden tugging at his wrists threatened to pull him further out. The brutal wind seemed intent on sucking him through the hole in the wall and whirling him away. Rain pounded onto the back of his skull as though he had thrust himself into a waterfall. He teetered on the edge of disaster, fighting for control.

The secret agent steadied himself. Physically and mentally. He spread his knees on the solid piece of furniture wedged against the inner edge of the window to facilitate the escape. Glad of the thick leather of his military-style *bracchae* trousers, which ended at his knees but seemed to grip the wood better than skin and bone. 'Puella?' he called as loudly as he dared. 'Puella, what's wrong?'

The young woman who had just slithered through the frame, her fingers closed trustingly around his wrists, was known simply by her slave name as *Puella Africana*. Her full burden swung below him as he waited for her answer. Threatening to drag them both to destruction as she writhed. And the time he had allowed for the escape sped by. But she was slight, he assured himself spreading his knees wider, willing the leather covering them to grip the treacherous tabletop. She would find her footing soon and solve both problems at once. The arms holding her in the meantime had seen him through years in the legions to the rank of centurion in the VIIth. In the arena as a *provocator*, armed and equipped the same as he was as a legionary. Lethally expert with the *gladius* sword that gave gladiators their name. With the *pugio* dagger that matched it. These arms and shoulders were more than equal to the task of holding a slim young woman steady.

'I can't find it,' she answered his whispered question. 'It's not here!' At once he understood the movement threatening to pull the pair of them to disaster. Her body writhed as her feet

1

sought in the darkness for the first rung of the ladder he had left leaning against the wall when he climbed silently into the villa in order to break her free.

The brutal wind which had extinguished the tiny flame of his tallow candle and entombed them in darkness, backed suddenly. Smacked him in the face like a fist. Weather like this was not unusual in the month of Mars, this close to the New Year which was only fourteen days past. But, thought the Spartan spy with a bitter smile, this particular cataclysm seemed especially powerful. Almost personal in its spite. Perhaps he should have made a sacrifice to Janus, Roman god of doorways, on entering. Even though he had come through the window. For this was the two-faced god's season. Janus oversaw beginnings and endings as well as entrances and exits. The spy was certainly entering and exiting without due reverence. Independently of the fact that he was stealing a valuable slave from one of the most powerful men in the city.

And perhaps he should have left something for the household deities and ghostly *lares* at the shrine in the *atrium* when he also stole the knife that had lain there. Tucking it into his belt as he glanced up at the wax death masks of past generations, all watching him accusingly. And at the family tree adorning the wall. Tracing the house-owner's ancestry back through more than four hundred years to the founding of the Republic. The theft of the knife had been an impulse. Something about the weapon made him want to discuss it with Quintus, the veteran *optio* in charge of maintaining and issuing the weapons he used. Quintus, last of a rich and noble clan who had nothing but the legion as a family. Who stayed on, therefore, long after he had earned his release. Quintus, who they teased affectionately, calling him the last of the *triarii*. The theft certainly appeared to have upset one god or another. Unless, of course, he reckoned wryly, the tempest had a significance which was larger than one Spartan secret agent, his actions and omissions.

Whatever the reason, the stormy darkness beneath Artemidorus seemed disturbingly threatening and utterly blinding. Though in truth there was little enough to see. An ebony-haired, dark-skinned woman in a drab sleeping tunic, dangling down a brown-brick wall above a black-cobbled passageway between two tall patrician villas. Her face two arms' lengths below him. Her feet still the height of a man above the ground, scrabbling over the brick in search of that elusive ladder.

But then, a lightning fork lit up the entire sky. Its brightness lingered for two full heartbeats. He saw the woman's face as she looked up at him, eyes wide. Legs spread as they searched for the ladder. The ladder itself, sliding away across the edge of his vision. Kicked by an unwary foot or blown by the ferocious wind. Gone, in any case. Distractingly, he also saw the way her tunic had ridden up to leave her naked from her shoulders down. The way the brightness gleamed disconcertingly off her rain-polished nudity. It seemed that her entire body had been gilded with thick gold paint.

As though the huge bolt of lightning held some power over the storm itself, the wind dropped to silence as darkness slammed back. Everything was still for the briefest instant. As the ladder clattered onto the ground with sufficient noise to wake the *ostiarius* doorkeeper's dog. The dog's barks were lost at once beneath the most deafening rumble of thunder so far. As it echoed into silence, the dog redoubled its warnings. There was a stirring in the villa. Artemidorus glanced over his shoulder. The open doorway into the upper room from which they were escaping was suddenly defined by distant brightness as the household came awake. It would be a matter of mere heartbeats before someone noticed that one of the slaves was missing. Particularly as she was the master's current favourite.

Artemidorus released his grip on Puella's left hand and she opened her own fingers, allowing her shoulders to sag and lower her toes a few more precious *unicae* inches. He eased his grip on her right wrist. 'Run!' he spat.

'I can't,' she replied, her words just loud enough for him to hear. Her tone calm and controlled in spite of the danger. 'I can't see.'

'Downhill,' he ordered. 'Follow the slope. Towards the Forum. I'll catch up.' He doubted she heard the final promise for she had loosed her grip in turn and was gone.

He slid back, raising his torso and unexpectedly stabbing himself in the left buttock with the stolen knife tucked against his spine. The soldier's part of his mind marvelled at a blade sharp enough to cut through his heavy woollen tunic and thick leather trousers and into his flesh like that. He had never before seen a dagger with such an unusual, cross-topped handle – or ever come across a blade of such temper or quality. It had cut through Puella's leather slave collar effortlessly. He was fortunate not to have slit her throat with it. He doubted even wise old Quintus had seen anything like it.

He smacked the crown of his skull on the top of the window frame. The pain in his backside and thoughts of his *triarius* weapons expert distracting him as effectively as the vision of Puella's gilded nakedness had done. The hard edge would have brought blood had he not been wearing the leather cap of a freedman. Like the unfashionable barbarian beard hiding his lower face, it was part of the secret agent's current disguise as a handyman.

He hardly noticed the pain in his head, for he was focused on swinging round and easing himself back along the tabletop and out of the window as quickly as he could. If he didn't catch up with Puella before the doorkeeper and his dog did, then the fugitive slave was in deadly danger. By Roman law she was guilty of theft – having stolen herself from her owner. She could expect to be whipped, branded as a runaway and perhaps even crucified. All the careful undercover work he had done during the last few days while fixing damage to the villa would be utterly undone. Repairing damage carefully designed to grant him undercover access not only to the villa but to the servants and slaves within it.

The best of good fortune had led the secret agent to Puella and the secrets she knew within a matter of days. It had taken no time at all to convince her to run away with him. Had it been any other member of the household who agreed so readily, the spy would have been suspicious. In his world, there was a counterspy for every spy. But there was an innocence about the girl that rang true; a deeper motivation he had yet to understand. In the meantime it was his responsibility to keep her alive long enough to pass on what she had heard and seen.

For the knowledge in Puella's memory was simply too important to be put at risk, though she herself had no idea how significant it was. The secrets locked within her could change the course of history. Or, perhaps, stop the course of history from being altered by the villa's owner and his murderous associates. But only if Artemidorus got her safely to his handler, the spymaster and military tribune Enobarbus. And, together, they got her to the general in time to present him with unarguable proof that must spur him to immediate, decisive action.

The secret agent dangling from the sill of the open window had a list of suspicions gathered as he worked in the household, and gossiped apparently inconsequentially with whoever would talk to him there. The girl lost down in the darkness had the undeniable proof. He was a *speculator*. She was a witness. A witness full of the kind of proof both Enobarbus and the general demanded before they would consider taking action. The only witness he had.

*

Sudden brightness shone out above him. The *ostiarius* no doubt – racing up here from his post at the front door, carrying a lantern. Following the chilly drafts and the sound of the rain pouring in. Just about to find a cut slave collar lying on the floor. The slippery table. The gaping window.

Artemidorus loosed his grip on the sill and kicked clear of the wall as he dropped. He landed hard but fell into a roll and came up running at full tilt. There were shouts of surprise and anger above and behind him. They faded quickly enough as he took his own advice and began to pound downhill towards the Forum, guided by the slope beneath his feet rather than by anything he could actually see. And by the smell. Even in the midst of a deluge like this, his nostrils, more used to the relative cleanliness of legion encampments, twitched at the gathering stench of the city's bustling heart.

But the darkness overcame the guidance of both the streaming slope and the gathering stink. Long before he caught up with the girl as promised, Artemidorus smashed into an invisible outcrop of wall that sent him staggering. The slick soles of his sandals slithered across the cobbles and he went sprawling. He pulled himself to his feet at once and stood gasping, regretting the absence of the solid *caligae* he wore with his centurion's uniform. Their studded soles would have given much more purchase. But then, he reflected with a tight smile, the studded soles of a soldier's boots would hardly have been the ideal for creeping around a patrician villa in the middle of the night seeking to smuggle a slave girl out of the clutches of her traitorous master.

Although Artemidorus stood still only for a moment, the hesitation was sufficient to bring the doorkeeper, his half-wild guard dog and a pair of brawny household slaves down upon him. They were running fast and sure-footed because the doorkeeper had a lantern whose horn panels allowed almost as much light to beam out as came from the flaming torches carried by his companions. The hound clearly had the girl's scent, for it was running straight and sure, its nose close to the cobbles. Its chain taut from shaggy neck to master's fist. The spy reached for the knife he had stolen from the shrine in the *atrium*. Glancing around for a good place to stand and fight.

But the darkness befriended him. The light from the lantern and the torches revealed an angled house-front with a recessed doorway. He stepped silently back into the shadows of the doorway and watched the three slave-hunters run heedlessly past.

'If she gets to the Forum, our task will be harder,' snarled the doorkeeper to his companions. 'The dog will lose the *canicula* bitch's scent.'

They growled in agreement. Not much more civilised or house-trained than the dog, thought the Spartan. He stepped out of the shadows once more and joined their party. He ran at the same speed as they did but half a dozen paces back at the edge of the darkness, which also followed them silently down the roadway.

It took them hardly any time at all to catch up with the fleeing woman. She materialised like a ghost from the household shrine at the forward edge of the brightness. She glanced over her shoulder and the brightness caught the whites of her eyes. The three slave-hunters gave a universal growl of avarice and lust. There would be a fat reward for the return of Puella Africana, no doubt. But the way her sodden tunic clung to her offered a more carnal, more immediate, promise. As though she understood the depth of her danger, she ran on faster, still looking over her shoulder in terror. So that she also ran headlong into an unexpected thrust of wall. She bounced off the brick outcrop, apparently sure-footed enough to survive. But then her sandals slipped and she fell headlong onto the streaming roadway. The doorkeeper slowed, his lantern high and his dog straining at its chain. His cohorts slowed beside him. And their unsuspected follower slowed also, keeping far enough back to be hidden by shadows and downpour. Close enough to hear what they were saying.

'Right. You two go back,' ordered the doorkeeper as he came to a halt beside the fallen woman. 'Tell the master I have her and will bring her back soon.' The broad, squat-bodied *ostiarius* was a freedman. He wore the same leather cap as the disguised spy. His companions were slaves. They wore neck rings and name tags like the one Artemidorus had cut from Puella's throat. They would obey immediately and fully. Their lives might depend on it. 'And take this brute with you,' he added handing one of them the dog's chain, swapping it for a nasty-looking club. Artemidorus stepped back into the shadows as they pounded obediently past. Only the dog shot him a suspicious, golden-eyed glance before being dragged away.

This section of the street became quiet almost at once. Except for the wind and the rain. Artemidorus stepped out of one shadow into another and began to close up behind the unsuspecting doorkeeper. He pulled the stolen dagger out of his belt, slipping the cross-topped handle into his right fist and

7

letting the blade rest vertically against the skin of his inner forearm, the icy touch of the flat steel reaching almost from wrist to elbow. He could see the weapon in his mind's eye. A *pugio* like the dagger he carried with his *gladius* on the belt of his centurion's uniform. Except for that unusual handle. And, perhaps, for the almost magical keenness of the blade – two honed edges coming to a sharp steel point. But what steel it must be! He wished he had time to examine it properly. Perhaps when he was back with Quintus at the VII's camp on Tiber Island after this was all over. One way or another. If he lived to tell the tale. As he took another silent step forward he wondered once more why it had been in the little shrine in the first place. Then he dismissed the thoughts and focused on the matter in hand.

The doorkeeper was too intent upon his apparently helpless victim to register anything less intrusive than a full cohort of soldiers marching up behind him. Hobnailed *caligae* and all. The spy had no trouble in creeping closer as the doorkeeper continued to poke at the stunned woman with the end of his club. The man had the bandy legs, squat spine and massive shoulders of a bull. The short, fat neck of an ox. The head on top of all this looked ridiculously small. But it was neither the head nor the shoulders that interested Artemidorus.

'You're in trouble, girl,' continued the doorkeeper. 'You know the mistress, Lady Porcia, has been in a foul mood since she got that knife wound in her thigh. And the master, Lord Brutus, has hardly been any better. And as for his mother the Lady Servilia... You'll be lucky if they only crucify you. I'd bet that they'll flog you half to death and let all us menfolk have you first. The master won't want to keep you for himself any longer. Not when you would rather run than pleasure him. No. We'll all have you, I'll bet. Freedmen and slaves. As often as we want.' The end of the club was pushing at the hem of her tunic now, easing it up her thighs. 'If you let me in first, though,' continued the doorkeeper, 'we might be able to work something out.'

Which was as far as he had got in his one-sided bargaining before Artemidorus stepped past him. 'What...' he demanded,

8

confused by the sudden intrusion of a large, square shoulder between himself and his victim. With his lantern in one fist and the club in the other, he didn't know what to do with his hands. He straightened, the tiny brain in the tiny head seeking to make sense of the unexpected situation. The stranger said nothing. Still facing away from him, he took one more step forward and half-turned. The last thing that the doorkeeper saw was a blur of the stranger's arm lashing back towards him at neck level. The last thing he felt was a sharp pain in the pit of his throat.

It was a move Artemidorus had perfected for his brief career in the arena. He called it *The Scorpion* and the manoeuvre had become so famous he had taken it for his fighting name: *Scorpionis*. As he stepped past the doorkeeper, he allowed the blade of the stolen dagger to slide away from his inner arm until it stood out at right angles behind his fist. Then he drove it backward as hard and fast as he could. The point went unerringly into the pit of the doorkeeper's throat. It passed through the tubes there and slid between the vertebrae buried at the back of his thick neck, severing the great nerve of his spinal cord without cutting the blood vessels on either side. Then it wedged between the articulated bones which joined his skull to his spine. A finger-length of blade protruding just above the collar of his tunic. He might as well have been beheaded. In an instant, his lungs forgot how to breathe, his heart forgot how to beat and his legs forgot how to stand. There was no sound. No blood. Nothing but an instant and permanent cessation of life.

The doorkeeper collapsed, the expression on his face one of mild surprise. The weight of his body pulled the handle of the knife from the spy's grip. Artemidorus caught the lantern as it fell and used his free hand to pull the dazed girl to her feet. She looked at the corpse and shuddered. 'Take me away,' she said, turning. Artemidorus turned at her side.

Then the pair of them froze. An unearthly animal scream rang out. Two red-gold points of light at the inner edge of the darkness showed Artemidorus that the doorkeeper's dog had escaped from the slaves and returned seeking its master. Its howls were probably all he'd get by way of an elegy. But the noise the animal was making would bring the rest of the household back in moments. He took one last look at the dagger wedged immovably in the doorkeeper's throat. Then he looked away. No point in lingering. Out of time.

Another bolt of lightning pulsed down, dead ahead. Lighting the downhill slope of the road to the Forum in front of them. Making the streaming water look like a river of gold. The picture was so striking that the pair of them hesitated, entranced, while it persisted – the brown brick walls on either side apparently gilded. Like the statue of Cleopatra so recently erected in the Forum beside that of the Goddess Venus Genetrix. The cobbled roadway ahead of them a river running deep with molten gold. Then, before the thunder could come – or the slave-catchers return – he said again, '*Run!*'

*

Puella obeyed automatically, her mind full of conflicting thoughts and fears. Seemingly unconnected to the body so thoughtlessly doing what her rescuer commanded. It was as though the storm had somehow entered her with all its wild and terrifying disorder. As though she was running from herself, as well as the peril she had got herself mixed up in. As though, in the end, she was running from Artemidorus and all the threats and promises, dreams and dangers he represented.

The doorkeeper's death shocked her terribly. She had seen death before, of course, on rare visits to the arena with Lord Brutus, Lady Porcia or the Lady Servilia. But those deaths had been distant, down on the sand. And full of religious significance; blood shed and lives lost to honour the gods. The doorkeeper's brutal execution had had nothing sacred about it. Indeed, she felt that she herself had caused it because her rescuer had done it to protect her. And he had done it within arm's reach of her. But that terrifying dagger blow had saved her from rape – and worse. For she had no illusions about what would have happened to her had the doorkeeper taken first advantage of her. A fate from which the man who got her into this chaos in the first place had ultimately preserved her.

Her rescuer. She glanced over her shoulder at him as he ran close on her heels, illuminating her path and his face with the dead doorkeeper's horn-sided lantern. This tall, powerful freedman with light-coloured hair curling out from beneath his leather cap, his thick red beard and his strange eyes that seemed one moment the colour of smoke and the next the colour of steel. This self-styled *libertus* freedman who showed no sign at all of ever having been a slave. Who moved, rested, did everything with a soldier's confident swagger. Who had transformed himself so rapidly, so magically, from a casual labourer to a heroic being filling her mind with fascinating stories. Who had come to fill her dreams as well.

In spite of her name, Puella Africana had never been further from Rome than the *latifundia* country estate just north of Capua in Campania owned by the Lady Servilia's second husband, the late Consul Decimus Junius Silenus, Lord Brutus's stepfather. Here in the northernmost of the areas known as *Magna Graecia*, she had been born on a whim of the consul's; the issue of a couple of Ethiopian slaves matched for colour and feature like a pair of horses destined to pull a chariot in a race or at a triumph. She never met her father who was sold on before her birth and had no memory of her mother who died from tertian fever soon after the infant Puella was weaned. But all her life, in the households first of the Lady Servilia and later in that of Lord Brutus, she had heard of the wonders to be found on the outer reaches of the empire she would never get the chance to explore.

Lord Brutus was spoken of as an able administrator. Though by reputation a governor – and landlord – noted for his greed. He often talked of his work with his uncle Quintus Servilius Caepio and, later, of another uncle, Marcus Porcius Cato. Father to cousin Porcia Catonis, whom Brutus had taken as his second wife. Much to the anger of his own mother, the Lady Servilia. It was strange that he surrounded himself with uncles and stepfathers when the identity of his own father was somehow open to question. So the gossip went. Cato and Lord Brutus were together in Cyprus and Cilicia, which were apparently untamed and fascinating lands. Full of wonderful sights, strange peoples and wild pirates. But the other household members who had accompanied him looked pityingly at her when she begged details from them. Keeping the master's accounts in Salamis or Tarsus was no different from keeping them in Rome, they shrugged. The same could be said of cooking his meals or tidying his quarters.

Moreover, Lord Brutus's occasional visitor, his brother-in-law the soldier-statesman Cassius, also told of his adventures escaping distant, dangerous Parthia. Leading to safety the last survivors of the seven legions Marcus Licinius Crassus lost so disastrously along with his head. All wiped out at the battlefield of Carrhae in distant Mesopotamia. Of his naval actions as Pompey's fleet commander destroying Caesar's navy off Sicily in the recent civil wars. But such tales were snippets overheard as she served men who hardly registered her presence. Like other, darker and more dangerous information. As they lay eating, drinking, reminiscing, planning and plotting.

Her Greek hero, however, with Ulysseus' red beard and roving spirit, talked to her. Directly to her. And more and more often as he came to know her better. Held her wide and ardent gaze as he told tales of battles, adventures and wonders in places even Lord Cassius had never visited. For, although he was a common workman now, Artemidorus had been a soldier. He could talk of Egypt, from the Pharos lighthouse of Alexandria to the Library; from the Theban Valley of the Kings to the wonders of the timeless Pyramids. And even the extravagances of Queen Cleopatra's court. Of wild northern Gaul and the long-haired barbarians haunting the black forests there. Of the legendary Spartacus and his army of slaves and gladiators. Of Cilician pirates with whom he had sailed as captive, against whom he had fought in his youth beside the Divine Caesar himself.

And the tales had won her, though she did not yet understand how each of them had been bait on a hook designed to tempt from her in return those very snippets of gossip that Artemidorus was currently making her carry to the men he said he worked for. The Tribune Enobarbus and the as yet nameless, mysteriously powerful figure they simply called 'the general'.

*

Even at this time of night, part way through the third night watch, the Forum was a hubbub. In spite of the torrential rain, storm winds, dazzling lightning and deafening thunder, the heart of the city was beating as strongly as ever. Wagons, forbidden during daylight hours, hauled goods from the nearby family-owned farms and patrician-owned *latifundia* to the shops that stood beneath the tall *insulae* blocks of flats. To the warehouses that stood behind them. Hauled stone and brick to the part-completed as yet unnamed basilica, beside which they entered the open Forum itself. To the *Basilica Aemeilia* which bustled all along its three *actus*, three hundred and sixty foot, length. The better part of fifty shops there alone. With the Macellum fruit market beyond.

The markets were open for shopkeepers to top up their stock rather than to conduct business. That didn't stop them turning a denarius or two of profit, however, by selling to the drovers, farmers and merchants anything they wanted to buy. And the gamblers, dice and knucklebone men, the prostitutes and pimps, bullies and footpads all crowded there. Also keen to relieve the yokels of their money. Warily watched by the *triumviri capitales*' police patrols out to fight fires and keep the peace under the orders of the local *aedile* magistrate.

Everything in the centre of the city was a roar of commerce and a blaze of light. Light which travelled far enough up the house-packed hillsides to give the two running fugitives a beacon to head for and the brightness to guide them. And the stench to offend their nostrils.

As Artemidorus ran at Puella's side past the tall, wood-scaffolded building site which was the nameless basilica, he felt the weight of tension begin to lift from his shoulders for the first time in one of the Divine Gaius Julius Caesar's new seven-day weeks. Like the law forbidding wagons within the city during the day, the calendar had been introduced less than two years ago and he wasn't quite used to it yet; still feeling vaguely robbed of the eighth day of the old week he had grown up with.

This time exactly seven nights ago, Artemidorus had thrown the first stone up onto the villa's roof with sufficient force to smash a roof tile. Like his expertise with sword and dagger, he had been trained by Quintus in the use of *pilum* spear, the bow and arrow, and the sling. The venerable *optio* had also schooled him in the simple skill of throwing rocks with consistent accuracy. On the first of the rocks was written, 'Brutus. See. Strike.' He also held another with, 'Shall there be a king in Rome while a Brutus lives?' scrawled on it. These messages were copied from the graffiti adorning some of the walls nearby. Messages which, according to spymaster Tribune Enobarbus, had been thrown into the *atrium* and even the *peristyle* garden of Brutus's house during the last few nights. The work of Gaius Cassius and his men. Like the graffiti. Which was why a couple of Artemidorus's colleagues were working undercover in Cassius' house as well.

The mission Tribune Enobarbus had given Artemidorus was simply to get into Brutus' household and find out what effect all these messages were having on the man who famously displayed on his *atrium* wall a family tree tracing his ancestry back to the man who had founded the Republic. Lord Brutus might be hesitant about joining Cassius' conspiracy, but he clearly saw himself as the latest son of an ancient aristocratic family whose forefather, Lucius Junius Brutus, had rid Rome of the last king more than four centuries earlier, founding the Republic of which so many patricians were so proud. A man likely enough, therefore, to die – or even to kill – in order to protect it. Which was why the Spartan spy had started throwing rocks at Brutus' villa seven nights ago.

It was the size of the rocks Artemidorus threw with Cassius' messages on them that damaged the roof. As he had planned they should. Damage which he, disguised as a freedman, offered to repair when he passed next day. Apparently by chance. An offer almost inevitably accepted by Brutus's household. After all, it was better to employ a cheap freedman to do dangerous roof work than to risk killing or crippling a slave who might be expensive to replace. The spy eased himself into the household routines, exactly as he had planned, while he came and went about his business. Discovering more damage than they had suspected; drawing out the time it would take to repair. As he began to find out crucial details of the plot in which Cassius was trying to involve Brutus, Enobarbus' fears soon proved to wildly underestimate the apparent reach and the danger of the conspiracy, and its immediacy.

During those seven days, Artemidorus swiftly built a list of patricians apparently directly involved. He had a roll of nearly twenty names within four days, and a growing suspicion that they wanted to act before the festival of *Quinquatria* on the 19th day of Mars, when the objective of all this murderous plotting planned to leave for a military campaign against the Parthians. A campaign and departure date which his old friends in the VIIth Legion, camped on Tiber Island, had been warned about long since. But as to Brutus, Cassius and their plans, he had none of the proof Enobarbus demanded before he dared take action against so many honourable, honoured, trusted and powerful men. Only a crushing certainty that time was fast running out.

Then Puella offered salvation. The beautiful, dark-skinned woman was her master's current favourite. She attended him on almost all domestic occasions – and sometimes even at social meetings. At home and around in the city. There was no doubt in anybody's mind that as soon as his preoccupation with Cassius' secret matter was over, he would take the nubile slave to his bed. Particularly as his wife the Lady Porcia, had somehow managed to cut her thigh. She had revealed the fact to no one, and had done little enough to treat it; like her father, a follower of the Stoic philosophy, to whom bodily demands – hunger, thirst, pain, ambition, joy and sorrow – were second to mental and spiritual fortitude. The wound was now badly infected. Her health was suffering. Her bed was closed to him, even though by all accounts his heart and mind were lately open to her.

In among all this gossip and rumour, Puella innocently revealed that she had been witness to several of the meetings about which the spy and his handler had only heard whispers. And if he would help her escape, she would tell her story to Artemidorus' Tribune Enobarbus.

On the darkest watch of the fourth night, therefore, with an ironic smile and an amused shake of his head, Artemidorus scrawled *'Brutus vigilat'* – 'Brutus wake up' on the largest stone yet and hurled it unerringly through the tiny upper window, utterly destroying it. The noise had made not only Brutus but the entire house wake up. And the window's repair had been added to the list of jobs the cheerfully accommodating workman was employed to do when he returned to the villa next morning. Yesterday morning, in fact. It had taken one full working day and part of the next to finish the roof repairs and replace the frame of the shattered window with one designed to lift out. Allowing silent entry for one – and equally silent exit for two.

But all that was behind them now. What lay ahead was a desperate race to collate all the suspicions, test the proofs and witness, and get it all first to Tribune Enobarbus and then to the man Centurion Artemidorus of the *Legio VII* still thought of as the general, in spite of the fact that he was currently no longer holding military office. But he was still the man who commanded Enobarbus and, through him, the entire network that Artemidorus worked for. The only man whose intervention might bring the terrible plot to an abrupt and fruitless end.

Co-consul of the Republic Mark Antony.

*

Artemidorus and Puella slowed as they entered the Forum. But they could not afford to stop. Pursuit would be swift and even more ruthless now. The runaway slave was accompanied by the murderer of a freedman. A freedman servant of the most powerful aristocratic household in the city. The full weight of the Twelve Tables of Law would come down on them thought the spy with one of his brief, wry smiles – and neither could hope for the great lawyer Marcus Tullius Cicero to defend them. For Cicero's name was written right up at the top of his precious list of probable conspirators. Just under the names of Cassius and Brutus, in fact.

Neither the fugitive slave nor her murderous companion were Roman citizens. Citizens could face the death penalty only for treason. Or for killing their fathers, as the famous trial of Sextus Roscius had shown nearly thirty-five years ago. In Cicero's first great case. Therefore Puella and Artemidorus, would be crucified if they were caught. Unless, as the doorkeeper had said, the slave was scourged, branded, raped or forced to suffer whatever fate her master, his wife or his terrible mother decreed. Unless the murderer was sentenced to *dejection* – being thrown from the Tarpean Rock. Or *projection* – being chucked into the Tiber to drown. Or decapitation. Or strangulation. Or being sent to the galleys. A fate in many ways worse than death.

The first obstacle to the fugitives' progress was a huge ox cart dragging high-stacked baskets of fish up from the Tiber wharves, heading for the *pisces tabernas* fish shops of the *Basilica Aemilia*. The massive animal emptied its bladder and bowels onto the ground as it passed them and the pounding rain washed the liquid away while instantly beginning to liquefy the more solid matter. The combined stench of fish and defecation was overpowering. And the association of the beast's activities seemed to stir something in Puella. She suddenly started looking desperately around. Her face betraying much more tension than it had shown as she hung out of the window. 'Where are you taking me?' she demanded as they passed upriver of the ox-droppings. Preserving their sandals as best they could. And were immediately caught in the scarcely more fragrant swirl of equally rain-soaked men, women, animals and vehicles. All laden with baskets from which issued an eye-watering array of stenches.

'As I told you, first to some friends, then on to the tribune…'

'No. *Exactly* where?'

'To the *insulae* over there.' He gestured to a tall building that loomed above the bright shops away to their left. 'Why?'

Then he understood. Puella was looking for the nearest public lavatories. He took a deep breath – instantly regretted it – and gave a mental shrug. A visit would slow their progress towards their most immediate goal. But it was unlikely their pursuers would look for them in the lavatory. A visit might give them a chance for a little more discussion. To clear up one or two points that still concerned him. Particularly about her motivation. And, as it chanced, the nearest one was close to the *insulae* he was planning to visit. 'Come on,' he said. He took her hand. As though she was a girl in fact rather than a young woman. And began to shoulder his way through the crowd.

The lavatory was ill-lit but they were lucky to find it lit at all. The dead doorkeeper's lantern added just enough brightness to emphasise the gloom. The latrine was continually cleaned by water running down into the great sewer of the *Cloaca Maxima*. So it smelt a good deal better than the Forum outside. With some relief, Artemidorus noticed that Puella did not pull a stick with a sponge on the end out of the *amphora* of vinegar near the door. She was planning on emulating only one part of the ox's performance, therefore. And, now he thought of it, Artemidorus decided that he could invest some time doing the same. Better now than later when it might not be so convenient. So they ended up sitting side by side on the icy stone bench with its openings on top and in front. The lantern sat between them. Puella gathered her sodden tunic around her waist unselfconsciously and Artemidorus held his lowered *bracchae* taut between his ankles, keeping them clear of the floor.

Artemidorus looked around the walls of the place apparently idly as he ordered his thoughts and planned his questions. Walls which were decorated with pictures, mosaics and graffiti. The mosaics, augmented by some of the paintings and almost all of the graffiti, illustrated a variety of sexual positions. The pictured activity was by no means as adventurous as that to be found in the public baths, but it was still colourful and lively. All around the room, men and women were pictured taking vigorous carnal enjoyment of each other. The flickering shadows strangely seeming to give them life. He on top. She on top. They, side by side – front to front. Back to front. Legs up. Legs down. Standing. Lying. Kneeling. Partially clothed. Utterly naked. Several couples in positions that would have been familiar to the dead doorkeeper's dog...

The spy dragged his mind back to the task in hand. He was taking Puella to see his most immediate associates, who were for the moment living on the top floor of the *insula* nearby, pretending to be a married couple. For the last few days they had been working in the kitchens of another of Enobarbus' list of supposed conspirators. Whose own kitchen staff had suddenly succumbed to a serious bout of food poisoning which fortunately was not passed to the rest of the house. A ruse Artemidorus had suggested – though he had no idea how Enobarbus had managed to pull off such a precise poisoning. Or get his own people into the suddenly vacated kitchen. The husband-and-wife team were called Telos and Cyanea. What they discovered in their undercover assignment would add yet more weight, he hoped, to what he suspected and what Puella remembered. Thus bolstering her confidence to reveal every detail of the facts she knew. But there were those few nagging points he wanted cleared up before they left the latrine.

They were by no means alone, but Artemidorus thought them safe enough from eavesdroppers. 'Are you running away from your master's attentions, like the doorkeeper said?' He asked. It was the one major element of her motivation they had not yet examined. And he had lived in the shadowy world of espionage for long enough to know that motivation was sometimes the most important element of all. Usually it was sex, money, fear, spite, revenge, pain or desperation. Occasionally – rarely – love, honour, patriotism. But which one of the great motivators moved Puella?

'No. Not entirely...' Her voice was steady, her tone thoughtful. As though she was preparing to reveal something she had dared not discuss in the Junian family villa itself.

'What, then?'

19

'Every time he has taken one of the girls to his bed, she has sickened and died soon after.' He had to strain to hear her answer.

'Is he diseased? He looks to me to be exhausted, not infected. Not like the Lady Porcia with her poisoned leg…' He probed further. Quietly. Gently. If she ever got to know him better she would learn that he was at his most dangerous when he was quiet. Gentle.

'It's not him.' She looked down. 'He seems as shocked and upset by the deaths as anyone else. It is… I'm sure it must be either…'

'What? *Who*?' he recast his question shrewdly. 'Not the Lady Porcia, even if she has been his wife for less than a year. Like her father she is a believer in the Stoic philosophy, I believe, more likely to accept the fact and bear the pain – as she has done with her leg.'

'No. I believe it is his mother. The Lady Servilia. She has not yet forgiven him for divorcing the Lady Claudia Pulchra and taking his cousin the Lady Porcia as his wife last June. She visits regularly and is civil to both of them. But there is still rage there… And moreover… She has a reputation…'

'… that she cultivates wolfsbane…' he suggested tactfully, nodding as he understood precisely what she feared. Rumours abounded about Servilia Caepionis, embittered ex-mistress of the Divine Julius. A mistress whose son, the Lord Brutus, Julius may even have sired in his distant youth. So went some of the gossip, at least. But the gossip about the Divine Julius, perpetual Dictator and Co-Consul of Rome, was endless. Sexually. Militarily. Historically. Speculatively. Politically. Dangerously.

Puella glanced at him, her eyes huge. There was the tiniest affirmative nod.

'… and Lady Servilia distils the juices…' he continued. 'How apt that it should be called The Mother-In-Law's Poison. Were the dying women incontinent? Did they complain of burning? Mouth? Face? Belly?'

Puella's eyes opened even wider in wordless confirmation. And he nodded wisely. Aconite, he thought. An even deadlier

20

poison than the hemlock drunk by Socrates. Such knowledge was mother's milk to the men and women living in the secret shadows he inhabited. The girl would be shocked, horrified, if she knew a tenth of the things he knew. A hundredth of the things he had done.

'Another thing,' added Artemidorus suddenly. 'Why was there a knife in the family shrine?'

Puella gave a bark of humourless laughter. Much more confident now. 'The Lady Servilia again. It was the second of a pair of knives she gave Lord Brutus and Lady Porcia. The first seems to have been cursed. No matter who used it, the thing cut them. To the bone. The cook, the kitchen slaves. The blade was almost magical, though in truth it was fitter for the battlefield than the kitchen. They say she had it sent from the East. From the furthest reaches of Alexander's empire. It may even have been that knife which wounded the Lady Porcia's thigh. I don't know what happened to it in the end. That is... No, I don't remember. Is it important?'

'Probably not...'

'But the second knife, Lord Brutus's, was out in the shrine so the household gods would bless it. Drive out the evil...'

'So, you think that Vesta, goddess of hearth and home, is more powerful than the Lady Servilia?' he teased, pulling up his trousers and grabbing hold of the lantern.

'Not in this world,' she laughed, shaking her head as she too stood up and adjusted her tunic. 'And possibly not in the next.'

II

The *ostiarius* of the *insula* where Artemidorus' fellow spies Telos and Cyanea were lodging was called Vitus. He and his dog Canem answered at the first knock. They both knew the visitor well and signified the fact with a nod of the head and a lick of the tongue. Then they turned their attention to Puella. She offered a hand to each one and they all seemed to become friends at once.

'She hasn't been here, Vitus,' said Artemidorus to the doorkeeper, nodding towards the girl. 'You haven't seen her.'

'I won't go around announcing her presence,' he answered. 'But if anyone serious comes looking for her, then they'll only have to ask forcefully enough.'

'I know,' said Artemidorus. 'They'll be able to beat it out of you with a feather. Fair enough. You don't owe us anything.'

The doorkeeper nodded. 'Visiting as usual?'

'As usual.' Artemidorus slipped him a gold Caesar denarius. The sort that the Divine Julius had issued to the legions that had crossed the Rubicon behind him. The VIIth among them. Without even seeming to look at the newly minted coin, the doorkeeper slid it into the leather purse at his waist. 'Some of that is for Janus,' warned Artemidorus.

The *ostiarius* looked sideways at the spy. 'I'll toss him for it. He can keep what he catches.'

Artemidorus gave a bark of laughter. The doorkeeper picked up a smoking tallow candle and led the way along a dark corridor towards a set of steep, narrow stairs. The dog trotted at his heels. The spy and the slave girl followed. He still held the lantern.

'You're up late, Vitus,' observed Artemidorus as the doorkeeper led them onto flight after flight of stairs. He had to raise his voice. The raving of the storm outside was matched by the various sounds and snatches of conversation coming through the flimsy walls inside. The spy wondered whether the slave girl would be shocked by some of what she heard. Lord Brutus's villa would be like the Temple of the Vestal Virgins compared to this.

'It's the weather,' announced Vitus after a while. 'That's why we're wide awake, Canem and me. One of these cheaply built *insulae* collapsed last week. It wasn't raining half as hard as this. No thunderbolts then either. Still managed to kill and injure a good number of the *plebeian* residents and the doorkeeper there. They dug him out last. Never found his dog. A good friend of mine. And the month before, another one burned down during that cold snap at *Terminalia* on 23 *Februarius*, the end of last year. Did you hear about that? Thought not. Yet more poor *plebs* and their families roasted like dormice at a feast. Both death-trap slums were owned by his worship Marcus Tullius Cicero. This one is owned by the Junii family as you probably know. Marcus Junius Brutus himself is the landlord. Tight-fisted *spurius…*'

Suddenly Artemidorus felt Puella very close behind him. Her breath on his neck. Panting. Shortened by exercise. Or fear. They had climbed five flights already and Artemidorus knew there were three more to go. Luckily the doorkeeper's pace was slackening as he began to puff and limp. Puella crowded even closer. She smelt of a familiar, fragrant herb. Hyssop, he thought as his nostrils flared. He hadn't noticed that before. Moved by a combination of compassion and sudden desire, he turned and handed her the doorkeeper's lantern. The light would make her feel safer, he thought.

'Lord Brutus's rents are higher than Cicero's but his buildings are not much safer,' the doorkeeper continued apparently unaware of the reaction he had caused by naming the landlord. 'At least we don't have to worry about fire tonight,' he observed at last, chuckling breathlessly as he led them to the top-storey apartment, his left leg beginning to drag more obviously. 'Here we are. I'm afraid it's only one room now, for young master Telos has been forced to sub-let the inner room to meet a rise in the rent. The rise in rent hasn't led to much civic improvement, mind. The roof still leaks so badly that the occupants below are more likely to drown than to burn.' He stopped on the threshold and turned, holding his light high. 'You know, there have already been complaints tonight about dampness oozing through the ceilings into the apartments downstairs on floors seven and six.'

'This is the home of my friends and associates Telos and Cyanea,' Artemidorus explained to Puella. 'You'll meet them in a moment but before you do it might be as well if I told you one or two things about them. Just as I have been working in the house of Lord Brutus...' he paused until he saw the full implication of what he had said sink in. The pause also gave him a moment to school his expression. To conceal a deeper truth. That he and Cyanea were lovers. Had been passionately re-enacting many of the illustrations from the wall of the public latrine for several months past. 'They have been working for his brother-in-law Cassius. They too have a list...' he frowned, wondering if he was taking too much of a risk explaining this in front of the *ostiarius* who, by his own admission, would reveal everything he knew to someone who frowned at him sufficiently fiercely. But they were on first-name terms. Moreover, Telos trusted Vitus. And Artemidorus trusted Telos' judgement. 'They have a list,' he emphasised. 'But no witness. No proof. Unless things have changed quite radically since I saw them both earlier this evening.'

Artemidorus turned and raised his fist to hammer on the door into the tiny flat. The doorkeeper turned away. 'Wait,' called Artemidorus. 'Vitus. Wait.' There had been enough light for him to see something disturbing. He lowered his fist and opened his hand. Used his palm gently to push at the door. Which creaked open an inch or two with a groan of tortured hinges. Sagged brokenly to one side. The door-foot scraped against the floorboards. Stopped. The flickering light showed a simple bolt, shattered. 'This has been kicked in,' said the spy, quietly, his voice a dangerous sing-song. 'Puella, you wait there. Many strangers about in the last couple of watches, Vitus?'

*

'No strangers that I noticed especially,' answered the doorkeeper thoughtfully, turning and bringing his tallow candle closer. 'People coming and going all night. You know how it is. I got more whores than cockroaches in some of these rooms. They don't all work in the *lupanarae* brothels.' He suddenly looked bigger. More threatening. He was responsible for the safety of the residents. He did not take kindly to this sort of thing. Like many in his trade, he was a retired soldier, late of *Legio VI Ferrata*, Caesar's Ironclads, Artemidorus knew. Wounded during the debacle in Alexandria. Lucky to survive; invalided out. Still walked with a limp, especially when his legs got tired.

With the smoky golden light from the candle behind him, Artemidorus pushed the door again. It screamed wider. Sagging door-foot juddering across the floor. Both men padded in – spy first then doorkeeper. Both moving like soldiers on a battlefield. One step in and they were shoulder to shoulder, tallow candle high, surveying the wreckage. Artemidorus frowned. The room seemed even smaller than he remembered it. This afternoon it had contained a modest wicker chest with some clothing in it. A bed just large enough for two – though Telos, he knew, slept on the floor. A straw mattress and a thin blanket. A terracotta bowl that contained their modest fish and *puls* wheat-porridge dinner during the first watches and their night soil in the later ones. No table – they sat on the bed to empty the bowl. No latrine – they squatted in the corner to fill it. A tiny wood-shuttered window under the eaves out of which they emptied it once again in the morning. Before scrubbing it clean at the nearest public fountain and filling it at the fish kitchen on the way home. A couple of horn spoons. Some wooden-backed wax tablets and a stylus for making notes. A cheap little lamp capable of giving just enough light to use the tablets. A pewter crucible and a ball of beeswax for repairing and reusing them. A man that he respected and a woman he loved. And none of it was as he had left it when the water clocks that counted the daylight hours stopped with the sunset and the first night watch began. When he had departed in the darkness to collect his ladder, to break into Lord Brutus's villa and bring Puella out.

'Looks like things might have changed since sunset,' said Vitus quietly. 'Quite a lot, in fact.'

Artemidorus grunted. Nothing that had been in the room as he last saw it was where – or as – it had been. The wicker basket lay spread, gutted. The clothing it had contained strewn all over the floor. The bed was in pieces, the mattress disembowelled and the straw scattered as though this was a home for horses rather than humans. The bowl was shattered. Artemidorus stooped and picked the largest shard up. Brought it to his nose as he studied the others. Some of them were smeared with blood. It had been broken over someone's head. Or in someone's face. It had contained the last of the fish supper. None of the night soil. 'First watch,' he said.

Vitus nodded silently, his eyes as busy as the spy's but seeing nowhere near as much.

Puella and Canem stepped silently into the carnage, adding to the light. Which was not necessarily a good thing. Neither one looked happy to be here. Artemidorus could see the girl's point at least. Since he brought her out of Lord Brutus's villa on the promise of protection and safety, she had been hunted, brutalised, nearly raped and watched a man die at far closer quarters than even the arena offered. Now here she was in a tiny room that reeked of yet more violence. No wonder she looked less than happy. And frozen to the bone, judging by the way her skin was gathered into goosebumps and her nipples stood erect.

A little lamp lay beside the shattered bowl, miraculously unbroken. The spy stooped and picked it up. Shook it. On hearing the sound of oil sloshing from side to side, he held it beside the tallow candle in Vitus' fist until the wick caught, then he knelt, carefully, and used the light to look more closely at the wreckage. Out of the scattered straw he pulled several writing tablets. They were of standard design – wooden boards covered in thin skims of wax, secured in pairs by cloth straps or metal rings so that the wax faces could close on one another and protect the writing on each surface. But they had been torn apart now. Some of the delicate wooden panels were broken in half, others splintered altogether. At least one contained a footprint – or part of one. Studded boot soles. Soldiers had done this. Or gladiators, perhaps. Someone wearing *caligae*, at least. He held their slick wax surfaces to the lamp flame, nodded, and piled them together, splinters and all. The next thing he did was to pick up some of the scattered clothing. First a woman's tunic. A day tunic, much more substantial than the sleeping tunic the shivering Puella was wearing. 'Here,' he said passing it to her. 'Put this on. It will be loose. But it's dry and it's better than the one you've got on.'

Puella took it. Put the lantern on the floor. Without a second thought, she hauled up the sodden one and slipped it over her head. Artemidorus caught Vitus' eye and the doorman hurriedly looked away as the young woman pulled the warm, dry garment over a starkly naked body illuminated graphically from below by the lantern by her feet. Apparently painted with gold once again. The spy pulled another tunic free of the mess and copied Puella's action. But whereas her new tunic was a little too big, his was too small, stretching over his torso like a second skin. As she looked at him Puella's gaze suddenly became almost as speculative as Vitus' had been as he had fleetingly observed her nudity. Something answering stirred in the spy. But he dismissed it at once. There were other relationships at risk here. Lives and limbs as well, he calculated. He had to keep his mind clear and focused.

'And you saw nothing?' he asked the doorkeeper. 'At least four, I would have thought. Large men. Soldiers or gladiators. Four coming in. Six coming out, given that they've taken Telos and Cyanea. And you saw *nothing*?' For the first time, he was beginning to lose faith in Telos' judgement of people.

'About the middle of the first watch,' explained Vitus, 'there was a big fight outside the fish stall down towards the basilica. The end one, near the Macellum fruit market. Couple of whores going at it like *gladiatrices*. I went down to look. So did half the Forum. They put on quite a show. I'm surprised Caesar didn't come out of his quarters in the *Domus Publicus* for a look.'

He was probably still at dinner with Marcus Aemilius Lepidus his magister equitum, thought Artemidorus, who followed Caesar's movements as closely as possible, information added to by meetings with and messages from Enobarbus. The last one of which should be somewhere among the rubbish on the floor, a tiny piece of parchment covered in the tribune's favourite code. Apparently the recently appointed *praetor peregrinus*, Decimus Brutus Albinus, was there as well – two of Caesar's best generals and closest allies. Truest friends to both co-consuls Caesar and Marc Antony. Though only Caesar had been at dinner; Antony, as ever, out and about. But Artemidorus did not allow the knowledge to distract him from the matter in hand. 'The old days were the best,' he said grimly. 'When they chained *ostiari* to their door post like dogs.'

Vitus shrugged. 'You may have a point,' he admitted. 'But on the other hand, I wasn't going to start confronting four big thugs – no matter who they were bringing in or bringing out. Especially as gladiators are allowed to carry swords in the city. And all I've got is a club.' He slapped the thigh of his bad leg. 'I had more than enough of swords on the docks in Alexandria.'

'I know you did,' allowed Artemidorus. 'But at least you might have seen them. Witnesses are in short supply.'

There was a brief silence.

'Then again,' said Artemidorus. 'We might have some witnesses yet.' He nodded towards the inner door that led to the second room. 'Who did Telos sub-let to?'

'Young couple with a baby. He's a baker.'

'Let's find out what they know. They must at least have heard something. These walls are thin as parchment.' As he spoke, Artemidorus crossed to the door. Knocked.

A silence, four heartbeats long. 'That's not good,' he observed grimly. 'That should have woken the baby at least…'

He pushed the door and it swung inwards.

He and Vitus stepped in together. The combined light of the candle and the oil lamp revealed all too vividly the contents of the tiny room. The destruction here was worse than in the outer room. And amongst the wreckage of the rickety furniture and all too modest possessions, there lay three bodies in an identical state of disrepair. A scarce-bearded baker, his child bride and their newborn baby, Artemidorus calculated. All so young. And none of them ever going to get any older.

At least Telos and Cyanea were not adding to the carnage in there. Or to the mess.

Puella came through with the doorkeeper's horn-sided lamp, adding more light. Revealing more detail. She gasped and retched. Vitus' dog Canem whimpered. The doorkeeper looked down at the lake of blood and body fluids slowly seeping through the floor. Suddenly the road to success and safety Artemidorus promised looked more like the road to hell.

'This explains why the tenants downstairs are complaining of leaky ceilings,' Vitus said. And his observation did nothing at all to calm Puella's sudden fears.

*

'Of course I'll have to report this,' Vitus observed dolefully, down at street level once again. 'And yes, I'll try and keep you and the woman out of it. But it won't be easy.'

'Abduction and murder. I'd be surprised if it *was* easy. Call on me if you need to. Just not Puella. Not that you'll know where she is in any case.'

'Right.'

The three of them were lingering in the doorway of the *insula*, looking out at the rain-soaked bustle of the Forum. Artemidorus was burning to be gone. A valued colleague and a woman he loved were in the hands of men who thought nothing of slaughtering whole families on the chance they might have witnessed something.

'The local magistrate's not the sharpest blade on the battlefield, though.' Vitus warned. 'He'll probably just reckon your friends killed the young family for some reason and then took off to avoid capture. He likes to keep things simple. He's pretty simple himself, our *aedile* Sextus Albanus.'

'That could work for us,' mused Artemidorus coldly. 'He wouldn't need to call anyone if he likes the simple version. Whether it's true or not.' He raised the lantern he had taken back from Puella and hefted the bundle of wax tablets wrapped in a couple of rags from Cyanea's bedding. 'Let's be off.'

'Where are we going now?' asked Puella, her quiet voice shaking. Still overcome with the sheer horror she had witnessed upstairs. No doubt beginning to see a pattern in all of this. A path like the one the Thracian poet Orpheus took seeking his lost love Eurydice. A path that led directly down into the depths of hell. 'Where are we going next?'

'To the *Carinae*.' Artemidorus answered gently. Using the tone he found most effective in calming frightened horses and talking to young legionaries in the moments before their first battle. 'There's a man in the *Carinae* district we have to see. It's a nice quiet, respectable place. You'll be safe there.'

'As long as there's no trouble overflowing out of the *Subura*,' warned Vitus. 'It's that kind of night. The gods are really restless. Everyone I've talked to thinks it augurs something bad coming.' He looked up, as though he could see up to the bloodbath on the top floor. 'The bad things may have started already.' He took a deep breath. 'I've even heard – you won't believe this but I swear I heard it when I was watching the battle of the whores...'

'You heard what?' Artemidorus was getting impatient and he let it show in his tone.

'That one of the lightning bolts hit the menagerie at the *Circus Maximus* and broke open some of the cages there. On top of everything else, there may even be some wild beasts loose in the streets. Lions. Tigers and such...'

As Artemidorus led Puella through the Forum once again, Vitus' words echoed in his mind. As soon as they moved out of the bustle outside the *Basilica Aemilia* and the Macellum market beside it and the darkness closed down on them, he began to suspect that they were being stalked. There was a tightness across his shoulders he had felt before. A familiar, almost ghostly warning that he had come to respect. It had saved his skin on more than one occasion.

Puella clearly felt the same. She spent as much time looking over her shoulder as looking ahead. Both of them probed the shadows at the outer edge of the little circle of light cast by the dead doorkeeper's lantern. Pausing each time lightning struck. Probing the further reaches revealed by the instants of greater brightness. The roaring of the thunder took on a dangerous tone. As though the storm itself were some great beast hungry for their flesh. The constant rushing and sluicing of the rain began to sound like the measured breathing of a massive predator. Drooling in anticipation of feasting on them. It was as though Vitus' warning had transformed the hunters they feared. From the much more likely footpads or slave-catchers. To the wild animals from the menagerie. It was strange. But it was what they were beginning to suspect.

Artemidorus became more and more uneasy, his mood darkened by the clear and mounting terror in his companion. Never had the gentle uphill path to the *Carinae* district seemed so lengthy. So complicated. So full of unexpected sounds and shadows. The open squares of the minor forums seemed especially threatening. For the walls on either side of the narrow, up-sloping roadways at least gave an illusion of protection. The lesser forums, however, were simply arenas full of shadows. Impenetrable beyond their fragile bubble of light. Full of endlessly threatening possibilities. Soaking and almost frozen once again, Artemidorus felt his scrotum tighten with a nervousness he had not experienced in years. And the sensation in his shoulders intensified as though there were ghosts trying to hold him back. But, he wondered, was he frightened for himself? For his companion? Or for his lovely, beloved Cyanea in the hands of nameless, numberless brutal murderers? The more he tried to reason it out, the worse his fears seemed to become.

So that it came almost as a relief when a band of men entered from one side of the biggest of the squares. Just as the two fugitives entered it from the other. For an instant, Artemidorus considered approaching them. Then his situation as a murderer accompanying a runaway slave brought him to his senses. He shaded the lantern with his parcel of tablets and pushed Puella back.

The new group of men rushed into the centre of the square and stopped there. Artemidorus was able to make out some details now. A circle of slaves and a couple of freedmen all holding lanterns and flambeaus. A set of *lictors* carrying their ceremonial *fasces*. Emphasising the central figure's importance and authority. But there were no axes in the ceremonial bundles, the spy noted. His standing and power were limited. As were those of almost everybody in the city. Within the Servian walls and the *pomerium*. In the centre, a tall man wearing a ceremonial toga with dark edges. An important figure, clearly, to be dressed like that and attended by so many. He suddenly pulled his toga wide. Uncovered the front of his tunic beneath it, then tugged the neckline down to offer his naked breast to the storm.

'Great Jove, god of thunder and the lightning bolt, I call on you now!' shouted the man in the toga. His voice wavered with excitement bordering on hysteria. His words carried even over the roaring of the wind and the pounding of the rain. His upturned face in the light of the flambeaus all around him seemed to be composed of Greek fire. Golden drops sprang up from his high forehead into a wavering halo and streamed down off his sleek hair. Bursting into his face and making his eyelids flicker. Running down his neck over his breast. Between his trembling fists and into the wadded cloth of tunic and toga. As though he was bathed in liquid flames.

'If what I do or what I plan offends the gods, then take me now, great Jove. Throw down one of your thunderbolts and take me. Take me *here and now!*'

The circle of men around him fell back a pace. Even the *lictors*. But their wariness, though understandable, was misplaced. Either Jove did not hear or did not care. Or even, possibly, approved of what the shouting man proposed. Certainly, the next great thunderbolt fell far from the square. Somewhere out by Tiber Island, if Artemidorus was any judge. He hoped his colleagues in the VIIth had done nothing to upset Jove either, for it looked as though the thunderbolt could well have fallen on them.

Instead, completely unexpectedly, a storm of hail came lashing down. Chunks of ice which seemed as hard and sharp as leaden slingshots came hurling out of the upper blackness.

Artemidorus felt the sting of them on his back and shoulders – and even through his leather cap. Puella gasped and hissed with pain. The man in the forum got the full force of it in his upturned face. With a cry of surprise and discomfort, he pulled his clothing straight and strode on, face down. His footsteps through the dancing whiteness on the ground at first faltering but then more purposeful. His actions once again becoming commanding and decisive. The vicious hailstones bouncing off his head and shoulders – as well as those of the men who followed him. After a moment, the hailstorm passed and he even seemed a good deal taller.

As the little crowd left the square and darkness surged back once again, Puella asked, 'Who was that? Do you know who that madman was?'

'Yes,' he answered. 'That's the man in whose household my missing friends Telos and Cyanea were working undercover. Did you not recognise him?'

Puella paused a moment, frowning with thought. Then her expression cleared. 'Of course!' she said. 'He visited Lord Brutus many times and we visited him as well. I served them wine and honeycakes. That was Lord Gaius Cassius!'

'Right. That was Cassius,' Artemidorus nodded. 'Off somewhere we can't spare the time to follow – but up to no good, I'll bet.'

*

The darkness that flooded back after Cassius and his retinue vanished seemed more threatening than ever. The lamp was clearly on its last legs – either starved of oil or drowned with rain. The storm intensified. The rain fell on them so fiercely that it hurt their shoulders, bruised as they were by the hailstones. Artemidorus considered lending Puella his leather cap – for that was protecting his head from the deluge. The lightning seemed almost continuous. The thunder never let up. As the stench from the Forum fell behind them, so a strange new odour began to fill the air, and Artemidorus was put in mind of the sea. Of the various ships in which he had sailed, in one capacity or another. Everything from Cilician pirate *liburnian* vessels to the huge *quinquereme* battle ships of the

33

Roman fleet. Everything from helpless captive to military *optio*. But always in disguise or undercover. Never quite what he seemed to be. Just like now, in fact.

Artemidorus's train of thought was interrupted by Puella. She grabbed his arm. 'Look!' she whispered. 'What is that?' Just for the briefest instant, at the boundary where the wavering light and the gathering darkness bled into each other, two unblinking discs of brightness appeared and disappeared almost as swiftly as the lightning. Even as the twin points of brightness vanished, it seemed to Artemidorus that some part of the darkness moved.

'Where are we going now?' asked Puella. And, in the same breath, 'Is it far?'

'We're going to see the *haruspex* and augur Spurinna,' he answered. 'And, no; it's not far. He's a knight of the rank of *equitum* and he lives in a villa not far from here.'

'Why are we going to see an augur? From the look of your recent past, you really don't want to know what your future is likely to hold.'

'I'm not getting my future predicted. Or yours. He's a colleague. We work together.'

'Oh.' She fell silent, clearly pondering the conundrum of why an aristocratic augur and a spy disguised as a common freedman would ever want to work together.

Side by side, they crossed the rest of the square, almost running – with some relief – into the mouth of the next narrow roadway. And straight into the middle of the gang that was waiting there. Half a dozen strangers surrounded the pair of fugitives with practised ease. Two dark lanterns were uncovered, putting the guttering glow of the one Artemidorus carried to shame. 'What have we here?' demanded a rough voice. The sudden brightness revealed an enormous man with the shoulders and arms of a bear.

Artemidorus didn't hesitate. He threw his lamp at the giant and charged after it. The lantern smashed into the massive footpad's chest. Oil sprayed over his clothing and flames licked hungrily at it. He should have burst into flames. Would have done so if there had been more oil and less rain. As it was, the lamp burst and died at once. The gang leader was surprised but by no means incapacitated. When Artemidorus hit him with the full weight of his charge, shoulder to belly, he staggered backwards. But he stayed upright and secured his footing by wrapping the spy in a bear-like embrace. The pair of them reeled back into the shadows but the rest of the gang followed, the light from their lanterns revealing a crossroad. Where there was just enough room to let them gather round the wrestlers. The bundle full of Telos' tablets flew into the flooding gutter and washed back to Puella's feet as she looked around, assessing their danger and seeking an escape.

The men not holding lanterns were carrying weapons. And at least one had a club that looked even heavier than the dead doorkeeper's. The runaway slave realised that there was almost certainly no way out of this for either of them. The spy who had promised to protect her was going to be beaten to death, either by his huge opponent's fists or by his gang's clubs. And she was going to be taken back to Lord Brutus's household after all. Probably only marginally more alive than her would-be guardian. She turned to run but the nearest gang member caught her arm. A big, dark man with a dangerous-looking club. Who passed her to one of the others. Who held her captive as they watched Artemidorus begin to die.

*

Artemidorus drove a fist into the footpad's groin, but the huge man only grunted and tightened a grip that threatened to upend the spy altogether. And break his neck, crush his ribs or shatter his skull on the stones of the road. The first club blow smashed down across the small of his back.

Artemidorus twisted his neck, looking for the club wielder. And found he knew the man. Like the giant holding him, the club wielder was familiar; he just could not quite place the face.

'No!' bellowed his huge opponent. 'I want this one all to myself. First a little fun with him. Then a little fun with his woman. It's been a busy night after all. And although I've had some exercise, I know you boys were upset not to get your hands on the girl. Well, not so much your *hands*…'

The club man fell back a step or two, his half-familiar face twisting into an ugly leer.

The giant relaxed his hold on Artemidorus for an instant, then grasped his tunic forcefully enough to tear the seams, and threw him down the roadway. As he landed, Artemidorus staggered backwards into the arms of the rest of the footpads who, with a raucous cheer, hurled him forward.

As he stumbled towards the titan standing at the crossroads, Artemidorus at last recognised his opponent. Like *Scorpionis* had been in his time, this was a favourite of the arena. Another gladiator named for his technique or aspect of his craft. This was the gigantic boxer *Cestus*, named for the metal-spiked leather bands that he wore round his fists and up his forearms. Which, the staggering spy noted, he was wearing now. His eyes widened with the revelation. If this was Cestus then his sidekicks also would be gladiators. And the club wielder's name was…

Cestus swung a huge blow with his right fist at Artemidorus's head. The spy ducked, feeling the wind of its passage just above his skull. Even through the leather of his cap. His mind was suddenly focused on the matter in hand so he forgot all about the club man. He could never beat Cestus in a straight contest. The enormous metal-spiked fists were as deadly as the *pugio* with the amazing blade that had dispatched the doorkeeper. Speed and agility were his only real hope. And that hope was a thin one. Cestus was unlikely to tire before he landed a good blow. And a tired Cestus would still be a hard man to beat. And even if he did beat Cestus, there was the rest of his gang to consider. And their weapons. Swords. Clubs.

Cestus swung a massive right and the speedy spy easily avoided it once again. This was not the arena. He was not supposed to stand like a stunned ox and get beaten to a pulp for the entertainment of the crowd. Or further to honour the gods. But Cestus didn't seem to see it that way. He had one fighting technique and he obviously used it wherever he was. He continued to swing one huge punch after another while his opponent ducked, dived and danced just out of his reach.

Artemidorus reckoned he could keep this up all night if he had to – while he got things figured out.

But the fact remained that if Cestus landed one good blow, then the spy was done. Even if that blow didn't kill him it would certainly cripple him and one or other of the succeeding blows would definitely smash the life out of him. And it looked increasingly likely that there was nothing he could do about it. Truly, he had chosen a bad night to get on the wrong side of the Roman gods.

'*Achilleus*, help me now,' he prayed to his own favoured Spartan semi-divine power. And the most apt of all, under the circumstances. For the great Achilles was famed above all things for his speed and agility. It was these strengths which allowed him to overcome the Trojan hero Hector. And he had only met his end when Prince Paris robbed him of them by shooting an arrow through his heel. Use Achilles' skills against his own huge Hector and he might yet come out of this alive. This was the thought that filled Artemidorus's head in the moment before his sandal slipped on the treacherous roadway and he fell helplessly onto one knee while the victorious giant strode forward at last to deliver the killing blow.

But perhaps the immortal Spartan hero heard him in a way that Jove had not heard Cassius. Or perhaps Achilles cared more for his lonely Spartan warrior, as far from home as Troy had been, and going to his death like a Myrmidon of old.

The huge panther that had been tracking Artemidorus and Puella arrived like a bolt of black lightning bursting out of the side street at a full charge. The massive animal hurled through the ring of robbers and took Cestus on his left side, rearing up almost to the boxer's height, huge pads armed with claws that reduced the boxer's studded fists to playthings. Its great square black head bigger than the gigantic boxer's own head, and armed with massive teeth. It stood as tall as his hulking shoulder and if it only weighed half as much as the gladiator did, the power of its charge more than compensated.

The huge gladiator was hurled against the corner of the wall that opened into the side street on his right. He span, helplessly, flailing uselessly with his huge fists as the beast held onto him by sinking its foreclaws into the flesh of his chest and back. It slowed him by sinking two pairs of fangs the size of big bone daggers into his shoulder and neck, releasing a huge fountain of blood as it did so. And it dispatched him by using the talons on its rear legs to rip open his belly and let his guts fall free. The once-terrifying giant was dead and largely dismembered before his body hit the ground. His bullying cohorts took to their heels, dropping clubs and lanterns as they ran, keeping hold of their swords.

Artemidorus stooped and grabbed a club and a lantern. Straightened, looking at the stricken Puella. 'The tablets.' He ordered. 'Get the tablets!'

Obediently, she stooped and retrieved the bundle from the gutter at her feet. But her eyes remained riveted on the gaping blackness that the panther had vanished into. The huge beast was invisible once again, but the way the dead boxer's legs were sliding into the side street left little doubt where it was. Or what it was doing.

With a mental prayer of thanks to the greatest of Spartan heroes, Artemidorus raised the lamp above his head and, with Puella close behind him, took to his heels again.

*

'It won't come after us…' Puella said. But she didn't sound too sure.

'I doubt it,' he answered, almost drunk with relief. 'Not before it has finished eating, at least. And that is one enormous meal.'

'That's disgusting,' she said, angrily. 'It sickens me even to think about it.'

She was clearly reacting to their narrow escape in exactly the opposite way to him, thought the spy. Perhaps it was the difference between men and women. He was a warrior, trained to laugh at death – even his own. She was a woman, raised to care and nurture. Even murderous giants such as Cestus.

'If the panther hadn't killed him, he'd be ravishing you now,' he observed almost brutally. 'With his thugs all lined up behind. And if his parts below were built on the same scale as those above, it would not be a comfortable experience. A bit like childbirth. But quicker. More repeatedly. And in reverse. I'd be dead in the gutter and you'd be envying me.'

'I suppose...'

She hadn't considered that. So he pressed his advantage with the persistence of a man so full of the best Falernian wine that there is no room left for good sense. 'So it's all to the good that something which might have been coming at you like the ram on the bows of a *quinquireme* is now reduced to a *Lucanian* sausage feeding the biggest cat I've ever seen.'

'That's disgusting,' she said again, but her tone had moderated.

'And his men would all have used their *weapons* on you as well...' he persisted drunk with relief. And even as he said it he remembered who the club wielder was. They called him *Syrus* The Syrian. He was one of the few gladiators to use a club in the arena. Only Syrian auxiliaries used clubs and maces in battle. The tight formations of the regular legions made the arc of such weapons impractical. And in any case, the *pilum* spear, the bow, the sling, the *gladius* and the *pugio* were more than enough. 'At least I saved you from that...'

'I suppose you did. You and your cat.' Her tone moderated even further.

Even so, he noticed that she was no longer walking so close to him. She was on his left side and he held the lantern in his right. The club in his hand swung between them. Even when he swapped them over she stayed back. He discovered that he rather missed the fragrance of hyssop she seemed to exude. 'I apologise,' he offered. 'I'm just so relieved to have come through all this. With you safe and neither of us damaged to any great extent.'

She did not move any closer.

'But of course we're not safe home yet,' he persisted at his most devious. 'And, talking of my cat as you call it, I've heard that those big cats do sometimes hunt in pairs...'

Ah! He thought an instant later. *The fragrance of hyssop. How lovely.*

'So,' she persisted as their shoulders rubbed gently together. 'Why are we going to see the soothsayer?'

'I told you. We work together.'

'Yes. But I've been thinking. How can a common freedman be an associate of a noble knight?'

'As I've explained. I am in disguise. Like an actor in a play. I am in fact a centurion with the VIIth Legion. *Primi ordines*, if that means anything. No. I thought not. It means I am a senior centurion. *Primus pilus*. First spear. In battle I lead the first rank – if I'm not off on assignment behind enemy lines. I stand one step below a legate, leaving aside birth – where you were born and how high up the social ladder is sometimes more important than experience and ability in these matters. Two steps below a tribune.'

'Then why are you not with your men? Where are they?'

'Camped on Tiber Island. I'm not with them because I have been reassigned as I have also told you, to the command of Tribune Enobarbus. He is a senior broad-stripe tribune and chief officer controlling all of us. He commands our network and reports in person to the general, co-consul, late *magister equitum* and General Mark Antony. Under Lord Antony's orders, we are all reassigned from our regular military responsibilities on occasion in order to undertake espionage assignments. It is a system first explored by General Scipio Africanus in the wars against the *Punic* Carthaginian Hannibal but more recently by the Divine Julius himself, and it has been very effective. The tribune and I are expecting to return to our posts in five days' time when the legions move out against Parthia by way of the *Getae* in Macedonia.'

'This tribune. Enobarbus. How important is he? Or did he get his position because of ability and experience?'

'He is of the *Marcii* family and claims descent from the Etruscan Kings of Rome – the *Marcius* clan. He is a patrician of senatorial rank.'

'And will he be at this soothsayer Spurinna's villa?'

Her tone was becoming more confident now and she was beginning to sound impressed. The spy was well used to reading people's thoughts, not that hers were at all difficult.

That she, a common slave, would be hobnobbing with senior officers of the legion, men of *equitum* rank and senatorial patricians. Perhaps even get a chance to meet the fabulous Mark Antony, military hero, late *magister equitum*, co-consul, general and close friends with the Divine Julius himself. Both men known for their weakness in the matter of beautiful women. And their willingness to indulge it. Whether their lovers were slaves or queens. Like Queen Pharaoh Cleopatra, currently and outrageously settled in Caesar's villa on the crest of Janiculum Hill, just across the river. With their bastard son and Caesar's only natural offspring Caesarion. Her eyes took on a distant, dreamy look as her vision turned inward. To the possibilities offered to women who caught the eye of men such as these. Perhaps this was not the road to hell after all…

But then it was.

Another flash of lightning lit up the roadway in front of them. 'Stop,' he ordered abruptly. She obeyed and he paused at her side, close enough to be obscuring most of her vision with his body. For he had noticed something that he didn't want her to see. 'Do you see the house opposite? That one over there with a torch burning above the door?'

'Yes…' she was uncertain again. Suspicious once again that there was more going on here than she understood.

'That is Spurinna's house. Go straight there, knock on the door and tell the slave that answers you are with *Septem*. They'll take you straight to Spurinna. Go there and wait for me.'

'*Septem*? Who is *Septem*?'

'I am. Both Spurinna and Enobarbus sometimes call me that: Seven. It's because I'm with the Seventh Legion. Say you're with Seven and they'll look after you. Now go. And take those tablets we found in Telos' and Cyanea's place with you. Spurinna will want them.'

Artemidorus stood where he was and watched as she obediently crossed to the house he indicated. She knocked on the door, spoke when it opened, and was admitted. Then he turned. On this street as on many others, there was building work going on. Several of the villas had rough wooden scaffolding erected around them, just like the new basilica on the south side of the Forum. These included the villa directly opposite Spurinna's.

With lantern high and club at the ready, Artemidorus crossed to this one. The house behind the pinned and lashed wood construction seemed empty. It was certainly dark and silent. But the house was of no interest to him. Neither was the scaffolding.

As Artemidorus approached, the wind whistled down the roadway and howled in the scaffolding like a pack of the wolves which had lived in the place when Romulus and Remus arrived as babies. And, hard against the scaffolding, secured so that the feet were well clear of the sodden ground, there hung a body. As the secret agent came closer, the relentless brightness of his lantern was augmented by another bolt of lightning. And he could see that the body was that of a man. A tall, slender man wearing a simple sleeping tunic that was clinging to his body, soaking with various liquids, light and dark. A barefoot, bareheaded man, terribly out of place in this deserted, benighted, stormbound street. A man who had been crucified here.

Arms and legs lashed into place then nailed through wrist and elbow, ankle and knee. Around his neck, hanging against the thick red breast of his tunic beneath the lolling, downturned head, there hung a notice. '*canit quasi alauda*' was all he could make out. There was more but the rain had washed it away, together with the blood that must have been on the ground, judging by the state of the tunic front. 'Sings like a lark,' he murmured, the words lost in the thunder and the rain.

He dropped his club and reached for the rain-straightened fringe of hair. As gently as a mother rearranging a sleeping child, he took hold of the sodden hair and eased the face up into the light. He stood for a moment, looking into the dead features. Then he lowered it again and turned. One glance had been enough to sear it into his memory for ever.

They had gouged the eyes out.

They had torn the tongue out.

They had cut the throat, last of all; probably even after they crucified him here.

The notice was the grimmest of jokes of course. He had sung like a lark. So they had taken his tongue. Larks' tongue. The greatest of delicacies. But you never ate just one of them.

And, worst of all, the murdered man was Telos.

III

The same servant who opened the door to Puella admitted Artemidorus and the bloody bundle slung over his shoulder. The spy and the servant knew each other. The spy was relieved to be talking to a level-headed youngster he believed he could trust. The servant hesitating only for an instant, confronted with a soldier disguised as a freedman he only just recognised carrying the recently murdered, brutally mutilated corpse of a man he also half knew.

'Show me to somewhere private I can put this, Kyros,' ordered Artemidorus, careful this time to use his free hand to pat the picture of Janus on the door jamb. 'Then summon your master and send someone for Antistius the physician.'

The servant, pallid in the light of his candle, went white as chalk as the full horror of what the spy was carrying hit him. 'It is Telos?' he queried, hesitating until Artemidorus' curt nod confirmed his worst fears. He gave one decisive nod in reply, his face setting into youthful determination. 'Yes, *Septem*,' he said.

Kyros led him to a side room at once, pausing only to light a lamp at one of the candles, brightening the villa's modest *atrium*. All of them guttering as the storm wind whirled through the open roof above the shallow pool of the *impluvium*. The torrential downpour made the surface heave and froth. The quick-thinking slave chose a side room *taberna*. A room with an ancient shop design used by one of the villa's past owners, though shuttered and private now that Spurinna the soothsayer was the current occupier.

Artemidorus was able to place the cold, wet body of his dead friend on the rough brick counter which was a feature of the room's original commercial design as a shop or tavern. The slave left the lamp and vanished to summon first his master and then the physician, who was also an occasional member of

Enobarbus' military style eight-man *contubernium*. The active heart of his far-reaching secret organisation.

The spy set to work arranging the body of his murdered colleague into some kind of order. Not an easy task, given the state of his elbows and knees. And the fact that he was still running with a range of liquids, mostly water and blood. Artemidorus was hardly better off. Though at least the blood wasn't his.

Spurinna started speaking as he crossed the *atrium*, able to see something of Artemidorus but nothing of Telos, as yet. 'I've sent for the physician and given your pretty companion over to some of my women. They'll get her dry, warm and fed. Then Antistius can examine her. I assume that's what you wanted, Seven…'

Artemidorus looked up as the augur entered the room and stopped speaking mid-sentence. He held the lamp high so that his colleague could see what was left of Telos clearly.

'I bet you didn't predict this, Soothsayer,' he observed.

Spurinna grunted as he joined Artemidorus at the corpse's shoulder. He looked down with the authority of a man professionally familiar with death. Albeit the death of countless animal sacrifices. Neither man spoke for an instant, then Spurinna continued. 'Antistius will be here soon, I expect. But he's going to be too late to help poor Telos, if that's what you had in mind. You need a priest, not a physician. And a change of clothing.' He clapped his hands and Kyros reappeared at once. 'Find a dry tunic large enough to fit my friend Seven here,' ordered the augur. His tone of command revealed him for what he was – every inch a Roman knight. 'And something for him to dry off with.'

Artemidorus glanced across at his companion as the slave boy disappeared. Spurinna the augur, *haruspex* and soothsayer was a strange compound of dreamy, other-worldly prophecy and sharp-eyed, down-to-earth observation. Part Roman knight, part Etruscan visioinary. In the time of their association, Artemidorus had come to understand and appreciate this apparently contradictory character. It was the sharp-eyed, insightful observer who informed the other-worldly prophet of the likely futures he was predicting. But it was the prophet who was listened to in a way that more down-to-earth observers were not. Especially by the Divine Julius. For Spurinna was Caesar's personal prophet.

Behind what Spurinna saw in the entrails of his sacrifices, in the flights of birds, the changes in the weather or in the dreams of his employer, there always lay a cold and inescapable logic. Had not Spurinna warned Caesar almost a month ago that he should beware the middle days of Mars? Caesar had laughed by all accounts, and called his prophet a dreamer. But the rumours Enobarbus was currently trying to prove had been swirling around more than a month ago. And Caesar was due to leave Rome for a lengthy campaign in five days' time. If the plots the tribune feared were going to come to anything, then they must come to a head almost immediately. And Spurinna saw that clearly. In every sacrifice. In the flights of birds. In the dreadful weather. In dark, prophetic dreams that haunted both Caesar and his wife Calpurnia. And if Caesar was less than convinced by Spurinna, his other-worldly prophet, Calpurnia believed every word. While Enobarbus had been thoroughly convinced by Spurinna the cold logician who informed him.

Especially as the ways in which the tribune and his general had tested the waters of public opinion recently had all added weight to Spurinna's darkest predictions. The crown Antony had offered Caesar at the *Lupercal* festival a month ago. That got boos from the crowd. In spite of the group placed nearby and bribed to cheer. Lucius Cotta's pronouncement of the deliberations of the Fifteen interpreting the Sibylline Texts that only a King of Rome could conquer Parthia had clearly offended a majority in the Senate. Even Caesar's current predilection for regal red boots as footwear was causing negative comment.

It was Spurinna's concerns, supported by these incidents, that had caused the three spies to be sent urgently undercover into the households of Brutus and Cassius, the social leaders, brothers-in-law and men most widely believed to be behind any plots that were being laid.

Which in turn had led to this.

Telos began dripping onto the tile floor and the noise broke the brief silence.

'I don't want Puella examined. And I don't want Telos healed or resurrected,' answered Artemidorus as though the conversation had never faltered. 'I want to know about his death. The order in which these things were done to him. How he finally died. Perhaps I might even learn something of the men who killed him. They still have Cyanea…'

He stopped speaking, suddenly seeing at least part of the point of this brutality. Cyanea. Any of Spurinna's associates finding Telos would bound to be distracted from whatever they were doing by concern about what was being done to Cyanea. And it must certainly be Spurinna or his friends, given where the body had been placed. Perhaps Cyanea's colleagues might even turn aside from their immediate plans to go in search of her before she could share Telos' terrible fate. Which might well mean that whoever had done this was worried that Enobarbus' spies must be closing in on them as their plans rushed towards fruition. Likely enough, if what the note on his breast said was true and Telos had sung like a lark before he died.

Kyros appeared with a sheet of rough woollen cloth and a tunic. As the spy dried off and changed for the second time that night, his mind continued to work. Something must have been said or done at Cassius' house which could have given the murderous patricians' game away. Something that suddenly meant there was a chance the new staff so conveniently placed in the conspirator's kitchen had seen or heard a crucial clue. A clue to whatever these brutes were worried about. And might well have passed the information on. That whatever Cassius was planning must be coming to its climax very soon indeed. A climax fragile enough to be threatened by Enobarbus' secret agents.

But no such message had been communicated, though there had been no time for detailed debriefing as Artemidorus rushed through the tiny room on top of the *insula* on his way to release and recruit Puella.

47

On the other hand, he thought as he handed the wet cloth and the sodden tunic to the waiting slave, the situation and Telos' terrible fate also made it more than possible that someone in Caesar's most intimate circle, someone among Mark Antony's friends or, most likely of all, someone working undercover for the tribune was in fact a double agent who had warned Cassius and his cohorts that there were cuckoos in his nest...

*

Artemidorus had reached this point in his rapidly darkening speculations when Kyros returned once more to usher the physician Antistius into the room. The medical man was slight but dynamic, even though he was by no means in the first flush of youth. Or even of middle age, thought Artemidorus. His frame was spare. His back stooped and his hair thin. But his eyes were blue and clear as water. He was the personification of the sharp-eyed, down-to-earth side of Spurinna's character. With a silent frown he pulled back his hood and swung his dripping cloak off his shoulders, revealing a warm-looking woollen tunic. After an instant, he strode forward, frowning with concentration already. Kyros, who had taken the cloak, retreated into the *atrium* with every sign of relief.

'This looks bad,' Antistius observed. Neither Artemidorus nor Spurinna answered the self-evident truth. 'If I'm going to examine the poor lad properly, we'd better strip him,' the physician continued. 'He's clearly beyond my professional help. So I assume you wish me to speculate as to how he got into this state. Where and when.' The physician rolled the sleeves of his tunic up and flexed his hands, hooking his fingers like eagles' talons. 'Where did you find him?'

'Over the road,' answered Artemidorus as they rolled the stiffening corpse onto its side. 'Crucified against the scaffolding around the villa opposite this one.'

'A message...' observed the physician grimly.

'Meant for me,' observed Spurinna. 'I think I had better alert the household in case this is also a declaration of war. And I'd better start to go through the bits and pieces you retrieved from their home. There might well be something important there –

and you don't need me for the meantime. I'll get your girl to help me, Seven – it'll keep her occupied and well away from here. From this…' He left the little room.

'Put his clothing and that message carefully aside,' ordered Antistius. 'They may contain information that the corpse does not. But I have known you for some time, young Artemidorus. Even before they gave you the code name Seven, if my memory serves. And I suspect you must already have worked out that he died where you found him. Though he was probably not tortured there.' The medical man's abrupt tone slowed, became more thoughtful. 'And how close to death he was when he was brought there to be crucified and killed is another matter altogether.'

'Yes,' said Artemidorus. 'The bleeding and the bruising make it plain enough that he was still alive when they nailed him in place. He was alive up until they cut his throat, judging from the blood on his chest. There would have been blood on the road as well. I looked before I took him down but the rain had washed the ground clean as far as I could see.'

'Alive, certainly,' Antistius nodded. 'But barely. He had already lost a lot of blood, I would guess. Simple practicality must suggest that although it would have been possible to take his eyes there and then, taking his tongue would have been all but impossible. And the dried blood on his lips and cheeks suggests that he was mutilated elsewhere.'

'His head was hanging down,' Artemidorus added. 'The rain poured onto the back of his skull but his face was protected.'

'Or the dried blood would have washed away like his lifeblood in the gutter…' The physician leaned forward over the dead man's torso. 'He's been beaten badly into the bargain.' He pressed the purple flesh over the curve of a rib. There was the faintest grating sound. The depression made by his finger stayed in place.

Hardly surprisingly, thought Artemidorus. Telos' chest and belly looked as though they had been clawed by the panther that killed and ate Cestus. There were lacerations, welts, round depressions almost like stab wounds everywhere from his throat to his groin.

'There are many bones broken,' the physician continued. 'These things were done over a number of hours, I should say. Which also makes it highly unlikely that they were done in the street. Though the streets have been pretty well deserted tonight, because of the storm.'

That's what you think, Artemidorus reflected – remembering the bustle in the Forum, Cassius and his attendants in the square, the robbers at the crossroad. The panther.

But Antistius persisted heedlessly, 'His corpse is very much like the bodies I have examined belonging to dead gladiators after battles in the arena.' Then he fell silent, rolling Telos onto his side to reveal another series of lacerations and small circular wounds on his shoulders and back. Wounds that matched the others on his chest and belly, Artemidorus realised.

'In fact,' Antistius said after a while, 'I think you might take some comfort – enough perhaps to satisfy a Stoic. Poor Telos must have been so near to death from the beating that he would hardly have been aware of the final atrocities.'

'So,' nodded Artemidorus. 'Our ever-astute augur was right. This has little to do with Telos and more to do with us. It is a message. A warning.'

'Or a declaration of war.' Antistius nodded. 'As Spurinna has observed.'

'And very possibly an indirect way of torturing Cyanea,' added Artemidorus. 'Especially if they've believed the cover story that Telos and she were a young married couple deeply in love.'

'You had better hope so,' Antistius grunted, as he bent over the livid corpse once more. 'There are other ways to torture a woman than by making her watch it being done to someone else. Much more direct ways.'

But his earlier words suddenly tricked something in the ex-gladiator's mind. Something associated with his own experiences this evening. '*Cestus*,' he said, remembering the huge robber that the panther had killed. 'He's been beaten by someone wearing *cestus* spiked gloves.'

'I do believe you're right. Looking at the state of his torso and belly, back and front, I would say that someone wearing a *cestus* on each fist spent some time punching him very hard indeed.'

Artemidorus thoughtfully picked up an arm. In spite of the damage done by the crucifying nail it was possible to see the marks of a rope stretching up the back of the hand and the base of the thumb. 'While he was hanging by his hands,' he added.

But then he noticed the state of Telos' nails. For a moment he supposed that the torturers must have tried to pull them out. Then he noticed the splinters beneath the torn and bleeding fingers' ends. 'No, wait,' he said. 'While he was tied to a post. He clawed it in his agony and nearly tore his nails off. A whipping post, perhaps.'

'That would explain the presence of wounds on his chest and back, but almost none on his sides. It would also explain the damage to his ribs. He could not swing to lessen the impact so he was crushed,' observed Antistius. 'The threads of his tunic are still in some of these wounds, so he wore it to the end. Which is another comfort I suppose.'

'As long as we can say the same for Cyanea,' added Artemidorus, picking up on the physician's earlier comment. A picture of her naked body lashed to a whipping post sprang unbidden into his mind and his breath shortened. The soft, warm, fragile naked body that he knew so intimately. The murderers' plan was working, he thought grimly: he was being distracted after all. Being tempted to desert his post, forget his duty and go after his kidnapped lover.

Dismissing the mental picture of Cyanea before he began to speculate what they might be doing to her and see it all in his vivid mind's eye, he crossed to the bloody rags of Telos' clothing. Beside the pathetic pile lay the message that had hung around the corpse's neck. He picked it up, frowning with thought, and brought it over to the light. 'Good grade papyrus,' he said. 'Top quality amphitheatre-made. Expensive. This fits in with everything else. No matter who did this to Telos, someone of rank and fortune was nearby. Only someone of senatorial rank can afford papyrus of this quality.

And even if they employ gladiators to do their dirty work for them, they still have people to hand who can write in a clear and flowing manner. Just look at the penmanship on this. It's the writing of a secretary or a scholar. It's never the work of a brutal thug wearing a *cestus*…'

He held it up to the light. Occasionally – very occasionally – a really expensive sheet of papyrus might have the family name or clan crest of the man who ordered it woven into its very fabric. He narrowed his eyes, willing the overlaid ribbons of Nile reed to fall into some kind of a pattern. A Latin letter or a Greek one. The more he looked, the less sense the woven patterns seemed to make. The closest he could come to anything relevant was a truncated Greek *mu*, its tail ripped off by the way the sheet had been torn. He was still examining the papyrus when Kyros returned. 'The master asks Seven to accompany me,' he said briskly. He turned to Antistius and added, 'Is there anything you require, sir?'

'Not at the moment,' answered the physician, too wrapped up in his post-mortem examination to do more than glance up.

Artemidorus followed the young slave out into the *atrium*. Judging by the pool of the *impluvium*, the storm was past its height. Lightning flickered but somehow seemed further off. Thunder roared more distantly, long after the flickers of light. The wind still raved, however. Artemidorus shivered, even though he was almost dry and his new tunic was thick and warm over the still-cold dampness of his leather trousers.

Kyros hurried into the rear of the house, leading the spy through to the cramped little kitchen which stood almost like an outhouse added to the back wall of the villa. The slave seemed surprised that his master should bring the slave girl and her bundle of blank wax tablets here. But Artemidorus was not. He knew what the augur was doing.

*

The splintered tablets were laid out on a series of thin slate trays, reassembled as best Spurinna and Puella could manage. Behind them on a raised shelf, sat the villa's main cooking utensil, a good-sized, pot-shaped clay *clibanus* oven. As Artemidorus entered, Spurinna was pulling the top of the oven up. Puella lifted one of the trays out into the light. The wax had melted off the tablets' backing to reveal words carefully written on the wood. Secret words which had been hidden by the thin wax layer above them. It was a device that Enobarbus discovered in the annals of Scipio Africanus – though whether it was he or his mortal enemy the Carthaginian General Hannibal who began the practice no one knew for certain. The wax covered the true message, which could only be read when the wax was removed. It would usually simply be scraped off, but Spurinna was taking extra care because the tablets were already so badly damaged.

Puella's tray joined several others which had been similarly treated. On which were written lists of words that meant nothing at all. The script was Greek, which the Spartan translated at a glance: ZFKKX, QRORIRP, KXPL…

'They'll be names,' said Artemidorus, picking up the least damaged of the wooden tablets.

'In code of course,' nodded Spurinna. 'It's your province rather than mine, Seven. Any idea which one?'

'We can try Caesar's cipher,' answered the spy, studying the writing on the wood with narrow eyes. 'That's the most likely. It's the one he uses for most of the reports and orders he wants kept secret. The general likes it too. And so the tribune trained me in its use and transliteration, though the trick of it is known only to a few of us. To whom I must add you now. But it is a heavy secret. Breaking it means death.'

'Almost everything we do seems to mean death,' said Spurinna. 'Explain your lethal secret, oh great *speculator*.'

'It's simple but efficient,' answered Artemidorus shortly. 'It's a transposition code. You move each letter three places to the right, so A becomes D and so forth. I'll try it on this first name here: ZFKKX. In Caesar's cipher that comes out as… CINNA. Now that looks very promising.'

'But what is Telos doing writing about a poet?' demanded Spurinna without thinking.

'Not *Helvius* Cinna,' said Artemidorus. 'This will be *Lucius Cornelius* Cinna. He's an outspoken critic of Caesar and all his works. *Lucius Cornelius* must be written on the matching, left-hand panel. One of these that have been reduced to splinters, I assume. What's next? KXPL. That comes out as NASO. Probably Publius Sextius Naso. Yes.'

He glanced up. Puella was frowning at him, clearly not quite understanding. So he assumed the manner of a schoolmaster and proceeded with his lecture. 'The full name must be written across each side of the tablet. *Praenomen* and *nomen*, on one tablet, then *cognomen* on the second. So we have the *cognomen*, surname, Cinna. But the first and clan names, the ones that tell us which *particular* Cinna, are on another piece. Which would have been attached, allowing us to read the full name right across, as I said; but which now have become separated and splintered. Hence the confusion about which Cinna is which…'

'Obviously,' interrupted Spurinna, impatiently. 'But until we've melted the wax off all of these, reassembled the splintered ones and matched one side against the other, we won't be able to get all of the names for certain.'

'Puella,' said Artemidorus. 'Are any of these names familiar?' He picked up more of the undamaged, still-warm tablets and translated Telos' Greek letters and Caesar's simple cipher in his head to read the list of names from them. 'Turullius, Petronius, Galba, Spurius…'

Wide-eyed, she shook her head.

'Then what use are you, girl?' snapped Spurinna, angry and frustrated.

'These are the small fry,' answered Artemidorus, springing to her defence. 'The minnows. Puella has been where the big sharks swim. She can tell the general about meetings she attended. Between Brutus and Cassius. Publius Servilius Casca. Quintus Antistius Labeo. Lucius Tillius Cimber. An incredibly dangerous mix of men happy to stand with the Republican senators who make no secret of their hatred for Caesar and men he considers to be loyal allies. What Puella knows, together with the list of names on these tablets, if we can piece them together, must spur the general into action. If we can get this all to Tribune Enobarbus and he can get it to the general in time.'

'In time for what, though?' demanded the augur.

'In time to stop whatever they are planning,' answered the spy.

'But we don't know precisely what that is or exactly when it will happen.'

'We'll know,' said Artemidorus. 'We'll know what it is when it starts. And that's the moment we'll know the best way to stop it.'

'But only if we get all this put clearly into order and it fits in with what your girl knows,' countered Spurinna, counting the sequence off on his fingers. 'If we can get it to the tribune and the tribune can persuade the general to take action in a heartbeat and alert the Divine Julius with evidence so clear and damning that it cannot be refuted.'

'Mark Antony has never in his entire life been shy of taking action in a heartbeat. I've seen him do it. On the battlefield as well as elsewhere,' said Artemidorus. 'Speaking as the senior centurion of the *Legio VII*.'

'True. But a good deal of that instantaneous action has landed him in a great deal of trouble.'

'Not this time,' answered Artemidorus forcefully. 'This time I think we're only in trouble if Antony *doesn't* act.'

'Puella,' said Spurinna, his tone of voice in marked contrast to the one he used earlier. 'Is there anything you overheard that might give us more of a clue? Not names. Not who was at what meeting or where... But what they actually said?'

Puella's gaze flashed to Artemidorus and then away again before he could even react. 'They have talked about attacking him on the *Via Sacra*, when he goes for one of his unaccompanied walks. I heard Cassius and Casca discussing this with Lord Brutus.'

'I see,' said Spurinna. 'But what I don't understand is how a household slave like you – even a favoured servant rarely far from her master's side – gets to know all of these important people by name...'

Puella opened her mouth to reply but Artemidorus took over the explanation. 'You don't understand the full formality with which Lord Brutus and Lady Porcia run their social lives.

Almost every guest is not only conducted to the meeting room, whichever room that is on any occasion, but is also formally announced with full name, by the *atriensis*, major domo. Even regular visitors. *Praenomen, nomen, cognomen.* All three elements.'

'Almost everyone. I see,' nodded Spurinna. Then he shrugged. 'So, back to the conversation…'

'My Lord Brutus argued that there would be no reason for a group of patricians to be all in one place, even on the *Via Sacra.*' Her eyes closed. Her voice deepened. With a shiver of shock and surprise, the spy heard the conspirator's very words issuing from the mouth of a slave. A slave Brutus must simply have forgotten was standing close enough to overhear what he and his guests were saying. 'So many aristocrats strolling along the *Via Sacra* together must arouse suspicion. That such an act under such circumstances in such a place would simply appear as murder. And he would only be involved in an enterprise that was obviously protecting the good of the Republic. That their action should appear to be a sacrifice for the good of the Republic; almost like the sacrifice that gladiators make when they die in the arena as an offering to the gods. That they must be liberators, not murderers. Liberators like his famous forefather. They call themselves *Libertores.* Liberators.'

A picture flashed into Artemidorus' memory. Of the family tree in Brutus' *atrium*, tracing his ancestry back to the Lucius Junius Brutus who led the uprising that rid Rome of King Tarquin the Great and founded the Republic four hundred years earlier.

'Interesting,' mused the augur. 'Though I don't believe Caesar has ravished any suicidal aristocratic matrons recently – as Tarquin's son raped Lucrece, with such fatal results for all.'

'Only because he has managed to fulfil himself with more than enough willing women since he could first achieve an erection, perhaps,' observed Artemidorus drily. 'Like the one visiting her son Brutus even as we speak. Brutus, who Caesar may even have sired when he was fifteen and Servilia, his first mistress, was little more than nineteen. Like the current mistress occupying his villa on the Janiculum Hill at the moment.' He gestured southward with his chin.

'Ah, the fabulous Cleopatra,' nodded Spurinna. 'Who has captured more hearts than Caesar's. Marc Antony's for a start, I understand. But proceed with your story, child. It is the twenty or so men who hate the Divine Julius that we want to know about – not the infinite numbers of women who love him.'

'On another occasion they discussed Marcus Tullius Cicero, with Quintus Labeo and Tillius Cimber. Cassius wondered whether Cicero should be asked to join the *Libertores*,' continued Puella obligingly. 'My Lord Brutus decided that Cicero would support the cause because he fears that Caesar plans to become the next King of Rome…'

'As Lucius Cotta has already suggested the Sibylline Texts may predict…' interrupted Artemidorus.

Spurinna merely shrugged. 'Carry on, child,' he ordered.

'But my Lord Brutus believed Cicero would be incapable of following a plan he had not made himself – that he was incapable of taking orders.'

'Lord Brutus has the measure of the man,' nodded Spurinna, much amused. 'Cicero's opinion of himself, like his sentences, hardly ever ends. He will follow no man…'

'And then there was the question of Lord Antony…'

The laughter drained from the augur's face. 'Lord Antony,' he repeated. 'Go on, Puella…'

'Cassius put most strongly the case that Lord Antony must meet whatever fate they have planned for the Caesar. They are co-consuls together and only Lepidus as master of the horse holds more power. The others there all agreed with him.'

'Did he?' the augur's eyes were narrow. 'Did they? And what did Lord Brutus say?'

'That they were to be physicians. Not butchers. That Antony is only a limb of Caesar's in any case. And once the head is off, the limb will be helpless. Even a limb that holds a *gladius*.'

'By that they must mean the legions,' said Artemidorus. 'The Seventh is on Tiber Island. Lord Antony as co-consul or Lord Lepidus as *magister equitum* can have them on the streets of the city within a matter of hours.'

'No wonder they want him taken down with the Divine Julius,' said Spurinna. 'I'm surprised they don't want Lepidus killed as well.'

'They do.' Puella answered. 'Tillius Cimber put that case most strongly and the Lord Cassius agreed. But my Lord Brutus gave the same answer as he had given for Lord Antony...'

'Looks like Cicero isn't the only one who will only follow a plan he made himself,' said Spurinna. 'Though at least Brutus punctuates his speeches. On the other hand, that doesn't make them particularly interesting or moving. He's no better as an orator than he was as a soldier.'

'But we can't rely on Cassius doing what Brutus tells him,' warned Artemidorus. 'Brutus may be of the ultimate Republican bloodline. And one of the most respected men in Rome even if he is no great orator. But he's an administrator. Cassius is a soldier – and a good one to have walked away from Crassus' Parthian slaughterhouse at Carrhae with ten thousand men behind him. He'll act if he gets the chance, no matter what Brutus has said.'

Spurinna nodded. 'We'd better get these tablets clean and assembled as quickly as we can – and then get them and this young oracle to the tribune as fast as possible. Do you know where Enobarbus is, by the way, Seven?'

'At Antony's house.'

'Oh. You mean at the palace on the *Clivus Publicius* he stole from Pompey's estate. After Cleopatra's brother handed Caesar Pompey's head on that beach near Alexandria? The one decorated with the prows of all those galleys?'

'Yes,' said Artemidorus. 'That's the house I mean. That's where the tribune and the general will be. Guaranteed. If everything is proceeding as planned.'

'And do you think that's likely?' demanded Spurinna. 'Tonight of all nights?'

Even as he spoke, the physician Antistius entered the crowded, smoky little room. 'Can I have you with me for a moment, Artemidorus?' he said. 'I've found a couple of things I really think you should see.'

*

'Have you cut many throats?' asked Antistius as they crossed the restless, but no longer storm-bound *atrium*.

The vision of Brutus' doorkeeper sprang into the ex-gladiator's mind. And the numberless others that *Scorpionis* had despatched in the arena. 'Not *cut*, no,' he answered. 'Not many.'

'But you have seen cut throats?'

'Enough…'

'Then perhaps you can explain what is unusual about this one…'

Telos was lying on his back, arms at his sides and legs straight out, closed together. His ruined tunic lay across his loins. The papyrus lay nearby, with its almost-*mu* woven into the fabric of it. Artemidorus noted all this only distantly, for his attention was focused on his dead friend's throat. Antistius had rolled the ball of his skull back so that the gaping wound was clear and easy to examine under the lamplight.

As he had admitted, the ex-gladiator and centurion had seen cut throats before. Cutting a throat was often the easiest and most merciful way to send a terminally wounded man out of howling earthly agony to the peace and quiet of the Elysian Fields. Whether in the arena or on the battlefield. Perhaps that was why the killing stroke was called a *quietus*.

'The two most effective ways of doing it are to cut across the front with a sharp knife, dagger or sword. Or to push the point of your knife or *pugio* behind the big tube immediately beneath the chin here and pull the blade straight out to the front. That's the best way in my experience. You cut all the blood vessels and end matters most quickly. If there is any resistance from the organs of the throat it hardly matters because the blood vessels are all severed in any case. Slicing in from the front can be more problematic. This pipe here is solid gristle, almost as hard as bone, and it can be tough to cut

59

through. I've seen men sawing and sawing while some poor bastard chokes and screams.'

'Fascinating. And this one?'

Artemidorus had been studying Telos' wound as he spoke. 'This was from the front, clearly...' The wound was wide, almost from ear to ear. And deep. All the tubes and vessels of the throat were neatly and completely severed. The muscles of the neck were cut and white points of bone showed where the blade had scraped across the spine. But most striking of all, the wound was clean. There were no rough edges. No torn skin. No signs of sawing at all. Telos had been given his *quietus* with one single stroke of a fantastically sharp blade. Hanging against the scaffolding, half dead already, his head held up by someone pulling a handful of hair. Surrounded, in all probability, by the five or so men it would have taken to hold him in place while he was lashed and nailed. Even fainting near death, he would have struggled. Almost certainly no room for a *gladius* sword or anything of comparable size, therefore. Just as there was no room for a legionary to swing a club in battle. So it was done with a knife or a dagger. Not a *gladius*: a *pugio*. And one clean stroke had cut to the bone.

Cut to the bone...

The phrase echoed in his mind and he understood what Antistius was telling him. The knife that did this had a blade of almost magical keenness. And as far as he knew there were only two blades in the whole of Rome like that. Brought from the East. From the farthest edge of Alexander's empire. At the orders of Lord Brutus' mother the Lady Servilia. One of them was probably back in Brutus' family shrine – if they had managed to pull it out of the doorkeeper's ox-like neck.

And Puella might just be able to remember what had happened to the other one if he pressed her firmly enough, he thought, turning without a further word and striding back out into the *atrium*.

*

Spurinna and Puella had melted the wax off all the tablets and splinters. The clean wood lay on the kitchen table and the pair of them crowded side by side, staring down. Which was a waste of time for at least one of them – unless Puella had been taught to read Greek. That, however, seemed unlikely to Artemidorus. The sharpness of her memory made him almost certain she was illiterate. Most household slaves had to remember complex messages, orders and directions without the support of notes. So their memories tended to get better. She had already proved to possess excellent powers of recall. And was clearly filling her mind with what Spurinna was saying as he translated Telos' coded list.

'It's confusing,' the augur was grumbling as Artemidorus entered. 'Naso seems to be on here twice. So does Casca. So does Brutus. Can there be more than one of each? Cassius is named here as Cassius twice but also as Longinus, which is his *cognomen*. It's a mess. And we can't even be sure whether all the names on here are conspirators or men standing against the conspirators. Cicero is on one of the tablets, but Antony, Trebonius, Lepidus and Albinus are on another. And as Puella admits she only knows the names and identities of *almost* all of them, we could still run into unexpected trouble.'

'The general and the *magister equitum* have to be above suspicion,' said Artemidorus, joining them. Almost unconsciously sliding his body between theirs; thigh, hip, shoulder and cheek close enough to Puella to feel her heat and smell the odour of hyssop that seemed to cling to her. 'Albinus is one of Caesar's closest friends. He was at Lepidus' villa tonight having dinner with Caesar as far as I know. Enobarbus says Albinus may be mentioned in Caesar's will – he's planning to adopt him, though it looks as though his great-nephew Octavius will be the principal heir. He rewrote it a few months ago. There may even be an updated document in the keeping of the vestals. No. I have no idea how he learns these things. Perhaps he's sleeping with one of Caesar's secretaries. Or all of them. Maybe even with a vestal. Who knows?

'Trebonius and Caesar have had their differences but he's Caesar's legate and proconsul. Caesar made him *suffet consul* a couple of years ago. He's almost as close to Caesar as Albinus is! That must be a list of men that Caesar can count on to support him.'

'We won't know for certain until we get all the splinters back together and the two sides of each tablet in the correct order. Until we manage that, poor Telos seems to have died for nothing.'

Spurinna's words prompted Artemidorus. 'Puella,' he said. 'Search your memory. The first knife. The one which cut everyone who used it to the bone. I need you to remember what happened to it.'

'I told you,' she said, with some asperity. 'I don't remember...'

'No,' he corrected her gently, thinking how tired, disorientated and simply terrified she must be. 'In the public toilet you said you weren't quite certain. I'm looking for a way to prod your memory. You haven't recognised any of the lesser names on the list...'

'The minnows,' added Spurinna helpfully.

'And you don't think you remember any of the other men whose names you knew...'

'The sharks...'

'...having anything to do with it. Not Cassius, not Casca, not Tillius Cimber or Quintus Labeo...'

'The thing was possessed. Why would Lord Brutus give it to a friend?'

'Perhaps one of them thought that they could tame whatever evil spirits inhabited the thing,' suggested Artemidorus. 'Did any of the men who visited Lord Brutus talk in such terms?'

She shook her head, tears beginning to flood her wide brown eyes.

'Spurinna, have we any other names that might prick Puella's memory?'

Spurinna handed Artemidorus a wooden tablet still hot from the oven and the spy glanced down it. 'Aquila... that's probably Pontius Aquila; he and Caesar are at daggers drawn... Do you recognise the name? No? Well then, Ligarius... Quintus Ligarius, I'd guess; Cicero's friend and ex-client. No? Spurius... Marcus Spurius I suppose... No? Haven't we discussed him already? Well, finally, what about this one? Basilus. That would be Lucius Minucius Basilus.

Born Marcus Satrius, adopted by his fabulously rich, incredibly aristocratic uncle. Took his name in consequence. Good commander; close to Caesar and also Cassius at one time or another. But, again, at daggers drawn since Caesar tried to pay him off when he didn't get command of a province this time round. As though he needed more money or social standing. Another friend of Cicero's too. Thoroughly nasty piece of work, they say. Likes to torture his slaves.'

'Him!' said Puella. 'I remember him.'

'What do you remember about him?' demanded Spurinna.

'Nothing to do with the matters you have been discussing, which is why I did not think...'

'But you are thinking now,' said Artemidorus gently. 'And remembering. What do you remember, Puella?'

'My Lord Brutus was telling his brother Cassius about the knife. How, as I said, it seemed to be possessed, cutting everyone who handled it, no matter how careful they were. This was before he discovered that the Lady Porcia herself was wounded in the leg...'

'And this man Lucius Minucius Basilus was there? Was part of the conversation?'

'Yes. He was very interested; excited. He asked where the knife was and my Lord Brutus said both knives were now in the shrine. Basilus had brought a slave with him, as was quite usual. He asked if the boy could go and get the knife and Lord Brutus agreed. The boy returned with both knives because he didn't know which was which but the handles were different so Lord Brutus was able to take back the one... The one...'

'The one I used to kill the doorkeeper...' prompted Artemidorus quietly.

'Yes. That one. This man Basilus took the other knife and pushed into his slave's leg. Just like that! A deep cut. It went through his flesh like a spoon through honey. I have never seen anything like it. The slave whimpered and his master laughed. He said something about the boy being well trained in suffering. Then he pulled it out and told the boy to get the wound seen to before he bled on anything important enough to merit a good whipping. My Lord Brutus was clearly shocked.

Perhaps more. He said at once that he did not want the knife returned. Basilus and Cassius left together, deep in discussion, about the knife I think. I suppose now that they took it with them...'

'Fascinating,' said Spurinna. 'This man Basilus has a reputation for brutality. But this goes beyond anything I have heard of him.'

'So either Cassius or Basilus has the knife,' said Artemidorus. Then he made the connection that the other two could not. 'But Cassius has no whipping post in his villa, nor any nearby it. I wonder if the brutal Lucius Minucius Basilus does?'

*

At the back of the *atrium*, where the next inner passage led through to the rear of the villa, the *pater familias'* chair was placed facing the *impluvium*, with its back to the *peristyle* garden. Open at the moment, this area, the *tablinum* or study, could be closed off on one side by curtains and on the other by wooden doors. Artemidorus came through from the kitchen and wearily folded himself into this large, comfortable chair, his mind deeply lost in thought. The storm had calmed at last. The pool had settled until its glassy surface mirrored the last rags of cloud scurrying across a starry sky which contained the promise of a full moon. It looked as though dawn was going to arrive early. Except that the light was silver, not gold. Sunrise was still some time away. But it was coming, thought the weary man. The moment the sun peeped over the horizon, the city's clock keepers set the water clocks to measure the hours and the day itself began.

The Ides of Mars was coming all too soon.

The wind had died and the flames on the lamps and candles in the *atrium* steadied and did their best to challenge the stars. There were no longer any discernible flickers of lightning and the thunder was so distant that the sound of it might have been imagination.

The exhausted secret agent had much to consider. The sudden eruption of violence made him as certain as he could be that the conspirators were on the point of acting. This was a fact that he had to get to Enobarbus as soon as possible. But it was only worth disturbing his chief if he came armed with sufficient evidence to make the tribune rouse the general to action. For as far as he could see, the general was the only man likely to stop Caesar following his usual routine – and walking into whatever trap the conspirators were laying for him.

Puella had a new level of evidence locked in her memory. Precise details of plots being hatched and the names of the men discussing them. But nothing as yet which said unarguably, *These men will do this thing in this place at this time. And Caesar will die because of it.* When she and Spurinna had completed the list of names contained in Telos' secret coded communication, then there might be enough of sufficient weight to make worthwhile a visit to Pompey's palace on the *Clivus Publicius* to rouse the tribune and his general.

But, as the conspirators had planned, the spy was torn. Not only between the certainty that time was running out and the worry that if he acted too soon he would do more harm than good, but also between the absolute importance of his mission and his overwhelming concern for the woman he loved.

He had no doubt that the fact he had only met groups of Cassius' and Cestus' men in the streets on this side of the Forum was no coincidence. Somewhere along the line he had come to suspect that the two groups were closely associated. And both were probably also associated with Lucius Minucius Basilus. Who liked to torture people. Who was the man in Rome most likely to possess both the twin of Brutus' dagger and a whipping post. The dagger at least must have been responsible for Telos' cut throat. Just as the whipping post was the most likely place for Telos to have been secured while the life was being beaten out of him. Added to the fact that Cestus' spiked fists were most likely to be responsible for his terrible wounds. And as *Syrus* the Syrian and Cestus had discussed just before the panther attacked, raping Puella would make up for the fact that they had been forbidden to touch the girl they had been near earlier. And if Cestus was the man who beat Telos, then the woman Syrus had been forbidden to touch could only be Cyanea.

And the place where all this happened had to be Basilus' villa, where, no doubt, there was a whipping post that was all too familiar to Basilus' slaves. Where there were likely to be sheets of top quality amphitheatre papyrus. With the Greek *mu* woven into them to celebrate the Minucius family's name and ancient aristocratic heritage. It had been part of his mission during the last weeks not only to go undercover in the leader's house but also to try and keep an eye on anyone else with a grudge against Caesar. Therefore he knew where Basilus' villa was. Not too far from here in fact, further up on the Esquiline Hill.

But when it came right down to it, he was not a free man able to follow his own desires. He was senior centurion of the *Legio VII*, under orders from his tribune, even if he was disguised as a common freedman. He was, as Spurinna insisted on reminding him, *Septem* the secret agent codenamed Seven, tasked with protecting Caesar until they all departed on the Parthian campaign in five days' time. He had his duty, which came before everything. Even Cyanea.

He pulled himself wearily onto his feet, therefore, and went back to the kitchen to see how Spurinna and Puella were getting on.

They were still busy fitting the pieces of splintered tablet together. But they had made some progress. 'We have a list of surnames, *cognomen*, Seven. All of the ones listed here,' announced Spurinna, who sounded pleased with himself. 'We're still working on the *praenomen* and the *nomen*, though. So we still can't be absolutely certain who we're actually talking about.'

'Surnames are a start,' said Artemidorus with a touch of impatience. He knew what Spurinna was up to – the repetition of his codename kept emphasising where his duty lay – and let Cyanea look after herself. 'Let's have the list.'

'Puella has memorised it,' said Spurinna. 'I haven't had an opportunity to get it written down yet.'

Artemidorus turned to the woman who was rapidly becoming the most indispensible element in any report he would take to Enobarbus. 'Well?'

'Lords Brutus and Cassius,' she said at once, her tone confident. 'Casca, Labeo, Cimber, Aquila. Basilus, Caelius, Bucolianus, Ruga.' She paused for breath, frowning with concentration. 'Ligarius, Galba, Naso, Parmenses, Petronius and Turulius,' she concluded.

'There may be more than one of each,' warned Spurinna. 'You know there are several names repeated. That may mean there are several conspirators all with the same surname. Brothers. Cousins. Fathers. Sons – natural and adopted like Lucius Minucius Basilus.'

'But at least sixteen for certain.' The spy persisted.

'At least sixteen. Maybe more than twenty.'

'All patricians.' He probed.

'All senators, in fact,' nodded Spurinna.

There was a moment of silence as the exhausted spy's mind caught up with Spurinna's apparently unthinking observation. 'Wait. Say that again…' he demanded.

'All senators…'

He swung from the augur to the slave girl. 'And Puella, what did Lord Brutus say about attacking Caesar on the *Via Sacra*?'

'That they could not do it because there was no good reason for a large number of patricians to be in a group all together there.' She frowned, still not making the connection.

'But there is one place where it is inevitable that there will be a large group of *senators* gathered together!' he breathed.

'In the Senate!' said Spurinna, his voice full of astonishment. 'It's so obvious! How could we not have seen…'

'When is the next meeting of the Senate?'

'Today! In the *curia* meeting hall of Pompey's Theatre. At the third hour or soon after. Later this morning!'

'That's it, then. That's where they will try to put their plans into action. At the meeting of the Senate, in Pompey's Theatre at the third hour. *Today*.'

Abruptly all hesitation, weariness and indecision was gone. He was speaking with the voice of the senior centurion of the *Legio VII*, alerted by the insights of the *speculator Septem* and his associates. Taking clear and decisive action at last.

'Gather your stuff together, Spurinna, and don't forget Telos' tablets. Lend Puella a cloak. We have to take her and all of this to Tribune Enobarbus. At once.'

*

In spite of his impatience to be gone, Artemidorus' experiences so far tonight advised caution. And the largest possible bodyguard of burly slaves that Spurinna's household could supply. The storm was over, the moon full and nearing its apogee. Nevertheless the men Spurinna roused lit flambeaus on Artemidorus' order. For he was wise enough to know that light would announce their presence and keep the shadows at bay. And those who lurked in the shadows. Swords were forbidden within the Servian walls – to all except gladiators and soldiers on duty. So the cook was upset once more as, not content with ruining her favourite oven, her master confiscated every promising-looking knife in her kitchen. But at last the party was armed and assembled. While Antistius saw to the disposal of Telos' corpse, the sizeable group going down to see Enobarbus and Antony at Pompey's villa left him to it.

There would be no report to the local *aedile* magistrate about Telos' death, thought Artemidorus as he led Puella, Spurinna and his men down the slope past the scaffolding on which the murdered spy had been crucified. No investigation. No charges. No legal redress for the slaughter of his friend and the kidnapping of his lover. But there would be retribution. There would certainly be revenge.

Then he put all thoughts of the past to one side and began to focus on the work in hand. The moon was as large as he had ever seen it. The whole of Rome seemed to be bathed in silver as the raindrops, puddles and still-running gutters gleamed and twinkled. The storm had left more than water in its wake. The last of the night was surprisingly warm. A wind from the south promising a bright and balmy early spring day, when the sun began to rise. Its gentle gusts at first smelt of the pine trees clothing the Palatine Hill and then of rosemary as it blew across some local Lucullan gourmet's herb-garden. Rosemary and, tantalisingly, of hyssop.

But soon enough they bore the familiar stench of the Forum. Even as the keening of the breeze in empty streets was replaced by the gathering bustle.

Artemidorus led his little cohort straight ahead with the central group of Puella, Spurinna and Kyros at his shoulders and the larger group of household slaves spread in a protective circle around them. Artemidorus was keeping to the north of the Forum itself, heading past the Temple of Tellus for Antony's house on the *Clivus Publicius*.

With little immediate to worry about, Artemidorus' mind inevitably returned to his other concern. Given unusual co-operation from the gods, he rather hoped he might come across the remainder of Cestus' gang. Especially Syrus the club man. Artemidorus knew his face, could find him and recognise him. Could beat out of him as necessary the final details of where Cyanea was. Of how Cyanea was. Although preoccupied, he led the little cohort across the benighted city at the double. Marching them at the legionary quick march which could cover more than twenty miles in a five-hour marching day. They were unladen and marching in the best possible conditions. So they reached the Temple of Tellus within half an hour and were outside Marc Antony's residence a few moments later. The prows and rams of the ships with which it was decorated shining like silver along with everything else nearby.

With Spurinna at one shoulder and Puella at the other and Kyros guarding his back, Artemidorus hammered on the general's imposing front door – as though he were an important guest too elevated to consider the more discreet *posticum* side entrance he would have used under most other circumstances.

After a while a sleepy *ostiarius* answered, easing the door open apprehensively. Hardly surprisingly, thought Artemidorus – given the rough-looking gang demanding entry.

'Rouse the Tribune Enobarbus,' he ordered. 'Tell him the *speculator Septem* is here with people bearing vital information for the protection of Rome and the Republic. And we need to see the Consul Antony on the most urgent business…'

'But the consul is not at home,' answered the doorkeeper nervously. 'And the tribune is not here either. Do you wish me to wake the Lady Fulvia?'

'Is she likely to know where the consul is?' The Lady Fulvia was notorious for her temper, Artemidorus knew. And she was unlikely to appreciate being woken by men on business with her errant husband.

'No, sir,' answered the *ostiarius*. 'I heard the Lady asking her serving women if they knew where Lord Antony was as she prepared to retire.'

'And do *you* know where the consul is?'

'No, sir. But I expect the tribune is with him…'

Artemidorus let out a frustrated sigh. To have worked so hard and accomplished so much, only to be disappointed at the final moment…

'Perhaps you would like to wait, sir. If your business is as vital as you say, the tribune and the consul will wish to be made aware of it at the earliest opportunity. The instant they return, in fact.'

'But you don't know when that will be.'

'It can't be much later, sir. The consul will wish to perform his ablutions, visit his *tonsor* for a shave and change his clothes before his first appointment. He always does, without fail. Especially as there is a full meeting of the Senate that he must attend this morning. At the third hour I believe…'

Artemidorus swung round like a beast in the arena. He felt trapped. Tricked by whatever gods there were. It seemed brutally hard to him. He had come here, following a path dictated by his duty, a very different path to the one he really wished to follow – the path that led to Minucius Basilus' villa on the Esquiline while there was still a chance of rescuing Cyanea. And to have come this far, leaving her in the most terrible danger, only to be invited to sit and wait… He was action personified. It was simply not in his nature to do what Antony's doorkeeper advised. And yet…

'*Septem*,' said Spurinna softly, 'Puella and I can tell the tribune everything he needs to know. You assembled the information but you do not need to deliver it. The pair of us can do that. Take a couple of my men to light your way and watch your back. You can be at Minucius Basilus' villa well before sunrise and at least find out if she's there.'

He swung back to meet Puella's wide gaze. Oddly, he felt he needed her permission too. For he had promised to protect her – and that might well mean standing by her in the face of Antony's anger. But she nodded. Gave a half-smile. '*Run!*' she said.

IV

Tribune Enobarbus stood at the outer edge of the balcony fronting Caesar's villa on the Janiculum Hill. His fists rested on the cool, wet top of the marble balustrade. They were clenched with anger and frustration. His eyes remained blind to the magnificence of the view he was looking down upon. Because they were turned inward to his raging thoughts.

Unobserved by the furious tribune, the Tiber wound past like a ribbon of molten moonlight under the low, star-filled sky. The island in the midst of it lay picked out with tiny points of gold from the VIIth Legion's watchfires. On this side, the lower slopes of the Janiculum Hill were clothed with jade-black pine trees whose scent lay heavy on the clearing air. Pushed into the tribune's face by a warm southerly breeze. Beneath the pines lay walks and gardens laid out and maintained by the man who owned them. Caesar. Beyond the gleaming river, Rome rose majestically on her seven hills. From this distance the great city looked like a queen's jewellery box. The buildings gleamed with roofs and columns all of pearl and silver. Streets of dead black shadow lay like an enormous spider's web between them. Green-black stands of trees like ebony-winged moths trapped within the obsidian threads. Here and there, specks of golden light moved like sunstruck raindrops along them. A throbbing gilded brightness pulsed at its heart. Where the bustle of the Forum persisted. And would do so until the sun rose to start the new day. The fifteenth day of Mars. The Ides. And if Enobarbus roused himself to look beyond the gleaming city, away to the east, the night-black sky was just beginning to pale with the first, distant promise of the coming dawn.

Enobarbus remained unaware of the beauty all around him. As he raged against the ill fortune that had robbed the one man he relied upon for forceful action of the ability even to stand. Until he was disturbed by a noise in the great reception chamber. The soldier turned and marched back into the beautiful building. The reception room was bright with a wanton extravagance of candles, lamps and flambeaus. Servants waited, the younger and weaker, seated half asleep with their backs against the marble walls. The rest standing in rigid ranks, praying, no doubt to be dismissed to their beds before the mistress arose and yesterday's duties ran seamlessly into today's.

A fire guttered in an inner grate throwing warmth and light unsteadily across the room. Enobarbus caught the eye of the *dispensator* steward. He was one of the few Romans still part of the household. Everyone else in the room was Egyptian.

Except for Antony.

Antony was seated in a chair so rich and ostentatious it was almost a throne. Indeed, when the villa's current tenant sat in it, it *was* a throne, thought Enobarbus. And all too many people down in Rome were fearful that when the villa's owner sat in it he too thought it should be a throne. For the person who had occupied the chair before Antony had been Cleopatra VIIth of Egypt, Pharaoh, Queen and Goddess. And the man who would sit in it after she had left was Consul and Dictator the Divine Gaius Julius Caesar – who also, perhaps, wished to be a king as well as a god. In Rome the former was far more powerful and fearful than the latter.

Cleopatra's departure was at the root of the problem Enobarbus was facing now. The Queen had made no secret of the fact that when Caesar left for Parthia in five days' time, she would already have vacated the villa. Everything she had brought with her from Alexandria more than a year ago was packed. The royal vessel was moored in Ostia, where the Tiber's delta gave Rome her closest seaport. She had made up her mind. And, independently of her regal standing and unquestioned divinity, she was a woman who did not waver once her mind was made up.

Caesar loved her, Enobarbus knew. Enjoyed the wit and challenge of her company. Was enslaved by whatever Greek and oriental variations on African sexual techniques she used. Techniques the staid and proper, unfortunately barren,

Calpurnia would never dream of. Loving and supportive though she was. Techniques through which he had sired a promising son upon her: *Caesarion*. But Little Caesar would be returning to Egypt with his mother, rather than invading Parthia with his father. Caesar had plans that did not include the Egyptian queen, in spite of the fact that he had erected a gilded statue of her beside the statue of Venus in the Forum. The plain truth was that Caesar was in no way upset by the prospect of Cleopatra's departure for he was leaving Rome himself.

Antony was different. Antony loved her in a way he could never love his wife Fulvia. Or any other of the women he casually and repeatedly bedded. Perhaps the root of the problem was that he had never bedded Cleopatra. She remained for him something as precious and unattainable as the moon whose light was silvering the world around them. But the problem facing Enobarbus now had more than one root. It had a double root like a mandrake – to which *strigae* witches, aptly enough, gave a magical sexual power.

On the one side of the double problem was the unattainable, departing Cleopatra. On the other was Antony's legendary love of wine. Tonight, when he had come through the deluge to take his leave of her, the two roots of the mandrake had come together. After the formal farewells, Cleopatra and Caesarion had retired and left him to his own devices. Mother and child had been in bed since moonrise. And now it was almost dawn. The interim which the broken-hearted Antony had filled with drinking. And an increasingly bellicose refusal to go home. Perhaps on purpose, perhaps by accident, he has simply drunk himself into a stupor. With the consequence that it was now difficult to be certain that he was even living. Nothing the increasingly desperate Tribune Enobarbus had done gave any sign of bringing the general to his senses.

Antony gave another stentorian snore. An echo of the one that had brought Enobarbus back in off the balcony. For an instant the soldier thought the noise might be loud enough to wake his commander. But no. Antony settled back into the

74

depths of drunken insensibility from which Enobarbus had been unable to rouse him.

Though the tribune had been circumspect in his actions. Antony was not a man to be slapped or shaken into wakefulness. Quite apart from the assault that would make upon his dignity as Co-Consul of Rome, there was also the fact that he had been a dangerous tearaway in his youth. If Enobarbus wasn't careful, he would wake the streetwise bully who had run with notoriously violent street gangs such as Publius Clodius Pulcher's. And anyone waking *that* Antony was unlikely to survive the experience. Not for nothing did he claim direct descent from Hercules. And, if he had left at home the lion skin he often wore – as Hercules wore that of the Nemean Lion slain with his own hands – he was still a man of enormous size and strength. More than capable of killing a man with his bare hands. If not a lion.

Raging with frustration, all too well aware that the dawn was creeping relentlessly up the sky behind him, Enobarbus looked around the huge reception room. And its very size gave him an idea. He turned to the sleepy steward. 'Do you think we could get Lord Antony's litter through those doors?' he asked.

'I should think so, Tribune. Do you wish the consul's litter brought in here?'

'Yes. And rouse the rest of his retinue. His *lictors* should make sure the axes in their *fasces* are sharp and easy to use. I don't like the feel of the night, and twelve well-armed *lictors* will make me feel better. Even if we have to dispense with some of them when we enter the *pomerium*. I'd like as many men with torches as you can find. And arm them as best you can. With *gladius* swords if you have them. We'll leave them outside the Servian wall if anyone should complain. And then I want half a dozen of your strongest but most gentle men in here. Now.'

Within moments the double doors opposite the fireplace were standing wide as Antony's personal litter was carried in. At the tribune's direction, the litter bearers put it on the floor beside Antony's chair. With the gentle care of a mother moving a sleeping child, the six strong men lifted the insensible Antony out of the chair and laid him in the litter. Enobarbus closed the curtains and gestured. The bearers lifted the litter and carried the sleeping consul out of the room with Enobarbus close behind. The twelve *lictors* were waiting in the anteroom outside, axes gleaming at the centre of the bundles of ceremonial wooden rods they carried. As the growing group of men moved through the anteroom and out of the villa altogether, twenty more strong servants gathered round them, flaming flambeaus in one hand, naked swords in the other.

As the main door to Caesar's villa closed quietly behind them, Enobarbus bid a mental farewell to Queen Cleopatra, with whom he was also more than half in love. And then he settled into the business of getting Lord Antony home in time for this morning's meeting of the Senate in the *curia* of Pompey's Theatre on the Field of Mars.

*

The villa belonging to Lucius Minucius Basilus on the Esquiline Hill was set back from the road. Although the ancient and impressive frontage was open, the sides and the rear were surrounded by trees. Artemidorus looked at their moon-bright canopies. As far as he could see they were all pine trees. Some rose straight up like tall green-black candle flames. Others opened and spread like massive mushrooms. It was these that overhung the roof of the Minucius family villa, which appeared to have been standing here as long as the ancient vegetation had done. He stood, deep in thought, while Kyros and the others stood in the circle around him, their flambeaus dangerously bright in the last of the predawn darkness – dulled as they were by the brightness of the setting moon. The spy had little time to linger or plan before someone in the villa saw the flaming torches and grew suspicious.

Artemidorus' plan of action sprang into his head almost ready made. The trees would replace the ladder with which he had freed Puella. But only if he could get out as easily as he got in. He needed something that would double for the ladder even though in the final analysis it had proved less useful than he had hoped. But once again the bustling industry that Caesar

76

had brought to Rome together with his fortunes in tribute, gold and slaves, offered the secret agent a chance to take action. For one of the villas on this road was clothed in scaffolding. Just as the villa opposite Spurinna's had been. Scaffolding made of wood held together by a combination of rough metal brackets and length upon length of rope.

'Kyros,' he ordered. 'Take a couple of these men and get me as much of that rope as you can.'

'Yes, Seven.'

'You two,' he said to the remaining slaves. 'Follow me in here.'

Without further conversation, Artemidorus led the two men with their flambeaus down the side of the villa, among the fragrant trunks of the massive pines. The tops of the trees soared in black outline against the starry brightness of the sky, dimming though it was as dawn threatened. The flambeaus gave an idea of how the lower branches of the wide-spreading canopy were positioned. And most of them were high above reach – especially those belonging to the trees that spread wide enough to overhang the villa's roof. Silently, his mind racing, the spy led the slaves through the shadowy grove. The ground beneath his feet soft with sodden pine needles. The trunks on either side layered with flakes of bark and running with fragrant balsam. At last the little group reached the rear wall of the villa. The trees stretched across the back to join the others on the far side of the building. Nothing that Artemidorus could see promised an easy climb up to a spreading canopy that would allow him to look down into the open roof of the villa's inner *peristyle* garden.

As he paused at the rearmost corner, frowning in thought, Kyros came bustling up with a length of rope looped over and over his shoulder, his companions on either side, their flambeaus blazing. The added brightness showed Artemidorus his best way up. A black pine, shaped like a candle flame, stood beside a tall stone pine shaped like an umbrella. The black pine had branches that started at ground level and should be easy to climb. The stone pine spread its canopy widely. On one side it mingled its lower branches with the top of the black pine. On the other it spread them across the villa's roof and from down here it looked as though its branches would support the weight of a man sliding along to their outer ends.

'I'm going up,' he told Kyros. 'Follow me with the rope.'

'Yes, *Septem*,' answered the slave unhesitatingly.

'And, Kyros, bring the sharpest knife we've got.'

Artemidorus pushed into the dark, sweet-smelling heart of the black pine and began to climb. The branches were thin and flexible, but by placing his feet in the angles where they joined the trunk, the agile spy was able to make his way upward quickly and efficiently. He felt the tall, thin trunk begin to tremble when he was little more than three cubits, six *pedes*, feet, up as Kyros began to follow him with the rope. By the time he was ten feet above the ground, the black pine was beginning to bend and twist under his weight. But when he paused to let everything settle down, he saw that the lowermost of the stone pine's sturdy branches were just above him, outlined against the sky by waning starshine. Steadying himself, he reached up and over until he could grasp it and swing out, letting it take all his weight as he heaved himself up onto it. Thankful for his thick leather trousers, he straddled the rough branch and slid carefully along and down it until he was able to grasp the trunk. Then he carefully pulled himself to his feet. Feeling the branch shaking beneath him, he turned to see Kyros' silver-edged shape humping itself towards him down the considerable slope of the thick branch. Moving in such a way as to make it very clear that the boy had no thick leather protecting his vital parts.

As he waited for the slave to reach him, Artemidorus looked around. The needle-like leaves and nut-filled cones obstructed his view a little – but not too much. The tree was the better part of ninety feet high. It gave a view over the lower slopes of the Esquiline Hill to the south and the west. The rapidly fading starlight showed nothing but a city seemingly cast in lead and pewter – and sound asleep. To the other side, the north-eastern vista was gobbled up by other groves of pines which clothed the gathering slope, between the villas that had stood there seemingly since Romulus was king. And hid, for the moment, the gathering brightness of the dawn.

Nearer at hand, the trunk he was holding onto seemed to split and spread a cubit or so above him, and by the time Kyros arrived with the rope, he had pulled himself up onto a higher branch that reached out promisingly over the roof of Minucius Basilus' villa. One behind the other, the two of them slid along this branch until it began to sway dangerously. Then Kyros waited while Artemidorus proceeded as close to the end as he dared go. But that was close enough.

The secret agent found himself a few feet from the branches' fan-like end, which, beneath his weight, was overhanging the inner edge of the villa's roof. From this position he had an excellent view of the *peristyle* garden. The moonlight might be waning but it was still bright enough to show the spy every detail of the garden. The columned walkway around its outer edges. The fragrant herb bushes and flower beds immediately within that. The brick-paved pathways that lay geometrically within the gardens. The well-tended square of lawn in the middle. And, at the end of the lawn where there usually stood a statue or a fountain, Minucius Basilus had erected a whipping post.

A whipping post to which Cyanea was tied. Her body sagged with fatigue and hopelessness. Shoulders bowed and face pressed against the post where her hands were secured. All he could see clearly was the back of her head, the tumble of her long, golden hair, her shoulders, and back. She was still wearing her tunic, so her would-be rescuer was pretty certain she had not been whipped or assaulted yet. At least, he prayed to his demigod *Achilleus* that this was so.

*

After a moment more of watching, Artemidorus was in action. He reached back for the rope Kyros was holding, took it and secured one end of it firmly round the branch. He threw the other end outwards and watched in lively satisfaction as it followed the curve of the branch and fell across the roof, down into the garden. He reached down to his belt and made sure that the largest knife from Spurinna's kitchen was safely there.

'Wait here,' he ordered.

'Yes, *Septem*,' whispered Kyros.

Artemidorus was in motion once again, sliding along the branch until he could grasp the rope and swing himself out and over the tiles of the villa's roof. Silently, he eased himself over the corrugated slope and down over the edge until he was swinging on the rope itself. Hand over hand, he lowered himself into the garden until the soles of his sandals were brushing the top of a rosemary bush, releasing its fragrance onto the still, cool air. A heartbeat later he was on the ground. He let go of the rope and turned, stepping out of the flower bed and onto the path. He ran on tiptoe across the grass towards Cyanea, reaching for the knife that would cut her free as he did so.

As he neared her at last she looked up, her eyes wide and desperate, her nostrils flared, her mouth sealed shut by a thick gag whose ends vanished beneath her hair. He knew then for certain what he had only suspected all along. That this was a trap. For there was no point at all in gagging someone at a whipping post. The screams of the victim were a major element of the scourging. Especially for someone who enjoyed inflicting pain, like the villa's master. The only point of gagging Cyanea was to stop her warning anyone coming to the rescue that this was a trap. He pulled the knife out and swung round, shoulder to shoulder beside her, his back to the post.

The wooden doors at the inner end of the garden opened and light flooded out as they did so. Not just light. A tall, cadaverous man in a toga, edged with purple, stepped out of a spacious but crowded *tablinum* study. Eight or so large and threatening-looking thugs behind him. As the thugs rapidly spread out on either side, looming between the columns, Artemidorus recognised their leader. Syrus the club wielder. Cestus' right-hand man. Clearly Cestus' replacement now that the panther had eaten the actual right hand in question.

A whisper of sound distracted him. The rope he had climbed down was gone. He hoped that Kyros had gone with it and stood some chance of getting back to Spurinna with the news of the trap. Because he and Cyanea clearly weren't going anywhere. Except to the Elysian Fields, perhaps. Mind racing, Artemidorus stepped forward. 'We know the whole plan, Basilus,' he said. 'My associates are talking to Lord Antony even now. Telling him everything. He will put a stop to this. You allowed Cestus to slaughter my friend for nothing.'

'We'll see…' answered Minucius Basilus, his voice as quiet as the hissing of sand blowing over silk.

He gave a tiny gesture and Syrus' men closed round Artemidorus. The spy gave in without a fight. A fight he clearly could not win. And even if he could, how would he escape? Even were he willing to leave Cyanea to face the wrath of the thwarted Basilus. Which he was not. The club man took his knife with no trouble therefore – and with an arrogant, victorious sneer.

'You were lucky Cestus didn't kill you,' said Syrus. 'You won't be so lucky with me.'

'We'll see about that,' answered Artemidorus with more confidence than he felt. 'The gods were on my side when they set that panther free. Perhaps they will stay on my side.'

'Poor old Cestus,' chuckled Syrus. 'Well, he might have been big. And he might have been strong. But that was about it. I mean, he was the one who beat your friend half to death. But the eyes. The tongue. The crucifixion. The note. Those were all my doing. And it was those things that brought you here. So maybe he wasn't the *sharpest blade on the battlefield*, as your friend Vitus the doorkeeper might say. And neither, it seems, are you. Oh, yes. I frowned at poor old Vitus. Really *frowned*. He was another one who sang like a lark. Priscus, tie this fool up.'

As the Syrian was speaking, his men roughly grabbed Artemidorus' arms. The one called Priscus said, 'Have you got any rope?'.

'No,' snapped Syrus. 'Go and find some, fool!'

There was silence for an instant.

'What do you want us to do with them, Lord Basilus?' asked Syrus, clearly hoping for the answer: *Kill him and do as you like with her*. Keeping her alive and untouched had simply made her a better bit of bait in the trap they had set, Artemidorus calculated grimly. But the trap was sprung now.

The skull-face of the villa's aristocratic owner tilted up. His hollow eyes regarded the sky for a moment. The air in the garden was stirred by a little wind. Artemidorus realised that it was almost daybreak. 'That is for Lord Cassius to decide,' Basilus whispered. 'I am due at his home at dawn so we have no time to linger. You and your men will escort me there. And bring these two along. And don't worry, Syrus. What they know and what they can guess is too important for them to live much longer. He will want them killed, I am sure. And you may take your time with them. And I will watch. With pleasure.' The only part of Basilus' face that did not look like one of the mummies of Egypt was his lips. They were full, red and glistening.

And he licked them at the thought.

V

'You knew it was a trap?' whispered Cyanea, as soon as her mouth was free.

'I suspected,' answered Artemidorus. He took a breath. Ready to explain what he had suspected and why. Distracted, as always by the simple beauty of the wide blue-green eyes. Of her face, worthy of Eurydice. Though he was no Orpheus, he would follow her to Hades and back, he thought.

She spoke before he could: 'And still you came?'

'Of course...' Again, he would have added more.

But, 'That's enough whispering,' snarled Syrus. 'You'll both have plenty to say to all of us. As soon as Lord Basilus lets us start questioning you.'

Artemidorus took the measure of the man for the first time. In a heartbeat, he noted the colossal shoulders and slim waist round which a thick belt sat loosely. Only there to gather up his tunic to the length his status required. And to carry the sheath for the sword which only soldiers on duty and gladiators were permitted to carry within the *pomerium* and the Servian walls. Massive thighs, bulging calves and big, square feet in their hobnailed *caligae*. Brawny arms and brutal hands. Square nailed and callused from wielding the club that gave the gladiator his name just as Cyanea's eyes had given her hers. Knuckles thick and scarred from punching and pounding those unfortunate victims the club had crippled.

Unlike Lord Brutus' doorkeeper, the head which sat squarely on the thick neck did not look too small for the considerable body. The face was youthful, fine boned. Surprisingly unscarred. Sharp cheekbones stood between black-bearded cheeks and ears that stuck out like the handles on an *amphora*. The nose was aquiline but almost delicate. It had not yet been broken, which suggested some skill in the arena. Or some luck. The eyes beneath the square-cut, luxuriant hair and single black bar of eyebrow were dark. Burning with passionate intelligence.

Like the downward twist of the full lips, they betrayed the Syrian's attitude to life. Revealed his excitement at the prospect of torturing two new victims. All in all a dangerous enemy. Motivated not only by Basilus' orders. And his money, no doubt. But also by simple enjoyment of wielding power and inflicting pain. The club man might be shorter than the Greek spy by almost a head. But by the look of things he was physically and mentally his equal. Younger; maybe fitter. The only edge Artemidorus had was experience. But he had plenty of that.

Unaware of Artemidorus' scrutiny, Syrus started to release Cyanea from the post. His gestures were rough, designed to hurt her as he worked out his frustration at not being able to torture her at once. His face folded in a frown of childish disappointment. She suffered in silence as his abrupt movements bruised the pale, soft skin. Of her arms. Shoulders. Breast. Working on her bonds with his cruel fists.

Priscus was slower, finding a length of rope and beginning to secure her would-be rescuer. Artemidorus thought that *Ursus* would have been a better name for him. The gladiator was as hairy as a bear. His shaggy head seemed to join his sloping shoulders without benefit of a neck. He moved in a slow slouch, dragging his feet. It was a wonder that the big paws at the end of his arms were capable of holding the sword he also wore at his right hip.

The skeletal senator lingered, observing the process of binding the prisoners. 'Had you been a little more quick-thinking,' he sneered at Artemidorus, 'then we should have enjoyed a most amusing time.' His voice was low, but it carried. He was, after all used to public speaking. In the Forum. In the Senate. The sibilants hissed, snake-like as he spoke, spraying a fine mist of spittle into the torchlight. His passions were the same as Syrus', thought Artemidorus. But his power and ability to indulge them were infinitely greater. As demonstrated by the stabbing of his young slave's thigh. They befogged his mind and interfered with his reason. He continued to talk too much as a cover to his lingering enjoyment of the spectacle his helpless prisoners presented.

'But your slow wits have saved you for the moment,' he continued. His gaze fixed on what Syrus was doing to Cyanea. Eyes glinting as he watched the beautiful young woman being rebound. 'As I said, I am due to attend the *deposito barbae* coming-of-age ceremony of Lord Cassius' son. Which begins soon. And I am by no means the only guest invited. Being tardy would disgrace me before many of the city's most powerful men. But I wish to refer to Lord Cassius before taking further action. Both you, woman, and your dead friend were members of his household after all. For a while at least.

'Therefore you two will accompany us. So that he can decide your fate. Even if I propose to make Syrus execute it according to my personal preferences.' He licked his glistening carmine lips again. Cyanea's arms were tightly tied behind her back now, squaring her shoulders and thrusting her breasts into prominence.

'I'll look forward to breaking you,' sneered Syrus as Lord Basilus turned away. 'Like we broke Telos. Bone by bone.'

'You might find that more difficult than you think, boy,' breathed the spy. 'Without Cestus to hide behind.'

By way of answer, Syrus picked up his Syrian club and drove it into Artemidorus' belly. The club was as long as Syrus' arm and covered with dull spikes at its end. A rough-and-ready weapon modelled on the club the legendary Hercules was often pictured wielding. But Syrus was no Hercules. No more than Lord Antony was. But at least the general was huge and prone to wearing lion skins in honour of the demigod he claimed to be descended from.

The ex-gladiator was expecting the blow and tightened his stomach muscles. But he folded over as though badly winded when it hit home. The muscles of his torso and arms bulged hugely as he fought for breath – just at the very moment that Priscus was finally knotting ropes binding his wrists behind his back. He wheezed and tore the ropes from Priscus' fists as he staggered into the villa on the heels of the departing senator. Retching and gasping as he went. Close behind

Cyanea. In the midst of Syrus' brawny companions. Vanishing before the startled gladiator could check the knots he had just tightened.

Artemidorus had been in much more pain and a great deal more danger many times before and yet he had lived to tell the tale. Usually because of careful thought and planning. Sometimes because of luck – or the good offices of his own favourite demigod, Achilleus, hero of Troy. This was all a calculated risk, he thought as he came up behind Cyanea's slim rear. But a risk well worth taking. It allowed him to help Cyanea escape – if she needed help.

And, more importantly, perhaps, if he could not be at the centre of the conference in Lord Antony's villa, then he was very happy to be at the centre of the suspiciously large gathering at Cassius'. For the youthful subject of the ceremony was at least a year too young to lose his beard. And this was the fifteenth of the month – the Ides. Not the seventeenth, *Liberalia*, when the annual ceremony that passed a youth into manhood was traditionally carried out.

It was the assembly of men at Cassius' villa, therefore, and not his son's ceremony, that was important.

*

As Cyanea and he were being hurried towards the heart of the conspiracy, the Greek spy was relying on Spurinna's young slave, the quick-thinking Kyros. To assess the situation as soon as the troupe of nobles, clients, servants, slaves, captives and gladiators came streaming out of the villa. To follow them all to Cassius' villa and observe the men assembling there under pretext of honouring the boy. Actually about some other, darker business. And to take news of what was happening to Spurinna, Enobarbus and hopefully Lord Antony.

There were handy men in the VIIth, led by Quintus among others, who would be happy to come to the spies' rescue. If Enobarbus decided the action was necessary. Or to stand between Cassius' guests and any harm threatened to Caesar himself. If the hesitant General and Co-Consul Marc Antony had arrived home yet. If he was in a fit state to make decisions.

If he could be convinced to order the action. To risk the utter enmity of the most powerful men in Rome. Men who would be his unrelenting political and personal enemies for the four-or-five-year duration of Caesar's imminent Parthian campaign if Antony miscalculated in any way. Or the information his *contubernium* eight-man unit of spies gave him proved inaccurate. In the meantime Cyanea and he were on their own. But none the worse for that, thought Artemidorus. For the moment at least. If everything continued to go to plan.

The crowd of men and one woman spilled out into the street, flambeaus blazing, *lictors' fasces* held high. Clients grouped around their patrician benefactor. Gladiators in a wall of muscular flesh around their prisoners. Artemidorus straightened apparently painfully and looked around as he staggered forward across the wet cobbles. Motivated by Syrus' club in the small of his back. The aftermath of the departing storm had left restless winds. They slammed around the streets in unexpected gusts which made the flames of the torches dance and flicker. But it had also left a clear sky and pellucid atmosphere. There would be no darkness before the coming of dawn today.

Which meant fewer shadows for Spurinna's cunning slave to hide in as he followed them all towards Cassius' city home. Or to linger in as he counted heads and noted faces. If only he had thought to bring Puella too, mused Artemidorus with a flicker of frustration. To see which of the so-called guests she recognised. He had thought ahead. But not quite far enough ahead. Distracted, just as his enemies planned. By Telos' horrific fate and the terrible danger to Cyanea. On the other hand, Puella would have shared their current fate had she accompanied him. Though the prospect of torturing two beautiful women, one with white skin and one with black, might have been too much for Minucius Basilus. Might even have given him a dose of the falling sickness that Caesar suffered from.

Artemidorus straightened to his full height, his face breaking into a fleeting grin at the thought of Basilus fainting from an excess of lust. One of the very weaknesses the Stoic philosophy warned against. The eastern sky above the Esquiline Hill was beginning to lighten with soaring streaks of red. As though Zeus himself, god of the sky, had had his throat cut like Telos. Or Eos, pink-fingered goddess of the dawn was wearing red robes today instead of her traditional saffron. As though her brother Helios' rapidly approaching sun chariot was bright with ruby flames instead of golden ones. High above the muttering of the clients and the trudging of the gladiators' hobnail boots, a lark suddenly burst into song. Somewhere, not too distantly, a cock began to crow.

'Hurry,' snarled Minucius Basilus. 'I don't want to arrive late!'

I'm with you there, Senator, thought the spy as he began to test his bonds, feeling already the play that resulted from having tensed his muscles just as Priscus tied the knots. It was a trick as old as time itself. But apparently young Syrus and his ursine associate had never come across it before.

*

During the walk to Cassius' villa, Artemidorus continued to work surreptitiously at the ropes binding his wrists. He wished to be taken to the chief conspirator's *domus* but he had no intention of being held as a helpless prisoner there. Just as he had not even begun to entertain the thought that Minucius Basilus, Syrus or their men would get the pleasure of torturing both himself and Cyanea to death. His thoughts were neither pointlessly grim nor self-indulgently negative. At the foundation of Artemidorus' view of the world and his place within it lay a weakness for the Stoic philosophy of Zeno and his followers. Which put him in step with some of his enemies, their teachers and their friends. From Cato, Porcia's father, through Marcus Junius Brutus, her husband, to Marcus Tullius Cicero, their friend.

No. The Greek spy did not entertain negative thoughts so that he could attain *eupathia* and come to terms with the passions they aroused; finding peace and spiritual balance as the philosophy dictated. But because those passions could prompt him to try harder. To push himself further. As they had done many times in the past. He expected to escape. Planned to do so, in fact.

The streets through which Basilus' attendants and their prisoners rushed were made restless by more than the wind. There was a stirring all around as the great city began to come awake. The ox wagons and mule carts would be hurrying to vacate the city's roads. To leave them free for the citizens, their clients and their slaves to do their daily business in. Glimpses down other thoroughfares and into other forums showed other groups of men already hurrying along. Most with a guard of *lictors*. All led by servants carrying flaming torches. It seemed to the spy that there must be hundreds of people heading in the same direction as they were. And, unlike many citizens around him, Artemidorus, the soldier, centurion of the VIIth, knew exactly what a hundred men would look like.

But Artemidorus' keen gaze was not interested in the hangers-on, the clients, *lictors*, torchbearers. It was the senators they accompanied whose faces he wished to see. Those men betrayed by their ceremonial togas who were placed at the core of each group like the seed in a grape. Many of whom must be at the centre of the plot he was fighting to stop. Like the pit at the heart of a poisoned olive.

He could recognise some of them because he had served under them. As he had served under Caesar. Antony. Lepidus, current *magister equitum*, third most powerful man in Rome after the co-consuls. The late unlamented Crassus, who he had not followed – thank the gods – to the slaughterhouse of Carrhae. He knew Gaius Cassius as a commander. Marcus Brutus as an administrator. Others he knew because they were public men whose faces were familiar to many, like Cicero. Still others he knew because he had stood on the steps of the Senate House with Enobarbus, noting the faces and the names the tribune listed to accompany them. For Enobarbus, as Antony's lieutenant, had accompanied him into the Senate on more than one occasion. As Sulla had taken Lucius Gallius Fango. As Caesar himself had taken Decidius Saxa. Both, like Enobarbus, aristocrats of *equites* rank as well as retired centurions. Both magistrates. Both later elevated to senatorial status.

The closer they came to Cassius' villa, the more numerous the groups of men hurrying alongside them; the more familiar the faces of the aristocrats at their centres. Artemidorus glanced down at Cyanea. Her eyes were as wide as his were narrow, soaking up the information like the practised spy she was. Antony would simply have to listen to them, Artemidorus thought. All he himself had to do was get them out and down to Pompey's villa before the general departed for the Senate meeting. Due to convene before the third hour in the nearby *curia* of Pompey's Theatre. Which stood on the Field of Mars outside the Servian wall, close beyond the Fontus Gate.

*

The roadway outside the villa, which was the city residence of Gaius Cassius Longinus and his family, was thronging. The last of the darkness banished by torches, held high to allow the actual guests to pass safely into the *ostium* entrance and through the *fauces* vestibule into the *atrium* inside it. The *atrium* was capacious but already crowded. Although the slaves and servants waiting outside seemed to have little to say, a lively hum of conversation issued from the aristocratic crowd within. Basilus' men all stopped together at the outer edge of the crowd in the street. The senator strode forward, however, and the mob parted before him like the sea beneath the keel of a ship. In the instant or two of stasis, Artemidorus noticed that the senators inside also parted readily, allowing Basilus to walk swiftly towards his host, preceded by Cassius' obsequious doorkeeper.

Then Syrus and his men peeled off, leading the two spies down the side of the villa towards the *posticum* servants' entrance. Priscus grabbed a flambeau and led the way. The path to the private entrance was a narrow one bounded by the walls of Cassius' villa and the one next door to it. The gladiators went three abreast. Syrus placed himself between the two captives. Immediately behind his bear-like companion who held the torch high and steady. As they moved away from Senator Basilus' influence, the atmosphere among the group changed subtly. A new urgency seemed to animate their actions. The frown on Syrus' face became one of concern rather than frustration. 'Priscus,' he called, his voice echoing between the walls.

Priscus glanced back. 'Yes?'

'I'm going to leave you in charge of these two. Keep them safe until the senator has talked to Lord Cassius and decided what to do next. Don't let them out of your sight.'

'Whatever you say, Syrus. But where are you going?'

'The rest of us are due at Pompey's Theatre at sunup. Lord Decimus Brutus Albinus is putting on a gladiatorial display there today and we're a part of it. We're running late already. Because of Lord Basilus' demands and this great oaf being so slow to come to the woman's rescue.'

'Right,' answered Priscus. But he didn't sound too happy.

'It's good money,' Syrus insisted. 'Albinus inherited a fortune from some relative or other. I'll keep your share safe for you. But don't let these two out of your sight 'til you either hear from the senators or from me.'

'As you say.' Priscus sounded happier at the thought of the money. The fact that the instructions had to be repeated made Artemidorus even more certain that Priscus, already fooled by his play-acting, wasn't a particularly sharp blade either.

The conversation took them to the side entrance of Cassius' villa. Syrus' men gathered round the doorway. Priscus hammered on the door and Syrus pushed the prisoners in as soon as it was opened. The light was dazzling. The heat and smell almost overpowering – the side door was between the servants' quarters and the *culina* kitchen. There was a heady odour compounded of rank sweat and fresh-baked bread. Lord Cassius or – more likely Lady Junia, his wife – had managed to replace Telos and Cyanea as cooks and kitchen hands. Hardly surprisingly, given the importance of the occasion – and of the men who had come to celebrate it. The last thing Artemidorus heard Syrus say was, 'Give me the torch. Remember. Don't let them out of your sight.'

Any hope the spy might have entertained at the prospect of being guarded by one slow-thinking gladiator instead of ten was dispelled at once. A couple of brawny servants stood behind the man who had opened the door. They regarded Cyanea with recognition but little warmth. They looked at her companion with naked enmity. 'Bring them through here,' said the servants' leader. 'Lord Cassius and Lord Basilus have told us to prepare a welcome for them. And appropriate accommodation. We have a room that will hold them until the ceremony's over and we can give them our full attention.'

Artemidorus and Cyanea were bundled along a short corridor and into a store which appeared to be part-filled with *amphorae*, barrels of various sizes, sacks and the occasional basket. All stacked or standing neatly around two walls with shelving on the third. That was the impression the spy got during the instant the door was open and the little space became full of light with shadows dancing across it. No sooner were they through the door, however, than they were expertly tripped and sent sprawling onto the stone flags of the floor. The door slammed shut behind them before they could pick themselves up. The windowless *cubicula* storeroom became utterly dark. There was a grating crash as a bolt on the outside was pushed home.

Artemidorus rolled over and pushed himself painfully into a sitting position. Over the distant hubbub of the busy household, he could hear his own breathing and the thunder of his heartbeat. The only other sounds were those being made by Cyanea. Everything about them familiar to the lover's ears. Except the circumstances, the pain and the fear. There were no other noises in the room. They were alone. In spite of his orders, Priscus had decided not to stay with them after all. A situation that seemed in equal measures promising and unlikely to last long.

Priscus was probably just looking for a lamp so he could actually keep his eye on the prisoners as directed. He did not strike the spy as a man who thought for himself very much. He would probably take Syrus' orders literally. Artemidorus had met many such men in the legions. They were useful soldiers, though they tended not to last very long. There could just be a chance, though, that Priscus might allow himself to be entertained until the aristocratic guests were gone and Lord Cassius' servants returned as planned. The treacherous senator's household seemed well disposed to the gladiators. If not to ex-cooks and their companions. There might even be some fresh-baked bread to tempt him unless the guests had eaten it all.

*

Artemidorus had no intention of waiting for either eventuality. He folded his supple body until his knees were all but touching his nose. Then, supporting his shoulders against the door itself, he passed his bound wrists beneath his buttocks. He sat once more and used the play in his loosening bonds to pull his tied wrists past his feet. His hands were now in front of him instead of behind. They were still tied. But, like Priscus' absence, this was a situation likely to change soon.

The supple spy's decisive action was not the only step forward. During the time it had taken to assess the situation and part-free himself, his eyes had adjusted to the dark. There might be no window in the storeroom, but there was at least an ill-fitting door. A blade of light cut through the darkness past him at floor level. Another much higher, showing some barrels about the same size as a man's head piled against the far wall. One or two beams came in past the jamb and around the handle. The lowest beam of brightness showed Cyanea's body moving on the floor as she writhed against her bonds. All curves and shadows in almost liquid motion. The other shards of light began to give Artemidorus a clearer idea of the room they were imprisoned in.

'Are you alright?' he asked quietly, easing himself to his feet.

'Bruised and battered,' she answered breathlessly. 'That *nothus*...'

'Not bleeding? Nothing broken?'

'No. How did you get up so quickly? I'm finding it difficult.'

By way of answer he crossed to her, stooped and took hold of her shoulder. Pulled her gently to her feet. Swiftly, he guided her forward, turning her sideways-on to the beam of vertical light coming past the door jamb. When her tightly bound wrists were clearly illuminated, he stopped her and started to untie the knots. As he did so, they shared a short, whispered conversation.

'Did you recognise those servants? They seemed to know you.'

'The one who let us in and did the talking was that *nothus* Balbus. He's the janitor's assistant. He tripped me up! I don't know the names of the other two.'

'They seemed to recognise you.'

'I've seen them around. They serve Lord Cassius. Working in the kitchen meant Telos and I had more to do with Lady Junia.'

'Are any of her slaves likely to help us if need be?'

'Not help, no. Lord Cassius is not as brutal as Basilus but he is severe. He's been a soldier after all.'

'Yes. A good leader. Strict disciplinarian...'

'And so is she. Strict. The slightest suspicion that anyone was helping us would mean a whipping at the very least. One or two might look the other way, though. And whoever's in the kitchen baking the bread you can smell probably wouldn't know me anyway – they must be new.'

'Unless the original cooks have recovered from their food poisoning and returned.'

'I suppose... But they wouldn't recognise me either.'

'Right,' he said, still worrying at the knots binding her arms. 'If we get out of here, is there anywhere we can hide? Preferably somewhere we can watch the guests from?'

'Yes. Telos and I used some of our time here to get up into the rafters and make a spyhole so you can see down into the *atrium* quite clearly. We had quite a bit of freedom to move around before Lord Cassius became suspicious of us. If we get out of here we should be able to get up there.'

'Good,' said Artemidorus. Then he fell silent for a moment. His fingers continued to work on Syrus' knots. Nimble and powerful in spite of the fact that his own wrists were still bound. Even so, the knots so viciously tightened by the frustrated gladiator required all his attention.

94

Which is why he missed the warning he would otherwise have received when the light coming from beneath the door was blocked by approaching feet. It was not until the knots vanished for an instant, blinked into darkness by a body immediately outside the door, that he realised what was about to happen. He danced away from Cyanea on silent feet, raising his bound hands high above his head. Guided by the beams of brightness that defined not only the portal but the wall on which it stood. His shoulders hit invisible solidity immediately beside the door at the moment the outer bolt was shot and the door began to swing wide.

*

Priscus came in with his attention focused on the flickering flame of the lamp he was carrying in his left hand. His right hand was curved into a protective barrier around it. He was clearly more worried at the prospect of darkness than he was about a couple of battered, securely bound prisoners. Whose fate was, as far as he knew, sealed. Whose spirit was clearly as broken as Telos' ribs.

He had taken three steps into the little room before Artemidorus' bound hands whipped down over his head. The rope he himself had tightened cut across his throat. Closed off all hope of shouting. Or breathing. Automatically, he reached for the makeshift garrotte with both hands. The lamp fell like a tiny meteor and shattered on the flags. Miraculously, instead of dying, the wick ignited the little pool of oil it had contained. The room was lit at once with weirdly flickering brightness and looming shadows. Artemidorus swung the surprised gladiator round until he could see that the corridor behind him was empty. Priscus hadn't brought a servant to bolt the door behind him. Nobody had suggested it. The gladiator hadn't thought for himself. Really and truly not the sharpest blade on the battlefield.

'The door!' spat Artemidorus.

Cyanea danced between the silently wrestling men and the little puddle of fire on the floor, swinging the door closed and leaning back on it, ruthlessly scraping the skin off her wrists as she fought to free her hands from the knots her companion had loosened.

Priscus reared backwards, seeking to smack his skull into Artemidorus' face but the spy saw the blow coming and hurled himself back with all his strength. Avoiding the blow and bringing his adversary even closer to death. Immediately, the desperate gladiator charged forward. But Artemidorus was ready for this as well. His right knee rose into the small of his enemy's back and his left foot left the floor. For an instant the only thing holding him erect was the rope cutting ruthlessly into Priscus' throat. The spy's left foot swung out and in, tripping the desperate man up. He went face first into a pile of sacks with the spy's full weight concentrated on that one sharp knee in the middle of his spine. There came a muffled roar as the agony managed to force a cry of pain past the garrotte, with the last of the gladiator's breath. Artemidorus hissed in pain as well. He had closed his hands into fists as Priscus tumbled forward so he didn't break any fingers. But the rough sacking scraped the skin off his knuckles.

Only now, when it was almost too late, did the slow-witted Priscus remember that he was carrying a sword at his belt. He began to buck and wriggle as he tried to get at the weapon's grip. The desperate spy threw himself back with all his force. Wrists complaining. Shoulders tearing. Fists beginning to go numb. Grinding the fulcrum of his knee into the dying gladiator's back. Desperate to kill his enemy before the clawing fingers could free the *gladius* from its sheath. Something the gladiator would find hard to do, for there was no room for him to pull the blade right out of its metal-bound leather scabbard. Or so the spy calculated.

Artemidorus was concentrating so fiercely that it came as a disorientating shock when one of the barrels, the size of a good big melon, smashed onto the back of the skull beneath him. Such was the force of the blow that it was a miracle the barrel did not burst. And another helpful intervention from his protector Achilleus, he thought. A trickle of *garum* fish sauce oozed out to mingle with the blood seeping from the back of the gladiator's skull. If the barrel had burst, it would have covered both of them with the stinking stuff. Making it all too easy to smell out the spy across the length of the fish market – and probably of the *Basilica Aemelia* as well. Let alone across the length of the *atrium* and into the rafters where Cyanea and he would be hiding as they completed their final tally of senators likely to be in Cassius' and Brutus' conspiracy. If they got out of here and completed this part of their assignment.

Artemidorus wrestled his bound hands from beneath Priscus' lolling head and stood up, opening and closing his smarting fingers. In the flickering light of the dying puddle, Cyanea reached for the knots with hands she had freed from her own bonds. And even though they had tightened again during the last few brutal moments, she was able to free him before the last of the oil burned out.

Artemidorus used the final few moments of brightness to return to Priscus. The fallen gladiator looked dead but it was impossible to be certain, even when the spy rolled the body over. He undid the belt and pulled it off with the sword. His first thought was simply to slide the sword's blade into the Priscus' breast and make sure matters were ended. But while he deliberated, Cyanea made his mind up for him by rolling their victim over once again and securing his arms as he had secured Artemidorus'. But with Syrus' rope and knots. 'Better to be certain,' she said. She glanced at the frowning spy. 'He was the only one of Syrus' men who refused to hurt Telos,' she explained shortly. 'If we haven't killed him, then whichever god he worships has intervened on his behalf. We should give him a chance.'

'Right,' growled Artemidorus. 'Let's go!'

*

Cyanea came out of the storeroom first, carrying a basket of early beans, onions, leeks and greens. Looking hurried but confident, as though she belonged. As though, like all the other house slaves and servants, she had a mission to complete on this most important of days. Artemidorus came out on her signal that all was clear. He was carrying one of the sacks on his shoulder to hide his face but he saw at once that he needn't have bothered; this part of the villa was effectively deserted. He would have put the burden down except for the fact that it was also hiding Priscus' sword. Which was trapped between the bulging sack-side and the spy's left cheek. Its cross guard reaching down behind his shoulder. Its grip secured against the flap of the leather cap he retrieved from beneath the trussed body among the other sacks in the storeroom. As soon as he was out, she turned and reached up to slide the bolt firmly home.

Together they began to move forward. The slaves' quarters were empty. There was far too much going on to allow anyone to rest or linger there. Everyone in Cassius' house would have a job to do today. And there would be a severe penalty for being in the wrong place, doing the wrong thing. Or doing the right thing at the wrong time. The entire household's feverish preoccupation was the fugitives' best hope.

Those few still in the kitchen baking a last batch of bread were too preoccupied to pay them much attention. Everyone else was crowded into the *atrium* or straining to see what was going on from the areas closest to it. Men at the front. Women at the back. Except for the boy's mother, Lady Junia Tercia, of course. The first part of the ceremony had reached its climax.

Artemidorus was tall enough to see an incredibly youthful boy, with a proud, almost tearful, Cassius immediately behind him, hanging his *bulla* child's amulet in the family shrine. Which, noted the keen-eyed spy, had a dagger standing in it beside the household *lares* or gods. Behind the pair of them, a couple of favoured slaves carried a selection of toys the youngster was now too grown up to play with. Which would also be offered to the gods as proof of his maturity. They were the usual lot. A wooden soldier. A horse with wheels instead of legs so it could be pulled along. An impressive looking chariot pulled by a pair of terracotta horses.

Beside the *pater familias'* chair in the open *tablinum* study area, the family's *tonsor* stood expectantly with his bowl of water, oil and razor. Waiting to shave the peach-down from the young celebrant's cheeks. Which looked at first glance, almost as soft as Cyanea's.

The spy paused, his mind racing. He knew how the ritual would proceed. Gaius Cassius junior would be shaved. A process unlikely to take long. He would then put on the *toga virilis,* the dress of a man. Then his proud father, with the guests in tow, would take him to the Forum and parade him there. So that Rome would be made aware that another virile man had survived all the dangers of childhood to join the ranks of the patricians. In the immediate future, therefore, several things would happen in rapid succession. The shaving. The robing. Then Gaius Cassius, father and son, would leave. The guests would follow. The women of the household, irrespective of rank, would remain. Even so, the villa would become relatively empty. As he started moving once more, following Cyanea towards the secret observation post she and Telos had made, Artemidorus coldly calculated exactly how much time they would have to spy things out.

And there was not a lot of it before the slaves and servants would be released from their current duties. The *nothus* bastard Balbus who let them in at the *posticum* and his burly cohorts would continue to follow the orders of their master and Minucius Basilus. The storeroom would be opened and Priscus would be discovered. As would the absence of his prisoners.

Logic appeared to dictate that the escapees should get as far away from here as fast as possible. Cassius' house was the most dangerous place in the city as far as they were concerned. Except for Basilus' villa. That was what the slaves would be likely to think at any rate. But, the spy speculated, was there any benefit in staying once the men had left? On the one hand, that would be unexpected. On the other, it might allow them to discover further details about what precisely was planned. Gaius Cassius junior would return. His father might well stay out. After all, he had an important Senate meeting to attend, in the *curia* of Pompey's Theatre.

'Here,' said Cyanea, turning away from the *atrium* into another *cubicula* being used as a storeroom, leaving the door ajar so they could see what they were doing. But this room was also lit by a couple of windows high beneath the eaves.

This one was full of *amphorae* ranging from ones almost as tall as Artemidorus to tiny ones hardly big enough to hold Lady Junia's perfume. They were arranged on shelves and in racks that stretched from floor to ceiling. The ceiling was dressed in squares of white stucco between black beams. Cyanea put her basket down, hitched up her tunic and used the end of one set of racks as a ladder. In half a dozen heartbeats she was up at the top, pushing an apparently solid section upward to reveal a rectangle of darkness above. She reached up unto the gloom. Kicked her feet free of the makeshift ladder. Wriggled like an eel and vanished. A moment later her face appeared at the hole. 'Coming?' she demanded teasingly. And was gone.

Artemidorus put down the sack which had sat on his shoulder while he watched this performance. He swung Priscus' belt round his waist so the *gladius* hung at his right hip and followed his companion upwards. The wood of the rack creaked beneath his weight. One or two of the *amphorae* rocked dangerously, but when he reached above his head and grasped the cunningly placed handholds that allowed him to pull himself up, all was still solidly in place. And a last glance round assured him that everything seemed just as it should be in the little storeroom. Except for a basket of spring vegetables and a sack of wheat.

As soon as Artemidorus was up beside her, Cyanea eased the square of ceiling back in place. Artemidorus expected to be plunged into darkness even more impenetrable than that in their erstwhile prison. But no. Cyanea and Telos had been busy lifting and loosening the tiles so the first bright sunlight of the new day, shining at last down over the Esquiline and onto the villa's roof, illuminated their way as though half a dozen slaves lined the tiny passageway with torches all ablaze.

Artemidorus paused at the first bright beam, twisting his neck to see out. And was rewarded by a dazzling glimpse of sunlight. The sight of the sun made him freeze in place. His mind raced and his heartbeat doubled. Like the beat of the drummer keeping the oarsman on a trireme pulling together suddenly going up to ramming speed.

On Tiber Island the VIIth would be stirring, the long night watches over. He could almost hear the *tubae* trumpets summoning the legionnaires from their beds, to their breakfast and their duties.

The timekeepers in the Senate would be setting their water clocks to measure the hours. And to measure the time allowed for speeches. Soon they would be checking their sundials. Because with the rising of the sun the new day had arrived. It was now officially the first hour of the fifteenth day of the month of Mars.

The Ides had begun.

VI

The realisation that the day had officially dawned spurred Artemidorus on almost magically. He turned and prepared to follow Cyanea to her spyhole overlooking the *atrium* of Cassius' villa.

But it struck him immediately how much slighter both Cyanea and Telos were than he was. It struck him literally as he smacked his head on a roof beam. Once again, only the leather cap that disguised him as a freedman saved his scalp from a nasty gash. But the pain made him doubly careful. Just as he was larger, he was heavier. He placed his feet as carefully as he positioned his head and followed Cyanea as swiftly as he could.

When he caught up with her, she was lying flat on her belly looking through a hole that seemed about the same size as her eye. As he arrived, she moved accommodatingly so that he could see what she saw. He pressed his face to the cool lath and peered through the perforated plaster on the far side.

The spyhole gave him a perfect view of the *atrium*. Gaius Cassius junior was just about to take his seat in his father's chair. The *tonsor* was oiling the razor's blade. Cassius senior was holding a box that would soon contain his son's first beard. And which was far too large for the task by the look of things. But the chair was elevated. The boy and his father still standing. Everyone was looking up. So their faces were easy to see. He recognised Publius Casca at once, and his brother Gaius. Quintus Labeo and Quintus Ligarius. Publius Naso and Pontius Aquila. He mentally ticked off more than fifteen of the suspects from the lists Telos and Cyanea had written on the secret tablets. Tablets that Syrus, Cestus and their brutal crew had splintered as they took the young spies to Telos' terrible fate. Tablets which he prayed Cyanea would be able to reconstruct and explain in telling detail as soon as he got her out of here.

But he noted the omissions too. For instance, Marcus Junius Brutus was nowhere to be seen. Probably still at home, mused Artemidorus, comforting the Lady Porcia. Dressing the wound in her leg perhaps. That thought made him squint a little as he tried to see the shrine with the boy's *bulla*, the household gods, the *lares*, the statuette of Vesta, guardian of hearth and home. And the dagger. Almost certainly the one that had fascinated both men according to Puella. The one Basilus had run into the slave's leg. The one that had been used to cut Telos' throat. Returned to Cassius by Basilus, obviously. The twin – except that the grip was slightly different – to the one Lady Porcia had used to cut her own leg and prove her Stoic strength of mind. Which had stood in Brutus' family shrine until he had stolen it.

Marcus Tullius Cicero was also notable by his absence. Though Enobarbus was of the opinion that the lawyer and statesman would be unlikely to be fully involved, for he had often spoken out against the unlawful killing of leaders and superiors. Though no doubt, the tribune suspected as did the spy, Cicero would be happy enough to see the deed done by hands other than his.

Gaius Cassius Longinus junior sat. The faces mostly moved down as he did so. Though some – Spurius, Galba and Naso – still looked up. Watching the proud father standing almost tearfully behind the chair rather than the nervous boy seated in it. Minucius Basilus hovering at his side like an evil spirit. The spy felt the back of his neck begin to prickle. There was an atmosphere here. A strange, almost wild, mixture of excitement and terror. It was a sensation he recognised. For he had known it all his life. It was the atmosphere that preceded a battle. Or a fight to the death in the arena. It was something he could sense almost as vividly as the stench of sweat and the sweetness of fresh-baked bread that greeted him on his first entry into Cassius' villa. He pursed his lips and almost shook his head. How could he possibly transmit a sensation like that to the all too hesitant Antony? Antony knew the sensation as well as any other old soldier – but would he allow himself to be convinced that what his spy felt here and now was genuine?

And yet he had to try. And he had to try at once. As soon as he and Cyanea could get out of here and back down to the villa that Antony had stolen from Pompey's heirs.

But then he caught his breath. For a latecomer was pushing his way through the gathered patricians. A tall man with a military swagger and an air of command to rival Cassius'. Artemidorus recognised him with a shiver of shock. It was General Gaius Trebonius. Artemidorus knew him from the siege of Massalia five years in the past. Trebonius had been in command of the land forces while Decimus Brutus Albinus – whose gladiators were putting on a show at Pompey's Theatre today – had commanded the navy. Both men had been Caesar's battle commanders then and were close to Caesar still. Though they had had their differences in the meantime, it was still a shock to see Trebonius here.

He moved so that Cyanea could replace him at the spyhole. 'The tall man who's just approaching the boy's seat. Have you seen him here before?' he whispered.

'No,' she answered after a moment.

'You're sure?' he pressed her. 'It's important. *He's* important. Gaius Trebonius. Another of Caesar's senior generals.'

'Never,' she assured him.

Artemidorus heaved a sigh of relief. Certainly, Trebonius' name had not appeared on the list from the shattered tablets. Or it hadn't by the time he left Antony's villa to come to Basilus'. But then, given the number of senators assembled below, it would surely be inconceivable for all of them to be involved in whatever Cassius and Brutus were planning. Logic dictated that some of the visitors must be innocent. Perhaps Trebonius was just an acquaintance of Cassius'. Another old soldier who liked to swap stories of the campaigns they shared in Gaul, Hibernia and Egypt.

The ritual shaving was soon over. The damp hairs just about covering the bottom of Cassius senior's box. Red-faced, the boy stood once more. The servants who had carried his toys to the shrine took the box and then helped Cassius senior remove the *toga praetaxa* with its broad purple stripe and array the young man in the pure white *toga virilis* that signified his passage from *impubes* youth to *pubes* manhood. There was loud applause and the young man bowed gracefully. The crowd began to surge towards the exit almost immediately. Cassius let his son lead the way and followed, going from one group to another talking earnestly. Artemidorus looked away from the hole, blinking. Cyanea took his place for a moment. 'They're all gone,' she said at last.

'Time for us to go as well,' he said. 'Back the way we came?'

'No,' she said. 'We made an emergency exit so we could get out without going through the villa.'

'Right,' he said. 'Lead the way.'

But before she could do so, there came a loud crash from the *atrium* below, followed by a good deal of lively conversation. Without thinking, the spy pressed his eye to the spyhole once again. The slave removing the first of the toys from beside the shrine – the chariot – had somehow managed to drop it. It appeared to be broken and the Lady Junia was making her displeasure very clear indeed. Artemidorus glanced over at the toys still resting beside the shrine. And, for the second time that morning, he froze. The toys were there; the soldier and the wheeled horse. The *bulla* was there. The statues of Vesta and the *lares* were there.

But the dagger was gone.

*

Artemidorus eased onto his knees, his mind racing. Only Cassius himself could have taken the dagger from the shrine. No one else, except, perhaps, Lady Junia, would touch anything in a place so sacred to the family. But not even someone as powerful as Cassius would walk the streets carrying a dagger in daylight.

'Did you see Cassius leave?' he demanded.

'He was just going out when I looked. Publius Casca and Minucius Basilus were with him. But now you mention it, I don't think he was going straight out into the street. There are a couple of other rooms before you get to the vestibule. It looked like they were going into one of those. But he can't possibly be in there for any length of time. He has to catch up with his son and the other guests.'

He'll be in there just long enough to tuck the dagger into his toga, thought Artemidorus. *A quick enough job with Casca and Basilus to help him.*

'And that was it?' he said. 'Just those three together?'

'Well, the man you pointed out to me. Gaius Trebonius did you say? He was just ahead of them. He might have gone into the room as well, I suppose.'

The need to get to Antony was now overwhelming. 'We have to get out of here,' he said. 'What's the quickest way?'

'This is,' said Cyanea.

She led the way forward, continuing to follow the straight line of the villa's traditional construction towards its frontage. At last she turned aside. 'We prepared an escape route here,' she said. 'But we never used it. We've loosened the bricks but left them in place. We just have to pull them apart, stack them in here, and we'll open a hole that will allow us to drop down into the alley beside the villa. On the street side of the *posticum*. We've secured a rope here that we can push out when the bricks are clear and climb down. We designed it for a swift, silent getaway.'

'Not swift enough. It'll take too long to pile that many bricks in here. And we're out of time. Let's just kick them out and make a run for it.'

'It'll be noisy…'

'Then we'll have to be quick.'

Artemidorus swung round so he could put his feet against the bricks Cyanea indicated. One good push and the central section vanished, crashing down into the alley that Priscus had led the gladiators and their prisoners into just before dawn. Daylight flooded in at once, accompanied by the morning breeze. Which still smelt faintly of fresh-baked bread. Cyanea worked at his side, kicking the last few bricks out of the way, leaving a long, low opening just below the overhanging eaves of the villa's roof. She pushed out the coil of rope secured to a roof beam. Swung round, lying flat on her belly. Shuffled sideways to the edge of the hole, grabbed the rope and was gone.

Artemidorus followed. Lucky to squeeze himself through an egress designed for Telos. But their actions had been so swift that the dust was still settling over the pile of bricks as he joined Cyanea in the alley. Which still seemed to be echoing with the thunder of their fall. A face appeared at the *posticum* behind them and vanished at once.

'That was Balbus,' said Cyanea. 'He'll be after us as soon as he can get someone to help.'

'We'd better hurry, then,' snapped Artemidorus. In motion as he spoke.

Cyanea was right behind him and they were running full tilt almost immediately.

But as they came out of the alley into the now deserted street, Balbus came charging out of the villa's main door, clearly intent on cutting them off. And Priscus was just behind him. Artemidorus was simply astonished to see that the gladiator was still alive. *He must have a head as hard as a ballista stone*, he thought. And the unkillable gladiator did not look happy. Hardly surprisingly. His throat must hurt as much as his head. Artemidorus reached a practised hand to his right hip and slid out the *gladius*, still running full tilt.

In answer, both the assistant janitor and the gladiator flourished clubs that looked just as lethal as Syrus'. The fugitives' flight began to slow. Cyanea ran to her left, crossing the street towards the villa opposite, heading for a side alley that might take them round their opponents. Understanding her simple plan at once, Artemidorus followed suit, staying on her right, so that he could protect her back. Holding the *gladius* low, as though he had a *scutum* shield in front of him. Ready for the upward killing stroke that opened his enemy's belly and slid up under his ribs.

Balbus and Priscus also ran across the street, ready to block Cyanea before she reached the alley. Coming to a halt with their backs to the opening. Holding their clubs high and ready. They didn't even need to fight, Artemidorus realised grimly. Just slow Cyanea and him until the rest of Cassius' slaves arrived. If Priscus was here then Balbus had already been aware that the prisoners had escaped. It was inconceivable that he hadn't roused the household. Those not out escorting Cassius *pater et filius* down to the Forum. Though, knowing Cassius, the senator would probably call the young man *teknon*, preferring the socially elevated Greek word for son. The remaining slaves would all be searching the villa. But Balbus couldn't have had time to alert them to this new development by anything more than a shout of warning as he ran out to stop the escape. The rest would be here soon, therefore. But they hadn't appeared yet. If only Cyanea and he could get past those dangerous-looking clubs in time, they might yet get away.

*

But then two figures stepped out of the alley Cyanea had been heading for. They wore cloaks and hoods that hid their faces. And they carried lethal-looking clubs too. Made from the handles of long-quenched flambeaus. Balbus and Priscus fell into their fighting stance. Ready to come to blows with Artemidorus and Cyanea. Unaware that there was anyone creeping up behind them. The anonymous strangers joined the fray at once. Laying their clubs with devastating force across the skulls of Cassius' men. The janitor and the gladiator went down without a sound. Artemidorus couldn't begin to imagine the headache Priscus would suffer when he woke up. In the meantime, the two fugitives didn't even need to slow as they leaped over the senseless bodies and swung into the alley with their cloaked saviours beside them.

After eighty paces, the alley opened into another major road and the four of them stopped on the corner. Now that they were not being closely pursued, continuing to run would only draw attention to them. The street parallel to Cassius' quiet domestic thoroughfare was a commercial one. Already busy, if not yet bustling. It should be easy enough to lose themselves in the crowd. But Artemidorus stepped back into the shadow. He sheathed Priscus' *gladius*. Paused, thinking. For they still had a problem. A freedman carrying a sword within the *pomerium* or Servian walls would attract almost as much unwelcome attention as four fleeing fugitives.

As they caught their breath, the slighter of the two cloaked men pulled back his hood to reveal Kyros' grinning face. 'I followed you when you came out of Basilus' villa,' he said. 'Because I didn't know where you were being taken. But I stayed here when everyone came out of Cassius'. I know where they're all going – to the Forum then the Senate meeting. And you were obviously not among them. So I thought it best to wait for you to appear. I never doubted you'd be out of there pretty quickly, Septem. Though I wasn't so sure you'd be bringing another lovely companion with you. I sent the others back but kept a couple of cloaks. And Narbo here because he's the biggest of the master's slaves. The best in a fight. Good thing I did.'

Artemidorus had been half-listening to this, for he was still preoccupied by the problem of Priscus' sword, which he was loath to lose. But then the simplest of answers occurred to him. A freedman could not carry a sword. But a gladiator could. He pulled off his leather cap, rolled it up and stuck it into his belt at the back. 'Narbo,' he ordered. 'Lend me your cloak.'

The slave obeyed. Revealing an olive-skinned, dark-eyed face framed with tight black curls both of beard and hair. Iberian, realised the widely travelled spy. Named for his birthplace, the port city of Narbo, no doubt. Refounded more recently by Caesar and filled with retired soldiers from the *Legio X Equestris Veneria*. His body was almost as muscular as Syrus'. Kyros had clearly made a wise choice of companion. Artemidorus swung Narbo's cloak over his shoulders, adjusted his tunic and assumed a belligerent swagger. He led the little group out into the bustle of the street like a drunkard looking for a fight. Almost magically the way ahead of them cleared. Just as well, thought Artemidorus. Cassius' household slaves would not stop looking for the fugitives just because they found the apparently lifeless bodies of Balbus and Priscus. He and his companions needed to mingle with the crowd and fade away as soon as they possibly could.

He shouldered his way forward with a well-practised arrogant sneer. If anyone risked challenging them, he would say that he was one of Syrus' troop. On his way to Pompey's Theatre for the gladiatorial display sponsored by Decimus Brutus Albinus.

Which, as all Rome knew, was due to take place there later today – to celebrate The Ides.

*

They reached Spurinna's villa without incident. As they moved through the streets, the city came fully to life around them. The crowds thickened. The lesser forums through which they passed were soon thronging. Shops and stalls – resupplied last night – were opening for business. The majority of the early customers were slaves with shopping lists. Almost all memorised by servants who could not read or write. Those trusted by their owners and better educated in finances had ready money in the household purses that they carried. But the majority negotiated with shopkeepers on behalf of their owners, running up accounts to be checked and settled later.

Artemidorus strode through them all like Spartacus, with Cyanea like the rebel's Thracian wife walking confidently at his side. While the other two followed behind. Until at last they turned into the street with the scaffolding against which Telos had been crucified. They crossed to the house opposite in a tight group. Almost as though the mutilated corpse still hung there. But Spurinna had not yet returned home. Neither he nor Puella had been seen since they all left to talk to Antony long before dawn.

Making a positive out of a problem as always, Artemidorus decided that going straight back to Antony's villa was the best course of action in any case. Now that The Ides was here and time so clearly running out. On they went, therefore. With equal urgency if a little less swagger. For within a very short time they were coming past the side of the *Basilica Aemilia* market and into the *Forum Romanum* itself. Their path took them to a junction with the *Via Sacra*. And here they paused. The Forum stood before them, with its arches and statues,

110

temples and public buildings. Its crowds of the great and the lowly cheek by jowl in the early morning.

Artemidorus looked left almost longingly. Towards the *Regia*. That strange-shaped, almost triangular building which housed at once the Temple of Mars and the office of the *pontifex maximus*. As chief priest and overseer of the Virgins in the Temple of Vesta standing just beside the *Regia*, Caesar himself was housed in the *Domus Publicus* which all but joined the two buildings. He had lived there for years. But recently, to support his position as premier general and dictator, he had moved the shields and spears sacred to Mars out of the *Regia* and into a special room in the *Domus*. There were those who suggested Caesar's legendary virility was beginning to fail and he needed a little help from the god, who seemed to have joined Venus as his Olympian patron.

But, virile or not, Caesar was no doubt getting ready to face the day. And all the multifarious duties that his multiplicity of offices made him liable for. Especially as Antony had famously stopped his attempt to hive off the title of Co-Consul and the duties that went with it to another of his old generals Publius Cornelius Dolabella. All independently of the fact that as general and dictator, he was about to mount a campaign in a far foreign land. Not even counting the further fact that his incredible energy meant that he habitually undertook to make a dizzying number of decisions. Decisions about who would bear which office in the city – and across the Empire – during the years of his planned absence. Decisions concerning which statues must be erected, what buildings finished and what public works completed before his return.

The most important of all, which must occupy some hours of his morning if not more, was attending the final meeting of the Senate before his departure on the Parthian campaign. His last Senate meeting ever, if what the spy suspected was true.

His path and Caesar's had crossed often enough in the past, and Caesar was famously approachable. But the thought of going straight to the *Domus Publica* and telling the man himself what he feared was going to be attempted by Cassius, Brutus and the others later today would be the height of folly and Artemidorus knew it. Caesar famously refused to listen even to Spurinna when the augur's predictions did not suit him. And there were rumours that the Senate meeting – if not preparing to kill him – was preparing to name him king.

Caesar's cousin Lucius Cotta, spokesman for the *Quindecimviri*, the Fifteen who oversaw the Sibylline Texts, translating and publishing their mysterious predictions, had pronounced less than a new week ago that only a king could conquer Parthia. And it was said he had more pronouncements in the same vein to lay before the Senate today. And even if Caesar had refused the coronet Antony offered him at the *Lupercalia* a month ago this very day, he nevertheless chose to wear personally designed triumphal togas, tunics, olive wreaths – and bright red *caligae* that only Kings of Rome had worn in the past.

No. Only Antony could possibly stop Caesar on a day like today. And the only way to Antony lay through Enobarbus. Who, if the gods were in a kindly mood, must be at Antony's villa on the *Carinae* on the lower slopes of the Velian Hill by now. Discussing what they had discovered with Spurinna and Puella. Ready to accept Cyanea's further testimony and get the general to stop the dictator attending the Senate meeting. At least until they could find some way of ensuring his safety.

But between here and the road to Antony's villa lay the length of the Forum. Where Cassius would still be parading his newly virile *teknon* son, accompanied by Casca, Basilus and the rest. Where, unless Porcia was at the door of the underworld itself, Urban *Praetor* Marcus Junius Brutus must come to occupy the *curule* stool and pass judgement on any civil cases brought before him. Almost all of the men Artemidorus was preparing to warn Antony about were assembled in the Forum, between him and his destination. Perhaps as many as twenty of them. And, if Cassius was any guide, they would all be carrying hidden daggers.

*

But then, thought Artemidorus, very few of them knew his face, his occupation or his current mission. A few more might recognise Cyanea – Cassius and his visitors, for instance. But hardly any would see anything suspicious in a kitchen slave out at the morning markets. It would be bad luck indeed for the little band to run into anyone that knew who they were. What they were up to. And who wished to stop them. Or worse. And, of these few, if any of them actually used their hidden daggers even to threaten him or his companions, their whole secret conspiracy would be unmasked. Even if they managed to kill him, Caesar would be safe. While Artemidorus would cheerfully give his life to save Caesar, few of the conspirators would stand a realistic chance against a retired gladiator armed with a sword. No matter how long they had served as commanders of the legions. Or how sharp their eyes, their wits or their daggers.

Thinking that this was an action he could not lose. Artemidorus strode forward once again, meeting the eyes of anyone in front of him with an insolent stare. No matter how white their toga or how purple its edges. And there were a good number of ceremonial togas in the Forum this morning. Even though he was never confronted by Cassius or his son, he was nevertheless glared at by Pontius Aquila, Casca, Turillius and Lucius Cornelius Cinna, conspirators all. Their cold glances were shot at him from the safety of their *lictors*. Had the bundles of *fasces* they carried contained ceremonial axes, as tradition dictated, then there might have been trouble. But there was nothing in the *lictors'* fists other than long twigs. In any case, none of the patricians coldly eyeing him saw anything other than an arrogant gladiator who clearly had notions far above his station. So Artemidorus and his friends passed on unmolested.

Until they met Minucius Basilis.

The instant the skeletal senator saw them, his pallid face went chalk white with shock. His right hand sped towards his left armpit and only stopped as he realised what he was doing. His fist rested hard against the folds of a toga that was exactly the same colour as his face. He turned to the largest of the *lictors* accompanying him and spat an order. The man passed his master's orders onto his companions and all of them came towards the four fugitives.

Losing none of his belligerent swagger, Artemidorus walked straight towards them feeling Kyros and Narbo fall in at his shoulders as he did so. He eased the cloak on his right shoulder and put his right hand on the hilt of his *gladius*. It was a gesture subtle enough to be missed by almost everyone else in the busy Forum. But the leading *lictor* saw and understood it. As a man armed only with a bundle of sticks.

And Basilus saw it. And realised that a fight between his men and Artemidorus in the middle of the Forum would put at risk the entire enterprise that turned upon the dagger beneath his left arm. And those beneath the arms of his fellow conspirators. His red lips twisted in a bitter grimace and he spat another order. The *lictors* stopped. With every sign of relief, they turned and reassembled around their master. Basilus swung away from Artemidorus and his companions. Stalking off across the Forum towards the Capitol and the Fontus Gate through the Servian wall. Which led out to Pompey's Theatre. And the *curia* where the Senate would be meeting in full session. In a little over two hours' time.

Artemidorus followed, planning to exit the Forum at the far end. Turning at right angles, heading back up towards the *Carinae*, the *Clivus Publius* roadway and the big villa built by Pompey. Where, if the gods were continuing to be kindly, Antony was waiting to talk to them. Then spring into action. But just as he was approaching the far end of the Forum, another of the conspirators caught his eye. And the sight made him pull up his hood as he continued to swagger forward. For, just as he had suspected, Marcus Junius Brutus, the *praetor urbanus*, senior judge, was on duty. Seated on the *curule* stool on the raised *tribunal* platform. With his *asseors* assistants seated below him and his *lictors* ranged behind him. Calmly hearing civil cases too complex to be judged by the local *aedile* magistrates. On an average day, this would fill most of the morning, but today, reckoned the spy, pulling his hood further forward still, he would only be here for another hour or so before following Basilus and the others to the *curia* of Pompey's Theatre.

During his time working on Brutus' roof and seducing away his slave Puella, Artemidorus had seen little enough of the senator's family. Mostly Lady Porcia until she had taken to bed with her wounded thigh. But he dare not risk Brutus recognising him. For the senator must be aware now of what Artemidorus had done. And, as the senior judge in the city, Brutus would certainly be able to have him arrested on the spot. And, unlike Basilus, he would not hesitate to send his six big *lictors* to do the job.

A prospect that suddenly became much more of a possibility. Basilus and Cassius appeared from the crowd, heading purposefully towards Brutus. One word from them and the *praetor urbanus* would detain the little group, strip away Artemidorus' disguise as a gladiator and arrest him for being in possession of an illegal weapon. All without arousing any suspicion at all about what his plans were for later in the day. And slam him in the *Tullianum* prison, as likely as not, with those poor commoners condemned to die. And the *Tullianum* was a good deal nearer than the general's villa. In reality as well as in possibility. By the time Antony was alerted to the situation and roused to take action and have his spy released, it would be too late to do anything further about the conspiracy.

There was no alternative but to get out of the Forum as quickly as possible. So Artemidorus dived into the nearest side street and began to weave his way as quickly as possible back through the maze of alleys and lesser forums towards the *Carinae*, the *Clivus Pullius* and the relative safety of Antony's villa.

*

Pompey had designed, furnished and provisioned the villa for his own use in the days before the civil war. Considering he was at that time known as *Pompeius Magnus*, Pompey the Great – one of the three most powerful men in the world – it was relatively modest. But by the standard of most of its neighbours it was palatial. Antony was rumoured to have drunk his way through the well-stocked wine cellar within days of moving in on the news of Pompey's death. And to have sold off some of the choicest furniture rather than run up yet more debts when Caesar insisted he pay a fair price for it.

Artemidorus knew the true facts behind the rumours. And that many had been started by sharp-tongued, quick-tempered unforgiving Cicero. But he always thought of them whenever he mounted the steps to the porticoed front of Antony's Roman residence, with the fore-sections of several ships built into the facade. He rather liked the image of Antony they portrayed. The general whose true spiritual home was the battlefield. In the command tent. Or at the head of his legions. Who took badly to civilian life with its petty political strictures and financial constraints. A bruiser who had grown up through a wild youth running with street gangs. Drinking. Fighting. Whoring. Some – probably Cicero once more – said thieving. Murdering. But maturing into a powerful force. A great leader. A generous heart who would give anything for a good friend or an old soldier.

But who treated the Senate house as another battlefield. Constantly losing ground to those, again like Cicero, who understood the rules of committees just as Antony understood the rules of engagement. A general who could lead his men to the far side of Hades if he felt so inclined. A man too big for the city. With a heart too big for one woman. With a reach that still might prove too great for the world. A man, indeed, very like his so-called ancestor Hercules.

With these thoughts swirling in his head, Artemidorus pounded on the huge, ornate door. Hearing the echoes of the blows repeating themselves down the length of the *ostium* and into the *atrium*. Before the last echo faded, the door swung open and the doorkeeper welcomed him. 'Septem. You are in good time. The tribune is here and wishes to speak to you at once. He is with the *haruspex* and his companion in the *peristyle*.'

'And the general?' asked Artemidorus as he led his three companions into a passageway that in another house would have been wide enough to serve as a room.

'The tribune will explain. He said I was to take you to him the moment you arrived.'

'The tribune was taking a lot for granted,' said Artemidorus, thinking how close he had come to *not* arriving on several occasions so far today.

He was speaking to Cyanea but Kyros answered. 'I don't think so, Septem. You know your reputation...'

'Do I?' asked Artemidorus, surprised. 'What reputation is that?'

'You are Achilles,' said Kyros, a strange tone in his voice. 'Just as Antony is Hercules reborn. You are Achilles. With no weakness in your heel.'

Cyanea choked on a laugh. 'No weakness in other parts either.'

'You are getting above yourself, woman!' He snapped with mock severity.

'In this house?' she answered. 'No woman could get above herself in a house where Fulvia reigns. They may not allow kings in Rome. But here is a queen!'

The doorkeeper led them through to the spacious *peristyle* garden where Enobarbus was seated between Spurinna and Puella. As soon as he saw Artemidorus, the tribune held up his hand, stemming the flow of their conversation. And rose.

The tribune Enobarbus carried an aura of restless energy. A compact, powerful body was clad in his soldier's uniform, of breast and backplate and studded leather *baltea* skirt over his tunic. The studs of his *caligae* grated on the mosaic of the floor. Tight gold curls, cut short, ready for a helmet. A perpetual slight frown furrowing his high forehead. Startlingly blue eyes. Full mouth. Decided cleft in his chin. He walked towards Artemidorus as the spy, still surprised by Kyros' flattering words, hurried to meet him. To report.

But as they met, Artemidorus found that he had a question that preceded the information he had to impart. 'Where is the general?'

Enobarbus' frown deepened. Artemidorus at once suspected that Antony had in some way failed to measure up to the image the tribune held of him.

'Bathing,' said Enobarbus.

'At a time like this?' Artemidorus, almost horrified, fought to keep the tone of his enquiry reasonable. It would not do to seem to question the general's actions or decisions.

'The moment he came home he went to Fulvia,' said Enobarbus. Also fighting to keep his tone reasonable. 'He spent the night with Cleopatra. Nothing improper took place, but the prospect of her departure has upset him deeply. The moment he returned, therefore, he went to discuss matters with the Lady Fulvia...'

Enobarbus paused. Artemidorus briefly wrestled with the task of understanding a man so complex that he loved two women at once. Loved them in such a way that whenever he was with one, he could not stop himself from admitting his indiscretions to the other. And, indeed, of understanding women who both loved the man in question sufficiently to listen to his admissions without resorting to the poisons favoured by Caesar's lover and Brutus' reputed mother, the Lady Servilia.

'They have gone through into the *balinae*.' The villa had its own private baths. 'The *frigidarium* is up and running. The *tepidarium* will be ready soon enough. It may take some time for the *caldarium* to heat up.'

'And we can't see him until he's finished bathing?'

'No. He and the Lady Fulvia have much to discuss. While he reinvigorates himself from the ex...'

Enobarbus had clearly been going to say 'excesses'. But he changed the word even as he said it.

'...experiences of last night. And prepares for the Senate meeting.'

'So Antony cannot be reached, even though he is at home.'

'That is the case. Yes. The Lady Fulvia is very clear on that point.'

Enobarbus was obviously going to say more. Perhaps unwisely. But Spurinna interrupted him. 'Tribune. It is my duty as augur and *haruspex* to Caesar to be at the *Regia* within the first hour. I have to declare the auguries for the day. And, if need be, read the entrails for more precise information from the gods.'

Enobarbus swung round to face the augur. 'All the predictions will be bad,' he said flatly. 'Until we can get Cyanea to give the general the full report of what she and Telos have discovered and he has decided on the action he needs to take, Caesar must not leave the *Regia* or the *Domus Publica*.'

'I understand,' said Spurinna. 'But Caesar has been hesitant to take all my auguries and predictions at face value. It may need more than my words to stop him going to the Senate.'

Enobarbus nodded. 'The only other element we have is Artemidorus. Septem, you must go with Spurinna to the *Regia*. Take Puella. If Caesar refuses to listen to Spurinna, you will have to see what you and she can do.'

'As you wish,' said Artemidorus. A centurion acknowledging the orders of his tribune at the start of a crucial battle. 'I will take Kyros and Narbo if I may. They are Spurinna's men anyway. I will send the fleetest of foot back if there is any important news.'

Enobarbus nodded. 'An excellent idea. I have some of my men with me – they are in the kitchen eating at the moment. If I have news I will send the swiftest of them to you. His name is Hortensius. He's a *tiro* – been with us less than a year. But he's fast.'

Artemidorus and Spurinna nodded understanding and agreement.

'Your objective, all of you,' concluded Enobarbus formally, 'is to ensure that Caesar does not leave to go to the Senate meeting before Lord Antony comes and talks to him. No matter what!'

VII

With Kyros and Narbo escorting them once again, Artemidorus, Puella and Spurinna hurried back down the *Clivus Pullius* roadway towards the Forum. The first hour of The Ides was coming all too rapidly to a close. Caesar would be up and about. Enjoying his famously modest soldier's breakfast. Probably consuming little more than bread and water. Dressing in his triumphal tunic with its golden palms; his bright triumphal toga and his regal red *caligae*. Choosing the victorious wreath that best concealed his receding hairline and thinning hair. Calling, no doubt, for his augur and *haruspex* to learn what fortune the coming hours might bring.

The augur, however, was running late. He had eaten nothing. The sacrifice and the augury should be taken as soon as possible. And fasting. Though, if time and circumstance allowed, the sacrifice could be eaten as a sacred meal after the divination was complete.

Spurinna's altar was set up outside the Temple of Mars, beside the *Regia* itself and close to Caesar's home in Rome, the *Domus Publicus* which stood between the *Regia* and the Temple of Vesta. The three buildings almost made one continuous complex. This had been done at Caesar's request. Spurinna usually sacrificed out on the Field of Mars itself. The sacrificial animal would have been cleaned and prepared. This being the month dedicated to Mars, his temple was among the preferred places for the auspices to be taken. It had been a bull at the *Lupercal*, in the *Ara Martis*, the main temple on the *Campus Martius*. It had been a boar on *Dies Natalis*, the first of the month. It would be a bull once more in two days' time, to celebrate *Liberalia* – and the coming to virility of all the fifteen-year-old boys in Rome. Boys other than Gaius Cassius Longinus junior. That sacrifice would also take place in the *Ara Martis* on the *Campus*.

Today it would be a white ram on an altar outside the temple in the *Regia*. And whereas many sacrifices to the gods were castrated or female, sacrifices to Mars were always fertile. Mars, god of growth and virility as well as of war and victory. Legendary father of Romulus and Remus. Protector of the city. But such sacrifices were sometimes difficult for anyone but the most skilled augur to handle. Mars was god of war and his sacrifices occasionally fought against the inevitable. Especially when wine and sacred vestal bread was scattered over their heads. But the augur's assistants would be there. Strong young men used to handling fractious livestock. Who would have drugged the ram's last meal if anything untoward seemed to threaten.

A range of other priests and concerned onlookers also would be waiting. The white ram would be waiting. With another, part-prepared also in case the first sacrifice proved to be ill-omened. Caesar himself might well be waiting. All that would be lacking was the man himself.

'Is it Achilles you pray to?' puffed the augur to the spy.

'Achilleus,' confirmed Artemidorus, giving the hero his Greek name. 'Yes.'

'Then pray that we can find sufficient warnings in the weather, the flights of birds, the feeding of the sacred chickens and the entrails of our sacrifices to slow the Divine Caesar. Until Lord Antony can come and stop him altogether.'

'The night was rough,' the spy observed. 'That's a good start.'

'It is,' agreed Spurinna. 'And the signs have been building up. I couldn't find a heart in the bull I sacrificed at *Lupercalia*. Before the business with Antony and the coronet. *That* went so badly the bull's entrails might even have been predicting it. The liver of the next sacrifice, a boar, on the first of the month, was badly malformed. Both of these signs were terribly unlucky. I warned Caesar then to beware the month of Mars.'

'And has he paid any attention?' asked Artemidorus.

'None that I've noticed. As usual.'

Puella struck into the conversation then. 'I heard that yesterday a great owl roosted all day in the Forum. Its wingspan wider than a tall man. Every now and then it would swoop screaming as though to carry off some woman or child. That must be a bad omen, surely...'

'Owls are birds of ill omen, certainly,' agreed Spurinna. 'But I hadn't heard about this one...'

'I heard something,' added Kyros. 'While I was waiting for you to come out of Lord Cassius' *domus*, Septem. There was talk of a man running around in the Forum at the height of the storm. With his hand on fire. Every time he held it up above his head, it would burn with blue fire. And yet it wasn't hurt. The skin wasn't even blistered.'

'That's certainly unusual,' allowed Spurinna.

'I've never heard of anything like it,' added Artemidorus. 'Or anything like a thunderbolt releasing animals from the menagerie at the arena, come to that.'

'And you've travelled all over the world,' added Puella. 'You have seen so many wonders.'

Had Cyanea been speaking, Artemidorus would have assumed she was being ironic or simply joking. But Puella seemed to be talking in earnest.

'But,' the spy observed, 'omens, like the storm, the owl, the animals and the burning man, are general. They might just as well be warning that something is going to happen to *me* as much as to Caesar.'

'With all due respect, Septem,' huffed Spurinna. 'Unless these wonders have been engineered by your demigod Achilleus, then they are *not* likely to refer to you. You are simply not important enough. The gods wouldn't bestir themselves to put on a storm because something was going to happen to you. Any more than they would bother with me. No wonderful events predict the deaths of mere mortals such as us. But *Caesar*... Now Caesar is different...'

'I take your point,' Artemidorus said. 'Quite apart from anything else, Caesar is a god.'

'I heard Lord Antony is chief priest of his new cult,' added Puella. 'One of Lord Brutus' guests was saying...'

'A god in waiting, perhaps,' interrupted Spurinna, beginning to slow as the Forum came into sight. 'He won't be properly a god until he's escaped from his mortal body.'

'You mean,' said Artemidorus grimly. 'Until he's dead.'

'Yes,' agreed the augur. 'That's exactly what I mean.'

'Then let's try and make sure his deification stays far in the future,' said the spy.

*

They entered the Forum at precisely the same point as Artemidorus, Cyanea and the other two had entered it earlier. It was busier than ever, the confined space heaving with people of all sorts, ranks and stations. But the crowds were mostly streaming away down the length of the Forum on their right. They were planning to turn left into the quieter spaces around the *Regia*, the *Domus* and the Temple of Vesta. And this time there was no hesitation.

But they had hardly taken half a dozen steps before a young man detached himself from the crowd and ran up to Artemidorus with every sign of recognition. Puella gave a tiny shriek and hid herself behind Spurinna as best she could. Kyros and Narbo closed ranks in front of her. The recognition between the stranger and the spy became mutual. The youngster was one of the slaves from Brutus' household. Artemidorus tensed himself for a confrontation. But the look of recognition changed to one of relief. 'Artemidorus,' said the young slave. 'Thank the gods. Have you seen Lord Brutus? Lady Porcia has set the house in uproar and she's sending messenger after messenger to see whether Lord Brutus is all right. I have no idea why she is so worried. But I must find Lord Brutus as swiftly as possible and report back to her. Have you seen him?'

'He's on the tribunal at the far end of the Forum,' said Artemidorus, unable to keep the relief from his voice. Gesturing forcefully with his right hand in the direction of the raised tribunal. 'He's hearing cases as urban *praetor*. Or at least he was until recently. If he's not there, ask at Pompey's *curia*. He also hears cases there. And that's where the Senate is due to meet.'

'The tribunal,' said the slave. 'I'll start looking there. Then Pompey's Theatre. Thank you.' And he was gone, vanishing into the crowd as though he had never been. Apparently without registering Puella's presence at all.

Before there could be any further interruptions or hindrances, Spurinna led them on. Not to Caesar's quarters in the *Domus* but to the door of the Temple of Mars in the *Regia*. And the space outside it. Which was not part of the Forum – and therefore was not bustling. But which was filled with the augur's assistants and a range of other priests, diviners and vestals. The assistants held the ram. The priests held the wine. The vestals held the sacred bread that they alone could bake.

Artemidorus paused, struck by the work Caesar had ordered to be done on the thick marble walls of the *Regia*. One of the oldest buildings in the city. The building that had once housed the ancient Kings of Rome. And also by the glittering, gilded statues he had more recently caused to be erected there. Companions to those further down the Forum depicting Cleopatra as Venus. But his calculated hesitation was motivated by more than awe. It also sprang from the need to ensure the four of them could vanish into the crowd if anything went wrong here.

For they would not be out of danger until they had made sure Caesar would stay safely at home until Lord Antony came. Until the conspirators realised that they had lost. And there was no point in sending Syrus and his murderous gladiators out to capture or kill them. Until Artemidorus could remove the disguise that identified him as a housebreaker, slave stealer and murderer. And until they had found some way of looking after Puella, the runaway slave.

Immediately outside the door of the Temple of Mars itself, an altar had been erected. Beside it was a blazing brazier. A sparking red mound of flame, smelling fragrantly of pinewood charcoal. Contained in a big brass bowl, held at waist height on sturdy legs. This bowl matched a second bowl – of gold this time – that stood on the ground beside the altar. One of the temple attendants hurried to greet the augur, and lead him ceremonially to the altar beside which lay a pure white ram, with its legs all lashed together – much as Cyanea's and Artemidorus' arms had been just before sunrise. Artemidorus half expected to see it fighting as energetically as they had done in its efforts to be free. But it lay still. Even when its legs were untied. It had obviously been drugged. For some reason the spy thought of Brutus' mother the Lady Servilia. Her drugs, potions and poisons. The stupefied creature's horns were decorated with ribbons and a garland.

Spurinna crossed to the altar, on which lay the tools of his trade. All sharp and gleaming in the morning light. As he did so, the priest who would actually cut the animal open also stepped forward. Another attendant hurried to the *Domus* to summon the *pontifex maximus*. And, as Spurinna arrived at the altar, Caesar himself appeared, dressed as Artemidorus had suspected he would be. In his full ceremonial robes, ready for a meeting with the Senate – or yet another triumph.

Tall, spare, dynamic. The personification of decisive energy. His face lean. Lips thin; mouth tight and pulled slightly downwards at its corners. Vertical creases joining square chin to pronounced cheekbones. Straight, sharp patrician nose, nostrils slightly flared. Bright brown eyes gleaming. Broad forehead rising above delicately curved brows. Crowned with a golden garland unsettlingly similar to the one the sacrificial ram had on its horns.

'Ah, Spurinna,' said Caesar, sounding cheerful, forceful and full of life. 'I seem to be surviving the month in spite of your predictions. I've made it to The Ides at least!'

'The Ides aren't over yet,' answered Spurinna.

Caesar laughed. His bright gaze swept over the bearded Artemidorus and the shy Puella with no sign of recognition – or surprise that his augur should be bringing strangers to the ceremony. 'Well, let's get on with it,' he said. 'I have a very busy day ahead of me and we're already running late. If I'd organised things at Pharsalus the way you're doing now, you'd be talking to Pompey the Great instead of me today!'

'That,' warned Spurinna severely, 'is an ill-omened thought, Caesar!'

'Oh don't you start,' snapped the ruler of the world. 'I've had enough of that from Calpurnia!'

'Really?' Spurinna's eyes narrowed as he rolled the folds of his toga back from his forearms. An assistant bustled up behind him and tied the *Gabine knot* which was designed to keep his clothing clear of any liquids splashing around during the sacrifice. 'What has the Lady Calpurnia been saying?' the augur asked. 'She is a wise and insightful woman in my opinion.'

'Something about a dream,' snapped Caesar, his sudden frown betraying to the spy, if to no one else, that he regretted having mentioned his wife at all.

'I will talk to her after the sacrifice,' decided Spurinna. 'The gods often speak to us in dreams. As well you know.'

'I also know that we often dream without any divine intervention at all,' snapped Caesar. 'And you know that as well as I do!'

So the subject was closed.

*

The ritual of the sacrifice proceeded. Silence was called for. Foreigners dismissed, though Puella remained. She was by no means the only attendant whose skin was dark. There was a place in the ritual for women as well – there were vestals in attendance after all. Music was played. Aromatic oils were sprinkled over the brazier. The flames roared upward. The perfume of pine was augmented by other, rarer scents. An assistant approached with a bowl of water, steaming in the cool of the morning. The celebrants, priest and augur washed their hands and forearms.

The golden bowl was lifted onto the end of the altar nearest to the fragrant brazier. The ribbons were removed from the ram's horns. Its forehead was sprinkled with wine and bread. It was made to seem an active part of the process. It was asked if it was ready to be sacrificed, as though the beast spoke Latin. It seemed to nod acquiescence, perhaps agreement. A silver hammer smashed onto its forehead between eyes and horns. Stunning it, perhaps killing it. It was immediately lifted by the attendants. Laid on the altar. It was rolled onto its back and held, horned head hanging inverted over the end opposite the golden bowl. Its throat open to the celebrant's knife. Artemidorus tried not to think of poor Telos.

The garland, so similar to Caesar's, fell to the ground unnoticed.

Attendants spread the ram's legs, front and back. The celebrant took his knife. Covered his face with the end of his toga as the ritual of sacrifice demanded. Spoke some sacred words so quietly that no one could hear. Except for Spurinna standing at his shoulder. The augur guided the priest's knife and with a single slash the taut barrel of the belly was opened. The priest who cut the creature's belly put down the knife and pulled the sides of the wound wide. Pushed his hands into the red-walled cavern, fingers clawed like the talons of a hunting owl. Tore the steaming entrails free. Lifted them into the golden bowl. Took up the knife again in hands that were crimson to the elbow. Moved to the far end of the altar and proceeded to cut the dying creature's throat. The faint sounds of pain and protest that the drugged animal had been making stopped at once. An acolyte caught the pulsing fountain of blood in another bowl with practised ease.

As *haruspex*, Spurinna stepped forward then to inspect the entrails in the golden bowl. He spread them across the gleaming surface, peering down. Frowning with concentration. But almost immediately, he straightened with a hiss of horror. 'See,' he intoned, his voice carrying like an actor's. 'The liver is terribly malformed! An entire lobe is missing! This is an omen that is even worse than the heart of the bull at the *Lupercal*. This is a warning of terrible danger. We must make another sacrifice!'

He lifted the entire dripping mess of viscera and threw it into the blazing brazier. There was a loud hissing. The smell of scent and charcoal was preplaced by that of roasting meat. He crossed to the attendant with the bowl of water and plunged his arms into the liquid up to the elbow. As he did so, he looked over his shoulder at the frowning dictator.

'Divine Caesar,' he said formally. 'You must not stir from here until the ritual has been repeated and a better outcome achieved.'

'This means nothing, Spurinna! The auguries were terrible on the morning of the battle of Munda two days less than a year ago. And I survived that all right! In fact I destroyed the armies of Pompey's sons and their supporters. It was a very lucky day! I really don't have time for a repetition...'

'You may have survived the battle of Munda, great Caesar, but you were in terrible danger that day – and you know it!'

Caesar, sighed angrily. Frowned thunderously. Capitulated under the steady, unrelenting gaze of his augur. 'Oh very well!'

'And, in the meantime, with your permission, I would like to talk to the Lady Calpurnia about her dream,' the victorious Spurinna said.

Caesar said nothing. He turned on his heel and stalked away into the *Domus*. Spurinna dried his hands and arms. As soon as he had done so, he crossed to Artemidorus. 'This is going very well indeed,' he whispered. 'I'm going in to talk to Caesar's wife now,' he added more loudly. Then he dropped his voice again. 'The dream she's had sounds promising. Wait here.' He turned and walked away, then stopped. Returned. 'No. I've a better idea,' he said so quietly that not even Puella could hear clearly. 'You're dressed and armed like a gladiator. You're my gladiator. My bodyguard. Come with me.'

'You need guarding against Caesar and his wife?' said Artemidorus. 'Won't they consider that strange?'

'If they do, I'll think of something. Just stand in the background. Use your eyes and ears. Not your mouth unless I ask you to.' He raised his voice. 'Puella, I might need you. Wait close by. No one's going anywhere until the next ram is readied and sacrificed in any case.'

He turned on his heel almost as abruptly as Caesar and done and followed him into the *Domus*.

After an instant more, Artemidorus followed them both.

*

The interior of the *Domus Publica* was spacious rather than palatial, thought Artemidorus as he followed Spurinna on the dictator's heels. It contained several rooms that were larger than those in the villas the spy had visited since helping Puella escape from Brutus'. It was designed at the front very much like the villas of Basilus and Cassius. But instead of a *peristyle*, it opened at the rear onto the Garden of the Vestals. There was an *atrium* of the Tuscan design, however, with an *impluvium* pool, off which most of the rooms opened. There was a *balnae* private bath, he knew. With a cold *frigidarium*, a cool *tepidarium* and a hot *caldarium*. But no *laconium* sweat room for massage. It was of an old-fashioned design, like the rest of the place.

And that was by no means all he knew. Caesar had lived here for sixteen years. Since his appointment as *pontifex maximus*. When he had moved out of his smaller residence in the *Subura*. Before he had amassed a fortune large enough to purchase, amongst others, the villa on the Janiculum Hill currently occupied by Cleopatra. Even though he was more often out of Rome than in it, he had managed to make the *Domus* his own. His office was here, manned by his secretaries. The official records of the city and the Senate were shared between here and the *Regia*. Deeper in the *Domus* were kitchens and rooms for his cooks, servants and slaves. His library and personal records room, where he did most of his own writing and dictation. His private rooms, where, like any other aristocratic citizen, he dressed, washed, ate, entertained, worked and slept. First with Pompeia, his second wife. Then with Calpurnia, his third, and current wife. The largest public room had been set aside to contain the shields and spears that he had moved here from the Temple of Mars in the *Regia*. Effectively a personal shrine to the god of virility and conquest. Caesar's new deity, standing beside Venus in his affections. There to protect him from the enmity of other gods, of lesser men, of simple ill fortune. Like Antony's demigod Hercules. Like Artemidorus' Achilleus.

Caesar stopped by the *impluvium*. He looked down into the silvery surface as it reflected the clear blue morning sky. Then he turned, frowning. And he spoke not to Spurinna but to Artemidorus who had been standing silently, taking it all in. Struck by a sense of awe at the sight of the sacred objects standing in the room dedicated to Mars. For he had heard tell of them without ever seeing them. They were weapons that everyone truly believed the god of war himself had wielded in the legendary past.

'You,' said Caesar. 'Do I know you?'

Artemidorus did not flinch for he had prepared himself for this. Had he been clean shaven, Caesar would have known him well enough. But the general had never seen him disguised like he was now. The bushy beard, red as a fox's tail, was a very effective mask indeed. 'They call me Septem, General,' he answered now, making his voice hoarse, unfamiliar. 'Because I was with the Seventh until I retired...'

'Ah the Seventh. Were you with me in Gaul and Britannia?'

'At Pharsalus, General.'

'Ha!' Caesar looked across at Spurinna. 'You should have let Septem here take charge of you this morning, Augur. The Seventh were on time when we defeated Pompey. You might have been on time today!' He turned back to the spy. 'And what are you doing now? I can see you're not out on Tiber Island with the rest of the Seventh.'

'I've done some work in the arena, General. Earned my *rudis* wooden sword. Retired. I do bodyguarding now...'

'He's my bodyguard,' interrupted Spurinna gently. 'I know you are interested in all your veterans, Caesar, but this is taking us away from the point. Wasting precious time. May I talk with the Lady Calpurnia about her dream?'

Caesar clapped his hands. Several attendants appeared as though by magic. They materialised from several different rooms. One even came out of the room containing Mars' sacred shields and spears.

'Ask the Lady Calpurnia to come here,' he ordered one of the female slaves. She vanished obediently. The others lingered in case they required. Caesar turned back to Artemidorus, clearly intending to examine him further.

Spurinna started speaking again, the slightest edge of desperation in his voice. 'The Lady Calpurnia had bad dreams you say, Caesar? Was there anything else unusual about last night?' His gaze took in all the attendants, although the question was directed at their master.

'All of the doors and windows suddenly burst open just before dawn,' volunteered one of them, nervously. 'All of them at once.'

'It was a stormy night,' snapped Caesar. 'Nothing wonderful in that!'

'The spears of Mars in the shrine started trembling,' said the young man at the shrine's doorway. 'At about the same time.'

'It was the thunder!' spat Caesar. 'Or perhaps the earth quaked. It's happened before.'

'But,' said Spurinna doggedly. 'These are still dreadfully unlucky omens.'

'What are unlucky omens?' demanded the Lady Calpurnia as she swept in from her dressing chamber.

'The doors and windows are talking to us!' spat Caesar. 'And the spears of Mars have been dancing around like drunken bacchanals in the shrine, apparently! I don't suppose the shields were drinking into the bargain, were they? Or was it just you who was drinking, Fabius?'

'Oh stop teasing the boy,' said Calpurnia.

'My Lady,' said Spurinna. 'About your dream…'

The Lady Calpurnia turned her steady gaze on the augur. 'I dreamed,' she said, 'that I was holding Caesar in my arms. And he was spouting blood from more terrible wounds than I could count. It was horrible. So vivid. So terrifying…'

'It was just a dream,' snapped Caesar irritably. 'A dream, not a vision! I myself dreamed that I was taken up to Olympus and shook hands with Jupiter himself! It was a very happy dream. But that is all it was. A dream! We discussed it when you woke me at some time in the third night watch.'

'And as soon as I slept again I dreamed that the gable that the Senate erected in honour of you tumbled off the *Domus* here and shattered on the *Via Sacra* where you love to walk. These are terrible dreams, my Lord. You must heed them!'

'Indeed, great Caesar,' said Spurinna, his voice gentle, his tone formal. His logic forceful. 'The destruction of a gable erected in your honour cannot be anything other than a bad omen. And, as for the Lady Calpurnia's dream of nursing your bleeding corpse – you hardly need an augur to explain that!'

'Please, my lord,' Calpurnia added her voice to Spurinna's. 'You know I am not superstitious. Or easily frightened. But these dreams were so lifelike…'

'Taken with the other signs, Caesar, they must persuade you! The bull at the *Lupercalia*. The boar on the first day of the month. And now the ram. Not to mention the storms, the wonders, the bursting open of your doors and windows. And you know as well as I do, though you choose to mock it, that the trembling of Mars' spears is one of the worst omens it is possible to receive. You must stay home today.'

'But I have so much to do!' answered Caesar, beginning to waver. 'So little time! And yesterday…'

'Yesterday?' asked Spurinna.

'Another bout of the falling sickness in the morning,' explained Calpurnia, her voice low.

'I recovered in time to go to Lepidus' for dinner with my old friend Decimus Brutus Albinus,' said Caesar. 'But I'd lost a day's work. I had to take the documents with me.'

'It's been getting worse,' whispered Calpurnia. 'The falling sickness…'

'What does Antistius say?' asked Spurinna, clearly shaken at the news.

'Nothing,' answered Calpurnia. 'My Lord refuses to speak with him.'

'Waste of time,' snapped Caesar. 'Whatever he advises will take too long to do. Or will slow me down. I leave for Parthia in four days and I have responsibilities as *pontifex maximus* on the seventeenth and then again on the morning of the nineteenth immediately before I pull out! Whatever Antistius says, I don't have time to waste…'

'You can work here today then,' suggested Spurinna. 'Instead of wasting time at the Senate. That way you will also stay clear of the evil auguries.'

Caesar sighed angrily once again.

Artemidorus actually closed his eyes. *Please*, *Achilleus*, he prayed. *Make him agree to stay...*

'Oh very well,' snapped the ruler of the world in the tones of an angry child. 'I'll stay. Spurinna, go and do your second sacrifice. Calpurnia, send a message to Antony. He'll have to go and tell the Senate in person that this morning's meeting will be postponed!'

Thank you, *Achilleus*, said the spy silently in his head. It had all been worth it after all. Even though he had not needed to rely on Cyanea's list of conspirators or Puella's testimony about the men who visited Brutus, the risks and the pain had been worth it. Even Telos' terrible death had been worth it. For Caesar was safe.

And he thought to himself: *mission accomplished!*

In the race to keep Caesar safe from whatever Brutus and Cassius were planning, they had won. A great weight seemed to lift from his shoulders suddenly and he took a deep breath of relief, breathing in until his ribs hurt.

He could hardly believe it. They had won!

VIII

As he waited for Antony to come out of the bath, Enobarbus walked through into one of the *cubiculae* leading off the *atrium*. Here Cyanea was seated at a low table that was mostly covered with the splintered tablets on which Telos had written the coded list of suspected conspirators. The other section of the table was filled with a sheet of papyrus on which the Lady Fulvia's secretary was writing down the names she dictated to him. He had placed his writing case on the floor, lifting onto the table only the pot of red samian clay that contained the ink and the bronze stylus he occasionally dipped into it.

The list was long, and hopefully nearing completion, thought the tribune. Even as it stood, it was likely to give Caesar pause. Even allowing for his notorious disregard for personal security. His refusal to bow to the will of the gods as revealed in Spurinna's auguries. His refusal to go about the streets accompanied by any more than his *lictors* – their *fasces* like everyone else's mere bundles of sticks with no axes at their hearts. His dismissal of his guards. It was as though the man was half in love with death.

'Is that it?' the tribune demanded. The tone of his voice tinged with the irritation his thoughts about Caesar caused. Cyanea looked up. Her frown matched his. But hers was a frown of worry. The anger in his voice had scared her. For an instant, Enobarbus was distracted by the beauty of her huge blue-green eyes. It was no wonder Septem had taken her to his bed almost the moment they first met. 'Is the list nearly complete?' he asked, his tone softened by her beauty.

'Nearly,' she answered. The frown became less worried. More thoughtful. 'But I was wondering. Should I add names from what Septem and I observed at young Cassius' coming-of-age *toga virilis* ceremony this morning?'

'Whose names were you considering?'

'There was one man Artemidorus was surprised to see there. General Gaius Trebonius.'

'Trebonius...' echoed Enobarbus, his habitual frown deepening once more.

'Trebonius?' demanded a new voice. Deep. Powerful. With a virile resonance. 'What about my old friend Gaius Trebonius?'

Antony came striding across the *atrium*, adjusting the final fold in his dazzling white toga with its rich purple borders. A costume that announced him as a consul as surely as the *lictors* waiting in another room to precede him in the streets.

Enobarbus shook his head in simple wonder. This was hardly the same man as the tottering wreck Fulvia had led into the baths at the rear of the villa. It was the exact opposite of the corpse-like comatose body he had brought back from Cleopatra's villa on the Janiculum Hill. This was the Antony who genuinely looked like a descendant of Hercules. Even without his lion skin. He stood the better part of four cubits tall and was built like a gladiator. The oils recently massaged into his skin in the *laconium* sweat room defined the muscles of his arms and legs. A thick neck rose out of shoulders that might have flattered a bull.

He had been shaved as part of the recovery process with Lady Fulvia in the baths. The lack of his customary beard revealed a broad jaw and square chin. His lips were by no means full, but the straight line of his mouth more often turned up than down. For he was of an open, cheerful disposition. His nose was straight, after the Greek style. Which was apt enough in a man claiming a Greek demigod as an ancestor. His cheeks were too full to present cheekbones. But his face was by no means fat. Nor was the rest of him. Any corpulence arising from his lifestyle in Rome was soon lost when he was out campaigning with his beloved legions. His eyes were wide set. Intelligent – some said calculating. Edged with laugh lines. Light brown, almost tawny. In spite of last night's debauch, the whites were clear. The brows above them were surprisingly delicately curved. If the ears behind the square jaw stuck out a little, they were not so pronounced as to make the helmet he wore in battle uncomfortable. The thick brown hair that topped his leonine head was recently washed and coiffed. As he swept past Enobarbus into the *cubicula*, the tribune smelt the lemony-pine resin odour of frankincense.

'Well?' demanded Antony. 'What about Gaius…' Characteristically, he stopped mid-sentence and changed topic like an acrobat leaping from one horse to another in the arena. 'What eyes! Who is this pretty little thing, Enobarbus?'

Cyanea slowly came to her feet under the co-consul's frank, appraising gaze.

'She is one of my *contubernium* unit of spies…'

'Ah. One of those women who sleep with unsuspecting men to learn their secrets as pillow talk, I hope. If so, I have many, *many* secrets…'

She blushed and looked down, a little overwhelmed.

Enobarbus closed his eyes, thinking that Hercules was not enough of a deity to define Antony. There was a fair amount of the drunken Bacchus and the insatiable Dionysius in that big body as well. 'She has been working undercover in the house of Gaius Cassius Longinus, General,' he explained brusquely. 'And she has brought a list of names for you to read. The names of men who are forming a conspiracy…'

'Oh not another conspiracy. Do we need to take this one seriously?'

'Someone certainly takes it seriously, General. Her partner was tortured to death, mutilated and crucified outside Spurinna's villa. We assume it was a warning to cease our investigations.'

'Really? Who would do such a thing?' demanded Antony as he took the list from the secretary's hand and began to read through it.

'Minucius Basilus. Well, his gladiators at least, led by men called Cestus and Syrus. But there is little doubt that Cassius ordered it.'

'Basilus, eh? He has a nasty reputation. Gets erect when watching slaves in pain. Preferably pretty female slaves. You were lucky he didn't get his hands on you, girl.'

As she had been directly addressed, Cyanea felt free to answer. 'He did, my Lord. But Septem rescued me.'

'Ah,' said Antony as though this explained everything. '*Septem*.' He changed horses once again. 'So, this list that men like Basilus and Cassius will kill for. Why are you thinking of adding Gaius Trebonius to it?'

As she was still being addressed, Cyanea answered. 'Septem and I saw him attending the *toga virilis* ceremony for Gaius Cassius junior this morning.'

'This morning? But that's two days early! And the boy can't be more than thirteen. What's Cassius up to?'

'Most of the men on the list were there,' said Cyanea. 'It looked like a perfect opportunity to get everyone together...'

'And Trebonius was there?'

'Yes, my Lord.'

'Well, he approached me a couple of years ago when Caesar and I were at daggers drawn. Wanted to know if I'd join in a plot to slaughter the old goat. But Trebonius was one of Caesar's closest allies – then as now. Only Decimus Brutus Albinus is closer, in fact. So I thought Caesar had probably put Trebonius up to it as a test of my loyalty.'

'We've been putting this list together from things our spies have seen and heard in the households of Cassius and Brutus,' Enobarbus continued. 'Marcus Junius Brutus...'

'Cassius and Brutus are brothers-in-law. Of course they'll get together...' Antony handed the list back to the secretary. He seemed only to have glanced through it but Enobarbus knew that all the names on the parchment would now be firmly fixed in the general's memory. Antony was a deceptively easy man to underestimate. As many had learned in the past. And many more were likely to learn in the future.

'It was you who ordered that we keep a close eye on these people, General,' Enobarbus pointed out, an edge of frustration in his voice. 'That order has cost one life so far. And now that we've found something you hesitate...'

'What would you have me do, Tribune?'

'Stop Caesar from attending this morning's Senate meeting, General,' answered Enobarbus flatly. 'The names on the list are all senators. The fact that they were desperate enough to kill in order to find out how much we knew. The fact that they left the corpse as a warning outside the house of another of our men. The fact that they all got together at Cassius' villa this morning on such a thin excuse. All of this must mean that they're getting ready to act. Today. It's the last chance for all these men to get together in one place with Caesar before he leaves for Parthia. It's now or never, General. And we believe it's now!'

*

Enobarbus had hardly finished speaking when Antony's doorkeeper came across the *atrium* with Kyros in tow. The young slave was almost as overcome as Cyanea at finding himself confronted with both Enobarbus and Antony. He stood for a moment, tongue-tied, until Enobarbus spoke. 'You have a message for us?'

'Yes Tribune. My master Spurinna has sent me on orders from Caesar himself. I have a message for the general.'

'If it's a message for me, then you'd better tell it to me,' advised Antony, amused by the boy's embarrassment.

'My Lord, Divine Caesar requests that you attend the Senate meeting in his place and on his behalf. He would like you to advise the Senate that he will not be coming to today's meeting.'

Antony's sculpted eyebrows rose in surprise. 'Is this your doing?' he asked Enobarbus. 'Has your *contubernium* of spies got to Caesar himself?'

'I don't know,' said Enobarbus, as surprised as his commander.

'It was the Lady Calpurnia,' volunteered Kyros. 'My master Spurinna augured disaster in his sacrifice this morning. He said there have been any number of ill omens. But Caesar would not listen. He was set on attending the Senate meeting. Then the Lady Calpurnia said she had dreamed a terrible dream and Caesar changed his mind. In the end it was nothing that my master foresaw. Or any of the terrible omens. It was the Lady Calpurnia's dream.'

'And I'm to go to the Senate, am I,' snapped Antony. 'And tell them all to go home until Caesar's wife gets a better night's sleep? I don't mind them hating me. Or slandering me – which Cicero does all the time. Or even plotting against me. But I will not have them laughing at me!'

Seeing Antony just about to fly into one of his lightning-quick rages, Enobarbus spoke forcefully and immediately. 'But, General, if you go to the *curia* where the Senate sits today via the Forum. Instead of going straight through the Gate of Fontus, then you will pass close by the *Regia* and the *Domus*…'

'And I'll be able to go in and talk to Caesar myself. Discuss a better reason for dismissing the Senate. Yes…' Antony clapped his hands and the doorway out into the *atrium* was suddenly filled with servants and slaves. 'Summon my *lictors*. Prepare my litter. Be quick about it!' Several servants vanished to do his bidding as he continued. 'Inform the Lady Fulvia that I am going to visit Caesar and then attend the meeting of Senate.' More vanished, but there were still a good few left. Antony turned away from them, but lost none of the dynamism that immediate action brought out in him. 'Enobarbus. You come with me. Boy, return to your master and tell him I am coming. He may pass that onto Caesar if he wishes.' Kyros vanished. 'Girl…' His voice trailed off as he looked at Cyanea again.

'Perhaps she can wait here for the time being,' suggested Enobarbus.

'Yes. A good idea.' He turned to the last few slaves in the doorway. 'Some one of you help this woman tidy these splinters away. You know the Lady Fulvia cannot abide a mess. Then take her to the kitchen. Get her food and drink. She can wait here until we decide what is to be done with her.'

He turned and vanished into the *atrium*, shouting orders as he went as though he was back in command of the outnumbered legions on Caesar's right flank at the battle of Pharsalus.

One of the slaves came in and started to help Cyanea with the splintered tablets. Another hovered, waiting to guide her to the kitchens. Fulvia's secretary stood, uncertain of what to do next. Enobarbus came further into the room and held out his hand. 'Did you add Trebonius to the list in the end?' he asked.

'No, Tribune,' the secretary answered. 'No decision was ever reached.'

'Cyanea?'

'Septem thought perhaps he was just there as a guest. Not a conspirator. I'd never seen him at Cassius' before.'

'Leave him off, then,' decided the tribune. 'But I'll take it anyway.' He clicked his fingers impatiently.

The secretary handed the pale sheet of parchment over.

'And I'll take that too,' he said, gesturing at the secretary's document case. The slave obediently placed his stylus and his samian pot of ink in the receptacles. Ensured the ink was tightly closed and handed it all over.

The tribune took it. Folded the papyrus into it. Shut it. Turned on his heel and strode out into the bustle the rejuvenated Antony was causing.

*

Antony's litter was large. As it had to be. The four litter bearers were all built like Hannibal's elephants. As they needed to be. Antony offered Enobarbus a lift but the tribune took pity on all concerned and walked beside the litter instead. And so, within a very short time, they were out in the narrow *Clivus Pullius*, heading down the hill towards the Forum.

Antony – like Caesar – habitually rode with the curtains wide so that passers-by could see him. And, every now and then, shout or pass messages to him. Again like Caesar, he preferred his *lictors* to precede him. Rather than surrounding the litter and keeping the *plebs* at bay. The consul knew he had enemies, but he refused to be intimidated by them. Yet again, like his friend and mentor Caesar.

But even with the *lictors* walking immediately ahead and the four elephantine slaves walking shoulder to shoulder on the inner sides of the carrying poles, Antony made slow progress towards the Forum. The streets were not wide. They were busy. There was simply no way even for the co-consul of the city to push past the throngs. But the sluggish progress at least gave the general and the head of his secret service time to talk.

'So...' said Antony.

His head was at the tribune's left hip, level with the military *pugio* dagger he was wearing there. As part of the relentlessly martial uniform he preferred. Though he was not, of course, permitted to wear his *gladius* on his right hip. Only gladiators could do that within the Servian walls. And the *pomerium* limits of the city. First defined by a furrow ploughed by Romulus himself. Later expanded by Sulla. In his right hand, however, he carried the secretary's writing case with the list of conspirators carefully folded within it. 'So,' said Antony again. 'You think this conspiracy is more dangerous than the others?'

'Yes, General. Cassius is an experienced soldier and an able commander. If anyone could organise such a thing it will be him. And the name of Brutus adds the weight of history to the project. As well as the height of social leadership. And, of course, the reputation of the man himself. Were we not going to the *Domus* with the intention of discussing with Caesar how best to explain that he will not attend today. And dismiss the Senate until a later time. Then I would be very concerned for the safety of the dictator. Very concerned indeed.'

'I take your point,' said Antony. 'I may have placed your *contubernium* of spies without much thought. But in that I did, and they have uncovered so much, perhaps I should keep what they have found in mind. Even if Caesar gets safely through today, there will still be plenty of opportunities to kill him before he sets out for Parthia. Or even when he's on the road. Look what happened to Lucius Julius Caesar and his brother Gaius in the year 678 since the founding. Both dead in the streets. Stabbed. Butchered. Not to mention Gracchus. Beaten to death with planks and staves. And, much more recently, my old friend Clodius Pulcher, hacked to death by Titus Annius Milo's gladiators on the Appian Way. Such an act of butchery that not even that viper-tongued windbag Cicero could defend him. Which is surprising given that the turgid turd started his career defending Sextus Roscius for the far greater crime of patricide. Saved him from *Poena Cullei*. From being sewn in a bag and chucked in the Tiber. That's the statutory punishment for such a crime after all.'

'Caesar says that cowards die every day,' Enobarbus observed after a moment's silence. 'But men who don't fear death only meet it once.'

'Once is enough, my friend. We just have to keep control of the place and the time.'

'Perhaps that's true for those we seek to protect, General. But I believe we can do little to control our own meeting with Pluto and Prosperine. Our entry into the Fields of Elysium. Or our ferry ride with Charon across the river Styx.'

'You speak like a soldier, Enobarbus. You expect to meet the gods of death in some battle that is yet to be fought. In some country that is yet to be conquered. Or in some war that has yet to be declared. But remember, a man is always in control of his own destiny, even in this. As long as I have a sword I can choose the moment that I fall on it.'

*

Artemidorus was standing between Puella and Spurinna when Kyros returned. The second sacrifice had gone no better than the first. Even though Spurinna had whispered his intention to find something positive in the entrails now that Caesar had agreed to remain at home. But, thought the spy grimly, maybe the gods were taking a more active part in this than even the augur estimated. For instead of straightening above the golden bowl with the news that all was well, Spurinna had taken a step or two back as though the great coils of sheep's intestines were a nest of venomous snakes.

Caesar was no longer interested in the proceedings now that his decision was made. So he did not see the concern – almost horror – on the face of his *haruspex*. Spurinna gathered up the offending viscera and hurled it into the brazier almost as though he was ridding himself of some dreadful plague. 'Take this creature and destroy it,' he ordered. 'Take them both. Burn them. Bury the ashes some place you wish never to flourish!'

He washed his hands and came across to Artemidorus. 'Never in all my years have I seen anything like it,' he whispered, his voice trembling.

'Do the auguries suggest Caesar could even be at risk here in the *Domus*?' wondered the spy, with unaccustomed superstition. 'The Lady Calpurnia's vision of the gable falling and shattering. The gable of this building…'

'I cannot tell,' answered Spurinna, sounding ancient suddenly. Ancient and unspeakably weary.

'Well, there is nothing we can do at the moment,' soothed Artemidorus.

'Except to wait,' added Puella.

'True,' allowed the spy. 'And to plan what we are going to do with you. We need a safe place for Puella to rest, Spurinna. Until we can settle the question of her being a runaway slave.'

'And of you being a slave stealer and murderer into the bargain,' added Spurinna. 'It seems to me that only a major case of civil unrest will cover up your various misdemeanours.'

'And of course that's the last thing we actually want,' said Artemidorus. 'In fact it's the main thing the general has put us into the field to prevent.'

'I don't follow…' said Spurinna.

'The only thing that could spark that level of unrest would be the murder of Caesar or something equivalent to it,' said the spy.

'Oh that's wonderful,' Puella chimed in. 'The one thing that could keep us safe is the one thing we are fighting to prevent.'

'Sort of like a suicide mission,' said Narbo, suddenly inserting an unexpected opinion.

'Oh, that's right,' said Puella. 'Look on the bright side why don't you!'

Which was the point their conversation had reached when Kyros returned. Breathless. Unable to speak at first. But clearly bursting with news.

At last he managed, 'Antony is coming. He ordered me to tell you, Master, so you could warn Caesar. Antony's coming here on his way to the Senate meeting.'

'Good lad,' said Spurinna. 'I'll go and warn Caesar. He may want to prepare...' He walked off before Kyros could catch his breath and complete his message.

'Lord Antony is concerned that the senators will laugh at him. And laugh at Caesar as well. If he has to tell them Caesar will stay at home because of the Lady Calpurnia's dreams...' gasped the boy.

Artemidorus was in action at once. Swinging round to follow the hasty augur. Caesar would be glad of the further details, he thought. At the least he would appreciate the time to think of an alternative explanation if Antony was concerned that the pair of them would be laughed at if they told the truth. His plan was to catch up with Spurinna and tell him the rest of the message. But the augur was too quick for that. So Artemidorus found himself following Spurinna into the *Domus* once more.

He discovered the two men in close conference, Caesar frowning, clearly displeased. The spy stopped just behind the augur's shoulder waiting for one man or the other to recognise his presence and give him the opportunity to speak. Which happened almost at once. 'Septem,' said Caesar. 'What do you want to tell us?'

Artemidorus relayed the second part of Kyros' message.

'So Antony is scared of being laughed at!' said Caesar, shaking his head.

'I think rather that he is worried that *you* would be laughed at, Caesar,' said Spurinna.

That's a dangerous thought, mused Artemidorus. But it had been suggested and there was no help for it now. Caesar frowned, his aristocratic Roman *dignitas* offended even by the notion.

'I have not,' grated Caesar, 'become dictator for life and co-consul of this city. Ruler over an empire that reaches to the edges of the world. The most powerful man there has ever been with the possible exception of Alexander. Offered a crown and called a god. All so that I might give any thought at all to what a collection of fawning sycophants and useless windbags might think of me. Or whisper behind my back!'

*

Antony and Enobarbus arrived while Caesar's angry words were still echoing in the *atrium*. The wily general sensed the tension in the air. And knew his old friend well enough to suspect that whatever had upset him was something he actually feared. Which was often the case with all men. So he put on his bluff soldier act. 'Now, what's this I hear about the lovely Calpurnia having terrifying visions?' he boomed cheerfully.

'She dreamed she held Divine Caesar in her arms as numberless wounds spouted blood,' explained Spurinna.

'How horrible,' said Antony in a pantomime of shock. 'I had no idea that she had such an imagination. The Lady Calpurnia has always struck me as the personification of matronly rectitude and Roman virtue.'

'That's what lends weight to Spurinna's reasoning,' said Caesar, beginning to calm down. 'She could not have possibly imagined such horrors. Therefore what she saw must have been a vision sent to warn me…'

'I can see the logic in that! It's as clear as what little I remember of Pythagoras' theorems. Or Aristotle's arguments, come to that.'

Caesar gave a bark of laughter. 'We don't have time to discuss the failings of your education, Antony…'

'Nor the excesses of my misspent youth! Yes, I know. I've been having this conversation all my life. First with Antony, my father. Then with the Lady Julia, my mother after he died. Then with my stepfather Lentulus until he was murdered by that venomous blowhard Cicero…' Antony allowed just a shade of bitterness to creep into the cheerfully self-conscious confession.

But Caesar laughed again. And the atmosphere in the *atrium* eased.

'So,' continued Antony, 'what do you want me to tell the senile ranks of our so highly respected senators? *Divine Caesar can't be bothered today so shut up and go home…* Something like that?'

'Tell them the truth!'

145

'That Lady Calpurnia has had a vision that advises you to stay at home?'

'No.' Caesar paused for a moment. Then drew himself haughtily erect. Freezing into positions like one of the statues depicting him, that were going up all over the city. 'That I have decided not to come. I, Caesar, have decided this. It is my will. And there's an end to it!'

Now it was Antony's turn to laugh. 'Oh yes. I look forward to announcing that. The look on their self-important faces will be a memory to treasure. Oh I hope Cicero is there! He might even burst with indignation! Tribune Enobarbus, you will accompany me. And it might be worth your while to bring a bowl of water and some rags of cloth to clean the floor after Cicero goes BANG!'

On this cheerful note, Antony turned and strode out of the *atrium* towards his litter, his elephantine carriers and his brawny *lictors*.

As ordered, Enobarbus followed him. But as he passed Artemidorus, he handed over the writing case he had carried here from Antony's house. 'Cyanea's list is in there,' he whispered. 'Just in case you need it…'

Artemidorus took the long, slim wooden box. 'What do you want us to do, Tribune?' he asked, equally quietly. Spurinna drew near so he could overhear the answer.

'Wait here. Whatever the general ends up actually telling the senators, they are likely to react in other ways than simply going *pop* like the ball in a game of *follis*.'

'I'll keep a close eye on Puella too,' said Artemidorus. 'She's not out of danger, even if Caesar is.'

'Good. But I want all of you watching the *Domus* as closely as you can. You are the only person here who's armed with anything more than a dagger Septem. And that might prove useful. Spurinna you stay close as well – and those two useful servants of his Kyros and Narbo. Septem won't have direct access to Caesar unless there's some kind of emergency. But his augur can come and go almost at will. Especially under the current circumstances…'

'Hey, Tribune!' came a distant bellow. 'I was only joking about the water and the cloths. Hurry up or I'll leave without you!'

Enobarbus' lips narrowed. His frown deepened. 'Keep good watch,' he ordered as he hurried out towards Antony's litter. Spurinna lingered as Caesar turned, heading into his office.

Artemidorus walked at the tribune's shoulder until the pair of them were outside the *Domus*. Then they split up as one went onto the Senate meeting and the other stayed on guard.

*

Enobarbus' VIIth Legion regularly marched fifteen Roman miles in an eight-hour day. That allowed time to break camp in the morning and erect tents (one per eight-man *contubernium* unit), raise defensive earthworks, dig latrines and prepare food at night. The distance from the *Domus Publica* to Pompey's Theatre was hardly more than half a Roman mile as the crow flies or as a Roman road runs. Outside Rome itself at least. Crossing the Forum, marching through busy, winding city streets and out through the constriction of the Gate of Fontus onto the *Campus Martius* slowed their progress, however.

Even so, the Senate's water clocks had hardly measured half an hour before Antony was leaping up the steps that led to the *curia* of Pompey's enormous theatre complex with Enobarbus at his shoulder. The first stone theatre in the city, built immediately outside the Servian wall. And the *pomerium* within which such structures were forbidden. It had been started eleven years earlier at the height of Pompey's wealth and power. Dedicated three years later when his slide to destruction and decapitation had already begun.

They had entered the vast complex of buildings, colonnades and gardens by one of the south entrances. The manicured lawns and fragrant fountains stood behind them as they headed eastwards towards the impressive *curia*. The water, constantly heated so that the fountains would not freeze in the winter, steaming a little in the still-cool morning, the odour of roses coming from it. Antony's *lictors* and litter bearers cleared out of the way as other senatorial litters jostled for space to deposit their important occupants. The colonnades around the gardens

PETER TONKIN

busy with senators and other visitors moving amongst the
artworks and statuary there. The original *curia* Senate House
near the Forum had been damaged by fire and was currently
one of Caesar's building and refurbishing projects. The
dictator had ruled that today's Senate meeting would take
place in Pompey's *curia*, therefore.

The broad front of the *curia* was also colonnaded and knots
of men gathered all along its length. The tribune paused as
Antony went on up the steps. At the far end, he could just
make out Marcus Junius Brutus, who, by the look of things,
was still hearing cases as he waited for the Senate meeting to
begin. And there, not far away from him was Gaius Cassius
Longinus, obviously doing the same. Both *praetors*. Senior
judges.

The next familiar face Enobarbus saw belonged to Caesar's
old friend and close associate on and off the battlefield,
Decimus Junius Brutus Albinus. Quite apart from anything
else, and in spite of his name, Decimus was a distant cousin of
Caesar's. And, therefore the one – admittedly remote –
member of the *Junii* and *Brutii* clans in whom Caesar and his
spy chief placed an absolute trust. His kinship to the dictator
was evidenced by his lean features and broad forehead. Like
Caesar's, his hair was thinning and beginning to recede. Also
like Caesar, however, he had a ready smile and an abundance
of easy charm. Though, unlike his cousin the dictator, he was
not reputed to have slept with many of the loveliest matrons in
Rome. Or a good few other women – and the occasional
potentate – out in the wider world. Or, of course, Cleopatra.

'Hey, Decimus,' called Antony cheerfully. 'You're here
early!'

'I'm here on double business,' answered Decimus. 'I have to
attend the Senate meeting in the *curia* of course. But I've also
got a group of gladiators putting on an exhibition in the
theatre.' He gestured to the monstrous erection at the far,
western, end of the *quadriportico* of the gardens.

'I'll maybe go and watch that after I've finished with the
Senate,' said Antony.

'Will you have time?' asked Decimus. 'I understand there's a full agenda. It may take all day. Divine Caesar has a great deal of business he wants taken care of before he leaves for Parthia. Cicero may put in an appearance…'

'That'll slow things down with a vengeance,' laughed Antony. The edge in his voice betraying his lingering hatred. Or it did so to Enobarbus if to no one else. 'Once the pompous blowhard opens his mouth, we're doomed to be stuck here well into the night watches!'

'And,' continued Decimus, good-humouredly shaking his head at Antony's gratuitous insult. 'Divine Caesar's uncle Lucius Aurelius Cotta also wishes to share with us more predictions from the Sibylline Texts. Which should be interesting. Especially as his last pronouncement was a scarcely disguised suggestion that Caesar should be crowned king.'

'Don't talk to me about crowning Caesar!' laughed Antony, apparently cheerfully. But with that edge still in his voice. 'Not after the mess I made at *Lupercalia*!'

'Oh. That was all your own idea, was it? I wondered…'

'You should have asked Caesar if you really wanted to know! I understand you were at dinner with him yesterday evening up at Lepidus' villa.'

Decimus laughed easily. 'Oddly enough, the question of kings and crowns did not arise. Just much less important questions of life and death. On the rare occasions we could raise his attention from the work he carried with him. He must have signed the better part of fifty documents while the rest of us were eating, drinking and conversing.'

'Well, whatever Lucius Cotta wants to say will have to wait,' announced Antony. 'Caesar's not coming. He's sent me to dismiss the Senate. So I'll have plenty of time to appreciate the prowess of your gladiators. Are they fighting to the death?'

'No,' answered Decimus distractedly. 'It's just an exhibition. But I've hired almost a hundred…' He turned away, suddenly preoccupied.

'A hundred gladiators. That must have cost a small fortune,' observed Antony to Enobarbus. Quietly. As they went on up

149

the wide marble steps towards the vast colonnaded front of the *curia*. 'I wonder what he's up to. Have you seen Caesar's list of appointees to all the major posts here and across the empire for the next couple of years? Is Decimus happy with his place on it I wonder? Or is the exhibition an attempt to attract Caesar's notice at the last minute?'

'What! Do you think the post of *praetor peregrinus* this year and Governor of Cisalpine Gaul next year won't be enough for him?' wondered the tribune.

'That depends on how big his debts are,' answered Antony knowledgeably. 'And, now I come to think of it, if your list of conspirators is correct, the parallel posts don't seem to be enough for Marcus Junius Brutus, do they?'

'But Decimus isn't on my list of conspirators. Any more than you are. Or Lepidus is. There have to be some trustworthy men in Rome after all!'

'Then the gladiatorial exhibition must be exactly what it seems,' concluded Antony. 'A show to amuse the *plebs*. And those of us with *plebeian* tastes.'

*

Enobarbus stopped at the door into the inner *curia* where the Senate was assembling, ready for the meeting that Caesar had called for today. Antony strode forward, his wise eyes assessing the number of senatorial backsides sitting on the benches and chairs. Senate meetings normally began at dawn, but today was a festival and so the senators might be expected to arrive later. Whether or not they had already attended the *toga virilis* ceremony at Cassius' villa and paraded round the Forum with the senator and his son afterwards.

It seemed to the tribune that the Senate's sacrifice revealing the auspices for today had not yet been taken, either. No matter how many senators were present, the session could not begin until yet another animal had been slaughtered and the messages from the gods hidden in its entrails had been read. So things were getting off to a slow start.

If the general wanted to delay things even further he could cry *numera*. And cause the number of senators to be counted. By the chief of the senatorial secretaries already bustling in and out of the huge chamber like a swarm of bees. The *numera* count establishing whether or not there was a *quorum* present. But, thought the tribune suddenly, a cry of *numera* might serve Antony as something more than a delaying tactic. If he was able to establish that a *quorum* was present, in fact, then he could dismiss the Senate as Caesar had requested without worrying whether or not all of the conspirators had turned up. The only problem, of course, was that late-coming conspirators would have to be told over and over that their last chance of killing the *Dictator in Perpetuam* was gone. Something that was likely to ignite an even hotter flame of murderous resentment.

The tribune could remember precious few times he had been glad that the need to make a decision was not down to him. And this was certainly one of them.

But then, suddenly, it was down to him after all.

'What do you think, Enobarbus?' demanded Antony. 'Shall I call *numera* now? Or wait for the auspices to be taken? I don't see Cassius or Brutus yet. Cicero is remarkable by his absence. Casca is in his place already. Keen in more ways than one if your list is accurate. And I see ten or more of the others named.'

'If you call *numera* now, we will at least spare a boar from being sacrificed...' suggested Enobarbus.

'And rob the Senate's augur of his breakfast. Not such a wise move, perhaps...'

'If Spurinna's auguries are anything to go by, the auspices will not be good.'

'But that won't stop the porcine vessel of bad news from being butchered and cooked,' Antony observed. 'Not all the augurs or *haruspices* are as punctilious as Spurinna. Or as *lean*.' He laughed. 'Caesar says he prefers *fat* men around him...'

Even as Antony spoke, Casca stood up and began to move across the auditorium, his toga failing to conceal his lean build. He exchanged a word or two with the skeletal Minucius Basilus. 'And I think I agree with him,' decided Antony. 'I wouldn't want those two standing behind me if things became dangerous.'

'So, General,' said Enobarbus, passing the responsibility back to his commander. 'Is it the augury or the *numera*?'

'At this stage, the augury,' Antony decided. 'I'm not sure there is a *quorum* present and I can't dismiss the Senate until there is. Casca is here – with a good number of Cassius' friends. But there's no sign of Brutus as far as I can see. Or Cassius himself. Maybe he's taken Cassius junior home for breakfast and a lecture about the social and moral responsibilities of a grown-up Roman citizen of senatorial rank.'

'No, General,' said Enobarbus. 'They're both here. Outside. Hearing cases on the colonnade.'

'Are they?' asked Antony. 'I didn't see them. Must be losing my touch. Or my eyesight.'

As Antony was speaking, the attendants completed several important functions. The water clocks were turned. The records brought in and the *amanuensis* who would record the proceedings, using shorthand created by Cicero's secretary, prepared his tablets and his stylus. This, observed Enobarbus, was a strikingly beautiful youth. A slave, he seemed to remember, in Trebonius' household. The dictator's gilded wood and ivory *curule* chair was brought in and placed on the raised platform at the front. Facing the assembled benches. And the work table that Caesar always liked to have to hand was placed in readiness to take the official scrolls and tablets he habitually carried around with him.

'That's a waste of time and effort,' said Antony. 'If only they knew it. Now, where's the augur and his altar?'

'Not far,' answered Enobarbus, though he knew the general's question was rhetorical. 'At the *Ara Martis* over by the *Villa Publica*.'

Tellingly, thought Enobarbus some time later, the Senate's augur had neither the standing or the reputation of Caesar's augur Spurinna. Nor the insight, it seemed. Certainly the messages he sent to the Senate made it clear that he saw nothing sinister in the entrails of the boar that was sacrificed in order to start the process of that day's Senate meeting. He seemingly saw nothing in the slaughtered animal, in fact, other than a good solid meal. As far as the hungry *haruspex* was concerned, Mars and all the other gods and goddesses were smiling upon the entire undertaking. Which, all things considered, seemed highly unlikely.

And the ill fortune that seemed to be hanging somewhere in the clear blue sky made its presence known almost at once. As a slave came panting up to them, red-faced and perspiring. 'Masters,' he gasped. 'Have you seen the Lord Brutus?'

'Yes, answered Enobarbus. He's at the far end of the colonnade. Why?'

'It is the Lady Porcia,' gabbled the slave, his eyes wide. 'I must find Lord Brutus and tell him. The Lady Porcia is dead!'

*

The sundial in the Garden of the Vestals behind the *Domus* had registered less than an hour having passed since Antony left before Decimus Albinus' litter appeared. The curtains around it were tightly shut so Artemidorus was uncertain who Caesar's unexpected visitor was at first. But the curtains parted and the occupant emerged. He recognised the high, broad forehead and receding hairline of Caesar's close friend and distant relative and breathed a sigh of relief.

Decimus Albinus' arrival by coincidence came at the same time as Puella's absence in search of a public toilet. Those in the *Regia* and the *Domus Publica* being closed to her. The spy was standing in the courtyard near the altar, deep in conversation with Spurinna, Kyros and Narbo. The augur at least being deemed worthy of a nod of recognition from Caesar's friend and relative. Then Caesar's doorkeeper was ushering the senator into the shady *atrium* of the *Domus* and the door closed behind them.

'I wonder what he's doing here,' said Artemidorus. 'Surely he should be at the Senate meeting or on his way to it. Unless the general has dismissed them all already.'

Spurinna shook his head. 'There hasn't been time,' he said. 'Perhaps he's just on his way. Passing by. Here to see if

Caesar's left yet. Wanting to keep him company. Talk some business maybe…'

Artemidorus shrugged. His eyes narrowed. He heard the tone in Spurinna's voice that told him the augur didn't fully believe what he was saying. Was on the edge of being concerned by the unexpected visit. After the auguries, dreams and wonders of the last few hours, anything out of the ordinary seemed sinister, thought the spy.

But the augur shrugged again. 'If it had been anyone else I might be worried…' he concluded. In a voice that sounded worried to the spy.

But he had hardly finished speaking when the door opened once again and Caesar's *ostiarius* came towards the little group. 'My master wishes his augur to come in,' he said.

Spurinna threw Artemidorus a look. 'You come too, Septem,' he ordered. 'I don't like the sound of this.' The spy nodded his agreement and handed the writing box containing Cyanea's list to Kayros.

As Artemidorus followed the augur into the *Domus* once again, patting the tile with Janus' face in the hope of some good luck, he could see all too clearly the basis of Spurinna's concern. The only reason for Caesar to be asking for Spurinna was because he wished to test the augur's predictions once again. His interpretations of the Lady Calpurnia's dreams. And he would only question those if Decimus Albinus was making him question the original interpretations and the decisions arising from them. Which in turn meant that Caesar was thinking of going to the Senate meeting after all.

The doorkeeper led them through the *atrium*. Past the busts and statues there. The spy's broad shoulder brushed a marble plinth that was as tall as he was. The marble bust of Caesar on top of it rocked. Then the spy and the augur were led into the large room dedicated to the god Mars. Mars' shields hung on the walls. Massive, colourful *scutum* shields as tall as a man; fit for a god to carry. His spears stood below them, also super-humanly massive. A statue of the god stood in one corner and a shrine in his honour stood in another. The attendant Fabius stood beside the shrine, seemingly ready to make some sort of sacrifice. The only thing missing was the head of the October horse which was nailed to the wall in the main shrine of the *Regia*. There had been a chariot race in praise of Mars in the *Campus Martius* only yesterday. But the winning horse was not sacrificed on that occasion. As it was in October.

Caesar and his cousin were standing by the statue deep in conversation when the augur and his bodyguard were shown in. The atmosphere in the room was, if anything, relaxed and cheerful. As might be expected in the baths, where two old friends were sitting side by side in the *caldarium* swapping ancient memories and the latest jokes.

'... if Calpurnia is asleep, poor thing,' Decimus Albinus was saying, 'then that's all to the good. I'm sure there'll be no repetition of whatever disturbed her last night. As you say, it was probably more to do with the storm than anything else. Like the way the doors and windows burst open. And the so-called trembling of the spears.' As he spoke, he went over and touched the nearest one. And they all crashed together to the floor. 'See?' he laughed, shaking his head. The slave Fabius rushed over and began to pick the sacred objects up. At a nod from Spurinna, Artemidorus went to help. As he lifted the first of the massive weapons back into place, the spy could have sworn he felt the spear haft trembling.

'Ah, Spurinna,' said Caesar, noticing his augur's presence. 'Decimus here has interpreted poor Calpurnia's dream in a much more positive way than the way you did.'

'Has he?' asked Spurinna carefully. Challenging Caesar's favourites was a risky business. Especially when they were relatives. And they were telling him what he clearly wanted to hear into the bargain. 'And how is that, Divine Caesar?'

'Why, it's obvious,' answered Decimus Albinus cheerfully. 'Calpurnia dreamed she was holding Julius' head because he is the head of the state. A head, I might add, that may well be wearing a crown before nightfall. If the rumours I have heard in the Senate house are true...'

'But I have refused a crown...' Caesar began, surprised by this sudden turn of events. Artemidorus, his hand still on Mars' massive spear met Spurinna's gaze. The augur's lips were thin. He wore a frown. But his eyes seemed calm in the face of impending disaster. The spy and centurion had seen that look in the eyes of soldiers approaching the battlefield.

'A coronet offered by that buffoon Antony,' laughed Decimus. 'Not quite the same as a crown offered by the Senate. On the advice of the Sibylline Texts. As interpreted by the Fifteen and explained by dear old uncle Lucius Cotta…'

'A crown…' repeated Caesar. And there was longing in his voice. 'King…'

'King outside Italy certainly,' said Decimus. 'The king we apparently need to ensure the Parthians' defeat. Perhaps even king outside Rome – outside the Servian wall and the *pomerium*. King of the world…'

'King of the world,' echoed Caesar, his voice like that of a man in the grip of a vision. 'King of the world…'

*

'But in the Lady Calpurnia's dream,' persisted Spurinna. 'The wounds spouting blood…'

'Caesar has poured his life's blood into making the city and the empire a better, vaster, richer place,' countered Decimus Albinus easily. 'Of course, as king, he will continue to pour golden benefits on Rome and all the lands she controls. It is a clear analogy. And, besides…'

'Besides?' asked Caesar, a dangerous tone in his voice suddenly.

'Consider, dear cousin,' explained Decimus, treading more softly now. 'Consider. The Senate met to honour you. Possibly with a crown as I say. Uncle Lucius ready to present the Sibylline predictions. Everyone tense with excitement and anticipation. Only to be informed you're staying at home because your wife has had bad dreams. Really. What would they make of such a thing? A joke? What would *Cicero* make of such a thing?'

'A speech,' admitted Caesar, his mood lightening again.

'A *very long* speech!' chuckled Decimus.

'And the gable?' demanded Spurinna, fighting to keep his voice level. To keep his tone respectful of Caesar's closest friend and associate. *Did the man not realise what he was doing?* 'The gable. Falling and shattering on the *Via Sacra?*'

'A gable erected by the Senate to honour the *Perpetual Dictator*! Of course it must come down. They will have to put up another one. Suitable to honour a *king*!'

'This all seems a much sounder interpretation of Calpurnia's dreams than yours, Spurinna!' said Caesar. And there was that dreamy timbre back in his voice again.

'Divine Caesar…' began Spurinna, his tone nakedly desperate now.

'I feel a little foolish that I allowed myself to be talked out of attending the Senate meeting.' Caesar said, with a shake of his head and a gathering frown. His mind returning from Albinus' tempting vision. The man of action kicking in.

'And such an important meeting,' added Decimus. Gratuitously. For he knew he had changed Caesar's mind.

Artemidorus felt a chill of impending disaster clutching at his belly. As though he was a sacrifice himself, with his guts torn out and spread.

Perhaps this was the will of the gods.

'The Lady Calpurnia…' the augur began. One last desperate move.

'Is sound asleep,' Decimus observed smoothly. 'If we do not disturb her, Divine Caesar will be back from the meeting before she wakes. And with such good news…'

'But Caesar,' Spurinna interrupted desperately, trying one last frantic roll of the dice. 'The auguries. They were as bad as the dream. Worse! You may be going into terrible danger!'

'Oh,' laughed Decimus Albinus. 'As to that, if Caesar *was actually afraid* of a bunch of fat old senators, I have a hundred gladiators on the stage at the far end of the theatre. Fully armed and close at hand. And happy to protect us both!'

'Right,' said Caesar. 'That's it. My mind is made up. We go. And we go now. Fabius, tell them to prepare my litter. And tell my secretary I will want this morning's work brought along with me. Go on, boy. Hurry!'

Fabius rushed out to obey the sudden list of orders. Like a soldier finding himself the target of a volley of slingshots. He rushed out of the room calling, 'Lucius? Lucius?'

'*Fabius*!' snapped Caesar, calling the young man back.

'Caesar?' He hovered in the doorway. 'Summon Lucius quietly! We do not want to disturb my wife!'

'Yes Caesar!' Fabius vanished again, whispering, 'Lucius? Lucius Balbus?' with hissing intensity as he called for Caesar's secretary. Balbus was already a rich and powerful man. He had houses of his own and was only attending Caesar in his post as private secretary today because of the enormous amount of business they needed to complete before the dictator left in four days' time.

The middle-aged Spanish Jew appeared at the doorway almost immediately, therefore. And was subjected to his own volley of orders.

Spurinna and Artemidorus exchanged despairing glances, trapped here until Caesar noticed them again and gave them either more orders or his regal permission to leave.

'Right,' said Caesar, turning to his beaming cousin Decimus. 'Let us go. My litter will be beside yours by the time we get the *Via*. And Lucius will follow with my work and his minions. Oh Spurinna. That will be all, I think. You and Septem here may go.'

Caesar and Decimus Albinus left the room then. Processing through the *atrium*, shoulder to shoulder. The *ostiarius* held the door open for them and they exited with hardly a nod to the Janus tile. Artemidorus and Spurinna followed. The spy's mind was racing. The augur seemed simply dazed. Lucius Balbus bustled past them. Fabius, still rushing to fulfil his master's orders vanished back into the temporary Temple of Mars. As he did so, his shoulder brushed the plinth that Artemidorus had touched earlier. The bust of Caesar rocked as the plinth reeled. Toppled and tumbled, shattering on the floor. The ball of the skull burst. The face remained almost whole. Except for a long crack running from his right temple to the left side of his chin. The noise of its destruction loud enough to cause Calpurnia to come half awake and cry out in her sleep.

By the time Artemidorus and Spurinna arrived outside, Caesar's litter was beside Decimus Albinus'. The cousins were exchanging a few last words before climbing aboard and heading for Pompey's Theatre. Kyros was watching them, his youthful face a mask of horror.

But his expression was as nothing compared to Puella's as she approached the little group. Returning from her visit to the public toilet in the Forum.

'Septem. You have to get to the tribune and the general as fast as you can!' Spurinna was saying. 'If Antony hasn't dismissed the Senate, you must stop him. And warn him…'

Puella arrived then. And something she had seen so horrified her that she interrupted the equestrian augur without hesitation. '*Who is that man*?' she demanded.

'The man with Caesar? His cousin Decimus Albinus. They are close friends and intimates. Why?'

'He is one of them! One of the conspirators! I have seen him! Only once or twice, but I am certain. I have seen him coming in secret to meet with my master Lord Brutus and Cassius.'

'This changes everything!' cried Spurinna. 'And explains the last few minutes into the bargain. Septem! You must find a way to stop Caesar altogether!'

'And if I can't?'

'Then get to the Senate house before him! Warn the tribune. Warn the general!'

'Right!' The spy was in motion at once. 'Puella,' he shouted over his shoulder. 'Stay here with Spurinna. Narbo, I think I may need you. Kyros. Come with me too. And bring the writing box. Bring Cyanea's list!'

PETER TONKIN

IX

Artemidorus ran into the Forum with his hand on the hilt of his sword. The cloak he had borrowed from Narbo flapped behind him, but a fold kept the weapon concealed. If stopped by the local *aedile* magistrate or his officious *vigiles* police he could still pretend to be a gladiator. But he would prefer not to be stopped. Anything that kept him from his mission would be little short of a disaster. And his disguise as a gladiator would not stand up to much scrutiny. Especially as he was running to catch up with Decimus Albinus' litter – and Caesar's which preceded it. And it was Albinus' gladiators with which he was pretending to be associated.

Kyros and Narbo were running at his shoulder. Kyros' hood was down, cloak also flapping. Like Artemidorus'. He was clutching the writing case that contained the deadly list. Which, thought the spy with burning bitterness, was at least one treacherous name short. He looked around, wondering if he dared stop for long enough to scrawl *Decimus Albinus* at the head of the fatal register.

They were well through the second hour now and the sun was high enough to be filling the square with light and heat. The heaving mass of humanity fighting its way through the heart of the city simply added to the temperature. And, once again, to the stench. But, thought the desperate spy, at least a couple of men could move faster than a couple of litters. They should find it possible – if not exactly easy – to get ahead of Caesar's litter. Pause for long enough to add Albinus' name to the list. And still be in a position to hand it to Caesar as the dictator caught up with them.

Caesar's litter was first of the two that Artemidorus, Narbo and Kyros were chasing. The dictator had dispensed with the services not only of his guards but also of the twenty-four *lictors* he was entitled to. As *praetor peregrinatus*, Albinus was entitled to six, but only two within Sulla's expanded *pomerium*, which reached well beyond the original boundary and the Servian walls to include the *Campus*. He had brought them, apparently more defensive of his *dignitas* than his mighty cousin, only to find that they were a solid, fleshy barrier between his litter and Caesar's litter just ahead.

At the left hand of Caesar's litter, Lucius Balbus and his men held several bags of scrolls and tablets – Caesar's work for the morning. Which he would scan and sign while he listened to the senatorial debates. He could get through a whole bag-full, thought the spy with a wry mental smile, once Marcus Tullius Cicero got under way. But the crowd of secretaries effectively made Caesar's litter even wider. And, although Balbus would call out now and then that the dictator was approaching, that information did not always have the desired effect of clearing the way.

Progress through the Forum, therefore, was slow for the litters they were chasing. As well as for the other senatorial litters heading out through the Gate of Fontus, north of the Capitoline Hill, the *Arx Capitolinus* fort and the Temple of Juno on top of the northern spur. It would almost have been worthwhile, thought the spy, to have missed the Forum altogether and gone south of the Tarpean Rock and out through the Carmenta Gate beneath the Temple of Jupiter on the southern crest of the Capitoline. But the Fontus was the most direct way, if the slower one.

The litters' progress was slowed still further by Caesar's notorious approachability. He might be hoping to be king of the world before nightfall, but Caesar saw himself as a man of the people. And therefore, as his litter moved through the thronging, perspiring Forum, one supplicant after another pushed towards the open side of his litter, asking for favours, passing messages, begging for charity. Caesar accepted them all. Answering the spoken ones with a word, a smile or a nod. Passing the written ones to Balbus after giving them the most cursory of glances. Putting one or two more pressing or private into the fold of his toga that served him as a pocket.

And it was this that finally helped the desperate spy make up his mind. His plan was good. They should go for it. 'Quickly,

161

Kyros,' he called. 'We have to get ahead of Caesar at all costs.'

'As you say, Septem,' puffed the young slave. Narbo was stronger, fitter. Like Artemidorus, he was not yet short of breath. But all of them were running with sweat now.

In the face of immediate action, Artemidorus somehow stopped being a disguised gladiator. He transformed almost magically into the senior centurion of the VIIth Legion. The crowd ahead of him might just as well have been enemy soldiers. Dodging this way and that, ignoring the startled cries of pain and anger he left behind him, he shouldered his way ruthlessly forward. Bouncing off men and women alike. Lifting or shoving children out of his way. Careless of whether anyone saw his *gladius* and tried to stop him because of it. Content that most of the citizens, servants and slaves who saw the sword at his right hip drew back automatically, fearing violence. His face folded into the frown it wore in battle. An expression that also helped to clear the way.

He barged his way past Decimus Albinus' litter. Then his *lictors*. He began to close with Caesar's litter as the open space of the *Comitium* came into view on his right, still a little way ahead. By the time they reached the tribunal on which Brutus had been delivering his *praetorial* judgements more than an hour ago, he was ahead of Caesar's litter too. Narbo and Kyros were still close behind.

Up ahead, the throng was being squeezed into the *Clivus Argentius* roadway. That led past the *Tullianum* prison on the left with the steep, rocky slope of the Capitoline behind it. And the *Curia Hostilis* on the right behind the *Comitium*. As the ancient roadway curved round towards the Gate of Fontus. Caesar's litter slowed still further. But the open area of the *Comitium* gave Artemidorus the space he needed. 'Kyros,' he snapped. 'I want the list, the stylus and, Narbo, your back to lean against!'

As quickly as he was able, the young slave offered the stylus and the papyrus. Narbo offered a shoulder as firm as the olive wood it resembled. Artemidorus spread the precious papyrus across the big slave's shoulder as he clutched the slick metal

of the stylus, praying to Achilleus that there would still be
some ink in the nib. The stylus was made of bronze. It was
about the same length as his *pugio* dagger, though slim and
sharp-pointed. And once again the immortal hero of Troy
answered the spy's prayers. There was still ink in the stylus'
sharp nib. In spite of the jostling crowds at his back, he
managed to add Decimus Albinus' name to the top of the list.
Then, for good measure, he added Trebonius' at the bottom.

He handed the stylus back to Kyros and swung round,
straining to see over the heads of the crowd. Yes! There came
Caesar now! His heartbeat raced from canter to full gallop.
With the precious scroll firmly in his hand he began to push
his way towards the litter.

*

'Caesar! Caesar! Hear me!'

'No, hear me Caesar. It is only a small request…'

'… a scroll for your attention, great Caesar. A matter of
some importance…'

As Artemidorus pushed his way through the crowd, the
clamour grew relentlessly louder and louder. Men and women
seemingly of every sort and station clustered round the litter
like swarming bees. For a wild moment, Artemidorus
considered taking out his *gladius* and hacking his way
through. As though the Romans in front of him were long-
haired Gauls. As though they were Spartacus' rebel gladiators.
As though they were ruthless Cilician pirates.

'Clear the way!' he bellowed, still in character as *primus
pilus* senior centurion, in full command of a cohort of six
centuries; a mere eight ranks down from full command of the
legion. And the citizens between him and the litter began to
obey. He tucked the precious papyrus into his belt and freed
both of his hands. Those who still hesitated he simply pulled
aside, taking men and women by their shoulders and tossing
them out of his way.

Until, at last, he was at the litter, looking down on a
frowning Caesar. He pulled the scroll of names from his belt
as Caesar glared up at him. 'Septem? What…'

'This scroll, Caesar. You must read it. It is of vital importance...' Artemidorus found it hard to talk for any length of time. The litter had not stopped – it was moving relentlessly forward and he was forced to walk along beside it. As the crowds of litigants closed in around them once again.

'Is this a message from Spurinna? Tell him...'

'Caesar. Do you not recognise me?' he cried desperately. 'Septem is an alias. A disguise. I am Centurion Artemidorus, *primus pilus* of the VIIth. I have been working with General Mark Antony and his tribune Enobarbus. What we have discovered is on that paper, Caesar. It is of vital importance to you. You must read it...' Even as he spoke, however, he was already being pushed back by the press of people. With a sick feeling in the pit of his stomach he realised that although he could outpace the litter by running through the outer fringes of the crowd, he stood little chance of keeping up with it here at the full-packed heaving heart of the multitude.

Caesar took the scroll and half opened it. Glanced uncomprehendingly down at it. Glanced across at Lucius Balbus, clearly wondering whether to pass the scroll to him.

'It is of vital importance, Caesar,' shouted Artemidorus. 'To you. To you alone!'

The unrelenting river of humanity overcame him at last and began to sweep him back.

The last he saw of Caesar, the dictator was pushing the vital scroll into the fold of his toga. As more and more of the people he lived to serve and hoped to rule closed around him with their interminable demands.

*

'Did he take it, Septem?' wheezed Kyros.

'He took it,' gasped Artemidorus. Breathless himself now. 'But he didn't read it. At least he didn't hand it to his secretary. He still has it on him. So there's a chance he might glance at it on his way. And arrive at the Senate forewarned. If not forearmed. Now we have to get to Enobarbus and the general.'

Even as he spoke, he was in relentless motion once again. But then he paused. Turned. 'Narbo. Go back to the *Domus*

164

Publicus. Tell them what has happened. Warn them of the danger. Tell Spurinna. Perhaps he can think of something...'
He had no need to add more. The solid Iberian was gone. He and Kyros turned back and ran on towards Pompey's *curia*, the general and his tribune.

As Artemidorus had calculated, the outer fringes of the crowds were much less of an obstacle than the close-packed press of bodies around the litters. The spy and the slave made better progress, therefore. The roadway they were following curved beneath the rocky side of the northern Capitoline spur with the Temple of Juno and the ancient fort of the *Arx* at its peak, which rose on their left. On their right stood the equally ancient *Basilica Porcia*. Ahead of them lay the square-legged arch of the Gate of Fontus which opened in the Servian wall and led out onto the *Campus Martius*. They ran through the gate, shouldering the populace brutally aside. Turned away from the portico which led up to the Temple of Mars where the *Via Flaminia* sped away northward, as straight as an arrow. Heading over the Appenines to the distant port of Arminium on the Adriatic coast.

Turning left at the junction and hurling themselves into the roadway that led westward along the southern side of the enormous Theatre of Pompey, they pounded along the cobbles with the huge marble wall rearing on their right. Until they came to the first of the southern entrances. Here they joined the throng seeking entry.

There were senators – some still in their litters, some on foot. Citizens and freedmen of all sorts. Some here for the meeting in the *curia*. Some here to enjoy the art and statuary collected from all over the empire. Much of it displayed in the colonnades that edged the ornamental gardens, which many of the others had come to enjoy. And, finally, there was a great press of people who had come to see the gladiatorial display that Decimus Albinus had arranged. Which included, thought Artemidorus with a shiver of revelation, the murderous Syrus and the men who had been at Minucius Basilus' villa.

They pushed through into the vast space. Artemidorus looked right and left, his gaze seeming to stretch away westwards to the theatre itself. Its massive frontage crested with the temple to Venus Victrix. Like Mars, one of Caesar's favourite deities. Beneath which the gladiators must already be going through the first of their exhibition matches. And away to his right, the wide marble stairway that led up to the colonnaded front of the *curia*. Like the Temple of Venus, and the other *curias* in which the Senate met all over the city, a sacred space. His eyes narrowed. The steps were busy with senators, their slaves and servants. But he was only concerned to find the general or his tribune.

He and Kyros had hesitated only a few heartbeats. Then Artemidorus was off again, running along the edge of the ornamental garden, outside the crowded colonnade, towards the steps. Neither Enobarbus nor Antony were there. They must be inside the *curia* itself, calculated the desperate spy. And if they were inside, that could only mean that Antony, as consul, had dismissed the Senate. Or was just about to do so. A gesture that was useless now. That was just about to be undone by the imminent arrival of Caesar.

Weaving in and out of the senators and their attendants, he took the steps two at a time until he reached the wide porch outside the big double doors of the place. Here he paused again. As an apparent *plebeian* – freedman or gladiator – he was forbidden entry. And he was armed with a *gladius* – so he was doubly forbidden. He peered into the relative gloom of the *curia's atrium*. All he could see was senators. In groups. In twos and threes. It was difficult to estimate whether they were going in to begin the session or coming out because they had been dismissed.

'Out of the way, *pleb*! What are you gaping at?' Came a haughty voice, shrill with irritation. Artemidorus turned to see Gaius Servilius, one of the Casca clan. Quintus Labeo was with him. Quintus Ligarius and Lucius Cinna were close behind. *The vultures are gathering*, he thought.

*

Deeper inside the building, lost in the shadows so that Artemidorus could not see him, Enobarbus watched as Antony marched forward. During the last turn of the water clocks, the

166

Senate had continued to gather. There must be a *quorum* now. But before Antony could send them all home, he would have to be sure. As soon as he spoke the words of dismissal, someone would be bound to cry *numera* and slow the process down as the precise number present was established.

As ever, once Antony had tired of trying to find a way round the obstacle, he would simply smash right through it. He crossed to the raised platform containing Caesar's chair and work table. He signalled the attendants there to remove the furniture, then crossed to the chief secretary. His movements and gestures made it clear he was asking for a count to be made quietly. Informally. But accurately enough to allow him to dismiss a *numera* call with his own count. The attendants hesitated, confused. The table and chair remained in place for the moment. The chief secretary nodded. Antony's count was under way.

In the meantime, the tribune was working on his own, much more sinister, headcount. No sign of Cassius or Brutus yet. They were still out on the portico, no doubt. Finishing their legal business for the day. Publius Servilius Casca and Basilus were there. Casca's brother Gaius swept in, his face pinched with ill humour. Another so-called friend and close associate of Caesar's who seemed all too happy to turn against him. Tillius Cimber, Pontius Aquila, Caecilus and Buciolanus formed a small, uneasy group. Heads close together. Tillius Cimber every now and then scanning the chamber. His eyes always settling on the low tribunal. On Caesar's empty table. On Caesar's vacant chair. As though something terrible was seated on it. Before they darted towards the entrance. After every nervous glance, he would fall into conversation with Pontius Aquila again. They were waiting for something. Someone. Their leaders. Their victim.

Quintus Labeo, Quintus Ligarius and Lucius Cinna followed Gaius Casca into the *curia*. Another little group who lingered, waiting.

The chamber was almost full now, and the tribune turned away. There were too many senators milling around for him to identify any more conspirators. He moved into the brightness of the vestibule, still deeply preoccupied. The entrance hall seemed almost as busy as the Senate chamber itself. Behind him he heard Antony's familiar voice raised over the bustle and the chatter. The consul was beginning the process of dismissing the Senate.

Enobarbus walked towards the great wide doorway leading out onto the colonnaded portico, deep in thought. At the forefront of his mind was the almost inexpressible sense of relief that they had saved Caesar. Even allowing for auguries, dreams and portents, there was no really accurate way to predict the future. But the auguries this time had seemed so clear. Even beyond what Spurinna had found time after time in the entrails of his sacrifices, there was talk of a little kingbird being torn to pieces in the *curia* yesterday. And someone had said something he had half overheard about Caesar's horses. Those that had crossed the Rubicon with him and been turned out to grass. Refusing to eat. Shedding tears... It was as though the gods were shouting warning after warning. And Antony's little eight-man *contubernium* of spies had made Caesar pay attention to their message after all.

But then, thought Enobarbus philosophically, perhaps Caesar would have survived the day without their interference and left for Parthia safely. Perhaps the conspiracy they had uncovered and feared so much would have come to nothing in any case. Caesar, beloved of Mars and Venus Victrix had escaped many an apparently fatal situation before. At Alesia. At Munda. Both battles where Caesar had placed himself – as was his habit – right in the centre of the action. Both battles that turned on a knife-edge. Both battles that could – should – have gone to pieces as Crassus' had at Carrhae. How close had Caesar come, time after time, to having his head taken, filled with gold and used as a prop in a stage play? Who could possibly know the will of the gods or the vagaries of chance? Or the inevitable turning of destiny?

They might even have preserved Caesar today only to see him struck down tomorrow. There was no doubt, Antony said, that the falling sickness was getting worse. Caesar was not a well man. The tribune had known others with the same

168

malady. It always grew worse and worse in his experience. The fits would come faster and faster. The swoons deeper and deeper. For all that the sufferer could perform wonders of energy and accomplish what seemed almost impossible in the hectic days between the fits. There came a time at last when the grip of the malady made the sufferer lose all control. Of his bladder. Of his bowels. And the end of it all was death. Which might come during a seizure. Or because of a seizure. If Caesar had an attack while on his horse, for instance. Or in the midst of battle. Or at any other time when a failure of sense could spell immediate or eventual death.

The tribune stepped out into the brightness of the day. He gave himself a mental shake. Such thoughts could only be ill-omened. A reaction to the greater, glittering truth. Whatever was destined to happen to him tomorrow, or in any of the days, months and years succeeding. They had kept Caesar safe today.

A tall, red-bearded man in a cloak came running up the marble steps towards him. Such was the tribune's preoccupation that he did not recognise his *speculator* the Centurion Artemidorus until the man was immediately in front of him.

And even then, the spy had to repeat his message before Enobarbus could completely understand.

'Caesar is coming, Tribune. You must warn the general. Caesar is coming! Caesar is coming I say!'

X

Artemidorus saw the horror sweep across Enobarbus' expression as the terrible news sank in.

'How long?' demanded the tribune. 'How long until Caesar gets here?'

'Not long. Once he's through the Gate of Fontus, the roads are not so crowded. He was leaving the Forum when I spoke to him, so he'll be here soon...'

'You spoke to him? What did you say?'

'I gave him Cyanea's list. I added Decimus Brutus Albinus and Gaius Trebonius to it. Puella says she's seen Albinus at several secret meetings but never knew who he was.'

'Decimus Albinus! You'll tell me Lepidus is one of the conspirators next. Is there anyone who's not plotting to kill him?'

'Lepidus is as firm as Antony I'm sure. But you must warn him. You must warn the general. He can't dismiss the Senate if Caesar is on his way!'

'Perhaps I should let him do it after all. There might be some hope in a bit of confusion.'

'A waste of time, Tribune. Even if he did dismiss them, there won't really be confusion. They'll stand around talking. In any case, they won't have had a chance to go anywhere before Caesar arrives. Can you get in there and warn Lord Antony?'

'I can try. I'm not supposed to go past the inner door into the chamber itself – only senators are allowed in there. And senatorial staff of course. Senate secretary and the lesser secretaries. Record keepers. Timekeepers with their water clocks. All of whom look like the kind of men who'd do that kind of job. You and I would stand out like a couple of long-haired Gauls. But if I can attract his attention. Catch his eye...'

'You have to try! If you don't, I will!'

'Both together then! Two are better than one!'

Shoulder to shoulder the two soldiers marched off the portico and into the vestibule. Artemidorus' cloak hid his *gladius* once more. The hood was down on his shoulders, though. His red beard might make as clear a signal as it had made a good disguise. They were going to find this risky enough as things stood, though – the *gladius* might make them stand out a bit too far.

They quick-marched through the crowd of senators making their slower way inwards and arrived at the inner door of the Senate chamber itself. They had no trouble in attracting the gaze of almost everyone they did not want to talk to. It was disturbing how so many pairs of eyes observed every movement by the door with almost frantic intensity. Artemidorus had experienced something like this when a pack of starving wolves suddenly registered his presence in a winterbound northern forest. And the fact that he was edible.

But Antony had his back to them, still in conversation with the secretary. With a sinking heart, Artemidorus saw that Caesar's chair and work table were being taken off his raised tribunal. The dismissal of the Senate was under way. But no one seemed to be preparing to leave. Just as he had predicted. Those senators that the two soldiers had passed on their way in were still coming past them into the chamber. Something that the secretary noticed as he looked over the consul's shoulder. Something which he obviously pointed out.

Antony at last swung round, his face folded into an unaccustomed frown. His gaze raking over the mob of white-togaed men still crowding inwards. But then it settled on the two interlopers by the door. The frown vanished to be replaced by a look of surprise. Enquiry. Enobarbus gestured. Antony hesitated. Exchanged a final word with the secretary. Swung right round and came to the doorway.

'What?' he snapped.

'Caesar has changed his mind.' Enobarbus said. 'He's coming after all.'

Antony blinked. That was his only reaction to the news. His expression didn't alter. But Artemidorus could almost see his

171

mind racing behind those deep brown eyes. 'How long before he gets here?'

'Not long,' answered Artemidorus.

'*Futo!*' Antony swore. 'I'd better get them back in their seats again.' And he was gone. He reached the tribunal, spat a word or two at the secretary. The secretary gestured to his acolytes. The work table and *curule* chair made a reappearance. It was this as much as Antony's bellow of, 'Fellow senators...' which appeared to drive the message home.

And the message seemed to go magically through everyone there. A stirring that spread like the wind through a field of barley. Heads nodded together and the message spread almost silently onwards. Out of the chamber, right across the vestibule, down the length of the portico. Caesar was coming. Was on his way. Would be here soon...

'We'd better watch out for him,' suggested Artemidorus. 'We can warn the general as soon as he comes into the theatre. Give him some notice at least...'

'Good idea.'

The pair of them wheeled round and marched out again. Through the vestibule. Out of the main door. Onto the portico. Across the marble width of it. Stopping at the top of the steps, looking down and to their left at the stream of people on foot and in litters pouring into the enormous space. Kyros came and waited near them, a couple of steps further down. He still held the writing case. And that fact suddenly struck a chord with Artemidorus. He swung round, his eyes wide. A surprising number of senators were also carrying long, thin wooden writing cases today.

But even as he made the discovery. Before he could take the next mental step. He was distracted once again. Brutus and Cassius were strolling along the colonnade side by side. Heading for the Senate chamber at last. Brutus was frowning and distracted. Pale. Shaking slightly. The man with the message about the Lady Porcia's death had obviously managed to reach the senator. Which was all the spy could think of to explain how Brutus looked. But that in itself was sinister. What business other than Caesar's murder could possibly stop a husband from returning home at once on receiving the news that his beloved wife had just dropped dead?

The spy surreptitiously pulled up his hood. It would not do for Brutus to recognise him now. There were enough unexpected elements in this situation without adding yet more. But a new random element was added at once. The pair of aristocratic conspirators were stopped by a senator Artemidorus recognised. His name was Popilius Lena. The spy had no idea whether or not his name was on Cyanea's list or in Puella's memory. The three men fell into a short but earnest conversation. When it was over, Brutus looked worse than ever. But his brother-in-law smiled easily and led him onwards and inwards. Into the gloom of the vestibule.

*

Brutus and Cassius vanished into the shadows just at the very moment that Antony hurried out. The general crossed the width of the portico in a dozen strides. 'Right!' he snapped. 'That's done. I'm going down to meet Caesar. He'll probably come by the south entrance. It's the nearest way. I'll try to talk him out of this as we come up. Enobarbus, I want you to go to Lepidus and tell him what's going on. As *magister equitum* he has the power to bring the Seventh Legion into the city if any trouble breaks out. The city is filling up with Caesar's old soldiers. If anything like what you suspect should actually happen, there's no telling what may come of it!'

'Nothing good. That's for certain,' observed the tribune. And he was off. Running light-footed down the steps towards the south entry. And the busy roadway through the Gate of Fontus. Then down to the Forum. And onward to the house of *Magister Equitum* Marcus Aemilius Lepidus. The only patrician left in the city that they all knew they could trust.

Antony hesitated. The wind taken out of his sails. He looked around the busy scene. Took a deep breath. 'You wait here Septem,' he said. 'I'll go now to greet Caesar the moment he arrives. You're not only *speculator* spy now – you're my *observabant*. My lookout.' And he was gone. Following in his tribune's footsteps down and across to the entry.

'What are we on the lookout for?' asked Kyros.

'Trouble,' answered Artemidorus.

And trouble arrived at once. In the person of Gaius Julius Caesar. Semi-divine being. Co-Consul of Rome. Perpetual Dictator. A man who would be king. Caesar walked through the south entry just as Antony arrived there. At his right shoulder was Decimus Brutus Albinus. At his left was his secretary Balbus and his acolytes. All of them laden with bags of scrolls and tablets. Without a second thought, Antony elbowed his way into the secretary's place.

Caesar walked determinedly forward. Trailing a crowd of clients, litigants and hopefuls like the tail of a shooting star. With the man at each shoulder competing for his attention. Perhaps because Caesar and Antony had not been on the best of terms recently, Decimus Albinus seemed to be winning.

Artemidorus swung round, scanning the length and breadth of the colonnade. Suddenly struck by the fact that Caesar's arrival somehow caused the busy expanse to empty. It was eerie. Disturbing. As though the senators all knew that something fearful was just about to happen. There were hundreds and hundreds of senators. Sulla had expanded the Senate to eight hundred. At about the same time as he had expanded the *pomerium* well beyond the ancient boundary that tradition said had been ploughed by Romulus to define the limits of his new city. The new line took in the *Campus Martius* and several sections on the far bank of the Tiber. But not Janiculum. And its rule was relaxed on Tiber Island where the VIIth Legion was waiting, fully armed. There were, perhaps, three hundred senators in the *curia* today. Though it was designed to accommodate several hundred more. And Cyanea's list named twenty-one conspirators. Now expanded to twenty-three.

It struck him then. Right out of nowhere. The writing cases. Cassius had almost certainly tucked his dagger into his belt beneath his toga. Had had little time or opportunity to do much else. As he and Cyanea could attest. As they had been watching through the spyhole in the villa's *atrium* at the time. Others, like Brutus, might well have done the same. Neither carried anything but papers. But still others might well have used their long, slim wooden writing cases to hide a dagger rather than a stylus. And it looked like there were many more writing cases than usual being carried into the Senate chamber. As with any daggers tucked in belts or hidden in the folds of togas, it was too late to do much about it now.

So Artemidorus and Kyros were powerless to do much more than keep watch. Artemidorus, the centurion, found this almost unbearable. He was a man of action. A soldier, used to giving and obeying orders. On campaign, the majority of his time might be filled with anticipating action and relatively little of it in actual combat. But those times before and after battles were always filled. With planning, preparing, weapons training, spying. Tending the wounded, collecting the bodies and burying or burning them. Spying on the departed enemy. If there were any left to get away. Planning for the next encounter. Training in the skills and tactics needed to face each foe. It was a relentless round of one activity or another. He had never been ordered to just wait and do nothing while events beyond his control relentlessly unfolded around him.

Caesar and his immediate group emerged from the cohort of well-wishers, clients and others who could have no business with the Senate. But then one man extracted himself from the bustle in the gardens and stopped Caesar. Chatting to him for a moment as the rest of the crowd melted away. It was Popilius Lena once again. The senator who had spoken to Brutus and Cassius earlier. A little bird of hope seemed to take flight in Artemidorus' breast. Perhaps Lena had somehow learned of the plot. Perhaps he was warning Caesar even now – giving Antony a chance to offer his word in confirmation. But no. Caesar shook his head. Lena turned away. The spy and his assistant were forced to watch the dictator's seemingly inevitable rush into danger once again.

To watch as Caesar began to mount the steps angled to head past them, deep in conversation with Decimus Albinus. Looking away from his would-be protectors. Apparently paying little attention even to Antony. Followed by his band of secretaries with their bags of tablets and scrolls. Mounting the steps. Hesitating for a heartbeat on the outer edge of the portico. Striding onwards towards the shadowy cavern of the vestibule. It seemed to Artemidorus that Albinus had even taken Caesar gently by the hand to lead him in.

The little group were just at the vestibule doorway when someone called Antony's name. Gaius Trebonius emerged from behind a pillar and Antony hurried over to him.

'Are you alright, Septem?' asked Kyros. '*The look on your face...*'

'He doesn't know,' said Artemidorus in a low voice. 'Antony doesn't know that Trebonius is on the list. I haven't had the chance to warn him...'

'Warn him now,' suggested Kyros, appealing to the man of action.

The pair of them crossed towards Antony and Trebonius. Only to see Trebonius slide a friendly arm across Antony's shoulders and lead him further away down the portico. Deep in conversation. Utterly unaware of the two desperate men following in their footsteps.

Almost frantically, Artemidorus sought to frame a sentence that would attract Antony's attention and alert him without alerting Trebonius. But then, he thought, did it matter at this point whether Trebonius knew their suspicions or not?

Artemidorus sucked in a deep breath. '*Lord Antony!*' he shouted.

*

'*Lord Antony,*' shouted Artemidorus at the top of his voice. But his words were drowned out by a scream from inside the *curia*. Another scream followed immediately by more cries. Shouts. Pandemonium. And then by a wave of senators running out into the portico like an invading barbarian army. At first it was hard to make out what they were shouting. One horrified phrase tumbling over another. The senators flooded down the steps and spread across the gardens. Antony stood, amazed. Trebonius had vanished. Artemidorus, on the edge of the stampede at first, found himself almost swept into it as more and more senators ran out. Ran, it seemed, for their lives. Kyros, younger and slighter than the powerful soldier was carried bodily away, lucky not to lose his footing as he was swept helplessly down the steps.

But here, in the outer fringes of the crowd, what they were shouting began to make some sort of sense to Artemidorus.

'Caesar!' they cried.

'Caesar is dead…'

Artemidorus began to fight his way across the portico towards Antony, who seemed to be frozen with shock. Pushing the hysterical senators away heedlessly. Using even more brute force than he had used to cross the Forum to Caesar's litter. It was like crossing a river in full spate. Crossing the Rubicon had been very much easier. As he forced his way through the terrified senators, their shouts of horror made even more sense.

'Caesar has been murdered…'

'…stabbed to death…'

'… on the floor of the *curia*…'

'…at the foot of Pompey's statue…'

Artemidorus' mind was blank with shock. That what they had feared and fought against for so long should have come to pass so swiftly. Like one of the bolts of lightning from last night. By all the gods – was it only last night? As his mind still reeled, his body just took over. He fought his way through to Antony's side as the last of the terrified men streamed out, still shouting. Caesar's secretaries amongst them. With no one now to serve; no one's words to write down. The Senate secretary and his men. The record keepers – as though what had happened was too terrible to record. The keepers of the water clocks. As though time itself had stopped.

'Caesar is dead…'

'Caesar is dead…'

Then, at the heels of the outpouring rush, came the murderers. Their cries echoed before them like the sounds of spirits lately released from Hades. Quiet and distant at first. Cavernous. Growing louder and louder.

'Liberty!'

'Freedom!'

'Tyranny lies bleeding!'

'Rejoice! Rejoice! The Republic is restored…'

They came out in a group. As tight-packed as a unit on the battlefield. Looking and sounding like Furies. Their hands and arms were red to the elbows, like augurs in mid-sacrifice. Most of them brandished their daggers above their heads. Some just clawed at the air as though they could rip entrails from the sky. But their togas had not been tied in the Gabine knot so the parts covering their arms were stained with blood. Sodden with it. So that the heavy cloth moulded to their skin as the blood still ran. Dripped. Sprayed in droplets each time they gestured. Blood that seemed shockingly red against the white of the chalked material. The fronts of their togas were red. Those sections covering their knees were red. Their boots were almost as red as Caesar's regal *caligae*.

Artemidorus saw all this in a heartbeat. But then the wise eyes of the experienced battle commander saw other details. Red-lipped gashes. Wounded arms and hands. Caesar had been unarmed. So they must have stabbed each other in their eagerness to get at him. At least one was bloodied from head to foot – fallen into the lake that must stain the marble floor.

The shocked spy began to register other splinters of dialogue then. In among the clamouring shouts of, 'Liberty!' and, 'Death to tyrants!' Shards of conversation babbled one over the other. Perhaps a dozen heartbeats covering them all as the murderers fled past him and stumbled on down the steps.

He recognised the hysterical voices too.

Decimus Brutus Albinus: 'He couldn't believe it when I stabbed him. *"You too, Brutus?"* he said… I laughed in his face…'

Publius Casca: 'When I stabbed over his shoulder he caught my hand. I never actually… But then *he* stabbed *me*! With his stylus…'

Marcus Junius Brutus: 'He called me *teknon*. In Greek. *My child*, he said. *Kai su teknon*… You too my child. He owned me for his son at the last moment. Accused me of patricide. He knew the terrible penalty for that. Where is Cicero? I didn't see him in the chamber. I may need him to defend me as he defended Sextus Roscius. Patricide… Cicero…'

Cassius: 'No one heard him, Marcus. And if they did, they won't believe it. Or they won't care. Not in the face of what we've just done!'

Brutus again: 'But wait I must address the people. I must make a speech. We planned...'

Cassius again: 'Too late, brother. The people are all running away...'

And the conversations faded as the frenzied men also ran away towards the beautiful, deserted gardens. And the exits packed with fleeing people.

Artemidorus' brain kicked into action then. As effectively as his body had earlier. With the ruthless logic of a soldier facing an unexpected reversal mid-battle. Caesar was dead and his killers running free. Antony would be next. It was a wonder they hadn't noticed him standing stricken in the shadow of a column. Then Lepidus, who was likely in the Forum waiting to greet Caesar, with Enobarbus at his side. Then any other friend of Caesar's who might stand against them.

He turned. Took the gaping Antony by his shoulders and pushed him ruthlessly back. His hand flew to the fastening of Narbo's cloak. 'Quick, General. Disguise yourself. Get away from here. Go to somewhere safe until we see how this plays out,' he hissed.

Antony took the cloak and swung it over his shoulders. Artemidorus reached for the freedman's leather hat that was still tucked into the back of his belt. He gave it to Antony, relieved to see that the general had shrugged off his incapacitating shock. The hat went over the distinctive, curly Herculean hair. The hood came up over it. The sole consul – no longer co-consul – became indistinguishable from any freedman and a good number of city slaves. He turned. Raced down the steps. Heading for the north exit as the murderers crowded into the south exit. Still shouting the terrible news to the shocked and terrified citizens.

*

Artemidorus turned on his heel. The portico was eerily empty. Strangely silent. One last record-keeper ran past, eyes wide. A strikingly beautiful, vaguely familiar boy. The voices

179

were all distant, fading towards stillness. A little wind stirred. Warm for early spring. Bringing from Pompey's massive gardens the scent of roses. He ran across the portico and in through the gaping vestibule door. The vestibule was vacant. There was a litter of writing boxes, bags of scrolls, scrolls themselves, like feathers restless in the breeze. Tablets. Many as trampled and splintered as Telos' had been.

The spy looked through into the *curia*. The cavernous chamber was also deserted. Silent. His boots made almost no sound as he ran across the threshold. But what sound they made echoed. The benches and seats were all vacant. The areas around them littered with things left, forgotten in the panic. He had seen encampments like this. Deserted in fear of an enemy attack. The tribunal was empty too. Caesar's work table and gilded chair lay on the marble floor a little way behind it. The table's legs were broken.

At first Artemidorus could not see Caesar at all. Then he remembered some of the words he had heard amongst the jumble of half sentences shouted by the fleeing senators. 'At the foot of Pompey's statue...'

Pompey's statue stood tall, on a square plinth bearing his name. A position to which it had been restored by Caesar's order. After it had been pulled down on the news of Pompey's defeat and death. The statue presented the dead general in the Greek style. Naked, but for a swathe of cloth like a cloak over his left shoulder, wrapped around his left arm and dangling almost to his knee. On the left side of his chest hung a *gladius*, angled back into his armpit. On his marble head a victory wreath. His slim, muscled body almost that of Mars himself. His left hand holding a ball that stood for the world, much of which he had ruled. His right hand reaching out for further conquests.

The shadow of that reaching arm fell onto the floor at the foot of the marble plinth. Fell across a bundle of old rags discarded there. Like a pile of washing too soiled to bother with. Left on the stones beside some riverside laundry. Only a soldier as experienced as Artemidorus would have recognised it at once for what it really was. As he ran towards it, he saw the red boots protruding at one end of it. A hand reaching out at the other. The statue's shadow seemed to spread. Becoming the shallow red lake that was the dead dictator's lifeblood.

Artemidorus slowed. Ever practical. Congealing blood was slimy. The marble floor would be as slick as ice. With careful, steady steps he reached the side of the fallen man. Squatted. Reached out with a hand so steady that he observed it with mild disbelief. Took the corner of the toga Caesar had pulled over his face. Like the priest performing the sacrifice on the ram whose intestines had foretold this. Gently lifted it.

Caesar's face regarded him. The eyes wide. Still. Fixed. The wreath he had worn was gone. The thinning hair and the skin of the skull beneath it were marked with more gashes than he could readily count. One reached down across the face from temple to chin. The nose was cut. The cheek gaped. The lips were split. The centurion had seen worse wounds. But this one was somehow more shocking. *This is truly what death looks like*, he thought. And more than one mere man had died here. The Republic itself may well have been murdered. By men who believed they were acting to preserve it. For he knew the friends of Caesar who had survived this outrage so far. And they would not forgive or forget. Caesar's death, he knew in his bones, was only the first of many. If this terrible act meant anything, it meant war.

Then he noticed something else. Trapped under a sodden flap of material that must be about level with the top of Caesar's thigh, there was a dagger. Without thinking, he reached down and slid it out from under the body. The handle was thick with blood but still he knew it. It was the dagger he took from Brutus' house. Which he had left wedged in the doorkeeper's throat. It had returned to him. Almost as though the dead man he had fought so hard to protect wished him to have it as a gift.

'Thank you, Divine Caesar,' he said. His words echoed hollowly.

And he thought, he really is divine now. Up on Olympus with Zeus, whom the Romans called Jove. Just like in his dream. And what is left down here is just like the Lady Calpurnia's prophetic vision. He shivered.

'*Septem!*' Kyros' voice came so suddenly that it almost made him jump. He replaced the flap of the toga over the dead man's face and stood. Turned. The boy was hesitating in the doorway of the *curia*. The fact that he had returned revealed much about his bravery.

'Yes?'

'Is that… Is that… *Caesar*?'

'Yes.'

'Dead?'

'Yes.'

'What are we to do?'

Artemidorus began to walk towards the boy, stepping carefully with his blood-slick boots. 'That depends on what everyone else is doing,' he said.

'The senators are all gone. Everyone who was in the theatre has gone I think. The murderers finally got out of the south exit and then stopped for a while.'

As the boy was talking, Artemidorus stooped. Picked up a handful of papyrus leaves. Cleaned the dagger that was Caesar's gift. Cut his finger doing it. Smiled. Such a blade. 'Did they?' He asked. 'Why was that?' He was at the doorway now, still walking. He tucked the naked dagger into his belt. Very, very carefully. Kyros walked at his side across the deserted vestibule out into the enormous, empty theatre.

'They were waiting for something…'

'Really? What?'

'The gladiators. Decimus Albinus' gladiators.'

Artemidorus stopped on the topmost step. Turned to the boy. How well this had been planned, he thought. A detailed plan worthy of Caesar himself. Though, the gods knew, that was the only type of plan that would ever have defeated him. 'The gladiators. Of course. How long ago did they leave?'

'They were still there when I came to find you, Septem. They may even still be there now.'

'Might they? Good. Now what I want you to do is this. Go and find Spurinna. He must take Narbo, you and Puella to a

safe place. His house will be safe enough. Cyanea is at
Antony's house. But she should be safe with the Lady Fulvia.
Especially if Antony has done what I suggested and gone to
hide somewhere else safe and secret. Enobarbus will alert
Lepidus. Who will bring the Seventh off Tiber Island and into
the city if he's got any sense. So that takes care of the
members of the spies in our *contubernium*. Except for the
physician Antistius. We may need him later. But, as it was
with Telos, not for his skill as a doctor.'

'And except for you, Septem. What are you going to do?'

'Me? Well, as I'm dressed as one now, I thought I'd become
a gladiator once again.'

*

Artemidorus ran as fast as he could to catch up with the
murderers and their escorts. He was no longer hampered by his
cloak. And the roads across the *Campus Martius* were empty.

The only thing that made him pause was Caesar's litter. It
stood just outside the south entrance. Alone on the deserted
roadway. Somehow it added to the shock and the sadness.
There were only three of the four litter bearers left. Clearly
one of them had run away. To break the terrible news to the
Lady Calpurnia, perhaps.

'Caesar is in the *curia*,' said Artemidorus. 'At the foot of
Pompey's statue. I want the three of you to get him in the litter
as best you can. And take him home.'

The three litter bearers nodded. Glad to have someone tell
them what to do.

The spy turned and ran on down the road after the gladiators
and the men they were protecting. He caught up with them just
outside the Gate of Fontus as the murderers rearranged
themselves. Brutus had been wounded in the hand, apparently
by one of the others. Rubris Ruga had been stabbed in the
thigh. The gashed toga the spy had noticed must have been his.
Publius Casca still had Caesar's stylus wedged in the flesh of
his forearm. Though this Artemidorus had not seen. Because
Casca, like many of the others, had wrapped part of his toga
round his arm like a shield. But now, wounds needed

bandaging. The next stage of the revolution needed confirming. Further plans needed to be put into action.

Most of the conspirators were swapping their bloodied daggers for the gladiators' swords, which were larger and more impressive. Easier for a mass of citizens to see. For, wherever else they were heading, they were certainly bound for the Forum. And the People of Rome whom they represented. In this as in all things. Or so they believed. The spy saw all this from the rear fringe of the mass of gladiators. He also saw Syrus and the band of men who had slaughtered Telos still close to the heart of the conspiracy. Crowded round Cassius, Brutus, Albinus and Basilus, swords out and eyes busy. The lead conspirators' counterparts. A moment or two later, the murderers and their men were in motion once again.

Artemidorus moved forward slowly at the very back of the crowd. If he was going to pass as part of this group without risking detection, he was going to have to find a better disguise. He started looking round the gladiators nearest to him. A helmet would be a good start. One with cheek flaps and maybe a nose guard. Or even a face mask.

The Fates, which had frowned unrelentingly on his enterprise so far gave a brief smile now. The nearest gladiator was a Samnite. He was wearing the helmet typical of his type, with a crest, a rim and a full face mask. On his left arm he carried a shield the shape of a teardrop, thick at the top and pointed at the bottom. In his right hand was a spear that he was using as a crutch. For, in spite of the greaves protecting his thighs and knees, he appeared to have been hurt in the mock combat Decimus Albinus had been staging. He was also, it seemed, an unpopular man. For none of the others nearby were offering to help him at all.

Artemidorus approached him with easy familiarity. 'Hey, Samnite. I see you're limping. Let me help…'

The grateful gladiator let the spy relieve him of the shield which felt surprisingly light compared with the army-issue *scutum* Artemidorus was used to. But then a *scutum*'s edge was bound in thick, sharp iron. The wounded man's left arm came over his shoulders and the pair of them limped on a little faster. The spy apparently thoughtlessly keeping the broad top of the shield up over his lower face and beard. Behind the shield and the mask of his bearded face, his mind was icy cold. The shock of Caesar's murder seemed to him like a declaration of war. A personal war – rather than the wider war he saw all too clearly in the not-too-distant future. But then, he realised, he had been at war with Cassius, Basilus and their associates since he found the body of Telos crucified outside Spurinna's house. Therefore he began to look for a place he could conveniently despatch the wounded gladiator and assume his full disguise. Although the pair of them were moving more quickly than the Samnite had been moving on his own, they were still some way behind the others as the murderers pushed through the Gate of Fontus, still shouting about the death of tyranny, the restoration of both peace and the Republic.

Immediately within the gate, where the rocky cliff slope mounted to the *Arx Citadel* and the Temple of Juno Moneta at the northern crest of the Capitoline, there was a colonnaded parade of shops. Those that had opened this morning were rapidly closing now. As the news of Caesar's death spread. One or two others had not opened yet at all. And a couple gaped emptily, untenanted. As the pair of gladiators came level with the first vacant opening, Artemidorus drove right with all his force. The Samnite stumbled sideways into the brick-walled cavern and crashed to the ground with Artemidorus on top of him. The spy threw the shield aside and pulled the dagger free of his belt. In a heartbeat, the long slim blade was sliding unstoppably into the Samnite's left side, just behind the edge of his breastplate. Level with the nipple on its moulded metal front. That beat was the last the Samnite's heart took. Artemidorus rolled the corpse onto its back, his hands busy with the laces tied under the chin to hold the helmet in place. He tore it off, exposing the face of a dark-skinned boy, eyes and mouth wide with surprise. Then he rolled the corpse onto its front and undid the laces holding the breastplate and the greaves in place.

As Caesar's murderers and their escort of gladiators entered the Forum, the Samnite caught up with them at last. Armour firmly in place. Shield on his left arm. Helmet on and face mask down. The only changes were that in the interim, he had recovered from the wound that made him limp. And that he seemed to have exchanged his spear for a *gladius* and a nasty-looking dagger.

XI

Enobarbus came along the *Via Sacra,* past the *Domus* and the *Regia*, heading for the eastern end of the Forum at the shoulder of Marcus Aemilius Lepidus. They were preceded by six lectors whose *fasces* did not contain axes. Within the *pomerium*, their number should have dropped to two. But Enobarbus had advised that they should keep the larger number. Other than that, the two men were without escort and were unarmed. This was, after all, the heart of the city. Their safety was guaranteed. During the daytime, at least. Especially as Lepidus was, as *magister equitum*, Caesar's deputy. And in Caesar's absence he spoke with his voice and carried his authority.

'Surely Antony is worrying over nothing,' the master of the horse was saying. Not for the first time. 'Whatever Spurinna's auguries, whatever the Lady Calpurnia's dreams, Caesar can never be touched. He is too astute at reading the mood of the Senate. And of the populace. The Parthian campaign will make rich men of everyone associated with it. From the lowliest legionary to the dictator himself. And Caesar will shower wealth upon the city as he always does when he returns in triumph.'

Enobarbus looked straight into the *magister equitum's* intelligent brown eyes. The dictator's deputy had a high, broad forehead. Slightly overhanging brow and a face that seemed to fall away to a narrow, shallowly cleft chin. He looked younger than his forty-four years, but was an experienced and successful soldier. By all accounts a strong and decisive leader. He was also level-headed and careful. And he had no intention of taking action until he had more information.

'I'm not so sure,' said Enobarbus. 'Co-Consul Antony is worried or he would not have sent me. There's something in the air…'

At the same moment as Lepidus and Enobarbus entered from the east, the murderers and their gladiators entered from the west. And the Forum in between burst into panic. Enobarbus had never seen anything like it. Probably never would, as long as he lived. The Forum was packed as usual. There were crowds of people from every rank and station. Senators rubbed shoulders with slaves. Freedmen and shopkeepers with *plebeians*, poets and retired soldiers. It was late morning on a warm day in the middle of the month of Mars. The Forum was getting hot. The citizens were getting sweaty. There was a strange, uneasy atmosphere. As Enobarbus had observed – there was something in the air. The moment Caesar's murderers entered, a wave of violent panic swept eastwards across the crowded square.

At first it was impossible for the tribune to see precisely what was happening. Automatically, he looked for somewhere he could climb onto. The most promising elevation that he could see was the scaffolding round a nearby building. Without a further word to Lepidus, he ran across and began to clamber upwards. As his altitude mounted, so his sight cleared. He could see a sort of pattern to it. There were gladiators at the far side of the square, coming in past the *Tullianum* prison building. Some of them seemed to be waving swords in the air. In front of them, senators were scattering. Women, screaming and running for their lives. Shopkeepers and stallholders doing their best to close up and protect their wares. And men of all sorts seemed to be rioting. Some of them looting.

As the gladiators came past the vacant space of the *Comitium* he realised that it was not they who were waving their swords but a group of men behind them. His eyes were keen enough to see that the hands and forearms of the men holding the swords were red. That the senatorial togas they wore were stained with blood. He recognised Brutus and Cassius in the lead.

He knew then. And the knowledge pierced his chest like the sharpest blade.

He jumped down and ran to Lepidus, who was standing, frowning, outside the *Domus Publica*. 'They've done it,' he said. 'They've murdered Caesar. There's a riot starting. You have to get to the Seventh on Tiber Island and bring them into the city. Now!'

'But...' said Lepidus, his face the colour of chalk. 'If Caesar is dead then I have no power. The master of horse is only deputy to the dictator while the dictator is alive!'

'Go anyway,' said Enobarbus. 'Alert them. Get them here! Or as close as you can. I'll try and find out more then I'll follow you. I'm still tribune. If they don't listen to you, they'll listen to me. And failing that, I'll try and find Artemidorus. He's senior centurion, *primus pilus*. The legion's legates and the other tribunes are all with their families at home as far as I know. In the absence of the general, he and I command the Seventh anyway!'

He stood for a moment, mind racing, watching as Lepidus and his six unarmed *lictors* sped past the Temple of Vesta and out of the south side of the Forum. Their best route, he knew, would run between the Temple of Castor and the tiny Lake of Juturna. Past Cicero's city dwelling on the *Nova Via*. Onto the *Vicus Tusculum* road. Which would take them past the *Forum Borium* cattle market and onto the *Pontus Aemelium* bridge to the far bank. Then turning back on himself to cross the *Pons Cestius*. It was the quickest way to Tiber Island and the VIIth.

These thoughts sped through the tribune's mind in an instant, then he was striding forward into the melee. The first thing he got was confirmation of his worst fears. 'Caesar's dead...' shouted someone.

'They've murdered him!' screamed someone else.

'Butchered!' Yelled a third. 'And they're coming for us! Run!'

But by no means everyone was running. At least not in the same direction. Those taking fright were racing north and south out of the Forum. Some few were running eastwards past Enobarbus. But no one was running westwards towards the bloodstained men and their gladiator guards. But no. Even that wasn't true. A group of senators he recognised as Lentulus

189

Spinther, Favonius, Aquinus, Dolabella, Murcus, and Patiscus were running towards them. Grabbing swords from the gladiators, joining in with the bloodstained men. The tribune realised that he could see this so clearly because the Forum was emptying with astonishing rapidity. Even those men rioting in order to rob the shops and stalls were running up towards the *Basilica Aemilia* or down towards the shops by the *Basilica Sempronia*.

The bloodstained murderers lingered by the *Comitium*. Marcus Junius Brutus climbed up onto the *Rostra* there. The platform from which the citizens of Rome were traditionally addressed. He spread his blood-washed arms. Which made the state of his bloodstained toga disturbingly vivid. 'Romans!' he shouted. 'Romans! Stay and hear the words of your liberators…'

But only his associates and Albinus' gladiators lingered by the *Comitium*. The Forum itself was all but empty. And the riot had moved to the shops along the fronts of the basilicas north and south of the central square. A cloud of smoke was suddenly borne in on the morning breeze. Brutus stopped talking. Looked about in shock. Obviously surprised that there was no one willing to listen to his speech of liberation.

Cassius called him down at once, and in the face of the gathering riot, they left the Forum and vanished into the pathway that ran south past the Temple of Saturn Aerarium, where the treasury was located and the *tabularium* records office.

Enobarbus did not bother following. That road led to only one destination. Instead he turned and began to follow Lepidus' footsteps towards Tiber Island and the Legio VII.

*

As soon as they turned towards the Temple of Saturn, Artemidorus knew where they were going. To the top of the Capitoline. There were several things up there which the murderers could use to their advantage. The first was the slope itself, climbed by narrow stairway cut into the rock or an equally narrow, stepped roadway. At the top of the roadway stood the Tarpean Rock. On top of a cliff so steep and high that condemned criminals thrown off it were smashed to death on the ground below. The rock stood at the corner of the square outside the Temple of Jupiter Capitolinus. A large building which was not only sacred but also capacious enough to house the self-styled Liberators and their bodyguards. As well as the small army of priests whose job it was to maintain the most sacred space in all of Rome.

Then there was a ridge running behind the *tabularium* records office to the northern spur where, on the *Arx Citadel*, sat the Temple of Juno Moneta, which was also the city's mint. Where there might well be a fortune in silver and gold waiting to be turned into coin. No matter where on the Capitoline Brutus, Cassius and their men ended up, no one in the city would be able to get at them. Even the VIIth would have a hard job securing the two temples in the face of well-armed, well-placed gladiators. Not to mention the priests. And the VIIth would only enter the situation if Lepidus and Enobarbus could persuade them to come off Tiber Island.

Indistinguishable from any of Albinus' other gladiators, Artemidorus began to work his way up to the front of the group. Placing himself amongst the gladiators was only the beginning. Next he needed to hear what the murderers were planning to do next. He eased forward carefully. It was easy enough while they were crossing the Forum, but the road that Brutus and Cassius chose was narrow, as well as being steep. Even so, the spy managed to work his way up to the fringe of Syrus' little group at the heart of the throng.

They turned right behind the Temple of Saturn and began to climb the lower slope of the Capitoline. The *tabularium* records office loomed above and on their right. As they followed the increasing incline along the great square building's southern side, Artemidorus began to hear snatches of Cassius' plans – and Brutus' concerns. 'It's not too late. We have the upper hand. You see how many are joining us. Find Antony now. Kill him. And Lepidus.'

'They are helpless. Antony is useless without Caesar. Lepidus is powerless. The moment Caesar died, the office of *magister equitum* ceased to exist. There is nothing they can do.

I will talk to the people. If they won't listen in the Senate or the Forum we can send messages and call them up to the square in front of the Temple of Jupiter. I can convince them that what we have done is for their own good.'

They reached the point where the roadway led off right towards the *Arx* and left up the steep gradient of the *Clivus Capitolinus* path that climbed to the Temple of Jupiter. The oldest and most sacred temple in the city. And the easiest to defend. The crowd of variously armed men became a lengthy snake as Brutus and Cassius led them left up the *clivus* towards the height of the Capitoline's southern spur and the great temple on top of it.

'What we need to do next,' Brutus was saying, 'is to get the message out to our friends around the city. Once I have talked to them and appealed to their patriotic and freedom-loving natures, they will rally to us.'

'Especially,' added Cassius, 'if we can find some way to bribe them. We have two things that they want. Money and power. Offer them either or both and we've won.'

'You'll have to be quick,' added Basilus, who was walking just behind them with the Casca brothers and Albinus. Unaware that the Samnite at his left shoulder was listening to every word and drawing his plans to frustrate any scheme they decided upon. 'If you don't get your men to take charge of the situation – and if possible the city – then it will be Lepidus who restores order. And once he does that, he and Antony will own the city. If that happens, we join Caesar. In death.'

'I am certain Lepidus is powerless,' insisted Brutus. 'The Seventh Legion will no longer obey him. Neither will the old soldiers in the city waiting to be assigned their lands as Caesar promised. He simply has no power.'

'Whether you are right or not, brother, we must act quickly,' Cassius decided. 'Basilus. Your gladiators. The Syrian and the rest. How reliable are they?'

'As reliable as gold and the promise of more gold can make them.'

'Very well. As soon as we are at the Temple of Jupiter, I want you to send them back to the city. I will give them a list of names and directions. They can alert men I have prepared. We will have begun to bribe the populace before nightfall. And also, Brutus my brother, we will have summoned up here as many representatives of the people and men of power as we can so that you can talk to them this afternoon. If we get this right, we can return to the Forum this evening and you can repeat your speech to the populace from the *Rostra*. Only this time there will be crowds of citizens there to hear you. Perhaps even the people's *comitia* itself.'

One of the newcomers shouldered his way past Artemidorus in his eagerness to join the conversation. The disguised spy recognised young Publius Cornelius Dolabella. One of Caesar's closest and least suitable associates. A drunkard, gambler, spendthrift and womaniser by all accounts. 'I will go down as well if I may,' he gasped. 'I know many more men who will join us…'

'Mostly men in taverns and brothels,' said Brutus austerely. Sneering at the young man's reputation. Which in matters of drunkenness and profligacy rivalled even Antony's.

'Precisely,' answered Dolabella unabashed. 'That's where I'll find Antony's friends and associates. And turn them to our side.'

Cassius gave a bark of cynical laughter. 'Very well,' he said.

'And, if you are going to return,' added Brutus, 'see what news there is of Porcia my wife…'

'I will,' said Dolabella grudgingly. One aristocratic eyebrow raised in disdain. 'But I will not be returning quickly…'

As they arrived on the wide flagged area in front of the Temple of Jupiter, the crowd of men spread out. Syrus and his cohorts lingered by Cassius just long enough to receive his orders and directions. Then they went back down the narrow path. Artemidorus in his Samnite disguise was tempted to join them. But the dead gladiator had not been one of their men. They looked like a tight team. A stranger would stand out amongst them and be viewed with suspicion. Dolabella also turned to retrace his steps. A couple of others joined him. Men whose togas were not stained with Caesar's blood. Murcus, and Patiscus by the look of things.

'Samnite!' called Cassius. 'Come here!'

Artemidorus crossed to him. Heart racing. He suddenly realised that, with the departure of Syrus and his men, he had become the gladiator standing closest to the group of conspirators. His keenness to overhear them had overcome his sense of caution. To a dangerous degree.

'Go with Lord Dolabella to Lord Brutus' villa. Bring word of his wife as fast as you can!'

'Yes, my Lord,' snapped Artemidorus, fighting to keep the relief out of his voice.

*

The Forum was deserted. It was early afternoon so that fact alone was remarkable. Disturbing. Even the rioters and looters seemed to have disappeared. Dolabella and his fellow senators stood staring around. Then the supercilious senator turned to Artemidorus. 'Samnite,' he drawled. 'Do you happen to know the location of Lord Brutus' villa?'

'Yes, my Lord.' The spy kept his voice gruff. His accent countrified.

'Go there. Find news of his wife and return to him.'

'Yes, my Lord.'

'*Really*...' Dolabella turned away as though the gladiator no longer existed. 'What *was* Brutus thinking of... Am I some slave boy to be sent on an errand?'

He and his two friends began to cross the Forum, still talking loudly. Like scared children whistling in the dark, thought Artemidorus.

'No,' Dolabella continued. 'I am next year's appointed consul. I am to succeed Caesar himself while Antony does whatever Antony does – if he survives. Before we start passing out money to the *plebs* and whoever else we can find, I think it fitting that I should get hold of the consul's insignia. Just to make sure I get what I was promised. What I deserve...'

Artemidorus hesitated. Torn. Dolabella was probably on the way to the *Domus*. That was where Caesar's consular insignia would be. He certainly had not bothered to bring them with him to the Senate meeting. Did he need to go to the *Domus* himself? What good would be served by following these treacherous, self-serving men? None that he could see.

Even as he stood, mind racing, events overtook him. Caesar's litter at last made its slow and stumbling entrance into the Forum. Two men held the forward poles, which bore the weight of the dead dictator's upper body. One man carried both of the rear poles, though the dead legs and feet were probably not much lighter. Artemidorus stood, transfixed. The litter bearers' fatigue and depression made them stagger as they walked. The litter swung a little from side to side. Caesar's arm hung lifelessly out of the side. Caesar's dead hand waved. *Come here*, it seemed to say. *Join me...*

Artemidorus obeyed Caesar's final command. He ran over to the stretcher bearers and walked beside the man who was carrying his end of the litter alone. He raised the mask of the Samnite helmet. 'Do you know me?' he asked.

'Yes, sir. You were at the master's *Domus* this morning. With the augur and the tribune...'

'That's right.' He grabbed the handle and took as much of the weight as he could while he talked. 'Unless your mistress gives you direct orders to the contrary,' he said to the exhausted litter bearer. 'I want you to do something as soon as you have taken Caesar home.'

'Yes, sir?'

'I want you to go to the house of Antistius the physician and bring him to the *Domus*. He will want to examine Caesar. Tell him Septem sent you.'

'*Septem*. Yes sir.'

Artemidorus walked a few more steps with the man, then eased away from the litter and its awful burden. Stopped still. Looking after the slowly moving men. As he watched Caesar's tragic progress across the deserted Forum, so Artemidorus' thoughts came clear. It all turned around whether he wanted to go back up to the Capitoline and spy out the plans that Cassius was making. Or whether he would serve Antony's interests better by going out onto Tiber Island and helping to rally the VIIth. Not to mention that, in the mix, he had agreed to find news of Lady Porcia. Which was a strong temptation because, during the time he worked undercover in Brutus' household he had grown to respect her.

It was not to serve Brutus, therefore, that he turned away from Caesar's litter and the supercilious Dolabella, and began to retrace the steps Puella and he had taken during the third night watch. To Lord Brutus' villa. As he hurried across the Forum and into the roads that he and Puella had fled down during the storm, he looked for hiding places where he could safely put the helmet and the armour he was wearing. It seemed to him that it would be better if the freedman Artemidorus came asking after the Lady. The man who had fixed the roof, who had heard terrible news of Lord Brutus and worrying news about the Lady. Rather than the faceless Samnite who could be anybody come from anywhere.

The new *ostiarius* did not know him, but the dog did. Its growl was a resonant echo of last night's thunder. 'Don't worry,' said the new doorkeeper. 'He growls at everybody.'

Then Brutus' steward entered the *vestibulum* behind him. 'Ah,' he said. 'Artemidorus. Have you heard about the events of the night and the day?'

'I know the city is in the grip of madness,' Artemidorus answered. 'They say Caesar has been murdered in the Senate. What else is there?'

'One of our slaves escaped last night. Through the window you were mending.'

'My work was not yet finished,' said the undercover handyman, as though his expertise was being impugned.

'But worse than that, the *ostiarius* who tried to bring her back was killed in the street!'

'How dreadful! How did the Lady Porcia take the news? I know she has not been well...'

'Oh! That is another story! She has been so worried about Lord Brutus that she seems to have had a seizure. She collapsed. At first we thought she was dead!'

'Dead! How terrible!'

'But we were mistaken. She had only fainted. She is recovering now. But in the meantime, what news from you? Is it true about Caesar?'

'It is.'

'And who would do such a dreadful thing?'

'I fear Lord Brutus himself may have been among the ringleaders. If I were you I would barricade your doors and make sure the house is safe. Unless the Lady Porcia has a better idea. There may be civil unrest. At the very least. And if Caesar's friends seek revenge…'

'Thanks for the warning! We will make the house secure as best we can.'

'Do. And if I were you I'd make plans to get out of the city as soon as you can safely do it. And take the Lady with you if she can be persuaded. Things are bad at the moment. But there is worse, far worse, to come!'

*

Oddly enough, in the midst of all that was going on, so much of it so tragic, the news that Porcia was not dead after all lightened the spy's spirit. And although he was sworn to bring Lord Brutus to account for his part in Caesar's murder, the thought of telling him his wife was still alive added further to the positive feelings. He had killed two men so far today with hardly a second thought. And found another he was fighting to keep safe slaughtered like a sacrifice. But the prospect of bringing news that someone feared dead was still alive seemed somehow to outweigh it all. He walked almost cheerfully back towards the Forum. And as he went, he pulled sections of the Samnite's armour out from where he had hidden them. And began to put them back on.

But then he came into the Forum once again to find it beginning to fill with people. And his positive mood began to dissipate.

It seemed that Dolabella had been as good as his word. He or his acolytes had been round all the local brothels and the bars by the looks of things. Handing out bribes as he had promised. Paying a range of drunkards and whoremongers to come and hear Lord Brutus. Wastrels, bullies and cashiered soldiers into the bargain. But clearly not only Dolabella had been busy. There were some more respectable citizens doing their best to stay clear of the rabble. The range of different togas spoke of *quaestors*, *aediles* and *praetors*. Aristocrats. Senators. Those, he assumed, who should have been at the fatal Senate meeting but for one reason or another had stayed away.

Distracted, he paused, looking for the one man so far remarkable by his absence. Marcus Tullius Cicero. But the great lawyer, orator and Republican was nowhere in sight. The reeking rabble and the patricians trying to stay clear of them milled around in front of the *Comitium* as though they expected Brutus to climb back up the *Rostra*. But that was not the plan. Murcus and Pasticus were trying to get the mob organised and heading up the *Cursus Capitoline* towards the Temple of Jupiter. Murcus and Pasticus alone, by the look of things. Like Cicero, Dolabella was not visible among the assembled mob.

Emboldened by Dolabella's absence and by his Samnite disguise, Artemidorus joined the fringes of the slowly moving multitude. And fortune smiled on him once again. He recognised one of the men he was walking beside. The man was one of the ex-legionaries currently filling Rome's bars and brothels while they waited for Caesar to assign them the farms and smallholdings they were entitled to at the end of their service. This one smelt of sweat and drink. But he seemed fairly sober.

Artemidorus lifted the hinged face mask of the Samnite helmet. 'Soldier,' he said. 'Do you recognise me?'

The legionary glanced at him. Was clearly just about to say *No!* But then he looked again. This time with recognition in his eyes. He stopped. 'Yes,' he said. 'You were my centurion when I was in the legion. Are you back in the arena?'

'No. I'm on a mission for General Antony,' Artemidorus led the man aside so they could talk while the rest of the group walked on. 'Do you know Lord Brutus?'

'Served with him in Cyprus.' The old soldier nodded.

'Good. When you get to the Temple of Jupiter, find him and tell him his wife is well. He's been told she is dead. But she just fainted. Tell him and he will reward you.'

The soldier gave a grunt of laughter. 'I doubt it. He spent most of his time in Cyprus raking the money in. I never saw him handing any out!'

'This is the kind of news that is bound to be rewarded!'

'Yes, Centurion. I'll give him your news. But why don't you tell him yourself?'

'Because I'm not coming with you.'

'I see. But what if he asks me how I know?'

'Tell him a Samnite gave you the message.'

'Oh. Right.' The soldier almost came to attention.

'Good luck,' said Artemidorus.

'Good luck to you, Centurion!' He gave a creditable salute, rejoined the crowd and was gone.

*

Artemidorus closed the face mask once again. Instead of turning right to go further up the side of the *tabularium*, he ran straight ahead and, out of sight of the crowd and their leaders, swung left. He ran down behind old shops of the *Tabernae Veteris* until he reached the *Vicus Tuscus* road that led down to the bridge across the Tiber just south of Tiber Island. Following unknowingly in Enobarbus' footsteps, he ran past the cattle market and out across the great stone bridge, glancing over his right shoulder at the galley-like bows of the island and the first of the temples behind them, the Temple of Aesculapius.

His hurried strides soon brought him to the far bank of the river where he turned right and after a few more moments was running back over the *Pons Cestius* onto Tiber Island itself.

The island offered scant space for proper army lines. It was busy with temples and buildings of all sorts. Many of these showed signs of recent military occupation. And what space there was between them was filled with legionary eight-man *contubernium* tents. But it was all as deserted as the *curia* had been when he had found Caesar's corpse.

Artemidorus ran across the marble-crowded space until he reached the *Pons Fabricius*. This narrower bridge spanned half of the width of the Tiber joining the east side of the island to the Field of Mars. It didn't take much imagination for the spy to see that someone had taken the VIIth Legion at least part way to the city. Lepidus probably. With Enobarbus at his shoulder, no doubt.

Artemidorus walked across the bridge, his mind racing. Trying to guess what the men of the VIIth would do when they heard that Caesar was dead. They would almost certainly want revenge. He could easily draw up a list of hotheads who would be all for invading the city, besieging the Capitoline and massacring everyone in the Temple of Jupiter on top of it. But by the same token, he could name a larger number of level-headed men who would want to wait for events to clarify themselves. Who would want to wait for orders from their commanders. There were a good number of men in the VIIth – many of them centurions like himself – who would understand the legality of their position and demand clear orders from someone with unchallengeable authority before they made a move. The only thing he couldn't work out was which of these groups would win out.

He found the VIIth drawn up in battle formation on the Field of Mars. The soldiers standing silently in the warmth of the afternoon, helmets and breastplates glinting. Swords sheathed on right hips. He ran past the silent ranks until he found Enobarbus and Lepidus in consultation with all the other centurions of the legion. An intense knot of debate grouped beyond the front rank of soldiers. Just as he arrived, the group broke up. He was too late to influence whatever decision had been made.

Frowning, he crossed to Enobarbus, who was now in full uniform like his men. Except that he was carrying his helmet under his arm. Its plume was almost as bright as the one that crested the Samnite helmet Artemidorus wore. He undid the laces, lifting helmet and face mask free as he approached the tribune and the *magister equitum*. 'Ah, Septem,' said Enobarbus. 'You have arrived at an opportune moment. We need to find the general.'

'Why? What's going on?'

'The Seventh will return to Tiber Island and await events. Or orders from the general. Orders given in person. The centurions decided in council that as Caesar is dead, Lepidus is no longer *magister equitum*. With one consul dead, only the other consul can order them into action. And that consul is Antony, of course. So if we want the Seventh to act, we have to find him. Have you any idea where he is?'

'No. He's in disguise and in hiding. That's all I know.'

As this conversation went on, the VIIth, under direction of their centurions – Artemidorus' century commanded by his deputy Oppius – wheeled around and marched back towards Tiber Island.

'Antony is wise,' Lepidus observed. 'If I can't command the legion, I think I'll go into hiding myself. If I was Cassius, I'd be trying to pick off Caesar's friends one by one before they could get organised. Our best hope for the moment is to stay out of sight. If you find Antony, tell him I'll follow any orders he gives. Abide by any decision he takes. Back him to the hilt...'

'Not a well-chosen phrase under the circumstances,' observed Artemidorus.

'But we'll give him the message when we find him,' agreed Enobarbus.

'And we'll stay with you and your *lictors* until you see what things are like in the Forum,' added the spy.

Things in the Forum were still eerily quiet. The Forum itself was deserted. Shops and stalls were shut, though some of them showed signs of the brief spell of looting that had happened earlier. Lepidus and his *lictors* hurried away eastwards, past the *Regia* and the *Domus*. Enobarbus and Artemidorus hesitated. 'I think I'll start at Antony's house,' the tribune decided.

'I'll follow you there so you know where to find me. Leave a message so I can find you. In the meantime I must see how things are doing at the *Domus*.'

'Good idea. See you later. At Antony's.'

*

The Lady Calpurnia met Artemidorus, dry eyed and enraged when the *ostiarius* showed him into the *atrium* of the *Domus*. 'I told him,' she said, with no preamble, recognising him at once. Even in Samnite armour with his helmet under his arm. 'You told him. Spurinna told him. As far as I can see the gods themselves told him. But he just would not listen! It's as though he wanted to die!'

Artemidorus didn't know what to reply. He had no idea how seriously to take the last comment. Could Caesar have wanted to die? In the unexpected, unlooked-for manner he had described to the treacherous Decimus Brutus Albinus yesterday evening? Was the falling sickness getting so bad? Was the man who wanted to control the world losing control of himself? Of his bladder? Of his bowels? It was too late to worry about it now. Useless to speculate.

'And to make matters worse – as though they could be any worse, that young wastrel Dolabella has been here demanding the consular insignia! He was promised it he said. Forced his way in and just took it. Before even Caesar came home! Thank the gods I had already received the terrible news and knew what he was talking about. Imagine if I had found out like that! Been informed of my husband's death by some young puppy coming in to take his badges of office!' She stood, rigid with indignation. Then returned to her original subject. 'He was getting worse, you know. With the sickness. Falling. Losing control. Very much worse. But he wouldn't ask Antistius…'

'Antistius,' he said gently. 'Lady Caplurnia, is he here?'

'He's with Caesar,' she said. 'In there.' She gestured towards the nearest room. 'The servants brought a table through from the *culina*…' She took a deep shuddering breath as the implications of what she had just said hit her. Her eyes flooded. She turned away. Clapped her hands. Was instantly surrounded by solicitous slave women from her quarters. They led her away, sobbing.

Artemidorus crossed to the room she had indicated. 'Ah, Septem,' said Antistius looking up as he walked in. 'I've been expecting you. You found the body I understand.'

Caesar was lying on the table, on his back. His wounded face pointed up at the ceiling. He was naked apart from a cloth over his loins. His eyes were closed. He had not yet been

202

washed or prepared for funeral. He looked as though he had been covered in dull red paint. Or damp terracotta dust.

'I was first into the *curia*, yes.' The spy could hardly take his eyes off the corpse. The head, shoulders, upper body were covered in wounds that gaped like red-lipped mouths. The red-lipped mouths of infants seeking their nurse's nipple.

'Lying on his front?' Antistius continued.

Artemidorus shook himself – mentally as well as physically. He shivered. His flesh rose. 'On his front,' he confirmed. 'And a little on his side. Not flat on the floor. Head turned to one side. Covered with his toga…'

'Dying is a private business,' the physician nodded philosophically. 'Or should be. Even a death like this.'

'…in a huge puddle of blood…'

'That I already knew.' The physician gestured to Caesar's toga. It was draped over the back of a chair. Artemidorus crossed to it. Looked down surprised. In fact there was less blood on the garment that he had expected.

'At the foot of Pompey's statue,' he concluded.

'The gods having their little joke.'

'Probably because he ignored all the messages they were sending.'

'The messages that you, Enobarbus and Spurinna were sending, you mean. And such a range of messages. I found quite a few papers in the folds of his toga. Most of them were petitions of various sorts. But one was a list of names. Very interesting. And, from what I hear, very accurate. The names of his murderers.'

'I gave him that.'

The physician nodded. 'I thought so. So the messages were not just supernatural ones that had been *coloured*, shall we say, by Spurinna and the rest of you.'

'We didn't make the weather last night. We didn't make the doors blow open or Mars' spears shake. We didn't send the dreams…'

'Of course not. And the Fates themselves must have had a hand in the fact that he carried the chance of salvation you handed him into the *curia*, unread!'

There was a short silence, then the physician turned back to his patient. 'I count twenty-three wounds. Head, shoulders, upper body. Arms. Face, of course.' He lifted the loin cloth. 'One in the groin…'

'That was Brutus,' said the spy.

'How do you know?'

'He left his dagger.' Artemidorus reached behind him and pulled Brutus' dagger out of his belt.

Antistius took it and placed it beside the wound at the top of Caesar's thigh. 'Yes,' he nodded. 'I'd have said this knife made this wound. It's Brutus' you say?'

'Mine now,' the spy retrieved the precious weapon.

'Well it missed the genitals. Missed the major vessels in the leg. Like most of the others, this wasn't fatal.'

'Most of the others? Not *fatal*?'

*

'That's right. Oh, he'd have bled to death eventually if left untreated. And his love life might have gone downhill given the damage to his face…'

'Cassius did that, I think.'

'… A miracle his manhood wasn't damaged though. But none of the twenty-two wounds here was the killing stroke. And you can see why. Take this one. Possibly the first, I'm not sure. It's come over his shoulder from behind. The dagger point has bounced off his collar bone. Cut the top of his chest here. But it's a shallow cut. Not much damage done. Someone must have pulled Caesar's toga out of the way or it wouldn't have cut him at all.'

'I'm sure that was Publius Servilius Casca. Caesar grabbed his wrist and stabbed his forearm with the stylus he was using.'

'I knew he was fighting back at some stage. Some of the wounds on his hands and arms are there because he was trying to stop the daggers. Catch them, even.'

'But there were more than twenty attackers, all grouped round him,' said Artemidorus. 'They all had daggers. But only Cassius and Brutus had daggers like this one. I've never seen a blade like it… He stood very little chance.'

'True. But they weren't doing much of a job of killing him. They were striking down from over his head. Hitting and cutting each other in all probability...'

'I saw a few of them wounded...'

'And striking downwards like that is not very efficient. Independently of the thickness of toga cloth on top of the shoulders. The bones of the chest, front and back, can act like armour when you strike down on them. The daggers mostly bounced off his ribs or his shoulder blades. Flesh wounds. Twenty-two flesh wounds. Even that one in his face. Gaius Cassius Longinus you say...'

'Twenty-two. I thought you said twenty-three.'

'That's right. Twenty-two flesh wounds. And one killing stroke. A soldier's stroke.' He rolled the body over slightly and the spy saw what he meant. Low in Caesar's side, below the ribs, but clearly slanting up into the chest cavity itself was a long, deep gash. 'The section of the toga that this went through was preserved from your lake of blood,' said the physician. 'It must have been uppermost in the angle that he fell at. But the amount of blood that issued from this wound stained the toga. From chest to hem. And that makes me absolutely certain that this was the stroke that killed him. And I suspect it was quite an early blow. Third, maybe, after Publius Casca's.'

'His brother Gaius, maybe. Because Caesar had stabbed Publius with his stylus.'

'Has Gaius been a soldier?'

'Haven't they all? I'm surprised Cassius didn't make a better job of it, though. He was a soldier's soldier.'

'Opened his face, you said. Maybe a different agenda. Like Brutus. All those years wondering if this was the manhood that fathered him like the gossips say.'

'Caesar called him his son as he died, apparently. *Kai su teknon*?. And you my child? His dying words. Scared the life out of Brutus. He came out calling for Cicero.'

'The Sextus Roscius patricide defence. Brutus must have been shaken.'

'More than a little. He'd just been informed his wife had died. She hadn't, in fact. But he didn't know that at the time.'

Antistius shook his head. 'The gods must be splitting their sides today. One joke after another.'

'What will you do now?'

'Wait for matters to become clearer. Then we'll start to clean him up. Prepare him for his funeral. Could be in several days' time. You?'

'Find Antony. The tribune's already looking. Will you be able you do something with his face? There will have to be a death mask made.'

'Don't worry. I know an expert in *imagines maiorum*. But in fact, I think I'd better have a full-body cast made. If you do find Antony and he can get control of the city, then I suspect there'll be a lot more statues to Caesar going up. And a full body cast will really help the sculptors.'

Something stirred in the spy's imagination at the physician's words. 'And the toga,' he said. 'Keep the toga safe.'

'As you wish,' said Antistius with a shrug.

And the gods laughed on. For of all the things the spy said or did during the next four days, his thoughtless demand that Caesar's toga be kept safe was probably among the most fateful.

But, as he came out of the room back into the *atrium*, Calpurnia reappeared, holding a box. 'Septem,' she said. 'Are you going to Antony?'

'Yes,' he said. 'If I can find him.'

'You will find him,' she said. 'And when you do, give this to him. The vestals brought it over on the news of his death. And Dolabella's visit shows me how much at risk it could become.'

'Of course I'll take it. May I ask what it is?'

'Caesar's papers. And, most importantly, a copy of his will. Well, notes, really, that he made while preparing the full document. The original has gone to my father, Lucius Calpernius Piso as tradition requires. He will oversee the funeral arrangements. I have also put in there the thing he kept closest to him whenever he was in Rome. The one thing more important, perhaps, even than his will.'

'And what is that?'

'The key to the treasury. Guard it with your life. And get it to Antony.'

XII

Artemidorus ran through the Forum once again, heading for the *Carinae* and Antony's villa. Coming from the *Domus* past the *Regia*. Through the eastern end of the open space. Preparing to turn right into the roadway that ran past the *Subura*. Which was fortunate, as the western end was packed. It was late afternoon now and the conspirators, at the heart of their cohort of gladiators, had dared to come down off the Capitoline once more. It seemed to the spy that the crowd that had climbed to the Temple of Jupiter had returned with them. And had been joined by many other citizens.

Brutus and Cassius were up on the *Rostra* and easily visible. He did not need to go any closer to know what they were saying. Their togas were still stained with Caesar's blood and Brutus' hand was bandaged. Nevertheless, he slowed. A third figure joined them. The stranger was wearing the official robes of a *praetor*, a senior magistrate. The spy slowed further, staring down the length of the Forum until he recognised the man's face. It was Lucius Cornelius Cinna. One of Caesar's more intimate circle of friends and relatives. Caesar himself had asked Cinna to take on the responsibilities, privileges and position of *praetor* for this year. Now in a pantomime he tore off his badges of office and removed his ceremonial robe. Theatrically hurling them onto the ground. The spy could not hear what he was saying. But he did not need to. As with Brutus and Cassius, the message was all too obvious. He gripped the box containing the will and the key more closely still and ran on towards the *Clivus Pullius* and the villa Antony all but stole from Pompey's estate.

The *ostiarius* opened the door gingerly. Only pulling it wide when Artemidorus raised the face mask and he recognised the visitor's face. 'Is the general at home?' asked the spy as the doorkeeper led him into the *atrium*. He unlaced the helmet and eased it off his head.

'No, sir.'

'Then I need to see the Lady Fulvia. If she's here…' It suddenly occurred to him that, like her husband, she might be in hiding. Who knew what names might still be on Cassius' kill list?

But no. 'Wait here, please,' said the doorkeeper. 'I will send someone to tell her.'

Artemidorus nodded, and stooped to put the Samnite helmet down on the top of a chest. Carrying that as well as Calpurnia's box was a bit like juggling.

Lady Fulvia swept into the *atrium* as he straightened. Antony's wife was no great beauty, but she had a striking, powerful face which reflected her character precisely. Her eyes were wide and intelligent. Her nose slightly hooked and thoroughly patrician. Her mouth was neither full nor thin-lipped. But it habitually turned down as part of the slight frown that usually lined her high, clear forehead.

She stopped in front of Artemidorus. Regarded him silently for a heartbeat. Then, 'Am I talking to my husband's senior centurion? Or to the tribune's most trusted spy?'

Artemidorus scratched his bristly chin. 'To the spy, my Lady…'

'Well, Septem, what do you want with me?'

'I have two missions, my Lady. Like the tribune, I'm looking for Lord Antony. But I have also been ordered by the Lady Calpurnia to give him this box. And in his absence, I'm putting it in your safekeeping.'

'What's in it?'

'A copy of Caesar's will. Or notes he made in drawing it up. The original document is with his father-in-law as tradition decrees. Some letters. The key to the treasury. They must go into the consul's keeping.'

Fulvia took the box. 'That's one part of your mission fulfilled,' she said. 'As for the other part, don't waste your time. I expect you know as well as I do where he's gone to hide.'

Before he could answer, she continued – voicing his suspicions for him. 'He's in Janiculum with his Egyptian whore.'

'If he is, that's the safest place, Lady. Cleopatra has a small army of guards and attendants. And Janiculum is outside even Sulla's *pomerium*, so they are all fully armed at all times.'

'Whether you're his soldier or his spy, you always look after him, don't you?'

'It is my duty, Lady. As soldier or spy.'

'The tribune said it was you who gave him the disguise he escaped in. Possibly saved his life.'

'As my duty demanded…'

'And now I find I have a duty to you. As your commander's consort. As his grateful wife. The tribune has gone to Janiculum. Antony is either planning to return with him. Or is bedding Cleopatra now that his love rival no longer stands between them. Either way, he will be home soon enough. You must wait here. Eat. Bathe. Sleep. You know when he comes back he will be like a whirlwind. And he will need you like his sword. Fresh. Clean. Sharp. Hold this for a moment.' She handed the box back. Clapped her hands once. A middle-aged slave appeared. His face was familiar. The steward in charge of the day-to-day running of the household. 'My guest the centurion needs food, a bath and sleep, Promus. See to it.'

'Yes, Lady,' he bowed slightly.

'And a shave if possible,' added Artemidorus as he handed the box back to Fulvia.

The steward showed him to the *triclinum* dining room with its central table surrounded by three *klini* beds. 'If you would care to take your ease, I will send in warm water and wine, then *gustatio*.'

'No. I will eat in the kitchen, thank you Promus. It will be quicker and better suited to the occasion. I take it the Lady Fulvia has eaten?'

'She ate earlier.' Promus nodded.

'Good. Then it's off to the *culina*. Lead the way.'

*

The kitchen was quiet. There was no family in the villa at present apart from Fulvia herself. And no guests apart from Artemidorus. The *culina* was a larger version of the room in Spurinna's villa where they had melted the wax off Telos' tablets. Artemidorus rinsed his hands in a bowl of water, then moved a stool over to the table. He was hungry. But he was also used to soldier's fare and had no desire to eat anything much other than the *puls* porridge and flat *emmer* bread already there. Promus produced an *amphor* of wine, a jug of water, another of olive oil. There were olives and fruit piled on plates beside the bread. Beside these, eggs and cheese. A copper goblet and a terracotta bowl with a horn spoon were placed before him and he proceeded with his meal.

Artemidorus poured wine and water into the goblet, swirling them together. 'Is there anything further, Centurion?' asked Promus.

'No, thank you.'

'Then I will go and ensure the *thermae* is reheated for your bath.' He turned to go.

But Artemidorus stopped him. 'My associate. The woman Cyanea. Is she still here?'

'She has joined the women serving the Lady Fulvia. Shall I ask for her to be summoned?'

'No. I just wanted to know she's safe.'

'She is safe. If you require anything further, just ask the *cocus*.' He gestured at a matronly figure in a cook's apron, who nodded at him cheerfully.

He tore a chunk off the *emmer* loaf and dipped the solid, chewy bread into his wine. As it softened, he took a handful of olives and chewed them carefully, spitting the stones onto the side of his bowl. His stomach growled. It had been two full days and an entire night watch since he had slept. And almost as long since he had eaten. He took a bite of the softened bread. The wine was good, even mixed with the coarse loaf. He took a sip. 'Are the eggs cooked?' he asked.

'Yes, Centurion,' answered the cook.

He took one, cracked the shell, began to peel it. 'What is the *puls* porridge flavoured with?' he asked.

'This bowl is flavoured with honey. This other with olives and cheese.'

'I'll have some of that. This food is excellent. The best I've tasted in many years.'

The cook smiled. They were friends. She ladled a huge portion into his bowl. He swallowed the egg, lifted his spoon and dug in.

As soon as he had eaten his fill, Promus led Artemidorus through to the bath. The centurion had heard tell of the baths Antony enjoyed in Pompey's house. They were modern and luxurious. He had heard they even contained a *palaestra* open-air exercise area at their centre. As well as a latrine. And a library. All this in addition to the usual arrangement of rooms. The *palaestra* and the library were tempting. But he used the latrine first.

Two male slaves awaited him in the *apodyterium* changing room. They helped him remove the Samnite armour he still wore. His belt with *gladius* and dagger. His tunic. His *braccae* trousers and his sandals. They led him, naked, into the *frigidarium*. This was so cold his flesh rose again. As he stepped into the icy water, his scrotum clenched. The breath was driven from his lungs as he sat. The pool was not large but it was beautifully appointed and decorated. Sea deities and legendary aquatic beings disported themselves with each other and a range of sea creatures. When he could stand the cold no longer, he stood up and went through into the *tepidarium* which was a good deal warmer. The tepid water in the pool began to relax him. The strain of the last few days and their tragic outcome began to ease. He floated contentedly, belly full of food and head full of wine. The pictures of nymphs and satyrs on the walls seemed to come to life. Doing what nymphs and satyrs do. In every conceivable manner – and a few he had never even imagined.

By the time he walked through into the *calderium* he was semi-erect. His head still full of erotic images. But the withering heat soon sorted that out. Just walking across to the central pool and the slaves waiting to wash him reminded him of his days in Egypt with Antony, Caesar and the VIIth. Where they had all, it seemed, begun to fall in love with Cleopatra. The fornicating nymphs vanished from his imagination. His memory was filled instead with visions of burning deserts bigger than *Mare Nostrum*. With dunes for waves. Moved by winds coming straight from a furnace. And burning sun in place of cool water. His body was instantly slick with sweat. He cupped his hands, filled them with cool water from a convenient bowl and dashed it into his face. Then he eased himself into the hot pool. Very, very slowly.

In every bath he had ever used, the bather returned to the *tepidarium* for massage, oiling and scraping with *strigils*. But the bath slaves led him instead into a *laconium* sweat room. Here there was a massage bed. A masseur and a masseuse. A matching pair of Nubians, their skin as dark as Puella's. But gleaming with a combination of oil and perspiration. They both wore loincloths and nothing else. They had prepared scented oils. *Strigils* warming in hot water. And Antony's *tonsor* stood beside them. An older man, fully if lightly dressed. With his razors, his shears and still more scented oils.

Artemidorus elected to be shaved first. It was a slow, uncomfortable process, for the red beard was full and thick. But the *tonsor* was painstaking, gentle and extremely careful. At last, he smoothed lemon-scented oil onto Artemidorus' cheeks, packed his razors and left. The spy sat for a moment wryly regretting that he had not sent for Brutus' knife. It seemed to him that its blade was keener than the *tonsor*'s sharpest razor.

Then, with his chin feeling strangely naked, he lay down on the massage bed and let the man and the woman go to work on him. The man was muscular but his hands were soft. His fingers experienced and knowledgeable. The woman was a revelation. The soldier had never felt so pampered as he did when she used fingers that felt like strongest steel covered with softest silk. Under her ministrations, he began to come erect again. As she saw this, she asked, 'Would the master like to enjoy me?'

Her hand went to her loin cloth.

'No,' said Artemidorus.

'My brother, then? He is as experienced as I am.'

'No. Thank you. Both.'

*

Promus was waiting in the *apodyterium* changing room. He held a light woollen robe. There was no sign of the spy's clothes. But his belt, *gladius* and dagger were where he had left them. The Samnite's armour and helmet stood in the corner. 'The mistress has ordered that your clothes be cleaned and mended while you sleep. Are you happy to continue wearing the Samnite armour or shall we send to the Seventh for your centurion's uniform when you get dressed tomorrow?'

'I'll know the answer to that when the general returns,' answered Artemidorus, tying the robe's sash. Stooping to retrieve his sword-belt and dagger. 'I'll know then whether he needs a soldier or a spy.'

'Very well. But you must be tired. Please come with me. A *cubiculum* has been prepared.'

The bedroom was surprisingly large. Such as might be offered to an important guest. Or a particularly favoured one. It was on the upper floor overlooking the *peristyle* garden. On the eastern side facing west so that the morning sun would not disturb the sleeper. The window could be shuttered and curtained. Promus proceeded to do this, after affording Artemidorus a glance at the beautifully manicured lawns and beds of scented herbs and flowers. The fountain was in the shape of a faun. Standing on one goat-foot in the middle of a rectangular pond. Framed by the shadows of the marble-columned colonnade. The entire garden given a golden glow by the slowly setting sun. Whose rays were briefly reflected in a big bronze mirror on a stand in the corner by the door.

But so was a strange, unsettling darkness. The exhausted spy realised that the sun was setting behind a bank of black clouds. It looked like another storm was on the way. It would soon be time to stop the water clocks and put them away until dawn, he thought. If there was anyone left to tend them. Then the closing of the shutters and the drawing of the curtains brought a restful darkness to the room. He put his weapons down carefully on the top of an ornate trunk standing knee-high at the foot of the bed.

A multi-flamed oil lamp on a bedside chest illuminated the paintings on the walls and ceiling which were of classical country scenes in the Greek manner. No doubt designed to give the bedroom's occupant restful thoughts on sleeping and waking. However, Artemidorus' imagination immediately peopled the verdant forests, shady groves, riverbanks, lakeshores and rolling hills with the orgiastic nymphs and satyrs from the *tepidarium*.

The bed looked extremely comfortable. Even the *ascender* beside it to help the sleeper step up into the thing was cushioned. The mattress thick and more than likely stuffed with down. Rather than the straw he was used to – on the rare occasions he slept in a bed. As opposed to a military cot. Or the ground. There were fat pillows. A pile of woollen blankets that promised warmth against the chill of the mid-Mars night. The counterpane was purple and covered with a pattern of gold thread. But, noted the spy regretfully, the bed looked big enough for two. Far too large for a man alone. Especially a man with a head full of rutting satyrs and infinitely willing nymphs. Perhaps he should have accepted the silken fingered masseuse's offer after all. But it was too late now. And, if the truth be told, he was simply too exhausted.

Or so he thought as Promus left him to climb into a bed that felt as soft as a summer's cloud. To discover that there were sheets of silk beneath the woollen blankets. And commit himself to sybaritic sleep. As he did so, the first downpour of rain rattled against the shutters. The first rumble of thunder snarled in the distance.

But then, some uncounted hours later, the sheets and blankets lifted. And, as he surfaced into half-wakefulness, a slim, cool body slid into the bed beside him. Soft breasts with nipples as hard as sling-shots pressed against his ribs and his left arm. The yielding length of belly, lightly furred at its base, eased along his side. Tickling the top of his thigh. He half opened his eyes. The room was filled with flickering brightness as fragile as the foil that gilded Cleopatra's statue in the Forum. That and looming shadows in which the frescoed rivulets seemed to shimmer. Lakes to undulate. Spectral nymphs disported themselves as they serviced rampant satyrs. One of whose number he could abruptly count himself.

Cyanea's lips closed down on his even as the lamplight glittered in her hair. She smelt and tasted of honey. Her eyes were wide and glistening but the shadows hid their true colour. Her tongue tip slid teasingly past his teeth and he began to respond even more fully. Her thigh slid across his belly and she eased herself on top of him. She sat up, cloaked with bedding. The swell of her breasts in the lamplight the same as those on Cleopatra's golden statue in the Forum. Almost of their own volition, his hands closed on the familiar firmness of her hips. His index fingers found the dimples that topped the firm swell of her buttocks.

Their bodies worked together, positioning her so she could straddle him. She eased back, accepting the merest tip of him into her. Stopping statue-still. Holding her breath. Teasing. With her moisture and her heat. Still forbidding him deeper entry, she leaned forward until her tresses caged his face like silk. 'Will you think of me as Cleopatra, queen of a thousand hearts?' she whispered.

'No,' he answered, laughing, as he effortlessly flipped her over onto her back. 'I'll think of you as a Sabine maiden to be ravished time and time again!'

He drove fully home as her sensuous giggle became an almost breathless gasp. And outside, over the city, another thunderstorm roared like an angry beast.

*

They had hardly finished *jentaculum* breakfast before Antony arrived. Artemidorus chose to eat in the *culina* kitchen again. This time with Cyanea at his side. He chose the honey-flavoured *puls*, and dipped his *emmer* loaf in milk to soften it. The slaves ate in the servants hall so the lovers were alone apart from the cook who continued to spoil the handsome soldier. And was happy enough to do the same to his lovely, green-eyed companion. And to feed her helpers who carried laden trays out and brought empty ones back. Clearly, thought

Artemidorus, there were worse fates than being a slave in Antony and Fulvia's household.

Enobarbus and his general arrived early in the first hour of the new day. Shaking from their cloaks the last raindrops of the departing storm. But, just as Fulvia had predicted, Antony was like a whirlwind himself. As he and Enobarbus consumed their simple *jentaculum*, they started drawing up their plans. And putting into practice the ideas they had clearly discussed the night before – and on the way down here from Cleopatra's household on the Janiculum. Artemidorus joined these deliberations as a matter of course. Especially when Fulvia brought her husband the box which the spy had carried here from Calpurnia. But at this stage, the most pressing need was for Antony to contact his friends and supporters while staying out of sight himself. Almost every slave in the household was tasked with taking messages to addresses all over the city. Starting with the ex-*Magister Equitum* Marcus Aemilius Lepidus.

At last Antony sat back with a hiss of impatience, his handsome face folded into a frown. 'This is all very well,' he said. 'But the men I really need to make some kind of contact with are up in the Temple of Jupiter Capitolinus. If I only had a way of finding out their current position and immediate plans…'

'You do, General,' said Artemidorus at once. 'I still have my Samnite armour. They know the Samnite. Brutus himself has entrusted him with vital messages. If I put on the armour, closed the face mask, loaded up with food and drink from your excellent kitchen, I would probably be welcomed with open arms.'

'You'll have to come up with a convincing story as to where you've been all night. What you were doing,' mused the tribune.

'A variant on the truth will probably suffice,' answered the spy. And it was as well for him that Cyanea was out of earshot at the time.

The water clocks in the Senate would have measured a further half an hour. If they were still running. When the

Samnite, helmet on and face mask down, appeared in the
Forum carrying a sack over his shoulder. Full of *emmer*
loaves. And an *amphor* under his arm. Full of wine. The rain
from last night's storm had washed the streets. But the clouds
that gave birth to it were long gone. The day after Caesar's
death had dawned clear and fair. A fact that Artemidorus
somehow found faintly disturbing.

As he crossed the open space, heading for the Capitoline, the
disguised spy became aware of a strange, almost sinister
atmosphere. He had once been on a Cilician pirate trireme that
was old. Semi-derelict. Abandoned. Adrift. And, he
discovered the hard way when he went down into the hold,
overrun with rats. There was that same secretive scurrying
about the Forum. By the time he reached the *tabularium*, he
found himself at the centre of a little knot of similarly laden
men. Clearly he was not the first to think of taking sustenance
to the murders and their guards. But, he suspected, he was the
only one using his generosity as a cover for espionage.

Up on the square outside the temple, there was quite a
bustle. Plenty of food and drink was coming up and slaves or
servants going back down. While one or two more patrician
benefactors stayed. Keen to associate themselves with
Cassius' faction. Like Dolabella, Cinna and their ilk. It was
easy enough for Artemidorus to dispose of the food and drink.
The conspirators had organised drop-off points in a vaguely
military style. They had almost all been senior officers at one
time or another. But, thought the spy with a secret smile, they
really needed some centurions and a senior *decanus* subaltern
or two to get things absolutely right. The temple's priests and
their attendants were willing enough. But no real substitute for
army know-how. Still, he took his time adding his burdens to
the pile and having a good look round. As he did so, Brutus
himself appeared briefly at the temple entrance. Then Cassius
joined him and they both vanished again.

The conspirators were all in the temple, clearly. The
gladiators formed an effective ring of swords around it. Only
carefully selected men were allowed to pass in and out. And
priests, of course. Organisation of supplies not very

impressive, thought the soldier. Security tight as a fish's anus. How could he get through the guards and into the temple? Let alone hear what the men inside were planning? He paused, deep in thought. Considered asking Achilleus once again for help. Or inspiration at the very least.

So that he did not react until his name was called out twice. 'Samnite! Hey, Samnite!'

He looked up. And there was Syrus. Club at his left side. New *gladius* at his right hip. The same threatening scowl he wore when Minucius Basilus had forbidden him to rape and torture Cyanea.

'What?' he kept his voice gruff. His tone belligerent. Every inch the swaggering gladiator he once had been. In the days he was known as Scorpius in the arena.

'Lord Brutus wants you. Come with me.' He turned on his heel and marched away.

So Achilleus had answered Artemidorus' prayer before it had even been uttered. He was being invited into the heart of Troy, like a warrior hidden in King Odysseus' wooden horse. But this warrior was going alone. With no guarantee of a positive outcome. He closed his fist over the telltale haft of Brutus' stolen dagger and swaggered after Syrus.

The interior of the Temple of Jupiter Capitolinus was a vast, shadowy, columned space. The men within it were dwarfed. Even in groups and crowds they looked insignificant. More than that, most of them looked dirty. Exhausted. Deflated if not defeated. He saw at once that they had not really planned beyond the murder yesterday. It had probably seemed so unlikely to so many of them that they would succeed so easily that they had no further plans at all. But, he thought, like Antony and Enobarbus, they would not be slow in adapting to the new circumstances they had created for themselves. He thought of the way Antony was sending messages all over the city, rallying support. Cassius would think of doing the same soon. If he hadn't thought of it already. Controlling the Capitoline was one thing. Whoever could control Rome would win in the end.

*

'Samnite,' Brutus looked the most exhausted of the lot. His skin – but not his filthy toga – looked as though it had been chalked white. There were dark rings under his baggy eyes. His stubble simply looked like grime on his cheeks and chin.

'My Lord?'

'Raise your face mask, man. I can't stand here talking to a metal countenance!'

The spy almost panicked then. Before he remembered Antony's *tonsor* and the good work done yesterday. Brutus had hardly ever seen the freedman who mended his roof and window. And if he had seen him – and bothered to remember anything of him – it would have been a beard as red as a fox's tail. Which had been the point of growing it, after all.

Artemidorus raised his face mask and met Brutus' gaze. Not the faintest flicker of recognition there. 'My Lord?' he said again.

'You did me good service yesterday. But you did not complete your task.'

'Did the soldier not bring my message, Lord?'

'He did. And it was very welcome as I am sure you can imagine. But why did you not bring it yourself.'

'I got waylaid, my Lord.'

Brutus frowned. 'Robbers?' he asked.

'Well, my Lord, it was almost robbery. The price was so high. But she earned every *denarius* in the end.'

For a moment the spy thought he had gone too far. Brutus was clearly offended at the ribald answer. But it had the ring of truth. So his face cleared after a moment. 'You can do me service once again,' he said. 'If you can keep away from the brothels for long enough.'

'My Lord?'

'I have three letters I want you to deliver for me. As you seem to know the city well.'

'Certainly, my Lord.' Artemidorus accepted them as Brutus handed them over.

'This first one is to my wife. This second is to Marcus Tullius Cicero. You know his house?'

'Who does not know Cicero's villa?'

220

'And this last, even more vital than the other two is to the consul, Mark Antony. You know his house?'

'I do…' Artemidorus felt that the words sounded strange. For he was winded by surprise. What was going on?

A letter to Porcia he understood. One to Cicero as well. Had Brutus not called for the lawyer as he came out of the *curia*? He must still fear a possible charge of patricide. Besides, if the so-called *Libertores* needed a solidly Republican apologist, Cicero was without doubt their man.

But *Antony…* Could it be some sort of trick? Some sort of trap?

'Well,' Brutus broke into his reverie impatiently. 'Don't just stand there. This is a vital task, man!'

Artemidorus turned and retraced his steps towards the temple door. But just before he reached it, a man stepped out of the shadows and stopped him. He found himself face to face with Gaius Cassius Longinus. The plot's ringleader looked tired. Strained. His high, broad forehead deeply lined. His eyes bloodshot. Like Brutus, he needed a shave. But there the resemblance ended. On Cassius' strong, square chin, the stubble seemed almost virile. The man radiated energy. Power. Almost to compare with Antony. And, on this occasion, threat. 'Two things,' he said abruptly. Like the decisive commander he was. 'First, we have not been able to seal those letters. That does not mean you can read them. To do so would mean death for you. Secondly, to Antony's letter add this message. We will be in the Forum at noon. With our gladiators as guards. If he wishes to parley, we will listen. If he wishes to fight, we will fight. Even if he brings in the Seventh Legion, there will be war in the streets.'

'I understand.'

Cassius frowned. 'Do I know you, Samnite?'

Artemidorus' mind raced. 'I served with you in Alexandria,' he answered. 'Before I retired and went into the arena.' A half-truth, but convincing.

Cassius nodded, satisfied. 'Tell Antony my message.'

'I will, my Lord.'

Cassius turned away and Artemidorus reached the door.

As he stepped out into the brisk morning air, he pulled the face mask down. Providentially. Just as he did so, Syrus fell in beside him. They marched out of the temple colonnade and down the steps into the square.

'You seem to have the ear of both Brutus and Cassius,' said Syrus. 'I have two masters also. Decimus Brutus Albinus and Minucius Basilus. Neither of them likes you. Neither of them trusts you. I will therefore be keeping a close eye on you as you come and go. And remember. I carry a club. And it's not for show. But I also have a *gladius* and a dagger and I know how to use them too. Whenever you're here on the Capitoline, I'll be just behind you at all times.'

Artemidorus said nothing. But he thought, *Good. That means I won't have to come looking for you.*

*

The letter to the Lady Porcia contained love, assurances and the sort of advice he had already given to her housekeeper in his disguise as the freedman. Bolt your doors in case of unrest. Prepare to leave the city if things get really bad. He scanned it as he walked towards Cicero's Roman villa. The letter to the lawyer was very much more interesting. He slowed as he began to read more carefully, glad that he was apparently alone as he strolled across the open grass behind the old shops of the *Tabernae Veteris*. And the building site that was Caesar's new basilica. Which was being built on top of the old *Basilica Sepronia*. The letter mentioned Caesar's last words and gave a little speculation on their legal implications if they became public knowledge. And if anyone in Antony's faction wanted to make a legal case of patricide out of them. But mostly the letter begged Cicero to come to the Temple of Jupiter as soon as possible. In case he could not do so, the letter also included a brief outline of the *Libertores'* plans.

They would negotiate with Antony, it said. As consul, he had charge of the city. And the city must be kept peaceful at all costs. They would hope that the Senate would be summoned soon. Brutus was certain – Cassius less so – that the Senate would back them. Publius Dolabella had already retrieved the badges of the office promised him by Caesar. It seemed to the *Libertores* that if Antony and the Senate would agree, all of the plans and appointments Caesar had made in preparation for his departure – and during the first year of his absence – should stand.

Decimus Brutus Albinus was the only obvious sticking point here and the great orator might like to prepare his most persuasive speech in support of Albinus. For, as one of Caesar's most intimate friends, Albinus had been given control of Cisalpine Gaul. The section of northern Italy that effectively reached up from the Rubicon to the Po and the Alps. A position from which, with the legions stationed there, he could control Italy if he wished to do so. Something Caesar's friends might balk at, given his association with the *Libertores*.

The rest of the letter referred to a speech Brutus had made and another he was planning to make – but all the references were to conversations the men had had in private. It was impossible to understand the details unless one had been privy to those conversations. Which the spy had not been. He folded the letter closed again.

'Syrus said you would read those letters, Samnite!' Croaked a familiar strangulated voice.

Artemidorus spun round to see the bear-like form of the apparently indestructible gladiator Priscus with another of Syrus' men close behind him. Somewhere along the line, Priscus had acquired a second sword. He advanced with one in each huge fist. In the arena he would have been called a *dimachaerus* two-sword. But it was his friend that took Artemidorus' attention. For he was shrugging off his left shoulder something that at first glance looked like a cloak. But the ex-gladiator knew what it was. It was a net. This was a *retiarius*. Fortunately he was not carrying the trident that completed his costume as a fisherman. But he was wearing the armour that protected his right shoulder and arm. And he also had a nasty-looking *gladius*.

Artemidorus saw all this in the instant that he turned, tucking the letters into his belt. He threw himself forward at once. Going to his *braccae*-padded knees and toppling onto his side.

Skidding along the slick dampness of the grass on his right hip. The *gladius* there guiding him almost like a ship's rudder. By the time he reached the *retiarius*, a heartbeat after he started moving, he had Brutus' knife out of his *pugio* sheath. Priscus' companion was still swinging his net and wondering what his opponent was up to. He was clearly not very experienced. Or he would have known. The one real weakness of the *retiarius* was his legs. Which, as with most fishermen, were bare. Artemidorus had cut the hamstrings behind his right knee before the net-man realised what was happening. Then he rolled over and came up with his *gladius* out to join the lethal dagger and meet Priscus blade to blade. Out of the corner of his eye he saw the *retiarius* topple as his leg buckled helplessly. But then all his focus was forward.

He ran at the shaggy giant full tilt. He was wearing full Samnite armour. Augmented by the breastplate. Priscus, in his guise as a *dimachaerus*, wore a helmet, arm protectors, solid belt and metal greaves on his legs. But nothing on his chest. The helmet that went with his costume, like the Samnite's costume, had a full face mask. But he had put it up to talk to Artemidorus and the speed at which things were happening took him by surprise. So when Artemidorus hit him full on, it was still raised. The four blades clashed together. Priscus' massive arms and shoulders held Artemidorus. Slowed him, but did not quite stop him. He drove his helmet full force into Priscus' face. The metal rim above the closed faceplate smashed into the giant's nose. The heavy crest pushed the open faceplate up until the hinges snapped then it slammed into Priscus' forehead with stunning force. He staggered back, dazed and disorientated. Blood pouring over his lips and down his chin.

Artemidorus glanced sideways. The *retiarius* was on the ground now, the huge muscle of his right thigh cut free of his knee was bunched in an agonising cramp. Looking like one extra buttock immediately below another. The boy was flopping about helplessly on the grass. Like a dying fish. He had even somehow managed to tangle himself in his own net. No threat there.

Artemidorus threw himself forward again at the stunned and staggering Priscus. His mind was racing as it always did in battle. Formulating plans. Assessing their effectiveness. The helmeted head was impregnable but the face and neck were bare and vulnerable now. The arms were protected and the swords would protect them further. The belt was thick and armoured, reaching almost up to his ribs. An armoured skirt hung from it protecting his groin. His greaves made his legs impregnable. The targets could only be face, neck and chest. He leaped for those with all his strength and speed.

And slipped on the slick grass.

*

He crashed to the ground with stunning force, winding himself badly. Had he not been wearing the helmet he would have knocked himself out. And died on Priscus' sword a couple of heartbeats later. As it was, he smashed into Priscus' legs. The massive gladiator was still staggering, trying to regain his balance. So he crashed onto the ground as well. Both men were too experienced and canny to lose their grip on their weapons. No matter how dazed or winded they were. And so they threshed on the ground, one half on top of the other, like wrestlers. Wrestlers with deadly hands.

There was no art to it. No spectacle. Priscus had the advantage of being heavier and being on top. Artemidorus had the advantage of being better protected and quicker thinking. Priscus tried to use the Samnite's technique, driving the crest of his broken helmet down against the metal faceplate below. The second time he tried it, Artemidorus moved his head at the last moment so that Priscus drove his own battered face against the peak of the Samnite helmet instead. Dazed, he allowed himself to be rolled half-over. But he brought his knee up into Artemidorus' groin. Only the thick crotch of the *braccae* trousers saved the spy from serious damage. And incapacitating pain.

The four blades ground together once again as the huge man forced himself back up on top of the spy. It was only because the dagger had that astonishing metal blade that it held the *gladius* without breaking. But the wrist beneath the fist that gripped it was no match for the bear-like power of the larger man. It began to give way. The *dimachaerus* pushed himself further on top, beginning to use his weight as well as his strength. Artemidorus sought increasingly desperately for inspiration. For if it came to a simple trial of strength then he stood very little chance.

But perhaps Achilleus was watching over him. For he reasoned very quickly that if he couldn't use physical strength then he had to use cunning and speed. Speed that had always been the source of his hero's power. No sooner had the thought entered his head than he acted on it. His left arm yielded, slamming back against the ground. Believing he had won, Priscus reared his sword arm back, ready to deliver the killing stroke. But in the instant that he did so, Artemidorus, anchoring himself against the big man's crushing weight, whipped the dagger up, round and into the gladiator's chest immediately below his armpit. Between ribs spread apart by the movement of the bear-like arm and shoulder.

The blade that had last tasted Caesar's blood sank into the huge man as though his flesh was as soft as cheese. By the time he tensed his arm for the down-swing, the dagger's cross guard was pressed hard against his skin and its point was through his heart. The arm slumped harmlessly into the mud. The battered, brutish face took on a look of mild surprise then the head slammed down. Driving its metal peak into the Samnite faceplate below once more. Bouncing off and sliding sideway like a ball rolling onto the ground.

Artemidorus lay motionless for a moment. Then he heaved the massive corpse aside and sat up. The *retiarius* was still flopping helplessly about. Wearily the secret agent stood. Stooped and pulled his dagger free. Went over to the helpless boy and cut his throat. Stepping clear of the spray of blood with practised ease. As he had done more times than he could remember in the arena and on the battlefield.

Though, he thought, he was so filthy and mud-stained now that a little blood would hardly matter.

But staying alive – for the time being – was only part of the problem. When these two failed to return, Syrus would send others after them. If they found bodies, Syrus would know what had happened. And the Capitoline would be closed to the Samnite. But if Syrus' men found nothing, then sufficient doubt might remain to allow another visit or two. After he had delivered Brutus' letters and got himself cleaned up. He looked around for somewhere he could hide the bodies. His best bet seemed to be the new basilica Caesar had been building over the old *Basilica Sempronia*. Hardly any distance north of here. On the south side of the Forum. The new building, designed to hold public areas, meeting places, law courts, banks, shops and offices had been under construction for a couple of years. But it was still something of a building site. And this morning it was a deserted building site. As almost everyone in the city was staying barricaded in their homes. Except people scurrying about in the service of either for Cassius or Antony. Or, like him, in the service of both.

Artemidorus untangled the net from the body of the *retiarius* and used it to secure the two dead gladiators together. Then, with a massive heave that almost destroyed his shoulder joints, he got the corpses moving over the slippery grass. By the time he got them to their final destination, his flesh at least was cleaner. He had sweated the mud away.

One section of the new basilica was still at the foundation stage. A deep trench into which the tufa blocks of the walls would be cemented. Eventually. For now, two nights of torrential rain had half filled it with muddy water. The bodies went in together, still bound by the *retiarius'* fishing net. They were both wearing armour so they sank out of sight at once. The surface of the water heaved and settled. Then it was as though they had never been. Their killer looked back along the track of crushed grass to the mud pit of the battleground. These things might give the truth away. But only if Syrus sent someone with a brain acute enough to read the signs. And brains seemed to be in short supply. Among the gladiators at least. Besides, there was nothing he could do to change things now.

Artemidorus went on his way, pulling three miraculously undamaged letters from his belt as he went.

Cicero's house was near the corner of the *Clivus Victoriae* and the *Nova Via* roads, beside the *Porticus Catuli*. It was high enough on the north-eastern slopes of the Palatine to afford views of the Forum. Various temples on its south side. The building site where Artemidorus had left the bodies. And the Grove of Vesta. Cicero was not at home, but his *ostiarius* grudgingly accepted the letter delivered by the filthy individual in mud-smeared Samnite armour. He would make certain his master got it with all due despatch, he promised. Closing the door as though the messenger had been a beggar of the meanest sort.

From there it was not too far to Brutus' villa. And the spy was getting his second wind so he took it at a jog. Through empty streets. Between blocked and barricaded doors. Brutus' new *ostiarius* was much more polite, though the dog began to growl thunderously as soon as he smelt the messenger. His nose stripping away any and all disguises the murderer of its original master might wear.

XIII

As soon as he arrived back at Antony's villa, Artemidorus handed over Brutus' letter. Described the contents of Cicero's. Passed on Cassius' message. Related what he had seen, done and learned. This time, instead of reporting only to Antony and Enobarbus, he found that he was also reporting to Lepidus, and others of Caesar's faithful friends. Aulus Hirtius was there, one of the men who dined with Caesar the night after he crossed the Rubicon. And Gaius Matius was there. Friend to both Caesar and Cicero. An obvious go-between. But also a wise and practical statesman worried about reactions to Caesar's death in the provinces and amongst the legions. And the Lady Fulvia was there, as much a part of the conference as her husband and his friends. But what made the greatest impression on the soldier was that Antony, Enobarbus, Lepidus and Hirtius were all in full armour. Antony as consul could be fully armed as of right. But the others should only be wearing armour if they were about to bring the VIIth back into the picture.

After delivering his reports, the message and the letter, Artemidorus took another bath as the Lady Fulvia's long-suffering wardrobe slaves tried to repair and clean his clothing once again. This time he hardly noticed the aquatic orgy or the fornicating satyrs. He was in too much of a hurry to get washed down, cleaned up, dressed and back to work. For things were speeding up again.

He had been absent for most of the morning. During this time, Enobarbus had sent a runner to Tiber Island. So, when Artemidorus re-emerged, clad in his refreshed tunic and rescued *braccae* trousers, he had a choice of armour. Would he be more use to Antony during the next few hours as a centurion or a Samnite? At least the two corpses in the foundation ditch at Caesar's as yet unnamed basilica kept the door open for more undercover work. Though it would be much more dangerous this time with Syrus doubly on the alert.

He arrived from the bath in the middle of *prandium*. The light late-morning meal was not taken in the *triclinum* dining room but around a table in the *tablinum* office area as the council of war proceeded and immediate plans agreed for the meeting with Cassius and Brutus in the Forum at noon. The table was piled with cheeses, olives and fruit. Loaves of *emmer* bread. *Puls*, porridge flavoured with fish and *gram* fish sauce by the smell of it. There were plates and bowls as well as cups in front of everyone. Promus and his kitchen staff were waiting to serve. But no one seemed to be eating or drinking much, except for Fulvia, who was nibbling at a fig.

'The final objective is clear,' Antony was saying. 'We're going to kill every man who had a hand in Caesar's murder. But we can't just rush at it. Revenge may have to wait a little. Perhaps even a long time. We certainly don't want the war in the streets that Cassius threatened. We've all seen enough of that. So we'll keep the Seventh in reserve for now.'

'I'll get them battle-ready on your order,' said Lepidus. 'So I can bring them in at a moment's notice if rioting breaks out.'

'Rioting against *us*, at least,' added Antony. 'I wouldn't mind a riot aimed at Cassius. Or Brutus. The *plebeians*, Caesar's old soldiers and the freedmen can become a powerful weapon. The *comitia* too. Especially as they all loved Caesar. Even better than a legion in the city streets.'

'Though harder to control,' observed Matius cautiously. 'Once they get going. Much harder.'

'True,' nodded Antony. But he didn't sound as though he cared much.

'So, what's our first step?' Asked Enobarbus.

It was one of the attributes that made Antony such a popular and successful leader that he did not pull rank or stand on ceremony. If you were at the conference, then you were welcome to have your say. And, as Fulvia's presence attested, he was not narrow-minded about who could attend. And add their thoughts.

'Brutus is convinced they can control the Senate,' said Artemidorus. 'But Cassius isn't so sure. What is your feeling on that, General?'

'Balanced on a knife-edge,' said Antony. The others nodded.

'Brutus may be in this for the Republic,' observed the spy. Who knew the truth of what he was saying better than anyone else there. 'Most of the rest of them are in it for what they can get. Like Dolabella…' There was another general nod of agreement round the table.

'Then risk it,' Artemidorus urged. 'Call the Senate to meet as soon as you can. While you still have undisputed power as consul. While you can still hand out some of the prestige and power they're after.'

Antony nodded. 'It's too late to call them to meet today,' he said. 'Especially as we have this meeting to attend in the Forum. The soonest would be tomorrow morning.'

'But not in the Pompey's *curia*,' Fulvia advised.

'Not with Caesar's blood still on the floor,' said Matius, his voice shaking with horror.

'Then where?' demanded Antony.

'As near here as possible.' Suggested Artemidorus. 'General, were is the nearest place that's large enough and consecrated?'

'The Temple of Tellus,' said Fulvia. 'It's just up the road.'

'There you are then, General. Agree to whatever they ask. Suggest a Senate meeting to ratify whatever is said. They'll go back to the Capitoline and the Samnite will go and get some idea of what they're thinking. Meantime you have Caesar's papers which give you access to his personal fortune. An outline of his will and the key to the state treasury. If you can't bribe a couple of hundred greedy senators with all that, then you're not the man I took you for!'

There was silence. And Artemidorus for one horrible moment thought he'd gone too far.

Then Antony burst out laughing. 'By the gods,' he said, slapping the table hard enough to make the fruit bowl jump. 'Septem you're a wonder. If I had half your devious cunning I'd be twice the general I am!'

*

The two groups met in the Forum at noon. The day was clear. The sun high and bright. Once again it was warm for the time of year. A gentle breeze gusted from the south. Had there not been two groups of men approaching each other, armed and ready for battle, everything might have been set for a perfect spring afternoon.

Cassius and Brutus approached cautiously from the south-west corner. Coming out of the *Vicus Jugaris* road at the foot of the Capitoline. Along the side of the Temple of Saturn. Surrounded by gladiators, their hands on sword-hilts. Clutching spears. Or tridents. Antony and Lepidus came equally carefully out of the *Argiletum* roadway opposite. Past the *Comitium* itself. Surrounded by carefully selected men from the VIIth. Hands also on the hilts of their swords. They waited beside the *Rostra* as the *Libertores* and their guards approached.

Artemidorus watched the process, narrow-eyed. He was in his centurion's armour and helmet. Fulvia had suggested that, in the face of the gladiators, Antony should be escorted by as many fully armed soldiers as possible. Short of calling in the entire VIIth. That meant getting as many men into military gear as they could. The secret agent's cheeks were protected by metal flaps. Which he had tied tight beneath his chin. A good deal of his face was therefore concealed. But his eyes, nose and upper lip were still uncovered. If Brutus, Cassius or Syrus saw him clearly then they would recognise him. And he would be useless as a spy. So he stayed well back.

Enobarbus approached the clear area between the battle lines as Antony's representative. He was met by Dolabella. The pair of them conferred. Agreed. Signalled. Antony and Lepidus went forward. To be met by Brutus and Cassius.

Apart from the two armed groups, the Forum was empty. Hardly surprisingly, thought Artemidorus. The atmosphere was threatening. In spite of the clement weather. As though another cataclysmic thunderstorm was just about to break. He had only ever come across tension like this during the opening moments of a battle. He began to go over in his head the battles he had fought in. Land battles and sea battles. Large battles and small ones. With thousands dead or dying. Or tens. Or, as with this morning, two.

As the sun moved slowly westwards, the atmosphere grew more tense.

The conference lasted until the middle of the afternoon. Then Antony and Lepidus returned to their side of the Forum, apparently satisfied. Brutus and Cassius retreated behind their wall of flesh and steel. The two groups left the Forum. Tension should have eased, but Artemidorus still felt that thunderous pressure in the air. At least he hadn't been recognised, he thought. So all he'd have to worry about when the Samnite went back into the Temple of Jupiter was whether Syrus had managed to work out what had happened to his missing men.

But before he changed into his disguise, Artemidorus once more became part of the group discussing what had been agreed and what would be done next.

'They were careful not to say anything against Caesar,' said Antony as they gathered round the table in the *tablinum* once again. 'So I said that although we were Caesar's friends our main aim was to maintain the peace both in the city and in the provinces.'

'That was wise,' said Fulvia. 'Do you think they believed you?'

'It was the point you made, Matius,' added Lepidus.

'And it was a good one,' agreed Antony. 'But to answer you, my dear, Cassius and Brutus both know that Lepidus and I are sworn to protect Caesar and to bring his enemies to justice. And that means his murderers of course. However, we also made clear that our immediate priority must be the city. It will take time for the news to spread to the provinces. But Rome already knows.'

'Talking of provinces,' added Lepidus, 'we discussed the problem of Albinus taking charge of Cisalpine Gaul. But presented it as an afterthought. We didn't want them to suspect we knew what was in Brutus' letter to Cicero.'

'So, we agreed that I would summon the Senate for a morning session tomorrow. In the Temple of Tellus. As you suggested, Fulvia. I'll send out runners once again. And the senators we notify first will send out runners themselves. Word will spread quickly.'

'But the atmosphere in the streets is still dangerous,' said Artemidorus. 'It could be a nasty night.'

'Right,' said Antony. 'What I'll do is this. When my runners have called the Senate, I'll send them out again to every *aedile* magistrate. Get them to build watchfires and put *vigiles* patrols out.' He straightened. Stretched until the straps on his armour creaked. 'And when I've done that, I will invite you all to experience my baths, and join me for *cena* in the *trinclinum*. Don't stand on ceremony. I could eat an ox, and I'm sure the rest of you could as well. And, if truth be told, I think I probably smell like an ox too.'

'That's better than smelling of sandalwood from the perfume of your Egyptian whore,' said Fulvia under her breath. Speaking the bitter words so quietly that no one else could hear them. Except, by chance, for Artemidorus.

*

A little after sunset, in the darkness before moonrise, the Samnite crossed the Forum, heading for the Capitoline. Without his usual swagger. A good deal of work had been done to his battered, muddy armour. As many dents as possible had been beaten out of his face mask. The feathers of his distinctive crest had been washed, dried, restored. Only the sharpest eyes would notice that the helmet had been through a battle. Like the rest of the disguise.

Artemidorus had been caught in a frustrating trap during the early evening. He refused the bath, preferring to help with the armour's restoration. He took his brief *cena* dinner in the kitchen. Then he finished working on his disguise and he changed into it. On the one hand he could not risk wearing anything that had obviously been through a bitter fight. Syrus would be bound to draw a deadly conclusion from that. But he also did not want to be stopped, perhaps arrested, by the magistrates Antony had alerted. As they sat by the watchfire burning at every junction and crossroad. Or by the patrols they were sending out to keep the streets quiet. So ideally he needed to finish and move out before the night guard could be posted.

Antony had offered him a pass. But that seemed of such limited value. It might get him as far as the Capitoline. But it would be too dangerous to take it into the temple with him. So, unless he could hide it and then reclaim it on his way back later, it was too much of a risk. Especially as he would have to hide it and find it in the dark. Besides, he felt that in the final analysis he could probably sneak past the city's watchmen. If they were out before he left.

But the Fates had other plans for him tonight.

He was moving through the shadows towards the Temple of Saturn. With the *tabularium* records office hulking against the starry sky on his right. And the darkness of the open lower slopes of the Capitoline just beyond. When he became aware of another figure also moving through the shadows of the old basilica on his left. A figure betrayed by the brightness of his senatorial toga. Which glimmered even in the starlight. His interest piqued, he fell in silently behind the stranger and began to follow him. So that when the patrol on the *Vicus Jugarius* road stopped him, they were almost side by side. The leader of the watch team uncovered the dark lantern he was carrying. The brightness was suddenly dazzling. 'The *aedile* said we'd catch some night crawlers if we waited in secret,' the watchman said. 'Now what do we have here?'

The stranger lifted his head into the light. To reveal the most famous face in Rome. 'I am Marcus Tullius Cicero,' he said. 'You have no authority to detain me! As for this man...'

Cicero turned towards Artemidorus and stopped mid-sentence. A rare occurrence by all accounts.

'As for this gladiator...' Cicero's voice dropped a little as he addressed the featureless metal mask in front of him. 'My doorkeeper tells me that it was a Samnite who delivered this to my house today.' He held up Brutus' letter.

'It was me,' said Artemidorus. 'I am Lord Brutus' messenger.'

The orator turned back to the watchmen. 'This man is with me. He is serving in the office of a bodyguard. The streets can be dangerous at night. Especially in times like these.'

'We know,' said the watchman. 'That's why we're on patrol.'

'Well get on with it, man! And stop delaying important people about vital senatorial business!'

'We'll have to report this to the *aedile*,' said the stubborn watchman, refusing to be bullied.

'You may report it to Mark Antony himself for all I care,' snapped Cicero. 'Now get out of my way!'

Beneath the featureless mask, Artemidorus smiled. This would certainly be reported to Mark Antony. If he got down from the temple alive.

Cicero strutted self-righteously past the watch and strode on down the road. Artemidorus followed him. The Capitoline Hill gathered above their right shoulders until the Tarpean Rock itself blotted out the stars. As they walked, so the lawyer bombarded his new companion with questions. 'You are one of Decimus Brutus Albinus' gladiators?'

'Yes, Senator.'

'Employed by him to put on a show at Pompey's Theatre yesterday?'

'Just so, sir.'

'And you protected the *Libertores* after they had executed the dictator?'

'We escorted them up to the temple, sir.'

'And you have stood with them ever since?'

'Except when Lord Brutus sends me on errands…'

'As he did today.'

'Yes. But that has come about largely by chance. I am not one of the inner circle. They are the gladiators who also work for Lord Minucius Basilus.'

'A nasty piece of work. Luckily it is only slaves he likes to hurt and kill. Or I might find myself fighting a case on his behalf. If he can afford me. Which by all accounts he certainly can.'

The lawyer turned abruptly right and began to mount the one-hundred-step stairway that led up to the Temple of Jupiter on the south side of the hill. Artemidorus stayed close behind as Cicero climbed the steps surprisingly rapidly for a man of his years. The spy wasn't certain but the lawyer must be in his early sixties now. Yet he was leaping upwards like a mountain goat.

In hardly any time at all the pair of them were in the square outside the temple. There were watchfires in every corner of the square. Like those springing to life at every crossroad below. And serving the same purpose. As soon as the two figures walked into the firelight, Syrus swaggered up to them. But the instant he recognised Cicero he stopped. His manner changed. Became humble. Almost servile.

'Your worship. I have orders to conduct you directly to Lord Brutus the instant you appeared. Would you kindly follow me, my Lord?'

Cicero condescended to do so. And Artemidorus followed Cicero.

*

The *Libertores* were preparing to spend their second night in the temple. Their supply of food had been augmented by bedding. Clean clothing. Basic washing facilities. Some of it supplied by the priests and their helpers. The rest by supporters. Nothing to compare with Antony's facilities, thought Artemidorus looking around. If the general had indeed smelt like an ox, he would not have been the only one in here. Then something struck him other than the smell. The number of the *Libertores* present was fewer than he remembered from his last visit. There was a fire in here and most of the murderers were clustered around it. But there was no sign of Dolabella that he could see. Nor of Lucius Cornelius Cinna. With an air of casual indifference, he began to probe the shadows. Mentally ticking off the names on Cyanea's list.

In the meantime, Brutus had risen, his face showing obvious delight as he recognised Cicero. 'Marcus Tullius... At last!' he said and came forward to embrace the lawyer. 'Now we have a voice worthy of our actions.'

'Let us hope your actions remain worthy of my voice,' answered Cicero, returning the embrace with some reluctance. 'But your own voice has been good enough so far by all accounts. Was it the speech that we discussed? A perfectly turned persuasive piece of rhetoric. Though I had no idea you were planning to employ it so soon.'

'I tried to speak three times,' said Brutus, an excited child reporting to the *pater familias*. 'On the third attempt I succeeded. On the *Rostra* in the Forum. The complete oration.'

'I wish I had been there,' said Cicero. 'In fact I wish I had known how immediate your plans were. It is a sad thing to come so late to a feast.'

'Well, you are here now. And a welcome guest at our table. And you will, I hope, be with us when the Senate meets in the Temple of Tellus tomorrow.'

'I will be there. But are you sure you will?'

'Certainly!' said Brutus. 'Antony and Lepidus have agreed…'

'Antony and Lepidus.' Cicero frowned. 'Now if I had been invited to the feast a little earlier, those are two courses I would certainly have urged you to include!'

'I urged him to include them.' Cassius stepped out of the shadows and stood framed against the firelight. His face all but invisible. Except for the glittering of his eyes. Reminding Artemidorus of Brutus' guard dog. He shivered and tried to conceal the fact.

'It would have been wise, I think.' Cicero nodded.

'But…'

'Yes Brutus. I know you wanted the one course in your feast to be carved as a sacrifice worthy of the gods. But I fear that all you have succeeded in doing is to let two deadly enemies escape. They will destroy you if they can. Have no doubt of that.'

'They are Caesar's limbs,' sneered Brutus. 'Powerless without him. Why Lepidus no longer has any legal standing or authority!'

'They are Caesar's war dogs and you have unleashed them,' Cicero warned. 'Be careful of your throats or they will tear them out.'

'My thoughts exactly!' snapped Cassius.

Brutus glanced at his friend and brother-in-law. Then at his friend and mentor. Frowned. But it seemed to the spy that the frown was one of confusion rather than of anger. Perhaps Brutus was having second thoughts. *I would be if I were in his place*, mused the spy. *Even if I didn't know what I know.*

'We can start making things clear tomorrow at the Senate meeting,' Brutus said after a moment.

'You're not going to that, are you?' demanded Cicero. 'In the Temple of Tellus? A stone's throw from Antony's villa? It's a trap! Can't you see that? Even if you get there unscathed, he's probably planning to cut you down as you cut Caesar down! On the chamber floor. In front of the Senate itself. He might even be able to claim legal precedent!'

'No!' said Brutus, genuinely shocked at Cicero's cynicism. 'We have safe passage there and back. Antony has given his word. And Antony is an honourable man! So is Lepidus. Both honourable men!'

Cicero shook his head. 'Let us say that you are right. Let us suppose that they are in fact honourable men. To whom is their first allegiance? To Caesar! They have both been given their office through him or by him. They have both sworn to protect him, or, failing that, to avenge him. That is their primary duty if, as you say, they are honourable men. I have to tell you that under the law as it stands, I could not convict them of any crime if they lied to you, cheated you, or murdered you in pursuit of that allegiance. As honourable men might do.'

'As with all the others,' added Cassius quietly, looking around. 'We can only be sure that they will keep their word if we make it too dangerous or costly for them to break it.'

'There is precious little honour in this business, Marcus,' said Cicero. 'I urge you to remain here with your guards tomorrow. While I attend Antony's Senate meeting and see what I can discover.'

Brutus shook his head.

It was clear to Artemidorus that this meeting had not gone as Brutus had planned. But there was nothing he could say or do to change things now. Sadder and wearier than ever, he turned and walked back to the fire. Shoulders slumped. A defeated general after a hard-fought battle. Cassius looked after him. Shook his head as well. But in frustration. Not disappointment. He looked at Cicero. The lawyer and philosopher shrugged. 'At least keep him here tomorrow. The Senate can meet without him. Or you, come to that. I will be there. A number of your friends will be there. We will sound out the feelings of the patricians at least.'

'What do you mean by that, Cicero?'

'The upper classes are not the only men involved in this. As Antony and Lepidus will know all too well. The city is full of *plebs* – freedmen and soldiers. They loved Caesar. They are dry kindling awaiting only the merest spark. Then we might well have a conflagration that will burn us all!'

Cicero turned on that and began to retrace his steps. Artemidorus followed him. They crossed the marble floor of the temple and strode out through the door onto the portico. The night was clear and the moon on the rise. Artemidorus' head was buzzing with the implications of what he had overheard. His eyes fixed on the brightness of Cicero's toga, as though he would burn a hole between the orator's shoulders with the intensity of his gaze. He followed Cicero across the portico, between the soaring columns and down the steps into the fire-bright square.

Cicero turned right and headed back towards the gate opening onto the one hundred steps down to the base of the Tarpean Rock. He was so preoccupied himself that he seemed to have forgotten all about his Samnite bodyguard.

So that he did not stop – or even seem to notice - when Syrus' arm went round Artemidorus' throat and the point of a dagger was pushed against the tender skin behind his jaw just below his left ear where his carotid artery pulsed.

*

Artemidorus lashed his head back. Syrus was too canny and experienced a cut-throat to be hit in the face by the helmet rim's iron edge. But he loosened his grip. Leaped back. Artemidorus span round. To find himself confronted by Syrus and three of his largest companions. All four charged at him and he was overcome almost immediately. A brawny gladiator held each of his arms. The third stood behind him, reaching round to loosen his belt. To remove it, his sword and the dagger. Syrus himself swaggered forward and undid the laces under Artemidorus' chin. Then he lifted the Samnite helmet off. His eyes narrowed as he regarded the spy's clean-shaven face. Artemidorus struggled against his captors' iron grip. Uselessly. The man behind him began to undo the straps of his breastplate.

'My first question is this. What have you done with Priscus and the boy?'

'I have no idea what you are talking about.'

'I think you do. I think you're lying. Because I think that's what you are. A lying spy!'

'I'm a gladiator just like you… A Samnite…'

'We found the Samnite's body in one of the disused shops just inside the Gate of Fontus. I knew you weren't him the instant I laid eyes on you. I came near to crippling him in our exhibition match. And suddenly he wasn't even limping! I've been watching you ever since. Coming and going. Listening. Looking. Spying. And now I see your face, I know exactly who you are. Did you think a visit to the *tonsor* for a shave would fool me? You're the red-bearded spy we caught at Lord Basilus' villa. Trying to rescue that little whore he was looking forward to whipping.' He stooped and picked up the club for which he was named. The man behind Artemidorus lifted his breastplate free.

'Cestus wouldn't let me use this on your friend Telos. He was having too much fun with his fists. But it's my turn now. So I'll tell you how this is going to go. I ask a question. Every time you lie. Or even answer slowly. I'm going to hit you with this club. I can keep it up 'til dawn. 'Til I have broken every bone in your body. Then I'll just throw you off the Tarpean

Rock. And no one will even know! If I judge it carefully, you'll still be just alive enough to enjoy the fall. And the landing. So, just to get you in the mood before we start…'

Syrus drove his club into Artemidorus' belly. He did so almost casually. Certainly not with full force. But he still knocked the wind out of the spy. Artemidorus would have fallen. But Syrus' men were holding his arms. So he curled into a foetal position. Gasping for breath. Hanging in the air.

Syrus waited until his feet touched ground again. 'So,' he said, swinging the club. 'About Priscus and the boy…'

The only plan Artemidorus could see was to make Syrus lose his temper and end this quickly. Because he had no intention of co-operating. And now that the gladiator had recognised him, there was no cover story that would convince his torturer. So he was looking at a wilderness of pain. He wondered how many bones would have to be broken before his resistance also broke. He had seen men tortured. His *contubernium* spy team even had a *carnifex* associated with it. An expert torturer ready for when the need for pain arose. He had never seen anyone hold out. They all talked in the end. Unless they died first.

'Why don't you just take that little twig you're holding and stick it right up your…'

The club slammed into his belly with enough force to make the men holding him stagger back. He curled into a ball once more. Fighting for breath. Hanging in the air.

'That wasn't actually your first blow,' said Syrus. 'That was just to shut you up while I think… Now, let me see. If you're wearing the Samnite's armour. Why don't we start with the Samnite's pain? Which of his legs did I break? And was it ankle, shin or thigh? Well, let's just start with ankle, as yours are still up in the air…' Syrus' club swung back and…

'STOP!' boomed a voice strengthened by years of oratory. 'What are you doing with that man?' demanded Marcus Tullius Cicero.

'We were questioning him, my Lord. He's killed two of my friends.'

'That's what gladiators do, you fool. Fight and die!'

242

'And he's a spy, my Lord. He works for Mark Antony. One of a team…'

'Is that true, Samnite? Do you work for Antony?'

'I am Iamus Artemidorus, centurion of the Seventh Legion. *Primus pilus*.' He admitted between agonised gasps. His feet touched ground again.

'Are you indeed? Put him down at once! Give him back his armour and his weapons.'

'But my Lord, they aren't even his…' Syrus whined.

'At once. Or it will be you who takes a flight off the Tarpean Rock! And you look more like Icarus than Daedalus. So it will be a short flight! You two, don't just stand there. Help him put it on.'

By the time he got his breath back, Artemidorus was once again in the Samnite armour with the sword and dagger at his hips. Helmet under his arm.

'Follow me!' snapped Cicero. And he strode off towards the temple.

Artemidorus followed, his mind racing. He was by no means out of the woods yet. But, as Cicero had got his weapons returned, at least he could go down fighting. Or, if necessity dictated, fall on his sword.

Brutus and Cassius were still by the fire, deep in conversation. They both rose as Cicero entered, each face showing their surprise that he had returned so soon. Cicero gestured for them to follow. And led them to a secluded corner. As he followed the three conspirators, Artemidorus closed his fist round the hilt of Brutus' dagger. They reached a spot that was far enough from the others so as not to be overheard. But still near enough to the fire for its light to let them see each other clearly.

'The gods have given us a gift,' said the orator, his voice unusually quiet. 'This is not a Samnite gladiator. This is a centurion of the Seventh Legion. A spy working for Marc Antony himself!'

'Is this true?' gasped Brutus, clearly deeply shocked.

Artemidorus thanked the gods that the *Libertore* still did not recognise the man who had pretended to fix his roof. Tightened his grip on the dagger. 'Yes, sir. That is true.'

'Then what are you doing here?' Brutus demanded.

'Doing what spies do!' snapped Cassius. 'He's spying! On us!'

'But you called him a gift from the gods, Marcus Tullius! What did you mean by that?'

'Think, man! If you capture a spy, what do you do with him?'

'Kill him!' spat Cassius.

'What a waste that would be, Gaius! No. If you catch a spy you turn him. Use him! What we have here is a line of communication that can go straight from us directly to Antony himself.'

'But we can't trust him! He's a spy!'

'We don't need to trust him, Gaius. We just need to give him a good reason to do what we want him to do.' Cicero turned to Artemidorus. Looked him straight in the eye. 'Convince him that our aims and objectives are the same as his and Antony's.'

'And what are those?' demanded Cassius. 'What's the common ground between Caesar's friends and ours?'

'To maintain the peace. To talk instead of fighting. To respect each other and each other's position. Instead of tearing each other apart. Like wild animals in the *Circus Maximus*. Don't forget the past. Just don't act on it. What's done is done. We need to move on. Together! If we get this right, the Republic will stand forever. And you, Marcus Junius, will be as famous as your ancestor who founded it four hundred years ago!'

'Is that what Antony wants, spy?' demanded Cassius, still not convinced. Spitting out the word *spy* as though it were something foul he was removing from his mouth. 'Peace and an eternal Republic?'

'Peace, yes,' said Artemidorus. 'I don't know about the eternal Republic.'

'We've already offered peace,' said Cassius.

'And yet you're still up here surrounded by guards!' observed Cicero. 'You call this *peace*?'

'I don't trust Antony!'

'And he doesn't trust you! But what I'm saying is that the centurion here is a bridge on which we can build trust. The very fact that we have unmasked him and let him live proves that! Send him to Antony with an assurance that there will be no more daggers, and we will have taken the first step! Don't you see?'

'I think it's a good idea,' said Brutus. 'We don't want to be stuck up here for ever. This man can help us come down...'

Some time later, Cicero was leading Artemidorus down the hundred steps. 'I don't think I convinced Cassius,' the orator was saying.

'No, sir. But he's willing to await events, I think.'

'An acute observation. But then I suppose acute observation is the spy's stock in trade.'

'I suppose so, sir. I've never thought about it.'

'Somehow I doubt that. But of course lying is also an important asset to a spy.'

'Sometimes, sir. If you can make the lie convincing.'

'But you will tell the truth to Antony. That the *Libertores* want peace. That there will be no more daggers.'

'I will, sir. It is a message he wants to hear.'

'I believe you,' said Cicero, stepping down off the last step and into the roadway of the *Vicus Jugarius*.

That's because it's a message you want to hear, thought the spy stepping down beside him.

Their ways parted then. The orator went home to his books and his bed.

The spy went back to his masters, aware that the gods had smiled on him yet again today. His head full of much more information than the message he was carrying.

And the absolute certainty that whether Caesar's murderers wanted peace or not. Whether the general agreed to their requests or not. Whether he listened to the wishes of the Senate or not. Whether he signed accords, ratified appointments, forgave past sins and misdemeanours or not.

245

Marc Antony was planning to slaughter every last one of them. And Artemidorus himself was duty-bound to help him.

XIV

The real trouble started early next morning. *Dies Veneris*, the seventeenth day of Mars. Two days after the Ides. *Liberalia.*

Everyone in Antony's household was up before dawn. That included guests, soldiers and spies. Especially spies. Antony summoned Artemidorus for another briefing before setting out for his Senate meeting. He wanted to have clear in his mind every detail of the message Artemidorus had brought last night. As well as his observations and his suspicions. Enobarbus was there too. As was Lepidus, who had risen early to join in the planning. Gaius Matius and Aulus Hirtus were not attending this meeting. They were getting ready to attend the Senate meeting. As friends and supporters of Antony and Caesar. Should they be needed.

As with most of the meals lately, *jentaculum* breakfast was taken in the *tablinum* while this briefing took place. And, as was again becoming the norm, everyone was fully armed. Artemidorus as a centurion, now that the Samnite costume was no longer any use as a disguise.

After they had gone through everything with Artemidorus once again, Antony and Enobarbus set out for the Temple of Tellus and the Senate meeting. Lepidus and Artemidorus were to go back to Tiber Island and bring back at least a *centuria* of legionaries. A hundred or so good men, fully armed. Enough to defuse any situation but not enough to frighten the *Libertores*. Antony wasn't certain that he wanted a whole five-hundred-man cohort on the streets yet. Or the entire VIIth Legion – which currently stood at nearly five thousand. It depended, he said, on how things went with the Senate. And the people. But a *centuria* would be good insurance against almost anything short of revolution. And it would give them a unit of similar size to Albinus' gladiators.

So Artemidorus set out with Caesar's ex-*magister equitum*. Who now held formal authority from the consul to command the legion. Or any part of it he wanted. The morning was overcast. Keeping the chill of a cold night trapped on the streets. But at least people were up and about. That was to the good, thought Artemidorus. Lepidus and he quick-marched down towards the Forum, planning to take the *Vicus Jugarius* past the Tarpean Rock down to the Carmenta Gate through the Servian wall out onto the *Campus Martius*. Then across the *Pons Fabricius* onto Tiber Island.

But they were just entering the Forum itself when a strange sight met their eyes. A senator, in full formal senatorial toga was running along in front of the old basilica as though multi-headed hound of hell Cerberus himself was after him. Artemidorus recognised trouble when he saw it. 'Lord Lepidus,' he said. 'Go for the legion as fast as you can. Get a *centuria* back here! The sooner the better.'

Lepidus broke into a sprint at once. As did Artemidorus. Running across the Forum, past surprised citizens, slaves and freedmen. Sprinting round proud patrician fathers showing off their sons in their new, adult togas. Before taking them home and heading for the Senate meeting. Hesitant to let even something like Caesar's murder upset their traditions. Somewhere, also, Artemidorus suspected, some die-hards would be carrying out the Procession of the Argei. A ritual so old that its origins and purpose were lost in time. Though he doubted it would have happened yesterday – the first of the two-day festival.

In the meantime, he was heading for the fleeing senator. As he came closer to the man he recognised him. It was Lucius Cornelius Cinna. Who had made such a performance of ridding himself of badges and robes of office. Things that associated him with Caesar. And who had made a speech calling the dead dictator a tyrant. Calling his killers heroic *Libertores*. The mob that he was fleeing from came boiling through the building site where Priscus and the boy lay hidden in a flooded ditch. As dead as the dictator. The senator shouted in terror. No one in the Forum took much notice. Certainly no one there had the slightest intention of helping him. Except for Artemidorus.

As he ran, Artemidorus was looking for somewhere the senator could hide. Preferably somewhere that could be barricaded. Defended until Lepidus came back with his *centuria*. Artemidorus' own *centuria* stood at eighty men. But they were tough. Experienced. Iberian. Like the bodyguards Caesar had so publicly dispensed with. Eighty of them would be better than a couple of hundred lesser troops. A hail of missiles flew towards the fleeing man. Mostly sticks and stones. A few came near Artemidorus. But he could afford to disregard them. He was in full armour. Helmet, breastplate, backplate, greaves. *Braccae* trousers. *Caligae* hobnail boots. *Gladius* and *pugio*, though he had no intention of using them.

Then he was at Cinna's shoulder. 'Do you know where you're heading for, senator? Somewhere you'll be safe?'

'Down here. My friend...' he said a name but his words were lost in another rain of stones. He shouted out with terror once again. And in pain. There was a nasty gash on the back of his head. Several of the stones hit the centurion, but his armour kept him safe.

Then the senator was banging furiously on a door. It opened immediately. Before the doorkeeper could even speak, Cinna bundled in. Artemidorus followed him. Tore the door out of the keeper's hands and slammed it. There was a bolt. He slid it home. 'We may need to barricade it as well,' he said. Calmly. In a conversational tone. 'That was quite a large mob. They don't look as though they'll just go away.'

No sooner had he spoken than someone threw themselves bodily against the door. 'Come out you traitor!' someone bellowed. 'We know you're in there.'

The *ostiarius* vanished. Cinna was long gone. Deeper into the villa. Artemidorus glanced over his shoulder. The senator was talking to someone in the *atrium*. Someone who didn't look too happy with the situation the senator had put him in.

'Yes,' chimed in another voice from the street outside. A woman's. 'Come out and tell us what a tyrant Caesar was. Tell us again how he's better off dead and we ought to kiss the hands of his butchers!'

'I have to warn you that the senator is under military protection,' called Artemidorus. 'There will be a patrol here soon if you don't disperse.'

'We don't want to harm you, Centurion,' said the first voice. 'I was in the legion myself. Just send that treacherous little *spurious* out so we can discuss Caesar's murder with him.'

'Really soldier? What legion?'

'The Sixth. *Ferrata*. The Ironclads. That was us.'

*

'Well I warn you, soldier to soldier,' called Artemidorus, 'that you're just about to meet some men from my legion, the Seventh. And they won't be very happy…'

'More Iberian lads. Just like us! When they see who's here they'll probably join in!'

'I doubt that! My men would never waver.' Even as he spoke, Artemidorus thought of Cicero's observation. Spies must be good at lying. He could in fact think of a number of his men who would just love to join the mob when they heard it was out to get Caesar's killers and their friends. If it came right down to it he could only be totally certain of Quintus, his old friend and weapons expert.

Conversation stopped then as the door was subjected to another battering. The doorkeeper returned with a couple of helpers carrying an iron-bound wooden trunk. They pushed it against the door. 'You'll need more than that,' said Artemidorus. Under the onslaught, the door was beginning to yield. The three men ran off.

But then the battering stopped. Artemidorus found the sudden quiet worrying. Especially when he heard the softer sounds of things being stacked against the portal outside. He understood at once what was going on. The mob was piling kindling against the front of the house. The doorkeeper and his friends returned with another wooden trunk to stand upon the first. 'Get water,' ordered Artemidorus. 'They're going to burn us out.'

The two men in the *atrium* were having a shouting match now. Artemidorus reckoned that if the house-owner had ever really been a friend of Cinna's, the relationship was coming to an immediate and acrimonious end. There had already been a host of relationships pushed past breaking point by Caesar's murder. And there would be many more before things were settled.

Suddenly his head turned. He came out of his brief reverie. He smelt smoke. 'Hurry up with that water,' he shouted.

The long-suffering doorkeeper and his helpers came back carrying brimming bowls. But before they could throw the water over the door the sounds outside changed.

'Look out!' someone shouted. 'Here come the soldiers!'

There was a confusion of shouting and scuffling. The sounds of feet running away. The sounds of *caligae* approaching. Hobnails marching across cobbles. Of kindling being kicked aside. Then a fist hammered on the door. 'Are you all right in there?' shouted Lepidus.

'Fine,' answered Artemidorus. 'You got here just in time. You three, clear the doorway. Senator Cinna, the mob has gone. It's safe to come out now.'

They exited the house and Artemidorus could see at once why Ironclad's mob had gone. There was a *centuria* of full-armed legionaries behind Lepidus. His own *centuria*, in fact. With Oppius, his replacement centurion standing grim-faced. And Quintus in the front rank. Though in battle he would be in the third. Quintus, in the most up-to-date, expensive armour money could buy. Looking like a man of iron himself.

A short time later, Cinna was out and walking across the Forum. Head high. Face fixed in a disdainful frown. Lepidus at one shoulder. Artemidorus at the other. Eighty stout legionaries, fully armed, at his back.

Enobarbus was waiting at the Temple of Tellus. The temple was old. Of a traditional design, modelled on the Greek. Built over the remains of a house once owned by a man, like Caesar, who wanted to be king. Executed for that very crime nearly four hundred years ago. As Tellus was the Earth Mother, it was fitting that a statue of Ceres, goddess of crops and

251

fertility, stood outside it. Marcus Tullius Cicero had more recently added a statue of his brother Quintus. The Cicero family home was nearby. Though Marcus Tullius himself lived on the other side of town.

Steps led up to a columned portico. The main building behind stood square and spacious. Tall doors opening onto the sacred space large enough to accommodate several hundred senators. On banks of temporary seating ordered by Antony and erected during the night. Antony, as consul, was in charge of procedure. He would be sitting on a dais at the front. Just as Caesar had sat in Pompey's *curia* a little less than two days ago. 'The consul is expecting you, Lord Lepidus,' said Enobarbus. 'Go straight in. It doesn't matter that you are armed and haven't got your formal toga. These are apparently unusual times.'

Lepidus gave a bark of cynical laughter. Nodded and entered. Cinna strutted at his side. Yet to thank either of the soldiers for saving him from the rioters. Artemidorus got a glance at the tiers of benches. The dais. Antony seated apparently at his ease. Dolabella on his feet beside him. Ranting about something. The door closed. 'We're to guard the building,' said Enobarbus. 'There may be some unrest.'

'There already has been. Cinna was lucky he wasn't torn limb from limb. Or roasted alive.'

'Some of the citizens are turning against the murderers,' observed Enobarbus. 'But the Senate seems largely on their side. For the moment at least. None of the ringleaders has appeared. In spite of what Brutus and Cicero said in their message. I suppose they are all still up in the Temple of Jupiter. Waiting to see which way the wind will blow.'

'That's probably just as well,' said Artemidorus. 'If the citizens go after hangers-on like Cinna, what will they do to Brutus and Cassius?'

The first citizens arrived just after the guards had been set. The grounds of the temple were ample. Soon the crowd gathering there grew large enough – and restless enough – to cause Enobarbus some alarm. Then they started calling for Antony. The tribune went into the temple and asked the consul

252

to come and talk to them. As he opened the door, Artemidorus heard the ill-tempered squabbling that had begun to characterise the Senate meeting.

A moment later, Antony and Lepidus both came out. Lepidus was in his armour. Antony was in his senatorial toga with his consular trappings. Enobarbus fell in at Antony's shoulder. Artemidorus at Lepidus'. As they reached the top of the steps, a range of voices, mostly male, started asking questions. Seeking reassurance. Wondering what was happening. What was going to happen. It was impossible to answer everyone at once, so Antony held up his hand demanding quiet. After a few moments, the crowd settled down. Antony drew breath to speak. But, before he could utter a word, someone bellowed, 'How do you know they won't kill you too?'

Artemidorus recognised the voice. It belonged to the old soldier from the Ironclads. The one who had led the mob chasing Cinna.

By way of answer, Antony simply pulled down the toga from his neck. To reveal his breastplate underneath.

*

A wave of amusement swept through the crowd. The atmosphere lightened. 'Citizens,' Antony shouted.

But once again, his voice was lost as members of the crowd started to demand that Caesar's murderers be brought to justice.

Antony held up his hand. Silence came more quickly this time.

'Friends,' called Antony. 'That is what we are debating at this very moment. Whether it was Caesar or his killers who served Rome best. Our aim is to come to an agreement that will bring peace. First to our city streets. Then to our provinces at home and abroad. But naturally it will take a little time to test these agreements and guarantees. Every man in the chamber behind me once swore an oath to Caesar. Some of the men here – and others elsewhere – broke that oath. So can their word be trusted now? It is a hard matter. And we must finish our debate. Let us do so, friends. Then we will tell you

253

what has been decided. But remember. I too swore an oath to Caesar. Both as consul and as friend. To protect him or avenge him. If I break that oath now it is only because I owe a greater loyalty. To you, to our city and to our empire!'

The old Ironclad's voice rang out again. 'Lepidus! Tell us what you think!'

Artemidorus leaned a little closer to the *magister equitum*. 'Take them back to the Forum,' he suggested. 'Talk to them there. Get them away from here.'

'Good idea,' said Antony. 'Artemidorus, take a detail from these guards and go with him. Twenty men or so should do.'

And so the morning passed. Lepidus, surrounded by Artemidorus' detachment, walked down to the *Comitium* and climbed onto the *Rostra* there. More and more people came pouring into the Forum. So many that Artemidorus soon lost count. The citizens who lived here, their families and slaves were being augmented by increasing numbers of old soldiers. Coming to the city to find out what was going on. All of them promised farms or smallholdings for their retirement. But promised by Caesar. And increasingly concerned now that whoever replaced him might be less willing to meet the dead dictator's commitments.

Lepidus found it hard to speak at first for he was overcome with emotion. Artemidorus climbed onto the *Rostra*. He stood beside Lepidus as he eventually managed to calm down and make himself heard. Artemidorus stepped back to let Lepidus speak. But he stayed on the *Rostra*. He was scanning the crowd. Hoping to link the familiar, often-raised, voice with the face of the old soldier from the VIth Legion.

Lepidus had little new to say. Like Antony, he told the crowd that the main objective now was to maintain the peace. That he had sworn an oath to Caesar but would break his word and stain his honour for the good of the People of Rome. 'Courage like that deserves reward,' bellowed that familiar voice. Artemidorus strained his eyes to see who was speaking.

'Like the *Libertores*, I seek no reward for any of my actions. Other than the good of Rome!' Lepidus answered forcefully.

'Perhaps you should be *pontifex maximus*. You seem well enough qualified to be chief priest!' It was hard to tell whether the suggestion was meant ironically or not.

Artemidorus had him now. Short dark hair. High forehead. Overhanging brows, thickly furred. Flattened nose. Deep-set eyes above strong cheekbones. Hard mouth in a short, dense black beard rising up olive-skinned cheeks. Medium build. Deep chest. He'd be the Cicero of his *centuria*. Up on everyone's rights, starting with his own. Every inch a troublemaker. *I could use a man like him*, thought the spy.

He climbed down from the *Rostra*. Paused, thinking. Lepidus was saying, 'Thank you for that thought, citizen. Perhaps we should save the suggestion for later.' It was obvious from his tone that he took the suggestion seriously. And was flattered. *Pontifex maximus* was an enormously powerful position.

Artemidorus took off his helmet with its bright, distinctive crest. An excellent rallying point on the battlefield. A distinct disadvantage now when he wished to creep up on someone. He turned to two of the legionaries nearby. The nearest was the reliable Quintus. 'Take off you helmets and follow me,' he said.

Lepidus was asking the crowd to disperse now. Because their presence was a distraction. Slowing down the delicate but vital negotiations they were all so keen to conclude.

Fortunately, he was unusually long-winded. Probably because he was still so emotional, thought Artemidorus. The crowd lingered, waiting for him to finish. And by the time he did, the centurion and his two legionaries were standing behind the troublemaker. Unsuspected. But close.

Lepidus turned and began to climb down off the *Rostra*. The crowd began to break up. '*Ferrata*,' said Artemidorus. 'I'd like a word with you.'

*

The *taberna* tavern, like the *lupanaria* brothel next door was little more than a single room shop with facilities upstairs. Artemidorus and the Iberian ex-legionary sat at a rough wood table. Surrounded by clientele who looked to be little more than slaves. Each of them had a bowl of wine in front of him. The man Artemidorus had christened *Ferrata*, Ironclad, preferred thin, bitter *posca*, though the centurion was paying and was happy to supply something more expensive. He himself preferred *Mamertine* wine. Far more expensive. So much so that he was lucky the tavern stocked it. But it was Caesar's favourite. *And what was good enough for Caesar...* thought Artemidorus. He sipped the rich Sicilian wine and looked the Iberian legionary in the eyes.

'A spy,' said Ferrata.

'What I am. What I would like you to become.'

'What's in it for me? If I say yes?'

'Twenty-five denarii a month. That's better than the eighteen or so you earned in the legion. And I guarantee a bigger plot of land when you finally retire. Your choice of location.'

'I was born in Iberia. On the coast. Between Barcino and Tarraco, the capital.'

'If that's what you want...'

'And twenty-five denarii...'

'A month.'

'Paid up front?'

'Paid when I know I can trust you not to whore it away and disappear.'

'OK, Centurion I'm your man. Do I need to swear the *sacramentum* soldier's oath all over again?'

'No. We'll assume the original one you took is still in force. What's your name?'

'They call me Otho.'

'I'll call you Ferrata. After the Ironclads.'

'What do I call you?'

'Septem.'

'Because you're from the Seventh. Clever. What do you want me to do?'

'Do what you've been doing. Go to the meetings. Listen to the speakers. Ask your questions. Tell me the answers.'

'Is that all?'

'It's all for now. But listen, Ferrata, I need you to go to places I can no longer go to. Up to the Capitoline. What are they saying at the Temple of Jupiter? If they come down into the Forum and start making promises. What do they promise? How do the other soldiers or citizens react? Keep close to the *Libertores*. It's them I want to know about. Understand?'

'I understand. I can do that. Where and when do I report?'

'Report at sunset. Consul Antony's house on the *Carinae*. You know where it is? Come to the *posticum* side entry. It's near the kitchen. You might even get fed if the report is good…'

The Iberian tossed back the last of his wine and rose.

'Oh, Ferrata…' Artemidorus stopped his departure with a word.

'Yes, Septem?'

'Next time you want to roast a senator, ask me first.'

*

Mark Antony was in a good mood. He felt he had outmanoeuvred the enemies of Caesar who now seemed to have spread through the Senate like a plague. And he was more than willing to explain his cunning in detail over *cena*. Which was taken in the *triclinum* this evening. Artemidorus also felt that the day had been a success, though he was less willing to discuss the details than his ebullient host. While the men were still out in the early afternoon, Fulvia and her handmaids had bathed themselves and Antony's sons. Antony and his men had bathed on their return. Artemidorus had been called from the *laconium* to hear Ferrata's report – which had been good enough to earn the ex-legionary a loaf of *emmer* bread.

Antony's dark curls were still wet as he disposed himself luxuriously on the couch he shared with his wife. Lepidus had returned home to his own wife and family. So Enobarbus and Artemidorus had a couch each. The latter feeling a little like a poor relation in his often-mended, recently laundered outfit. Especially as he had missed out on the massage.

'There were really only two propositions before the Senate,' Antony was saying as he munched on a handful of olives. Spitting the stones into a bowl at his side. Into which, Fulvia was putting the shell of the egg she was peeling. 'And the propositions were these. To brand Caesar as a tyrant – in which case his murderers had no case to answer. Or to accept that Caesar was not a tyrant but pass a motion to exonerate his killers. For the maintenance of peace. And the good of Rome.'

'Under the laws of the Republic, a tyrant who seeks individual rule is by definition condemning himself to death. As the fate of Spurius Cassius attests,' said Fulvia, knowledgeably. 'It was on the ruins of Spurius' house that the Temple of Tellus was built. Spurius was executed in the early days of the Republic because he wished to become a tyrant. A king.'

'Just so, my dear,' nodded Antony. 'And that is why it was so cunning of me to hold the meeting there. Everyone present knew that story. And knew the price of tyranny under the law. There was a powerful motion presented that Caesar be declared a tyrant. Many senators spoke in favour of the motion. Starting with Cicero who is already the voice of the *Libertores*. I just sat quietly and let them get on with it. One after another. They had no idea of the trap they were walking into. It was astonishing!'

He paused as Promus and his acolytes removed the *gustatio* first course. The eggs, olives, mackerel and mint accompanied by honeyed wine were replaced by a selection of roast birds, carved at the table into manageable sections. There were chickens, ducks and geese. Larks for those preferring something more delicate. There were also beans and more salad of mallow and rue. With a *Calenian vinum dulce* wine.

'I let them finish, and then I struck,' he continued, gesturing with the drumstick of a goose. 'I said that if the Senate wished to convict Caesar of tyranny, then they should do so. And I would personally oversee the reappointment and re-elections that would result. Because if Caesar was officially condemned as a tyrant, then every single appointment and office he had awarded must be null and void. Every bequest he had made must be returned. Every town and city throughout the provinces must send back the gold and silver he had lavished on them. A process made simpler, perhaps, by the fact that every governor and provincial official appointed by him must also return to Rome for reassignment. Every soldier placed on a farm by him must move off it and come back for resettlement.

'And that's where Dolabella started. He was up on his feet like a startled cat. I had let him share the dais with me because his appointment as consul – on Caesar's authority – had begun with Caesar's death. And he suddenly saw all that power and wealth slipping out of his grasp – after only a day! Poor boy. I thought he was going to burst into tears. Well, he convinced them in the end. His eloquence – and the fact that every man there would also have to give up his honours and stand for re-election all over again. So. The long and the short of it is that Caesar was suddenly no longer a tyrant. All his plans and appointments stand. But, for the sake of peace in the city, the country and the provinces, the men who slaughtered him are formally pardoned.'

'The news went up to the Capitoline with astonishing speed,' Artemidorus informed them, setting aside the fleshless thighbone of a duck. 'Because, according to my man Ferrata, Brutus and Cassius had called a meeting outside the temple by mid-afternoon. There was another big crowd there to hear them. According to my man, Brutus did most of the speaking. He spoke eloquently and I'm certain he had asked Cicero to look over what he was planning to say. He said he and his associates would stay on the Capitoline through fear of the people. And described the attack on Cinna. He said, *Yes*, he had broken his oath to protect Caesar – or avenge him. But he had only sworn that oath under duress. This is the legal bit I think Cicero must have advised on. It has the Ciceronian smell about it. Because Brutus, like all the others, feared Caesar's power. So his oath was by definition null and void.

'And was he right to be frightened of Caesar?' Artemidorus continued. 'Yes. He described Caesar as a despot. He listed the number of people Caesar slaughtered in his conquests. Powerful people. Princes in their lands. Like Vercingetorix, Prince of Gaul. Brought to Rome by Caesar. Imprisoned for five years. Then strangled to death as part of a triumph. He also apparently mentioned Lucius Flavius and Gaius Marullus, both tribunes of the *plebs*, stripped of their office and exiled for removing diadems from Caesar's statues! Who would not fear someone who behaved like that?'

The roast birds were cleared away. To be replaced by a tray of fruit. One of Fulvia's women came in with Marcus and Julius, their sons. A three-year-old and a baby. Fulvia kissed their cheeks. Antony ruffled their hair, clearly embarrassed at showing affection in company. The children went off to bed. The conversation continued.

'But it was towards the end of the speech that Ferrata observed something I think is of vital importance,' said Artemidorus. 'He says that Brutus suddenly asked all of the old soldiers present to make themselves known. Even Ferrata was surprised at how many there were. Brutus started talking directly to them. He told them Caesar had instituted a purposely divisive policy to ensure that his old soldiers never had a chance to turn against him no matter what he did. Or what he planned to become. He explained that the smallholdings, villages and towns Caesar had promised them already for the most part belonged to local people. Peasants. Farmers. Villagers and citizens. Who already lived where the soldiers were promised their land. So under Caesar's plans, the old soldiers would always find themselves at odds with their neighbours. Never really settled. Never able to leave their homes, their wives or families unprotected. Brutus said he had seen it happen in many of the provinces where he had worked. But now he and the *Libertores* were going to put that right. Whoever owned the land a soldier had been promised would be paid a fair price from the public purse. So old soldiers would be welcomed. Bringing riches and decent profits with them. Would settle comfortably. Live peacefully.'

'And that went down well, did it?' demanded Antony with a frown.

'Ferrata says the soldiers cheered.'

Antony's frown deepened. He swore under his breath earning a glare from Fulvia. 'That was clever. I was counting on the old soldiers to stay restless. Now I'll have to think of some way to get them back on our side. Because, remember, no matter what I say or do, the objective remains to execute every single one of Brutus' band of murderers. One way or another.'

*

But as the next day passed, Artemidorus saw the power to complete Antony's revenge beginning to slip further and further from the general's grasp. Soon after dawn, having consumed the briefest breakfast, Artemidorus, Enobarbus and the *centuria* which had been camped nearby, went down to the Forum. Artemidorus watched uneasily as the *comitia* of commoners formed. Called together by Antony to ratify the decisions that the Senate had taken yesterday. Lepidus arrived. He stood with Artemidorus, Enobarbus and the soldiers. Dolabella appeared and joined his co-consul up on the *Rostra*. Technically equal and as much in charge. His position as Caesar's replacement having been ratified by the Senate yesterday along with everything else.

Artemidorus immediately sensed the tension between the two men. But Antony's trap for the Senate had also caught Antony himself. He and Dolabella disliked each other intensely. But the only way to remove Dolabella from the consulship was to condemn Caesar of tyranny. And that was the one thing Antony could never do. So the two enemies had to forge an uneasy alliance in the face of the greater threat.

The general stood grimly silent therefore. While Dolabella seemed to give off a self-satisfied glow. Safe in his powerful position for the moment. Dreaming no doubt of the fortune he could make. Accepting payments for favours done. Bribing and being bribed. And the *comitia* of the People of Rome formed in the Forum at their feet. An overcast and vaguely threatening morning started to become more and more restless.

Then, just as the spy began to hope that things would get no worse, Cicero arrived. As soon as the people of the *comitia* saw him, they started cheering. When Dolabella invited him onto the *Rostra* and asked him to speak, there was nothing Antony could do. Artemidorus knew exactly what the lawyer and orator would say. He was, after all, the voice of the

Libertores. But there was no way that he could predict what the outcome of Cicero's speech would be.

By the time he had finished speaking, the orator had laid much of the blame for Caesar's death on Caesar himself. On his arrogance. His thoughtlessness. His ambition. He further suggested that Caesar had been weakened by the falling sickness. Which, as everyone knew, was getting rapidly worse. So he could even have engineered his own execution. As a way of escaping the horrible extremities that he feared were otherwise soon to destroy him. He explained what the Senate had agreed in yesterday's session. But in such a way as to make it seem that they were being generous to the dead man. And that the *Libertores* had really done everyone, including the sickly Caesar a favour. The last few days, he suggested, were like the storms that had gripped Rome for two nights running. Terrible and destructive at the time. But over now. And soon forgotten.

By the time he had finished, the hundred throats of the *comitia* were calling with one voice, for one thing. That the *Libertores* to come down from the Capitoline. Cicero immediately offered to carry the message himself. But as he came down from the *Rostra*, he noticed Artemidorus. 'And the centurion here will accompany me,' he announced. 'He is already known to Brutus and Cassius. In one capacity or another.'

Once again Antony was left with no choice but to agree.

The crowd of the *comitia* parted for the two men as they walked south, towards the Capitoline. 'Antony seems to be losing his grip on events,' said Cicero, as though there was no one but Artemidorus there to hear him.

'I wouldn't underestimate the general,' Artemidorus answered easily. He caught the eye of Ferrata. Neither man gave any sign of recognition.

'Oh but he makes it so easy to underestimate him,' Cicero continued. They were nearing the outskirts of the crowd. Entering the throat of the *Vicus Jugarius*. The Capitoline hulked threateningly above them. 'What are his estimable qualities? That he can drink more than a *centuria* of normal men? Whore more widely than an entire *cohort*? Sit elbow to elbow with the commonest soldier at table? I hear on one campaign he drank horse urine and ate things that would turn the most intrepid gourmet's stomach.'

'Have you ever been on campaign yourself, sir?' asked Artemidorus gently.

'With Strabo, Pompey's father. And with Sulla.'

'Never outside Italy, then?'

'I have travelled widely, Centurion, if that is what you are insinuating!' Cicero strode on down the *vicus*. Past the opening of the *Clivus Capitolinus* and the untended slopes of the *aquimelium*.

'As a scholar, sir. In comfort I would guess. Not as a soldier on campaign...'

'So, by extension of your logic I am in no position to judge what men might be forced to do on the march. Starting with your general. Antony. Once again, Centurion, I find I may have underestimated you.'

Cicero turned right and began to run up the hundred steps.

*

Brutus and Cassius were nervous. Perhaps even scared. Probably as much to do with exhaustion as anything else, thought Artemidorus. He watched them from a distance, locked in conversation with Cicero. They knew the soldier and spy too well now to allow him within earshot of their conference. Just to make certain, Syrus stood beside him, with the three who had held him yesterday. The Syrian swung his club. Easily. Threateningly.

'You know our business isn't finished, spy,' he said, keeping his voice low. 'Priscus and the boy lie between us, no matter where you hid their bodies. We will have a reckoning, you and I.'

'You and your three friends, if I remember correctly. Shall I bring three of mine too? Or will even numbers scare you and your little helpers away?'

The Syrian fumed in silence. Not daring to go any further by word or deed for the moment. For Cicero, Cassius and Brutus were all looking at Artemidorus as they spoke.

But although they made sure he could hear nothing, they couldn't stop him looking around. Which he did. Pointedly ignoring Syrus and his empty threats. And as far as he could see, the number of *Libertores* had diminished even further. The gladiators were here, but he could no longer see their employer Albinus. Syrus and his group were here. But where was Minucius Basilus? At home, he guessed. With their families. In clean clothes. Bathed. Fed. Having slept in their beds. Who could have calculated that one moment's madness on the morning of the Ides would lead to three sleepless nights and days hiding in a temple?

Cicero broke into Artemidorus' reverie. 'They will only go down if there are hostages to guarantee their safety,' he announced, walking towards the spy, dismissing the gladiators with a wave. Cicero's lips were thin. He was clearly unhappy with this answer. Perhaps he had underestimated more than just Antony, thought the spy with a wry smile.

'Will you take this answer to the consuls, or will I?' he enquired.

'We will take it together, Centurion.'

As they walked back down the hundred steps, Artemidorus asked. 'Have they named the hostages they want?'

'They have. They want Marcus Aemilius Lepidus junior. And Marcus Antonius Antyllus.'

'So it's lucky for Publius Cornelius Dolabella that he hasn't any children yet,' said Artemidorus, frowning.

'I see their reasoning. Their nervousness,' Cicero fumed. 'But I cannot condone it. Young Lepidus has yet to wear the *toga virilis* – unless he went through the ceremony yesterday. Which I doubt. And young Marcus Antonius is a mere baby. How does this make Brutus and Cassius look? Like frightened children!'

'And the weaker they look, the stronger Antony looks,' added Artemidorus. With some relish.

Antony received the news in stony silence. Lepidus with simple fury. But their hands were tied. 'Very well,' said Antony. After a while. 'Enobarbus, alert Marcus Aemilius' wife to send young Lepidus here with a slave or two to keep

264

him company. Septem. Go and tell the Lady Fulvia what's going on. Make it fast.'

Artemidorus ran into the *Carinae* at full speed. He was out of breath by the time he reached Antony's villa and hammered on the door. He had just enough wind left to tell Antony's doorkeeper, 'I need to see the Lady Fulvia. At once.'

Promus came into the *atrium* to see what the commotion was all about and went to summon Fulvia.

'What is it?' Fulvia demanded as she swept into the *atrium* a moment later. 'Promus said it was important. Is Lord Antony all right?'

'Yes, my Lady. He sends a message.'

'And what does the message say?'

Artemidorus could see no gentle way of breaking the news. 'The only way to get Brutus and Cassius down off the Capitoline as the *comitia* demands is to give them hostages. To take their places. In the Temple of Jupiter where they've been hiding. They want young Lepidus. And they want Antyllus.'

Fulvia looked at him with something close to horror on her face. 'Antyllus! But he's only a child. Scarcely more than a baby!'

'There is no alternative, my Lady. It is the will of the people. The *comitia* has spoken. The *Libertores* must come down. This is the one condition they demand. Lord Antony and Lord Lepidus have agreed. That is the end of the matter.'

'But Antyllus!'

'Antony suggested that young Lepidus be accompanied by a slave he particularly likes and trusts. Is there anyone in your household...'

Fulvia stood frowning for a moment. Then she turned and vanished into her quarters.

When she re-emerged, she was leading Antony's three-year-old son by the hand. 'His current favourite is just collecting together everything he will need if he's going to be up there for any length of time.' She took a deep breath. Began to speak. Hesitated. Stooped. Picked up her son and hugged him to her. Pressing his cheek against her own. Staring at Artemidorus with an intensity he found a little unsettling.

'Yes, my Lady?' he said.

'Septem,' she answered, her voice low and vibrant. 'You have done so much for us. For Lord Antony already…'

'What is it you want me to do, Lady Fulvia?'

'Go with them,' she said, speaking in a rush. Aware that she was asking something difficult. Perhaps dangerous. 'Go with them. Stay with them. Bring them back. Bring my little boy home safely to me.'

'Well, my Lady,' he began doubtfully. Quite apart from anything else, he was surprised that a matron such as Fulvia, with her reputation for propriety, would let him see beneath the social mask she usually wore.

But before he could finish speaking, Antyllus' current favourite came out carrying a bag of things he might need, when she accompanied him up onto the Capitoline.

It was Cyanea.

XV

'I'm stuck there like you until things move on,' said Cyanea. 'I can't sit around all day so I help out. And the child's taken a liking to me.'

'Better you than someone who's never been through anything like this before, certainly,' Artemidorus allowed, grudgingly.

'And you're going to be with us,' she added.

'Unless Antony has other ideas. He's my commander after all.'

They were part way down the *Argentium* roadway, heading for the Forum. Antyllus was riding on Artemidorus' shoulders, playing with his helmet crest. The soldier had tight hold of the child's ankles because the helmet's prominent neck guard could knock him off his perch if they weren't very careful.

'Not likely, is it?' continued Cyanea briskly. 'He wants the best for the boy. And he does not want to upset the Lady Fulvia.'

'It's just that the people in charge up there are the people who were all waiting to rape you the last time you met them,' he explained grimly. 'And in the meantime I've killed two of their friends.'

'You've been busy!'

'You don't know the half of it!'

'And I probably don't want to,' she added. Because she already knew him all too well.

They reached the Forum at the junction with the *Comitium* meeting area. Antony was waiting impatiently on the *Rostra*. Dolabella was talking to the crowd that formed the *comitia*. As soon as he saw his son, Antony came down. He lifted him off the centurion's shoulders and held him gently against his breast. Even though it was covered with his armoured breastplate. 'What did Fulvia say?' he asked quietly.

'That Cyanea should go with him…'

'Of course…'

'And that I accompany them. Guard them. Bring the boy back safely.'

'And are you willing to do this, Septem? There's nothing but enemies up there.' He spoke quietly and glanced across to where Cicero was standing. Apparently listening to Dolabella's eloquence. His face folded into a critical frown.

'Yes,' said Artemidorus. 'Unless you have another assignment you feel is more important or better suited to my skills. I gave my word to the Lady Fulvia.'

'No, Septem. Looking after my boy is even more important than looking after me. And I can't think of anyone I would trust to do the job more than you.'

'We just need to wait for young Lepidus, then,' said Artemidorus with a nod. And an unspoken promise to look after the boy better than he had looked after Caesar in the end.

Then Enobarbus came shouldering through the crowd with young Lepidus junior behind him. Accompanied by a slave who looked like Hercules' big brother. Antony gave a laugh of genuine amusement. 'You might not be needed after all, Septem! This youngster seems to have brought a one-man legion!' But then he quietened, his mood darkening once more. 'But we'll need brains as well as brawn. And you gave Fulvia your word…'

Cicero accompanied them again. This time he led them up the road beside the *tablinarium* and onto the steep *Clivus Capitolinus* road. Perhaps as a gesture to Artemidorus, who had Antyllus on his shoulders. As soon as they entered the square in front of the temple, they were surrounded by the remaining *Libertores*. Cassius seemed particularly pleased to see them. 'You see?' he said to Brutus. 'I said they would do it!'

'I didn't doubt they'd do it,' said Brutus angrily. 'I just questioned the necessity! If they'd given their word…'

'They gave their word to protect Caesar!' snapped Cassius. 'Look where that got him! We don't want to end up the same way.'

'An interesting approach to logic Gaius,' said Cicero. 'As the man most responsible for the breaking of that particular oath. But we do not need to debate the point. Your conditions have been met. Lead us all down to the Forum so that Brutus and you can address the *comitia* before they all get bored and disappear.'

As the *Libertores* followed their leaders down the roadway towards the Forum, the gladiators gathered increasingly tightly around the hostages and their protectors. Young Lepidus stood as close to his giant companion as possible. It seemed to Artemidorus that the youngster would have held his protector's hand if his pride had allowed him to do so. He glanced at Cyanea as he lifted Antyllus from his shoulders. 'You!' she snapped at the nearest gladiator. 'Clear the way! Antony's son wishes to view the temple. This is an excellent opportunity to broaden his education! One is never too young to learn!'

The gladiator fell back a little sheepishly. No doubt remembering his own mother or nurse. Cyanea swept through like a felucca under full sail and Artemidorus followed, with the child still in his arms.

They were on the temple steps when the cheering in the Forum started. The applause went on and on. Artemidorus gently put the child down and straightened. That seemed to him to be a very bad sign indeed. Antony may have won the game yesterday. By cunning or by chance. But he seemed to be losing today. One roll of the dice after another.

And on that very thought, an icily familiar voice said, 'You just can't seem to keep away from me and my trusty club now, can you? And how nice of you to bring your whore back too. We have so much unfinished business with both of you.'

*

Enobarbus had never seen Antony look so worried. Though to be fair he was doing a good job of masking his obvious concern. His tribune saw it clearly enough. Few others did. As the cheering went on and on, the *Libertores* gathered round the *Rostra*. First Cassius and then Brutus mounted the steps. To even wilder applause. Antony strode forward. Raised his hand demanding silence. But got no reaction. 'Friends,' he shouted. 'Romans…' But the ecstatic *comitia* just shouted him down.

At a loss, he looked across at Dolabella, who also came forward to try and get himself heard. Again, to no avail. 'Shake hands,' bellowed a voice from the crowd. 'Shake hands to show us you are friends.'

At once the crowd took up the chant. They were neither angry nor threatening. But they would not be denied. The chanting went on and on. Antony at last swung round. With scarcely concealed anger, he shook first Brutus' hands and then Cassius'. Under whose fingernails Caesar's blood was still thick and dark. Dolabella followed suit. Then Lepidus did the same. The *comitia* continued to shout their approval.

But when Brutus went forward to speak, the crowd quietened at once. Except for a hum of lively expectation.

Antony walked nonchalantly to the *Rostra* steps. Descended as though he was simply giving Brutus more space to make his speech. Strolled across to Enobarbus. Stood, apparently casually, beside him. 'We're losing this battle a little too quickly for my liking,' he said under his breath.

'The war's not over yet, General,' answered the tribune bracingly.

'Maybe not. But now is the time for an action to secure at least part of our retreat. Go over to Janiculum. Caesar's villa. Make sure Cleopatra leaves at once. I know she has been planning to go. She has a ship waiting in the harbour at Ostia. But if she hasn't started to move, then she must get under way. Now.'

'But, General…'

'Don't you see? If this all goes against me, then she will be a target for the mob. They hate her. They only accepted her because of Caesar. Now he is gone she is naked. Defenceless. I could protect her if all goes well. But if it goes badly…' He shook his head. His face a worried frown. 'The risks are too great.'

'Queen Cleopatra can protect herself, my Lord. She has her guards… her soldiers…'

'Tribune! The only escape from this situation I can see is to find some way to turn the mob against the conspirators. It will be difficult and full of risk. If I fail, then I will be defeated and if she is still in Caesar's villa she will be in danger from Cassius who hates her and who will have the power to destroy her. If I succeed then the mob will tear apart anyone they hate. Starting with the enemies of Caesar, certainly. But by no means stopping there. And they hate Cleopatra. Can you not see, man? If she is still in Caesar's villa by the end of the *Quinquatria* festival, which starts tomorrow, then there is no end to the danger for her. Especially if Caesar's new gladiatorial games on the next days after it get the people inflamed...'

Enobarbus crossed the Forum to the *Vicus Jugarius* and ran past the Capitoline, under the shadow of the Tarpean Rock, and out through the Carmenta Gate onto the *Campus Martius*. He knew he would find here the only section of the VIIth Legion not camped on Tiber Island. A small cavalry detachment with fleet-footed Iberian horses from *Hispania Ulterior* province. A unit which would simply not fit on the temple-crowded island. Once he was with the cavalrymen, it took mere moments for him to have the fastest of the Spanish stallions saddled. Then, just as Caesar used to do, he vaulted onto its back.

Gripping with his thighs, he caught up the reins and guided the animal over the *Pons Fabricius* at a brisk trot. He picked his way across Tiber Island carefully but easily and crossed the wider *Pons Cestus* at a gallop. The horse needed no urging to take the hill road up to Janiculum as though at the forefront of a charge. He pulled the creature to a halt outside Caesar's villa and dismounted. The stallion stood quietly, nibbling the close-cropped lawn. The door opened before he reached it. A slave hurried out to take the horse's reins. Another, bowing, waited to guide him into the capacious *atrium*.

The whole of Caesar's villa seemed to be bustling. Though there was nothing obvious. It was a feeling. A sensation. He turned to the slave beside him. 'The Queen...' he said.

'… is here, Tribune.' Cleopatra VII Philopator, Pharaoh of Egypt and the most powerful woman in the world, completed his sentence for him. Her voice somewhere between music and magic. Treating him as though he was an intimate. A friend. As always.

He turned and she stole his breath. She made the simplest attire look like a robe of incalculable worth. This one was a plain mourning gown. For Caesar. She was not beautiful. Her face, like Fulvia's, was too strong for that. Her nose too pronounced. Her chin too determined. But her eyes were so dark it was hard to see where their black centres began. Her lashes so long there was no need for the kohl that lined them on ceremonial occasions. Her lips were full. Her mouth at once firm and yet alluring. Prone to twist into a smile at almost any occasion.

And her voice…

At twenty-five years old, she was in her prime. And the perfection of her prime. Yet she retained an irresistible girlishness. A lust for life. She ruled the richest kingdom on earth and yet she took joy in the simplest pleasures. And, it seemed, that everyone who knew her loved her. Every man, at least. Among which number stood Antony. Artemidorus. Enobarbus himself. 'Your Majesty, Lord Antony counsels that you leave this place at once. Things are slipping out of his control in Rome and he fears for your safety.'

'If things are slipping out of Antony's control then he should be looking to his own safety.'

'He will do that, Majesty. But only after he is assured of yours. Can you leave at once? I know your royal vessel is waiting at the harbour in Ostia…'

'Much of the household has already embarked.'

'Then leave, Majesty. Leave now. While the *Via Salaria* is safe and easily passable between here and Ostia. Or do you plan to use your barge and sail down the Tiber?'

'I will take the road. It is less than twenty of your Roman *miles*. I can be aboard well before dark.'

'Would you like me to accompany you, Majesty?'

'I am tempted, naturally. But I have my household guards. I will be safe.' She raised her voice very slightly. 'Charmian! Iras!'

Her two handmaids came immediately. 'The tribune brings orders from Antony. We must leave at once. I wish to be safe aboard my *quinquereme* by sunset. Then we will leave on the first convenient tide. Iras, prepare Caesarion. Enobarbus, please assure Antony. We will be aboard by sunset and sail for Alexandria on the first tide.'

'I will, Majesty. But may I wait until I see you safely on the road?'

'You are as careful as Caesar was. I shall miss him. And, when I arrive home I fear I shall miss Antony as well. But yes. You may wait and watch until I have left.'

'May I send one of your men to tell Antony of our plans?'

'If you wish, oh *careful* tribune.' She gave a sad little laugh that almost broke his heart.

*

Marcus Lepidus senior had clearly spared no expense in his son's education. The youth was extremely knowledgeable. He was also a gifted orator. His voice was mellifluous. Easy to listen to. Seeming to belong to someone older than his years. Like his precocious knowledge and understanding. He loved explaining things. Did so in fascinating depth and detail. And he got on very well with children. The day passed surprisingly easily for Artemidorus and Cyanea, therefore. Almost educationally. They strolled around the Temple of Jupiter Optimus Maximus Capitolinus together with the young man's gigantic protector, listening and learning quite a lot. It was even better than being accompanied by one of the small army of priests who maintained the place. However, Syrus and his gang followed close behind them. Suspicious of every word and act. But Artemidorus doubted that the erudite boy added much to their store of knowledge. Such as it was.

But the child's fascination with the things all around him, and the youth's willingness to explain about them, gave Artemidorus and Cyanea some time to themselves as well. First they went over to young Lepidus' protector. 'Everyone just calls me Hercules,' he told them cheerfully when they asked his name. 'Well, the Romans do. The Greeks call me Heracles. And there are a fair number of Greeks in Lord Lepidus' household. I'm in charge of the young master's physical training. Running. Swimming. Wrestling. Boxing. Riding. Military aspects like sword-play. Javelin. Sling. Bow. How to work in armour.'

'Sounds like my own youth in Sparta,' said Artemidorus nostalgically. 'Does he have to kill a wolf to earn his *toga virilis*?'

Hercules laughed. 'No Centurion…'

'Roman children have it so easy…' Artemidorus shook his head in mock despair.

'Do Spartan youths still kill wolves?' asked Hercules. 'I thought that tradition died out long ago. That Sparta is…'

'A place which holidaying Romans visit? For pleasure and instruction? Maybe so. But my family believed in the old ways. And here I am…'

'Who has filled this boy's head with all this knowledge?' asked Cyanea.

'His father, mostly. Though he has a Greek tutor called Kalikrates for mathematics, oratory, logic…'

Under young Lepidus' tutelage, they admired the outer architecture. In the Greek style. Built by Sulla after the original temple burned down. But dedicated by Catulus after Sulla's retirement and death. It was the oldest consecrated space in the city. After walking around the outside, they entered through the huge double doors. Into the magnificent inner space. Left a little littered and untidy after the *Libertores'* occupation. Though the priests were doing their best to keep it clean if not tidy. But it was still filled with a dazzling array of statues. Shrines. Religious objects. Musical instruments. Objets d'art. Triumphal offerings. Battle flags. Banners. Legionary eagles. Golden crowns. Mosaics and frescoes. All of which the enthusiastic youngster knew all about.

'Much more of this and young Antyllus' head will split,' chuckled Artemidorus.

'I think mine already has,' laughed Cyanea. 'But it's time for the child's *prandium*. So he can rest his mind while he fills his stomach.' She produced soft bread and cool milk. Which the child ate and drank greedily. Fortunately, Lepidus was as careful of his son's body as he was of his education. Antyllus was still tucking into his midday meal when a slave arrived from the *magister equitum* with a basket full of bread, cheese, fruit, water and wine. More than enough to go round.

The meal, which they enjoyed on the temple steps in the early afternoon sunlight, seemed to be yet another matter that Syrus and his men would want revenge for. Neither Basilus nor Albinus, apparently, were taking proper care of the gladiators' bodily needs. Certainly not today at any rate. Syrus, thought Artemidorus, had a lean and hungry look. And he was by no means alone in that.

After their meal, Lepidus senior's slave took the basket away again. Then young Lepidus bounced up with renewed enthusiasm and took them on a guided tour of the temple's outer space. Which was filled with almost as many wonders as the temple itself had been. And yet more priests. As well as the better part of one hundred hungry gladiators. Which was all to the good, thought Artemidorus. Hungry men are not sharp. Hungry men do not stay. Unless Albinus or Basilus sent up some food soon, the gladiators would lose their fighting edge. And then the *Libertores* would begin to lose their gladiators.

Artemidorus followed young Lepidus. Half listening to the boy. Indulging in sporadic conversation with both Hercules and Cyanea. His mind actually occupied with Syrus. He and the gladiator had a reckoning coming. There was no doubt of that. He tried to calculate whether he should bring matters to a head here and now. The temptation to do so was great. For once the *Libertores* felt safe, the gladiators would be dismissed. Then he would lose sight of Syrus. Until he found himself with a dagger in his back. Or his throat cut. Or his head beaten in, down some dark alley one night. Until he found Cyanea raped and murdered. Probably tortured. Unless she simply disappeared. Via Minucius Basilus' whipping post.

And the whole purpose of Cyanea's, Hercules' and his own presence here with the youngsters was to hasten the hour when the *Libertores* would feel secure. And therefore dismiss the gladiators. Which was when he would lose sight of his enemy.

But Syrus had his gang with him – though he was three men down counting Cestus. There were still at least three others besides the club man. Who might well come to his aid. Avenge his death. And he had no idea how many of the other gladiators would be on Syrus' side in a confrontation. Furthermore, there were the youngsters to consider. Antony and the Lady Fulvia had sent him up here to guard Antyllus. Not to put him in the middle of a bloody brawl. He frowned, wrestling with the problem.

'What are you thinking about?' asked Cyanea quietly. Her tone worried.

'How to get rid of Syrus. Permanently. He's a danger. A distraction.'

'He's certainly taking everything personally. Everything you say or do.'

'He has plans for you too, remember.'

'Don't I know it! But I have plans for him. Similar to your plans, I suspect.'

That brought him up short. He knew what Cyanea was capable of. She might even be able to take the club man down. Alone. She would certainly have the element of surprise against the arrogant fool. Who clearly saw her as nothing more than a toy he wished to play his evil games with. And if she did, that would take care of his gang as well. Which muscle-brained gladiator would want to avenge a man killed by a woman?

But before he could take that thought any further, the servant Lepidus sent with *prandium* returned. This time without his basket of food. But with news instead.

'It is all agreed,' he informed them, excitedly. 'The gladiators are to be dismissed. As are the legionaries Lord Lepidus brought over from Tiber Island. There is no need for anyone to keep their guards. They are all friends now. Lords Brutus and Cassius are to dine with Lords Antony and

Lepidus. In friendship. Lord Antony suggested it himself. All of the *Libertores* have been invited to dine with one friend or another. You may all come down and return home.'

*

Fulvia insisted that Artemidorus join them for *cena*. One way and another, he was rapidly becoming one of her favourites. Having saved her husband and protected her son. He was almost a family member in her eyes. And she feared that the strain of entertaining Cassius would make the meal a long-drawn agony for all of them. Which Artemidorus could alleviate.

Antony acquiesced. Indeed, her insistence gave him an idea. 'Enobarbus must join Lepidus,' he announced. 'That way I will have extra ears at both meals.' He sent a messenger to Lepidus before he went into the bath. Satisfied that he had found another positive element in a situation that could have been entirely negative. Artemidorus joined him in his ablutions. Cassius did not, for he was still in the Forum. Antony was pleased about this, for he found that he could discuss his plans and fears with the centurion almost as easily as he did with his tribune.

'Enobarbus will return from Janiculum soon,' said Antony as he and Artemidorus strolled, naked, from the *apodyterium* changing room into the icy *frigidarium*. Artemidorus was pleased to note that even a consul's scrotum clenched at the chill. He and Antony eased themselves carefully into the water. 'I sent him up there to make sure Cleopatra left swiftly and safely. He sent a message to tell me all was well. And that he will return soon and brief me in more detail. That is one positive thing in a day that has otherwise been near disastrous.'

'How so, General?'

'To be forced by such men into sending my son as hostage…'

'But, General, even Cicero observed to me that hiding behind a youth and a child made the *Libertores* look weak.'

'That's something I suppose. But the *comitia* were still far too welcoming of Brutus and Cassius for my taste.'

'We heard the cheers on the Capitoline,' admitted Artemidorus.

'They came near to deafening me!' Antony heaved himself angrily out of the water and strode, streaming, through to the *tepidarium*. Artemidorus followed. This time he hardly noticed the naked nymphs and fauns.

They relaxed, side by side in the warm water. 'It seems that all Rome wants is peace,' continued Antony. 'Peace at any price. That's why the gladiators and the legionaries have all been dismissed. Though once again I'd have preferred to keep my men. But no. The *comitia* insisted... Can so many of them have hated Caesar so much that they will not even consider vengeance?'

'They are frightened,' said Artemidorus. 'They don't know which way to turn. They want to hide their heads like children scared of the dark. They want you to tell them everything is all right. That's all.'

'But everything is not all right. These men have slaughtered my friend. My mentor. I know we had our differences – what men have not? But we settled them. Like men. How can they... how can anyone... think I will just forgive and forget?' Antony's voice was shaking with emotion. His word seemed to echo.

'Make them believe you will.' Artemidorus spoke calmly. Hoping to smooth things over. If the general was still in this mood when Cassius arrived, then he might well do more harm than good.

'I may not have any choice,' said Antony more reasonably. 'I'm isolated in the Senate and now my actions are dictated by the *comitia*. Who, like those self-serving patrician hypocrites, are only looking out for themselves.'

'But that's not entirely the case, is it, General?' asked Artemidorus carefully. 'You outwitted the Senate yesterday and forced them to ratify Caesar's plans. Which the *comitia* supported today. And you have outwitted the *comitia* by going further than they had even considered by inviting Cassius, Brutus and the rest to dine. At a social occasion such as that you may discuss many topics otherwise closed to you. You will be in an excellent position to discover what the *Libertores'* plans are. You and Lepidus, myself and Enobarbus.'

Antony rose thoughtfully, climbed out of the pool. Walked into the *caldarium*. Artemidorus followed him. They eased themselves side by side into the steaming water. Even more gingerly than they had entered the frigidarium's icy pool. 'That's true,' Antony allowed. 'When Enobarbus comes to brief me I will alert him to that possibility in case he can guide the conversation at Lepidus' table. And these so-called *Libertores* will have to draw their plans pretty quickly and carefully. Unless they have done so already. Which I doubt, looking at the way they've handled things so far. Because old Lucius Calpurnius Piso, Caesar's father-in-law, is proposing to publish his will tomorrow. And I have seen a copy. Of the preparatory notes, at least. As you know. He named Albinus as one of his beneficiaries! Did you hear? *Albinus*! Treacherous little cockroach. Then Caesar's funeral will take place the day after tomorrow with a formal public cremation on the *Campus Martius*. Outside the city walls as tradition dictates. They're building the pyre as we speak. Piso is very much in charge, so tradition is very much to the fore. Pompous old fool that he is...'

They moved through into the *laconium* and lay on the massage benches. The *tonsor* waited in the corner, razors at the ready. And the brother-and-sister masseurs stood ready as well. Antony gestured to the brother, who came and started working on his broad, square shoulders. Artemidorus was more than content to relax under the silken, steely fingers of the sister. Oddly enough, the sensuous pleasure that filled his body under the probing pressure of her massaging, oiling and *strigil* scraping also seemed to sharpen his mind.

'And you will get other opportunities to address the people before the funeral,' he observed. 'Your knowledge of the will's contents will give you a chance to plan your speech carefully.'

'It's a pity Calpurnia and her father are against the idea of my doing a funeral oration over his body in the Forum,'

Antony complained. 'As are the *Libertores*. That goes without saying. Though I think I might be able to convince Brutus to let me say a word or two. Still... Without the body...'

'But you don't need the body, General,' said Artemidorus softly. 'Antistius has kept his toga. And has made a complete wax effigy of the corpse.'

*

Artemidorus came out of the bath, oiled, scraped, shaved and relaxed. To find that Fulvia had replaced his battered, often-mended uniform tunic with one of Antony's. Which embarrassed the centurion. But amused the general. And, indeed, the tribune, when he arrived soon after. Even though he was now the worst dressed of the three. And he was too late to fit in a bath into the bargain. Especially as his twin priorities were now to brief Antony on Cleopatra's departure. And to be briefed himself on his unexpected but almost immediate date for dinner at Lepidus'. With Brutus as the other guest.

'Lepidus is going to put Brutus on the same couch as Caesar used, four nights ago, on *Dies Martis*, the fourteenth,' said Antony. Amused by Lepidus' dark irony.

'I must remember to ask Brutus what sort of death he'd prefer,' said Enobarbus. 'Like Albinus asked Caesar that night. Or so I hear.'

'Long and painful for both of them. If I have anything to do with it. Which I plan to,' said the general.

Promus arrived then, informing Artemidorus that there was someone at the *posticum* to see him. So while Antony was briefed by Enobarbus, Artemidorus was briefed by his own secret agent. Ferrata. Who earned another loaf of *emmer* bread and this time a small *amphor* of wine.

As Enobarbus was being shown out, Cassius arrived and was shown in. He had come directly from the Forum where he had been talking to the crowd. Who received his words enthusiastically once again. Especially when he arranged for the gladiators to be dismissed. Prompted by the sight of Lepidus' *centuria* of soldiers marching back to Tiber Island. But he was hardly dressed or prepared appropriately for dinner with one of the most powerful men in the world. He had not been shaved since the morning of the Ides. He had not bathed since the afternoon before that. His toga was bloodstained. No longer anything like white. Had been slept in. Stank.

'My dear man!' said Antony with characteristic, unthinking generosity. 'Please feel free to use my baths.'

'I am not here to bathe. I can do that at home,' snapped Cassius. 'I am here as a gesture of good faith which you yourself suggested. I am here to dine. Which I hope we can do quickly. Then I can go home to my wife and family. Only then will I be able to change out of this toga and bathe.'

'Well,' said Antony affably. 'I hope you haven't still got your dagger hidden under there!'

'I have indeed,' Cassius growled. 'And it's a big one that I'll be happy to use on you if you're thinking of becoming another tyrant like Caesar!'

Antony laughed a little hollowly. Clapped his hands. Cassius might not be here to bathe, but fortunately Antony was a courteous and punctilious host. Promus arrived almost at once with a bowl of steaming water and a slave whose job was to wash the guest's feet and hands. Very thoroughly.

Antony was a gourmet of almost Lucullan proportions. And on the way to his bath he had ordered his cooks and Promus to outdo themselves in the matter of food. And, particularly, wine. Cassius had the reputation of being a modest eater. And an abstemious drinker. But after four days on the Capitoline, he was likely to be unusually hungry. And thirsty.

No sooner had the honoured guest placed himself wearily on the *lectus* couch in the beautifully appointed *triclinum* dining room. Next to that occupied by Artemidorus and opposite the third occupied by his host. And the chair beside it where his hostess was seated as tonight was a formal occasion. Than slaves appeared with bowls of iced water. Everyone washed their hands again. The slaves gave each person two cloths. One to dry their fingers. Another to wipe their mouths. Then a tray groaning with *gustatio* was carried in by three servants. Promus followed with an *amphor* of honeyed wine.

'You must try the wine, Lord Cassius,' suggested Antony. 'It is *Mareoticum*. Queen Cleopatra herself brought it from

Alexandria. Soft and sweet and good for the digestion. It will complement the thrushes stuffed with truffle perfectly. And you might like the sea urchins.'

Cassius was too courteous to refuse. Especially after having been so rude in answer to Antony's joke about the dagger. And, although he only sipped the liquor, it had an immediate effect on his empty stomach. So much so that Artemidorus began to suspect Antony of trying to make his guest drunk. *In vino veritas*, as Alcaeus the poet observed, he thought. Unlike Brutus, the lifelong Stoic, Cassius had the reputation of following the Epicurean philosophy. Had famously converted to it four or so years ago. Not necessarily always in the matters of appreciating fine food and wine. But in his ideas of liberty and justice.

However, Cassius seemed to be grudgingly impressed by what Antony's servants were setting out before him. His wish that the meal be over quickly receded. He gestured at the roast thrush and a slave dismembered it for him, placing it within easy reach. Pouring a little pepper sauce over it. Cassius leaned forwards and took a piece, savouring it. Clearly trying to control his hunger. For fear of betraying any weakness.

Conversation was at first strained, almost monosyllabic. There seemed to be little room for social chit-chat. In the face of the momentous events they were all caught up in. And yet those events also were difficult to approach in any way. It was, thought Artemidorus, as though Scipio Africanus and Hannibal had sat down to discuss elephants and alps.

But Fulvia at least tried. 'Your wife, the Lady Junia. Is she well?'

'She was well enough the last time I saw her.' Cassius reached for another morsel.

'And your son, Gaius junior?'

'Assumed his *toga virilis* on the morning of the Ides.'

In the face of his grudging answers, Fulvia refused to give up. 'Lord Brutus' wife, the Lady Porcia,' she said. 'I hear she has been unwell. Have you had news of her?'

'Not since your spy, here, informed Brutus she was not dead after all,' answered Cassius, taking a long sip of Cleopatra's priceless wine. 'As had been told to the poor man by some of his over-excited slaves. Fortunately in error.'

'How dreadful! He must have been so worried!'

'He and I had other matters on our minds. At the time.' He drank again, preoccupied by his thoughts. Gestured at the sea urchins. The slave serving him broke one open and passed him a spoon to eat it with. He wiped his fingers, took the spoon. Ate. 'These sea urchins are very good.' He dropped the shell on the floor. Another grudgingly courteous gesture. He reached for another piece of the stuffed lark. Its bones joined the urchin shell on the floor.

'I'm sure you did,' said Fulvia innocently. As though she had no idea what these matters actually were. 'More wine? Promus, our guest's cup…'

'But your plans, Lord Cassius,' asked Artemidorus. His eyes narrow as he calculated how far he could go without alerting Cassius to his deeper designs. His hidden agenda. The information Ferrata had supplied. 'What do you and Lord Brutus intend to do next?'

'Do? Why nothing! Everything is done! The tyrant is dead. And declared not to have been a tyrant at all. For reasons of political expediency. Rather than actual fact. The Republic is reinstated. The people are free. There is nothing left to do. Except to keep our daggers sharp in case more not-tyrants like Caesar appear.'

'But Caesar's dictates stand,' probed the spy quietly. Pretending not to notice Antony's thunderous frown. 'You and your fellow *Libertores* are declared innocent of any crime. And the Republic goes on forever?'

'Just so! As Lord Brutus observes, it has lasted four hundred years so far. It may well last four hundred more. Lord Brutus likes to think in centuries.'

'You yield all power to the Senate and the *comitia*?' Artemidorus persisted.

'That is how the Republic functions! Has done for four hundred years as I keep saying. Yes. A little more wine. The truffle stuffing was superb by the way, Lady Fulvia. I may ask to take a little home with me.' Cassius became more expansive. Took another draught of the wine.

'And plans,' he said, harking back to Artemidorus' earlier comment. 'There were no *plans*. Beyond the act itself. It was a spontaneous outpouring of Republican sentiment against a tyrant who planned to have himself declared king. We do not allow kings in Rome. The Servian walls were built to keep such despots out. That's why Sulla expanded the *pomerium*. Despots, autocrats, potentates, pharaohs or emperors. All forbidden.' He gave a bitter laugh. 'That is one reason that Caesar's Egyptian whore was kept in his villa on the Janiculum. She calls herself a pharaoh. We do not allow pharaohs in the city any more than kings. In Rome the people rule. And the people alone.'

'I understand the *comitia* wishes to give both yourself and Lord Brutus great rewards for what you have achieved,' said Artemidorus after a moment. Changing the subject carefully as Cassius and Antony exchanged frowns. 'Honours. Titles. Treasure. Land.'

'Reward!' snapped Cassius, his voice seeming to linger over the word. 'We did none of this in hope of reward! Accepting anything would only cheapen the act. The freedom of Rome is all the reward we sought. Lord Brutus has explained it all. Over and over again.'

'And this is also your view, Lord Cassius? I understand Decimus Albinus and Minucius Basilus have differing ideas to Lord Brutus'.'

'This is the view of all the *Libertores*!' Cassius gestured forcefully. A little wine slopped out of his cup. 'Lord Brutus has talked to them. Made them understand. Even if our refusal offends or upsets the *comitia*. Or, indeed, the Senate itself. We must hold firm. Stand together. Above such petty concerns as rewards! Money. Power. Social standing. Villas. Estates. What are these beside *honour*. *Pietas*; our duty to our mother and father – Rome! That is Lord Brutus' view. And he speaks for us all!'

Promus and the servants removed the first course and returned with the *prima mansae* main course. The food was on the theme of the elements. Air was represented by a range of roast and stewed birds, variously stuffed and sauced. Many still dressed in their colourful feathers. Parrots. Doves. And to one side, a flamingo. Water by a sturgeon, stuffed with eels. And a turbot full of shrimp. Earth by roast hares and rabbits. A badger. Boiled, returned to its skin. A ham boiled with bay leaves and figs. Served in a crust shaped like a boar. Fire by a pair of peacocks in all their glory, fully feathered. Tails fanned wide. Standing in for the phoenix.

And the *amphor* of wine accompanying it was even larger than the first. 'The best Falernian,' said Antony. 'Well aged. It's probably older than I am. You must try a little, Lord Cassius. It is particularly good with the gamier meats. Like the badger…' This time Cassius did not need any further prompting to eat. Or drink. Or talk.

By the time Cassius left in his litter, his escort carrying several food-filled parcels, he had talked quite a lot. And in due course Enobarbus reported that Brutus, too, had said more than was wise at Lepidus' table. With good wine and careful prompting. The three men and Fulvia sat together round the table in the *tablinum*, talking far into the night.

At last Artemidorus summed up what they had learned and what they believed. 'So,' he said. 'They had no real plans beyond the murder. They believed it would all end there. And now that they find this is not in fact the case, their united front is beginning to crumble. Brutus is taking the moral high ground. He did it all for *pietas* and the Republic. Any kind of reward will sully his pure action. Lessen his honour. Cassius is more pragmatic, in spite of what he says. He may well take whatever he is offered. And the others are in it for anything they can get. So they are already tearing themselves apart. Already in danger of offending the *comitia*. The people they say they did all this to serve and set free. And, in the meantime, if we move swiftly, we have the opportunity to turn the tables on them. And we have two potent and potentially deadly weapons we can use against them.

'Caesar's will.

'And Caesar's funeral.'

XVI

'We don't need to spy on the murderers anymore,' Artemidorus said at breakfast next morning. 'I thought it over and talked it through with Cyanea last night. We need to know the plans of four other groups, though. That way we can make the most of our chances during the next two days.'

'Oh, that's what you two were doing!' said Enobarbus round a mouthful of honeyed *puls* porridge. '*Talking…*'

Artemidorus ignored him. Though it was lucky Cyanea was in the kitchen, he thought. To spare her blushes from this crude soldiers' talk. He frowned. Irritated more than embarrassed. It seemed out of character for Enobarbus. Though Antony, he knew, had a reputation for coarseness. Subtlety, like oratory, had never been a strong point with him.

'You *talk* like that too often,' Antony sniggered, like an actor on his cue. 'And one of you will end up with a bad back.'

The spy ploughed on regardless. Moving into his intelligence officer role. 'First, we need to know what the legions are thinking – maybe planning. Next we need to know what the people, and the *comitia* are thinking. Then we also need to know what Piso, Lady Calpurnia and the Lady Atia, Caesar's niece and Octavian's mother, are planning for the funeral. Caesar left the plans for his funeral with the Lady Atia, I think.'

'I have a copy in his papers, just as I have a copy of the notes for the will that old Piso's going to present later today,' said Antony. 'They're both just outlines but they give some idea.'

'But Caesar didn't expect to be murdered of course,' Artemidorus continued. 'So the three of them might have made some changes. We really need to know just how far along they are with the preparations for tomorrow's ceremonies. Especially you, Lord Antony, because you will almost certainly be involved. You are the most appropriate man in Rome to give his oration. You were, after all, his co-consul, his friend and his relative. Though I know the blood relationship is distant. But it still exists.

'And lastly, we need to confirm what the gods have in mind. Though as you know, I always prefer to double-check on their guidance personally where I can. As I did, for instance, with Caesar.'

'Well, taking the last one first,' said Antony, suddenly more quiet and thoughtful, 'we can ask Spurinna. His predictions for Caesar seem to have been as accurate as yours. The gods spoke to him as clearly as your intelligence gathering spoke to you. Not that any good came of it. Spurinna has been sacrificing on the altar to Mars out on the *Campus Martius* every morning we've been in the Temple of Tellus and sending word to me. He's seen nothing unusual so far...'

'So we can keep consulting him,' Enobarbus said, breaking off a piece of *emmer* bread to dip in his warm honeyed goat's milk. 'I don't know how we're going to check on the funeral arrangements. They are intensely private. We can't just walk into the *Domus* and ask. Not even Lord Antony can. Until he's invited...'

'We can offer to help,' suggested Artemidorus. 'Cyanea is wasted here, even if young Antyllus has appointed her his new favourite. And if we're contacting Spurinna anyway, we can ask him to send Puella. Kyros can escort her in case of any trouble. Preparing the body is traditionally woman's work and they are both thoroughly capable. And I'm sure the Ladies Calpurnia and Atia will need all the help they can get. It's a huge project after all and time is short. And we'll have two sets of eyes on the process.'

'Good,' said Antony. 'That might work.'

'We can count on Quintus to keep a close ear on what the Seventh is up to,' said Enobarbus. 'And young Oppius, your replacement, will alert us as to anything the council of centurions decides.'

'That just leaves the people and the *comitia*,' said Antony. 'Can we rely on this new man of yours? Ferrata?'

'Yes. He seems solid enough. But I think he'll be swamped. There are people streaming into the city from everywhere. Some of them were coming for the *Quinquatria* festival anyway. Especially with the gladiatorial games. Teachers and some children on holiday. More teachers to collect their pay. Artists, weavers, poets – everyone whose work is sacred to Minerva. They all have a holiday on her festival.' He paused, suddenly, a dried fig halfway to his lips. 'And that gives me an idea too. Can we send a message to Lepidus? His son's tutor Hercules is on holiday today. He could join the team. He seems quick-thinking as well as skilled in all physical and military matters. And he's huge. An excellent ally if we can borrow him.

'But, as I was saying...' he continued as he bit into the fig and chewed thoughtfully. 'A large number of the newcomers are old soldiers worried about the land grants Caesar promised them. I'm not sure how many there are – but quite a few. Too many for one man to handle, certainly. Maybe even for two. I think we need someone else out there on the ground besides Ferrata. And Hercules if Lepidus lets us have him.'

'Well, who do you suggest?' asked Antony. 'We seem to have assigned every member of the intelligence *contubernium* and then some.'

'We have one more undercover operative,' said Artemidorus. 'We aren't at odds with Albinus' or Minucius Basilus' gladiators anymore. Not that they're likely to be out on the city streets. They'll be practising for the four days of games in the arena that Caesar added to the festival. Where, if fortune smiles, one half of them will kill the other half. So, the long and the short is this: once again we have the Samnite.'

*

Enobarbus stood beside Spurinna at the sacrificial altar on the *Campus Martius*. It was still Mars' month so sacrifices were dedicated to him at least in part. And were consequently virile. Though today's festival of *Quinquatria* on *Dies Solis*, Sun Day the nineteenth day of Mars four days after the Ides, was sacred to Minerva. The sacrifice, a young bull, lay disembowelled on the altar. Its empty belly gaping. Its entrails were spread across the largest of the sacrificial bowls and Spurinna was bent over them, his hands and arms red to the elbow. As Caesar's murderers' had been. A calculated gesture, mused the tribune, remembering Brutus' insistence that Caesar was not a victim. But a sacrifice. 'Tell Antony there is nothing to be feared today.' Spurinna interrupted his dark thoughts. 'The omens seem fair.'

'He'll be glad of that. The so-called *Libertores* are all back in the Senate this morning. For the first time since the murder. To hear Piso reading Caesar's will. After they've congratulated themselves and each other. And Antony himself, as likely as not. For maintaining the peace. So far.'

'Is there anything else Lord Antony requires of me? Today is one of my busiest. I can hardly count the women who call on me to give them predictions on this day. Above all days. Praise to Minerva and *Quinquatria*! I gave Puella a happy prediction earlier. Before sending her over to the *Domus* with young Kyros as your message requested.'

'Thank you. No. There is nothing more Antony requires of you today. If the gods are satisfied, then so is he. And so will your helpers and the priests be. That is a fine-looking bull. He will make good eating! A pity I can't take him over to my legionaries. They hardly ever get to eat meat.'

'That's probably just as well,' said the soothsayer. 'Meat is bad for them. Everyone knows that.'

Enobarbus did not go directly to the Forum or to the Temple of Tellus. He knew well enough what was going on in the Senate meeting there. As he had told Spurinna. He would almost certainly not be needed until Piso read the will. In the meantime, he walked across the Fabricius bridge he had ridden over yesterday on his way to see Cleopatra. On Tiber Island he soon found the men of the VIIth Legion. Camped in and around the temples there. And the two he needed to speak to.

After briefing young Centurion Oppius and their arms expert, ancient Legionary Quintus, he returned over the *Pons Fabricius* and made his way back towards the city. As he neared the Carmenta Gate, however, he really began to understand the point Artemidorus made earlier. The road was extremely busy. The city heaving. He had to queue to pass through onto the *Vicus Jugarius*. And it was a long, slow dawdle round the Capitoline and up to the Forum.

He had never seen the city centre so busy. The shops and stalls had been closed in fear of rioting and looting since the Ides and until today. Now they were all open for business. And doing a brisk trade. The *tabernae* inns must be as tightly packed as the locals' *insulae*. And as for the *lupanaria* brothels – the girls would be making their fortunes. Though they might not be able to walk for a week or so afterwards. Especially if this incredible mass of people stayed here for Caesar's extra four days' of gladiatorial games.

But, he noticed as soon as he entered the Forum, there was a kind of current. As though the crowds were a river of human bodies. Moving slowly but relentlessly towards the Temple of Tellus. As he pushed ahead, he looked around for Ferrata and the Samnite. And this man called Hercules that Artemidorus described. But he could see none of them. In spite of the apparent size of the tutor. And the distinctive headdress on top of the faceless Samnite's iron-visored helmet. How strange, he thought. That the moment Septem put on the Samnite's armour he seemed to become someone else entirely. And that realisation stirred something in the military intelligence officer. It was one of the reasons Septem made such an excellent secret agent. When he went undercover, he almost disappeared.

But the tribune was not above doing a little undercover work himself. Because he was not fully armed, only those who knew him could guess at his profession or seniority. So they spoke freely and excitedly all around him. And answered his questions with unthinking candour. There were men and women from the *latifundia* farms around the city. Most come for the holiday. Some with baskets of produce to sell. Some to hear more news of Caesar. And of his will. There were representatives of the local Jewish community who had been granted rights and freedoms by Caesar and who had come to repay him with their prayers and lamentations. Who planned to stay and repeat their ritual elegies each evening until the funeral games were over at the very least.

But most of all, there were the soldiers. Recently retired from the legions. There were Galicians from the IIIrd, Gauls from the VIIIth, Iberians like Ferrata from the VIth and the IXth. Especially from the VIth. Because Caesar had disbanded the legion after the hard-fought battle of Munda. Ferrata and his friends wanted confirmation that their land around Arelate would be delivered as promised. That the proposed settlement of *Colonia Iulia Paterna Arelatensium Sextanorum*, would stand as Caesar planned it should.

The single topic of conversation they all shared was Caesar. What had he promised them? Would his promises be kept? Who were these *Libertores* who had murdered him? Why had he not been avenged? Where were his friends in the Senate? All of whom had formally sworn a great oath to honour, serve and protect him? Where were his friends on the streets?

By the time he reached the Temple of Tellus and shouldered his way through the crowd there, his face was folded into a very worried frown indeed. The presence of the soldiers seemed to have shifted the balance somehow. Yesterday the mood of the crowd had been lighter. They had been amused at the sight of Antony's breastplate under his ceremonial robes. But these men were angry. And a good number of them were armed.

He really had to get to Antony and warn him.

*

Artemidorus watched through the eye slits of the Samnite face mask. Enobarbus ran up the steps onto the portico of the temple. Frowning. Apparently too preoccupied to notice that he had actually pushed right past him. Samnite headdress and all. He was standing beside the statue of Ceres. Hercules was over by the statue of Quintus Cicero. These were the only places where it was possible to stand and watch the crowd without being jostled or swept away. The spy had no idea where Ferrata was. But he suspected he would be somewhere in the heaving mass close by.

There was an atmosphere of lively expectation, tinged with an edge of impatience. And a current of anger which surfaced every now and then in confrontations and shouting matches. But no actual fights. Yet.

As Enobarbus was shown into the temple, Artemidorus got a brief view of the interior, as he had done yesterday. Antony and Dolabella were sitting in gilded *curule* chairs. Side by side on the dais. Facing the packed senatorial seats. In front of the two consuls stood the tall figure of Caesar's father-in-law Lucius Calpurnius Piso. Also facing the Senate. Holding a papyrus scroll. Obviously reading from it. Then the doors closed once again and there was nothing more to see.

A rustle of expectation ran through the crowd. Many of them had seen what Artemidorus had seen. And they knew as well as he did what was going on behind the closed temple doors.

Piso was reading Caesar's will to the Senate.

Artemidorus fervently hoped that the contents of the actual document were not too different from the digest Antony had received along with the other personal papers from Calpurnia. Or a good number of the plans they discussed late last night and early this morning would come to nothing.

But time dragged on and the doors of the temple remained stubbornly shut. The crowd in the temple grounds continued to grow. And those who had arrived first started to become even more restless. Their irritation spreading rapidly throughout the gathering multitude. An irritation, Artemidorus calculated grimly, exacerbated by the fact that it was getting hotter. As the sun crept up towards its noonday position in a lightly overcast sky. People were becoming thirsty. Hungry. Increasingly desperate to relieve themselves. And the nearest public latrines were quite a way distant. Like the nearest *tabernae* taverns.

To pass the time and take his mind off bodily functions, he tried to work out what must be happening in the Senate meeting. Piso would be taking his time reading the will. He was an old-fashioned, punctilious man. Seemingly much older than his late son-in-law. Though they were actually the same age. When, at last, Piso finished reading the will, the Senate would have to vote on it to ratify it. But wait! Would they actually debate and vote on it section by section? Or would they wait until it was all read and then debate and vote? It was taking so long he began to suspect that they must be voting on each individual section and bequest.

And once the will was voted through or voted down, that was only the beginning. Were there appendices? Codicils? Who were the executors? Were they to the Senate's liking? More debate. More voting. Then, once the will was dealt with, there would be the matter of the funeral. A pyre was already being erected on the *Campus Martius* beside the tomb of Caesar's beloved daughter Julia. But there would need to be a lively debate about the procedeure for taking Caesar's body from the *Domus* to the pyre. Where would the body be displayed? Who would do the oration? Caesar had no close male relatives in Rome. But Cassius, Brutus and the rest would not be happy at the prospect of allowing the next most logical candidate do the job. Because, as they had already discussed, that candidate was Antony.

Preparations at the *Domus* would be well under way, especially with Cyanea and Puella helping. But who would actually pay? State funerals like Caesar's were lengthy and expensive. Sulla's had been a carnival. A performance. A circus. The funeral games alone had lasted days. And Sulla had been accompanied to the Elysian Fields by the spirits of hundreds of gladiators slain in his name. If the expenses were coming out of Caesar's personal fortune that was one thing. If the Senate voted for the Republic to meet the cost, then that was something else again...

Artemidorus' reasoning had reached this stage when the doors opened. Antony and Piso appeared. With Enobarbus a couple of steps behind Antony. For a moment the crowd went wild. Shouting, cheering and applauding. Then Antony held up his hand and there was instant silence. Silence so intense it was almost like a sound. 'Friends,' he said, his voice carrying easily over the expectant hush. 'Here is Caesar's father-in-law Lucius Piso. I urge you to listen courteously to him as he reads Caesar's will. But before he does so, I wish to inform you of several things. First, the will has been accepted and ratified by the Senate. Like all the rest of Caesar's appointments, decisions and bequests have been. There was debate about some of the provisions. But in the end they were all accepted. Secondly, I must inform you that I have been named – and duly appointed – as one of the executors of the will. Alongside Lucius Piso himself.'

The crowd burst into loud applause at this, and cheering broke out again. Until Antony raised his hand once more.

'As executor, I now have many duties to perform. But there is more. The Senate have agreed that Caesar's body will be displayed in the Forum tomorrow. At which time, I will present a brief oration. As the Senate has agreed. At the urging of Marcus Junius Brutus, whom I thank. Then the body will be taken to the *Campus Martius* where Caesar's funeral pyre is already being built. Furthermore, the Senate has agreed that the Republic itself will meet all the costs of the funeral. After which, the four days of *Quinquatria* games that Caesar himself instituted, will be dedicated to him.

'Friends, as you will understand, there is much for me to do. I have been summoned to the *Domus* to engage in the preparations for the funeral tomorrow. So I must leave you.

'But, as I say, I urge you most strongly to listen quietly and calmly to Lucius Piso. Quietly and calmly, friends.'

And having delivered that short speech he ran down the steps and strode through the crowd that parted for him. With Enobarbus immediately in his wake. Brushing past Artemidorus and marching onwards.

But Enobarbus lingered for an instant before following. 'What did you think of that?' he breathed.

'I think it was carefully designed to start a riot,' Artemidorus answered.

Enobarbus gave a bark of laughter. 'You wait,' he said. Throwing the last words over his shoulder as he followed his general before the crowd closed in once more. 'You wait 'til Piso reads the will!'

*

Piso's voice went with his appearance and his reputation, thought Artemidorus. It was thin, precise. Punctilious.

'I have here the will of the Divine Gaius Julius Caesar,' he said. Almost inaudibly. Then he cleared his throat, spoke louder and repeated himself. '…Gaius Julius Caesar, *Pater Patriae*, *Pontifex Maximus*, Consul of Rome, Dictator for Life…'

'Get on with it!' yelled a voice from the crowd. And the cry was immediately taken up, drowning out Piso's attempt to list all of Caesar's honours and titles.

Wounded, Piso waited for calm to be restored. Then he continued. 'I Gaius Julius Caesar, *Pater Patriae* et cetera, et cetera…' He was not going to risk the indignity of being shouted down again, 'do hereby will and declare the following. First Bequest: That two thirds of my personal fortune, lands, properties and estates other than those mentioned below, I bequeath to my great-nephew, Gaius Octavianus, grandson of my beloved sister Julia and son of my niece Atia Balbus Caesonia. Who I hereby adopt as my son and heir. To whom I also bequeath my name, Gaius Julius Caesar. To him and to his heirs in perpetuity…'

The crowd stirred. Artemidorus found it hard to read their mood. Some of the soldiers knew Caesar's great-nephew, whom they called Octavian. He was a sickly but intrepid nineteen-year-old. Currently studying in Apollonia. He had been with his great-uncle on some of his campaigns. Most recently in Spain. Where he had arrived in spite of illness. Shipwreck. And a dangerous journey through enemy territory. He was a popular lad. Everyone seemed fairly content with his nomination as principal benefactor.

But then, almost immediately, things started to slide out of control.

'However,' Piso read, raising his voice once again, 'should any sons be born to me before my death – but by my death should they be left as babies or infants yet to assume the *toga virilis* – then I place their raising and education under the guardianship of my dear friends and associates Marcus Junius Brutus, Gaius Trebonius and Gaius Servilius Casca…'

'Hey,' shouted someone. 'Weren't these three amongst the ones who murdered him?'

Artemidorus thought the voice sounded like Ferrata's but he couldn't be certain.

'Yes!' shouted others in return. 'They were all *Libertores*… Murderers…'

'*Leaders* of the murderers…'

But the momentary interruption stopped when Piso held up his hand again. '…to each of whom I leave money and valuables to the sum of…'

Whatever the sum amounted to, it was lost beneath the howls of outrage. More shouts. Much louder. Even Artemidorus was shocked. That so many of the men he trusted so completely – willing even to give them guardianship of some infant son – should be among his murderers! And that he was bequeathing them not only his trust. But also his money and valuables. This was a detail that had not been included in the outline amongst Caesar's documents. He wondered how badly Antony had been shocked. Then he began to wonder what other shocks and surprises were coming. As Piso called for silence so he could continue reading.

Suddenly Enobarbus' parting words took on an extremely sinister implication. *Wait 'til Piso reads the will.*

Piso waited for silence to return before continuing. 'Second Bequest: The remainder of my personal estate I bequeath to my next nearest living male relatives, Lucius Pinarius and Quintus Pedius, to be shared equally between them.' There was nothing controversial here, so the crowd settled again.

'Third Bequest: To the People of Rome, to their families and heirs…' Piso paused, clearly expecting some reaction. But there was none. Other than an expectant hush. 'I bequeath my villa, walks and gardens on the Janiculum Hill beyond the Tiber for their use and enjoyment. Also in perpetuity.'

'But that's where he housed Queen Cleopatra!' said a lone voice, full of wonder.

'Cleopatra!' said another, awed. 'And he's given it all to us!'

That was the last articulated sentence Artemidorus heard before wild applause began again. But even beneath the cheering, he heard snatches of conversation. The beginnings of real confusion. Anger. Outrage.

'...But Brutus said he was a *tyrant* seeking to rob us...'

'...steal away our freedom. But now he gives us freedom to walk...'

'...it's not right! They lied. The *Libertores*. He wasn't a tyrant. They didn't do it for us at all...'

The centurion's stomach clenched as it sometimes did when the tide of battle suddenly turned against him and his men. There was real, immediate danger here.

Piso's hand went up once more. This time it took longer for the crowd to settle. But when he said, 'Fourth Bequest: To every adult male citizen of Rome...'

Everything went absolutely still. Surprised, Piso looked up and lost his place. So he began again. 'To every adult male citizen of Rome in Rome at this time, from my personal fortune, I bequeath three hundred *sestercii*, or seventy-five *Attic drachmas*. To be paid in coin. As at my triumphs.'

Artemidorus looked around at the stunned faces. Three hundred *sestercii* wasn't quite as much as Caesar had given at the last of his triumphs on his return from Spain. But it was still more than Ferrata and his soldier friends earned in almost half a year. The cheering started again. This time it was so loud that the disguised spy heard none of the comments that his neighbours were making. But he was certain there were some. He could almost smell the anger and outrage. Almost taste it.

This time Piso had to wait a long time with his hand in the air.

Then he continued. 'Addenda to the main Bequests: I name as my principal heir in the second degree, in case that Gaius Octavianus cannot for any reason accept my bequest to him, my trusted friend and close associate over many years Decimus Junius Brutus Albinus. Whom I hereby adopt as my son and to whom I also bequeath my name: Caesar.'

The stunned silence at this news allowed Piso to complete his reading. 'In pursuance of which, I name as my chief executors, my father in law, Lucius Calpurnius Piso

Caesonius, and my friend and associate Marcus Antonius who I also name as my heir in the second degree.'

Piso straightened. Filled his lungs. 'This is the will of Gaius Julius Caesar,' he shouted. 'As agreed, authorised and endorsed by the Senate of the Republic of Rome. On behalf of the People of Rome. On this *Dies Solis*, four days after the Ides in the month of Mars, *Ab Urbe Condita* since the founding of the city 710.'

*

'Why didn't they riot?' asked Enobarbus. 'I was certain they were going to riot.'

'It was the last bit, I think. It just seemed to stun them.' Artemidorus shrugged. He didn't really understand it either. 'It seemed to me that they were on the very edge. That almost anything else would have set them off. But that final section simply took the wind out of their sails. It was very strange. To see a crowd behave like that!'

'What? About Antony being executor? Or that he was heir in the second degree? That came close to stunning Antony – it wasn't in the outline he's read.'

'No. The bit about Decimus Brutus Albinus. It was the irony. The scale of the betrayal, I'd guess. That one day Decimus Albinus should be held up by Marcus Junius Brutus and the rest as the heroic heart of the *Libertores'* plot. The man who finally talked the over-ambitious tyrant into attending the fatal Senate meeting. In spite of the terrible auguries. In spite of the warning dreams and wonders. Who actually led him into the chamber by the hand. Like a lamb to the slaughter. Who supplied the gladiators as a bodyguard for the murderers.

'Then, that only four days later, this same Decimus Albinus should be named Caesar's heir. Adopted as his son. Bequeathed Caesar's name. It seemed to focus all the rest of it. That so many of the men mentioned in the will as close and trusted friends should have taken their daggers to him. Brutus, Trebonius, Gaius Casca. And Decimus Albinus worst of all. It was more than they could comprehend. It simply seemed to stun them. And so they went away quietly. And did nothing.'

It was late afternoon. The two men were in the *tablinum* of Antony's villa, where they had met after the crowd dispersed. So silently. So sinisterly. There was no sign of Antony. Or of Cyanea. Who were both almost certainly still in the *Domus* getting ready for tomorrow. Only Antony had been invited to the preparations which were intensely private and the responsibility of the women. So the tribune had been sent away.

In Antony's continued absence, the *cena* that Fulvia presented was simple. Eggs, olives and salad. Bread. Fish, meat, *puls* flavoured with *garum*, intensely salty fish oil. Fruit. Water and wine. Quickly but courteously consumed. Which suited both men. The streets might be quiet, but the atmosphere in them was still tense. As soon as they had eaten, Artemidorus and Enobarbus went out again, side by side. Unarmed. With no disguise. Their objective to go to one or two of the taverns favoured by soldiers and to listen to the conversation there.

'The atmosphere was like this on the eve of the battle of Munda,' said Enobarbus. 'We had eight legions and Pompey's son Gnaeus had thirteen. They were in the stronger position uphill from us. But that wasn't going to stop Caesar. That's just about the worst I can remember.'

'The eve of Crassus' last battle against Spartacus,' said Artemidorus. 'I've never known tension like it. It was near the village of Quaglietta on the bank of the River Sele. In Brundisium south of Rome. It was against a slave army so it was never named as an official battle. No triumph. Crassus crucified six thousand of the survivors though. All along the *Via Appia* to Capua.'

'You sometimes wonder whether the gods ran out of patience with him. He got what they decided he deserved at Carrhae. Lost seven legions, his son and then his head. Do you think the gods ran out of patience with Caesar too?'

'No. Look how they tried to warn him. Even with Spurinna presenting him with the darkest possible auguries. There were the signs. The dreams. No. The gods were always on Caesar's side. He just refused to listen to them.'

'He listened to Dercimus Albinus instead,' said Enobarbus bitterly. 'It makes you wonder, doesn't it?'

'Wonder what?'

'How they knew to send Albinus in. How much he already knew…'

'They said Telos sang like a lark,' said Artemidorus wearily.

'Yes. Maybe that was it…' the tribune didn't sound absolutely convinced. 'Hard to believe though. Telos was one of the toughest men I knew.'

This conversation took them to the Forum. It was unusually quiet. There were people going about their business, but conversation was hushed. There was no laughter. No singing. No plays being performed. Even the dice and knucklebone men were notable by their absence. Despite the fact that there were hundreds of country bumpkins in town to fleece. The tribune looked around, narrow-eyed. 'I think we'll stick together,' he said.

'Maybe we should have come out fully armed,' said Artemidorus.

'In an atmosphere like this, wearing a sword is asking for a fight.'

'True enough. And no one we want to hear from is going to have a loose tongue around a fully armed centurion and tribune.'

Side by side they walked towards the *Basilica Aemelia* and the *taberna* where Artemidorus had recruited Ferrata. And there he was, seated at a table surrounded by half a dozen old soldiers. Probably, like him, retired from the disbanded Legio VI. Ferrata. The tribune and the centurion eased themselves into the group. Very well aware that they were of the wrong rank and from the wrong legion. But when Enobarbus offered to buy drinks all round, the atmosphere became less hostile. Never welcoming, though. Never warm. But a couple of *amphorae* of the bitter *posca* wine the soldiers favoured went some way towards breaking the ice.

'What I don't understand,' said Ferrata, 'is how they could just forget an oath like that.' He was clearly picking up on an earlier conversation.

Which the others joined in. 'If I'd broken my *sacramentum* oath while I was still in the legion they'd have crucified me.'

'Quite right too. An oath is an oath.'

'Well, it is for poor lowly no-accounts like us. Clearly not for patrician *mentulae* senators.'

'Most of them generals into the bargain! *Cunnae*!'

'Like that *nothus* Albinus! Glad I never served under him!'

'That's because you get seasick, Valens!'

'No. I mean. To stand by Caesar against the Veniti and at Massilia. To be nominated heir in the second degree. Adopted! Given his name. The name of the man you swore to protect. But who you've just slaughtered. It beggars belief...'

The conversation went along these lines for some time. Until the wine ran out. At which time Artemidorus and Enobarbus moved on.

The conversations in the other *tabernae* favoured by old soldiers was along similar lines, though. Especially in those inns frequented by soldiers who had served under Albinus. A hard-driving, ambitious, unpopular leader. One of Publius Clodius Pulcher's thuggish street gang members in his youth. Like Antony. But unlike Antony, lacking charm and the common touch.

They did not follow the soldiers from the taverns as they staggered to their next destinations – the *lupinariae* brothels.

Instead, they began to wander back towards Antony's villa. It was getting dark now, but there was still enough light to see without the aid of lamps or flambeaus. The evening was cool and the Forum all but deserted. Citizens, slaves, freedmen, families, visitors all at home, in their taverns or their brothels. Eating, sleeping, drinking or whoring.

The two men fell into a quiet conversation about past adventures. Past missions. Past battles.

When their next battle was suddenly thrust upon them.

*

Syrus stepped out of a side street, swinging his club, with his two biggest associates just behind him. 'So,' he said. 'The rumours running around the *tabernae* were true. A couple of General Antony's officers trying to mix with the legionaries,

301

gladiators and other low-life brothel sweepings. Like us. Trying to stir up trouble against the *Libertores* like Senator Basilus, were we?'

'Having a drink. Listening to the gossip,' answered Artemidorus, looking around for an escape route. To fight these men would be to die. Possibly swiftly. Probably painfully.

'And from the gossip we've heard,' added Enobarbus, 'there isn't much stirring up to be done. What will Senator Basilus and his friends do when you are dead in the arena? Who will your *Libertores* hide behind then?'

'You'll never know,' sneered Syrus. 'Because you'll be dead in the gutter. Skulls broken open. Brains trickling away. *IMPETE*!' He bellowed and swung his club up. The three gladiators ran forward. Attacking as ordered.

The two empty-handed soldiers fell into their fighting stance. Knowing fists would be no real defence against clubs, spears and swords. Watching their death come charging down on them.

But Syrus had hardly taken two steps when a familiar voice called, 'Septem! Hey, Septem!'

Artemidorus turned. There at the end of the roadway was Kyros. Just coming up out of the Forum. Escorted by what looked like a combination of Antony's *lictors* and Spurinna's slaves. Two of whom were carrying blazing flambeaus. Obviously escorting Cyanea and Puella home. Three gladiators against two unarmed men was one thing. Against half a dozen others was something else again. The gladiators eased their murderous charge down to a casual stroll. Lowered their weapons. Came swaggering past their intended victims. Walked on down into the Forum as though nothing had happened.

Artemidorus watched them. Nostrils flared. Breath short.

As Syrus passed Kyros and his charges, he leaned in and said something to Cyanea. Then walked on, laughing. His friends joined in. As though he had just said the funniest line from the funniest play that had ever been written. 'That must have been a line from Plautus at the very least,' said

Enobarbus. 'From *The Persian*, maybe. Or Terence's *Mother in Law*.'

'I thought we were going to end up more like Pacuvius,' answered Artemidorus, straightening. Quoting the playwright's famously modest epitaph. *'Here lie Artemidorus' bones. I just wanted you to know that.'*

'Ah. Pacuvius. Cicero's favourite,' said Enobarbus. 'But not really what you'd call a fount of hilarity...'

They followed their would-be murderers down to Kyros, the *lictors*, torchbearers and the women.

'What did he say to you?' Artemidorus asked Cyanea. In the light of the torches she looked pale. Diminished somehow. Terrified. 'Did he threaten you?'

'No. It was nothing...' she answered.

'He said something about songbirds,' explained the ever-helpful Kyros. *'Alaudae.* Larks.'

'That doesn't sound funny,' said Enobarbus.

'It's not,' said Artemidorus. 'That was the note he pinned to what was left of Telos. *He sang like a lark.'*

'Syrus tore his tongue out,' said Cyanea with a shudder that shook her whole frame. 'And his eyes... After Cestus broke all his bones. With his fists. Those terrible spiked gloves...'

'No wonder you look upset,' said Enobarbus.

Artemidorus slid his arm over her shoulder. 'It's all right now,' he said quietly. 'You're safe.'

'It's not just the gladiator,' explained Kyros. 'She's been like that since we collected her at the *Domus*.'

Later, in bed, Artemidorus cradled the still-shaking Cyanea gently in his arms. There was no talk of love tonight. No risk of bad backs. 'What was it?' he asked. 'What upset you so?'

'It was Caesar,' she answered. 'Caesar's body. Puella and I were told to complete the washing. There were priests and vestals there to bless it. Spurinna sacrificed. Lords Antony and Piso, the Ladies Calpuria and Atia were all there performing the ceremonies. Antistius was there completing the wax impressions. But it was Puella and I who did the final washing and preparation. And Oh! The poor man. How he must have suffered! The wounds!'

'I saw them, *carissima*...'

'As we washed away the last of the blood, they seemed to open wider. Like little mouths. Their throats deeper. Darker. They seemed to be crying out to me. That this should have been done. By his colleagues. His companions. Men he counted amongst his closest allies. To a man who never wronged them. Who forgave his enemies. Promoted his friends. Twenty-one little wounds. Bone-deep on the top and back of his head. Into his shoulders, back and breast. Into his hands and arms. Then that one across his face. And the terrible wound in his side. Antistius said *that* was the one which killed him. It was so deep. I could put my fingers in it. My fingers. Right in...'

She was still sobbing when Artemidorus finally fell asleep.

XVII

Dies Lunae, Moon Day, the fifth day after the Ides of Mars and the day of Caesar's funeral dawned bright and fair. Artemidorus woke before sunrise. Eased himself away from Cyanea. Peeling their naked skin gently apart. She was curled like a baby. Her back to his belly. He did not want to disturb her. For she had passed a restless night. Crying out in her sleep. Obviously suffering sad and frightening dreams. Like the dreams Calpurnia had suffered six nights ago. He hoped that whatever Cyanea dreamed was not so clearly ill-omened.

But if ever a day was doomed to be ill-omened, today was that day. He thought grimly. As he went to visit first the latrine and then the *tonsor*.

He expected to be the *tonsor*'s first customer. But no. Lord Antony had been shaved, eaten a light *jentaculum* and already left. Fully armed beneath his mourning robes. Ready for the funeral in more ways than one.

This information was given to him by Enobarbus who was also shaved and dressed. As fully armed as Antony. But without the funeral robes. Neither of the secret agents had any specific responsibilities in the funeral. But both were well aware that Rome was like the funeral pyre out on the Field of Mars. The slightest spark could set it all ablaze. Their only problem was that they really did not know Antony's plans. As discussed with Fulvia late into the night. Discussed with Fulvia but not with them.

The simple question was this. If Rome was set alight, would Antony want them to fight the fire? Or fan the flames?

Over a light breakfast of warm bread, milk, honey and fruit, they discussed the coming day and how they should place themselves within it. Though Enobarbus' armour and sword-belt showed the drift of his thoughts on that subject. Artemidorus emulated him. Though they decided to leave their helmets here. For the time being.

'It would help if we had a more precise idea of what was going to happen,' said Artemidorus.

'Well, the funeral, obviously...' said Enobarbus.

'No. I meant on the larger scale.'

'Ah. I can't tell you much. But I know someone who probably can.'

'That's just what I was thinking. Let's go.'

Spurinna was at the altar on the Field of Mars. Sacrificing another bull. This one was pure white. A signal of the importance the augur was putting on today's conversation with the gods. Beyond the altar it was just possible to see Caesar's funeral pyre. Also in the shape of an altar but far larger than the one Spurinna was using. They would need ladders to get Caesar's body upon the top of it, thought Artemidorus. Longer ladders than the one he had used to free Puella five nights ago. Beyond the huge pyre towered the tomb of Caesar's beloved daughter Julia. Who had died in childbirth. Giving Pompey a son. Who had also died within days. Two deaths that seemed to drive a wedge between the two mourning men. Two small occurrences on which a civil war had turned. It was always the small things that did the most damage, he thought.

It was here that the two spies caught up with their general. 'I'm sorry, Lord Antony,' the augur was saying. 'The wishes of the gods are by no means clear. On the one hand I can see no threat of disaster predicted in these entrails. On the other hand I can see no promise of great good fortune either.'

'So,' said Antony. 'It looks as though the gods are content to leave matters in our less exalted hands. For today at least. Well. Sacrifice another bull and send me word if the gods change their minds. In the meantime, look to the skies. The flights of birds. The disposition of the clouds. Any approaching storms...' He turned away from the augur and faced his secret agents. 'You two, come with me,' he ordered.

This was the decisive, occasionally hot-headed Antony the soldiers knew from the battlefield. They fell in behind him obediently as he marched back towards the forum. He seemed to have dispensed with both *lictors* and litter today. Able to move faster and achieve more without them. 'I could have done with a little more guidance than that.' He flung the words over his shoulder.

'Perhaps Hercules is still asleep,' suggested Enobarbus.

'Very funny!' snapped Antony. Then he relented. Picked up on Enobarbus' slightly ironic thought. 'But even so, you would expect Mars to be keeping an eye on his favourite – even a dead favourite. And Venus Genetrix. Caesar does claim to be descended from her after all! As does the whole Julii clan.'

The three soldiers entered the busy Forum shoulder to shoulder. Workmen on the *Rostra* were just putting the final touches to the funeral shrine that would hold Caesar's body. For at least part of the ceremony. It was a perfect small-scale copy of the Temple of Venus Genetrix. Divine founder of Caesar's Julian line. The temple itself stood nearby. Caesar had promised it on the eve of the Battle of Pharsalus. As a gift to the goddess in case of victory. It had been dedicated less than two years ago. On the last day of his controversial triumph after Pompey's death during the civil war. A year before the battle of Munda brought it all to an uneasy close. With the defeat and death of all but one of Pompey's sons. Which generated the most controversial triumph of all.

The difference between the shrine and the temple was obvious. Apart from the scale. Behind the tall building's eight-a-side columns stood the square, marble-faced walls of the inner temple. In the smaller shrine there was nothing comparable. A place for a couch. A coffin-shaped box behind it. Its lid was open and someone was standing there. Artemidorus recognised Antistius the physician. And beside Antistius stood a spear from whose point hung a long, soiled-looking white cloth. The man who had treated dead Caesar's wounds closed the box carefully. Adjusted the strange white cloth. Came down off the *Rostra* and vanished into the gathering crowd.

*

In front of the *Rostra* stood a *praeco* herald. His voice was raised over the noise of people bustling about and talking excitedly. His job was not only to announce the imminent funeral as planned for later that day. But also to advise anyone wishing to leave gifts or sacrifices in honour of Caesar to take them by any route they preferred out to the Field of Mars. And leave them by the funeral pyre there.

'It's going to be a long enough day without waiting for half the city to sacrifice their trinkets to the Divine Caesar,' said Antony.

'And by the end of it, what do you plan to have achieved?' asked Enobarbus bluntly.

'I was hoping the gods would guide me on that.' Antony shrugged.

'But they haven't. So the choice is yours, General,' said the tribune.

'Today is your last chance, Lord Antony,' Artemidorus urged. 'If you haven't broken the power of the *Libertores* by sunset then you'll have lost and they'll have won.'

'I know that...'

'So,' pressed the secret agent and centurion. As the soldier, suddenly. Rather than the spy. 'What are your battle orders?'

Antony stopped. Looked around. Made sure he was not being overheard by any nearby strangers. Faced his companions and began to speak rapidly in a low voice. 'I thought they'd riot yesterday. At the reading of the will. It seemed to me that the will proved everything Brutus and Cassius said about Caesar and his ambitions was one lie after another. I didn't think for a moment I'd have to point it out. I really believed the people would see that. And react accordingly. Without any intervention from me that would look suspicious to the *Libertores*.

'Yet they just stood still. Then went quietly away. Even the old soldiers. I could hardly believe how calmly they took it. My main hope was to start a riot without appearing to have done so. And it didn't work. Now, I have one more chance to start one today. But I can't pretend not to have done so. Not any longer. If I go down that road it will be obvious to everyone.

'I have gone through the whole thing with Fulvia. We think the best way forward is to try and emulate the funeral of

Fulvia's first husband. My friend Clodius Pulcher. He was murdered too. On the Appian Way. There was none of this formality about his funeral. Fulvia displayed his body at their villa. Showed the people his wounds. Then stood back and let them loose. You remember the riots that followed?

'Our best hope is to do the same today. I have everything in place. But I'll have to judge the temper of the crowd so, *so* carefully. Because once I start, it will be obvious what I'm trying to do. The *Libertores* remember Pulcher's funeral and the riots that followed it as clearly as I do. And if it doesn't work then I'm certain Brutus will finally listen to Cassius, Trebonius, Albinus and Basilus. And Cicero, come to that. Those gladiators will come after me. Fulvia and the children. Lepidus and his family. Perhaps even you and yours. Everyone they think might be a Caesarian. Gladiators at the very least!

'Remember what Cicero did at the end of the Catiline conspiracy? How many did he kill out of hand? Without trial? Five! Patricians and senators. Strangled in the *Tullianum*.' He glanced across at the nearby prison building as he named it. 'No formal accusation. No trials. Execution on his say-so. Despite Caesar's defence of them in the Senate. Including Publius Lentulus. My stepfather! I even had to plead with the little cockroach to get him a decent burial!' Then he concluded, his face still reflecting some of the outrage he had felt as a nineteen-year-old in seeing his family so brutally destroyed. 'He can be absolutely ruthless. He'll urge them to proscribe and execute us all.'

'You'd have to run,' said Enobarbus. 'And if you run, you've lost everything. You might as well fall on your sword and have done with it.'

'Right,' said Artemidorus. 'So, leaving the citizens on one side for the moment as an unknown quantity, we have two immediate objectives. Get enough soldiers in here to keep you safe if need be. Even from the *Libertores*. Including Cicero. And find a way of slowing or stopping Albinus' and Basilus' gladiators.'

'We can't use the Seventh Legion, though,' warned Antony. 'I've thought this through. Discussed it with Lepidus. Talked it over with Fulvia as I say. The Seventh can only come in if we do manage to start a riot. Ostensibly to keep the peace. Any earlier than that and it will look like a coup. Like Sulla all over again.'

'No. I wasn't thinking of the Seventh,' said Artemidorus. 'I was thinking of the Sixth. The Ironclads. *Ferrata*. They've been disbanded. No one will think you are trying to stage a coup using old soldiers. And I have some idea of where they'll be.'

'Taverns or brothels, I should think,' said Antony, brightening up. 'At least that's the way it was in my day. And the gladiators?'

'At least we know where they'll be. At the *Circus Maximus*. The games start today. For the *Quinquatria* festival. And for Caesar's funeral. But wait! I've just thought... Lord Antony, didn't you announce that the Senate had agreed to pay for the funeral out of the public purse?'

'Yes. That's right...'

'Then it's entirely possible that the gladiators don't work for Albinus anymore. They work for the Senate and People of Rome. What difference would that make?'

'I'm not sure. But it's a good point. How can we find out?'

'We could ask...' suggested Artemidorus. 'Just simply go down there and ask.'

'Right!' said Antony. Fizzing with energy once again. 'You get the soldiers organised and find out about the gladiators. And I'll take care of all the rest.'

*

Ferrata looked as though he could scarcely stand. Let alone guard Antony's back. 'By Jupiter that was a good night,' he said. 'I just wish I could remember more of it. We established that she was a better *mulier equitans* horsewoman than an entire cavalry unit. Especially when it came to riding *me*. Then my memory goes hazy.'

While Enobarbus was regaled with what else the legionary could remember of his visit to the brothel next door, Artemidorus ordered him the best breakfast the *taberna* could provide. Not out of simple charity. They needed the old soldier up and out. Organising his fellow legionaries from the VIth. As with Artemidorus' wine of a couple of nights ago, this inn could produce the odd surprise. So Ferrata was soon tucking into sweet *libae* rolls, with dried figs and Egyptian melon. Drinking honeyed *mulsum* wine instead of the bitter *posca* of yesterday evening. And, surprisingly quickly he was back to his old self.

'Yes,' he said. 'I can organise Valens and as many of the old Ironsides as you want. But I can't arm them all. I mean we've all got our *pugio* daggers. Some of us have our *gladius* swords. But that's about it.'

'That's fine,' said Artemidorus. 'I've thought of that. You need to go out to Tiber Island. Take Valens and however many men as you can recruit. Ask for the Centurion Oppius and the Legionary Quintus. First *centuria*. Tell them Septem sent you. Septem and the Tribune Enobarbus. They'll supply whatever you need. But remember. No badges, banners or eagles. You cannot even begin to look as though you've come from the Seventh.'

'Wouldn't want to,' said Ferrata, mightily offended. 'I have my reputation to consider. And the reputation of the Sixth.'

They split up then. Ferrata went in search of Valens and his other friends. Artemidorus and Enobarbus began to make their way towards the *Circus Maximus*. The *Vicus Tuscus* Tuscan Road took them round the western slopes of the Palatine, down towards the river and the *Forum Borium* cattle market. The forum was conveniently placed. Between the Tiber, straddled at this point by the Aemelian and Sublician bridges. And the square western end of the *Circus Maximus*.

It was convenient because the forum housed more than the cattle it was named for. The menagerie was close by, housing the wild animals that had not managed to escape during the storm six nights ago. Which were destined for the circus. This was also where the horses were stabled that took part in the games. The horse races. The wild beast hunts. The gladiatorial contests, ridden by *equites*. And of course the incredibly popular chariot races. Each of the four chariot teams, Red, White, Blue and Green, kept their horses here. As well as maintaining clubhouses up in the centre of the city itself. Where enthusiastic supporters could meet like-minded men. Get drunk in good company. And go out to beat up the supporters of opposing teams.

'Which team do you support? I've never asked,' said Enobarbus as the forum came into view.

'It's a dangerous question,' answered Artemidorus. 'The Blues.'

'Thank the gods. Me too,' laughed the tribune.

They finished the conversation as they entered the forum, with its rich smell of cattle and their droppings. The noise of their lowing. The chatter of their handlers. And the men and women here to look or to buy.

They turned left, with the river to their backs. Heading up the slope towards the square western end of the circus. Which towered dead ahead. The main, central entrance was high and topped with a statue of a chariot drawn by a pair of horses. The bronze charioteer stood tall. Looking over the cattle market towards the Tiber. The Janiculum Hill. The villa which had housed Cleopatra. And the spacious, pine-shaded gardens Caesar had just willed to the People of Rome.

Five lesser entrances opened on either side of the main one, all topped with statues of gladiators. Inside the circus itself, the chariot racetrack stretched away. More than two thousand *pedes* feet. To the even larger entrances at the far, curved end. Partially concealed by the columns and obelisks that rose from the wall in the middle of the racetrack. On either side, the stands stretched away. Largely unoccupied as the games had not yet started. The lower stands were masonry. The upper ones were wood.

At the near end of the chariot circuit there was a wide space. Floored with sand. Where pairs of gladiators were rehearsing their individual combats. Which later in the day would be put on for real. Now it was just sweat raining onto the sand, thought Artemidorus as he neared the arched entrances. Later it would be blood. Immediately inside the circus he could make out a pair of litters and their porters. And a couple of familiar figures. Standing on the marble flagstones of the area behind the starting gates. Which would be erected later when the gladiatorial contests were replaced by chariot races. One figure was huge. The other youthfully slim. 'Good morning, Hercules. And young master Lepidus,' said Artemidorus as he neared them. 'What are you two doing here?'

'My father has come to arrange some details of the funeral games,' young Lepidus answered, turning round and smiling. 'He and Lord Albinus are discussing whether Albinus' troupe will take part in these games. Agreeing a price for them to do so, I think. Now that the Senate has ruled that the games will be financed from public funds. We accompanied him because Hercules thought I could learn a lot about various types of combat simply from watching these men practise. They are supposed to be the best. They come from the leading school in Campagnia.'

'So did Spartacus. And most of his army. You could certainly learn a lot from watching such men practise,' agreed Artemidorus. 'More than you can learn from watching them die, I think.' His tone was preoccupied. His eyes narrow. Scanning the carefully moving pairs of men for a Syrian club. But he couldn't see anyone who looked like Syrus. Or who resembled the members of his gang.

As he completed his swift survey, Lepidus senior and Albinus came strolling over. Locked in apparently companionable conversation. Artemidorus wondered whether Albinus had the slightest idea what Ferrata's legionary friends thought of him. Or what Antony was planning. Probably not. Or he wouldn't be getting rid of his gladiators. 'That's settled, then,' he was saying as he approached.

'A fair price, I think,' Lepidus nodded.

'As it comes out of the public purse.' Shrugged Albinus.

The treacherous senator's gaze swept over the two soldiers with no sign of recognition. He got into his litter and was borne away.

Lepidus looked after him. 'He did his best to cheat the public purse out of far too much,' he said. 'He's incredibly greedy. Especially as he's so rich in the first place. But it was a fair price in the end, I think.'

Lepidus was really talking to himself. But Artemidorus joined in the conversation. 'I don't see any of Minucius Basilus' men out there, Lord Lepidus,' he said.

'Oh Basilus wouldn't part with his gladiators at any price,' said Lepidus. 'So they won't be taking part in the games. He says he's still got a use for them. An account he wants to settle.'

*

'Right,' said Enobarbus. 'It's clearly not just Antony who's living dangerously today. And ironically enough, his plan is a double-edged sword as far as you're concerned.'

'I see that,' nodded Artemidorus. 'If there's no riot, Antony loses – but Syrus and his men will have only a limited chance to get to me. On the other hand if there is a riot, Antony wins. And I'm likely to turn up among the roll call of rioters' victims. Head broken open. Brains in the gutter…'

'That's what the man said. And it's exactly what I was thinking,' agreed Enobarbus.

'But on the positive side,' countered Artemidorus. 'If there is a riot, everyone will be on the lookout for trouble. Including me. *Especially* me, now. And the Seventh will be on the streets.'

As they talked, the two soldiers were retracing their steps though the cattle market and up Tuscan Street. The Tiber lay on their left, skeins of mist like spiders' webs rising from its limpid surface into the cool morning air. The Palatine rose on their right. The Capitoline reared ahead with the Temple of Jupiter on its crest. The road followed the *Velabrum* valley up to the Forum itself. And as with yesterday, the two men soon found themselves being swept along in a river of humanity all heading the same way.

The Forum was packed but not yet as full as it had been in the recent past. The shops and stalls round its edges were all open and doing brisk business. Their wooden counters piled with everything from seasonal fruit and vegetables to tiny models of household gods. At this season, winter apples, broccoli and artichokes; models of Venus, Minerva and Mars. The two soldiers were able to cross to the *Rostra* and take up position in front of it. Facing the crowd. Then, as the sun rose over the rooftops and pine trees clothing the upper slopes of the Esquiline, the forum filled to capacity. The *praeco* continued to advise the crowd that the funeral procession would soon begin. The ceremony would soon be under way. And those with gifts and sacrifices should take them out to the pyre on the Field of Mars.

No sooner had the first long golden sunbeams illuminated the *Rostra* and the model of the temple to Venus on top of it than the buzzing chatter of the expectant crowds was stilled by deep, mournful music. It seemed that every head in the Forum turned at once to look towards the *Domus*. The low, sad music of *tubae* military trumpets and *cornua* horns rang across the heart of Rome. Seeming to come from every corner and echo against the sky. As the doors to the *Domus Publicus* were thrown wide.

Piso, as Caesar's father-in-law, led the procession out of the shady *atrium* and into the morning light. The crowd parted to let the procession cover the short distance between Caesar's home and the shrine awaiting him on the *Rostra*. Spreading out into the side streets and up onto the slope of the *aquimelium* on the Capitoline as they did so. Artemidorus could feel the emotion of the crowd shift and swirl. Like a sailor reading the wind. Someone cried. Almost a scream. High pitched. Man or woman? He could not tell. But the sound was taken up. And spread.

Caesar was borne out into the light, feet first. On an ivory couch. Carried shoulder high by what looked to be every *aedile* magistrate in the city. All in mourning robes. The dead dictator's corpse was little more than an outline beneath a gold and purple funeral cloth. At each side of the couch walked a torchbearer, as tradition dictated. Blazing flambeau held high. The flames pallid, almost ghostly in the morning brightness. But bringing memories of the far-off days when funerals were held exclusively at night.

Behind Caesar's corpse came his widow Calpurnia and the Lady Atia. Then Antony, alone. And behind him, rank after rank of men lamenting in one way or another the death of

Gaius Julius Caesar. The first rank bore the long military *tubae*, pointing upwards to left and right. Larger than those used in legionary camps. Their sounds deeper. Darker. The gold of their wide mouths gleaming. Then the *cornua*, wrapped like gilded snakes around the bodies of the men who played them. Behind the musicians, came a choir, singing dirges. Behind them, the mourners. Professionals. Their numbers fleshed out with actors. Many in tragic masks. Playing their parts well. All costumed in funeral robes, weeping and wailing. Almost as loudly, thought Artemidorus, as the crowd through which they were passing.

Then, as tradition dictated, the jesters. Many in comic masks. Jumping, juggling and joking. Artemidorus could not make out what their jokes were. But he could see very plainly that no one much was laughing at them. Behind the jesters, almost as though they too were part of some grim joke, came rank after rank of senators. Artemidorus searched their solemn faces to see if any of the murderers were brave enough to attend. Brave enough or foolhardy enough. But no. There was no sign of any of the so-called *Libertores*.

Behind the senators came Caesar. And behind him, Caesar. Then Caesar. Then Caesar. And, finally, Caesar. The effect was disturbingly disorientating. It took an instant for Artemidorus to realise that the line of Caesars was made up of actors wearing wax masks of Caesar's face. The masks were of highest quality beeswax. Carefully painted. They were unsettlingly lifelike. Furthermore, the men had been chosen for their physical similarity to Caesar. They were wearing Caesar's face. And they were also wearing his triumphal robes. They processed through the Forum in the order that Caesar himself had celebrated his triumphs. First over Gaul. Then over Cleopatra's brother and her other enemies in Alexandria. Then the Pontus triumph. The African triumph. And lastly. Still most controversially, the Spanish triumph memorialising his destruction of Pompey's sons at Munda. Which he had celebrated through these very streets only five months earlier.

As the funeral was a family affair, though not without political weight and implications, there was no further political involvement apart from the senators already there. Any other patricians, politicians or foreign dignitaries who wished to observe the proceedings had to mix with the common men and women in the Forum. Consequently, thought Artemidorus, there weren't many patrician faces about. Other than those tacitly declaring themselves friends of Caesar by walking with his mourners. Or carrying his corpse. Not that that was much of a surprise. Given the way the man whose life they were celebrating had died.

*

By the time the last Caesarian effigy was in the Forum, Caesar's body was up on the *Rostra*. The ivory couch was laid in its place in the shrine modelled on the Temple of Venus. As chance would have it, this stood immediately above Artemidorus' head. And therefore out of his view. But the instant the body was settled, there came a great commotion. A squad of armed soldiers pushed into the square. What looked like an eighty-man *centuria* of them. Fully armed. With helmets and shields. Bursting out of the *Clivus Argentarius* road. Quick-marching in well-ordered ranks.

As Artemidorus and Enobarbus moved out of their way, they took up station all around the *Rostra*. On a bellowed command, each man pulled out his *gladius* and beat it against his *scutum* shield. The sound was overpowering. The crowd wavered dangerously back and forth. Settling only when it was obvious that the anonymous soldiers presented no immediate threat. That they were here to honour Caesar. Not to avenge him.

From his new position, Artemidorus could now see the *Rostra* clearly. And those assembled behind it. So he noticed at once that Fulvia had joined her husband. And had brought Cyanea with her. Escorted by Promus and some of Antony's house slaves. But it was not Antony who began the next section of the funeral. Marcus Fossilus, the oldest and most widely respected of the senators who had followed the body slowly made his way up onto the *Rostra*. He stood beside the

shrine that held Caesar's corpse. He painstakingly unrolled a
scroll. And began to read from it. His voice was stronger than
his aged body led the spy to expect. But still it quavered.
Almost as though the man was scared of what he was reading.
It took a moment for his words to sink in. Then there was a
kind of muttering from the crowd. Artemidorus looked at
Enobarbus, understanding the ancient senator's nervousness.
The tribune shrugged. Neither man had expected this.

The senator was reading out the oath that the entire Senate
swore on behalf of the People while honouring Caesar on his
return from Spain. The senator's words came and went under
the growing murmur from the crowd. '*Pater patriae*... Father
of your country... Immortal leader... Benefactor to all...
Sacrosanct... Inviolate... We swear to honour, obey and
protect you...' Having read the oath, senator Fossilus made no
comment. He simply turned and left the *Rostra*. The
atmosphere in the Forum, thought Artemidorus, was such as
could be felt just before the first thunder of a terrible storm.
And yet, still the people did not move. No one came forward
to lead them. To lance the boil of outrage with the needle of
violent action.

Fulvia pushed Antony. The general climbed onto the *Rostra*.
With obvious reluctance. He stopped by the shrine. Looked
down at the corpse. Which was doubly invisible now. From
the Forum, certainly. Hidden by the height of the platform and
the angle of the couch. Covered by the purple and gold cloth.
'I have been chosen to give this oration,' Antony said. His
voice carrying over the crowd. In the same way as it carried
over the ranks of his legions just before a battle. But without
the flair and excitement that the prospect of immediate action
usually gave it. More like the speech of a student of oratory
trying to impress an exacting tutor. 'A consul to speak for a
consul. A friend for a friend. A kinsman for a kinsman. But is
it right, friends, that an oration for such a leader should be
spoken by just one man? No! Caesar's funeral should be
spoken by all of us. By the Senate. By the People of Rome
whom they represent. By those of you who make up the
comitia. By every citizen, freedman and slave.' He took a deep

breath. His gaze swept the silent crowd. Artemidorus thought he detected a scintilla of desperation.

'We have heard the oath the entire Senate swore mere months ago,' Antony continued. 'The titles they gave him, *Pater Patriae* … Father of his Country… and all the rest. The honours that they heaped on him. The titles. But only at your request. He did not ask for any of them. The only thing for which he had any ambition was for the good of Rome and *you*, her people.'

He took another breath and began to recite the oath once again. Slowly. Clearly. Emphasising the titles awarded to Caesar. The promises to protect him. To avenge any wrong done to him. Then, when he was finished, he pulled from his belt another scroll. Unrolled it. Added, more weightily still. 'And these are the names of the men who swore this oath. To protect Caesar from all harm. Beginning with the names of the men he personally forgave for taking up arms against him and siding with Pompey or his sons in the civil war: Gaius Cassius Longinus. Marcus Junius Brutus. Quintus Ligarius…' The list went on. And on.

Then Antony added, 'And these are the names of the men who fought at his side, whom he supported, advanced, loved like members of his own family. Some of whom, indeed, he *adopted* into his family. And who also swore this great oath. Decimus Junius Brutus Albinus. Gaius Trebonius. Publius Servilius Casca Longus. Gaius Servilius Casca…'

Artemidorus could see all too clearly what he was attempting. As they had discussed. Nothing he had said or done went beyond the remit that the Senate and the *Libertores* had agreed. If the People remained in this trance-like stillness. Trembling on the edge of riot but still taking no action. He could be accused of nothing. But the expression on Fulvia's face was one of intense frustration. It looked as though it was time for Antony to dispense with subtlety. In her opinion at least. After all, she was only asking him to dare to do what she had already dared and done.

As though Antony could read Fulvia's mind, he finished reciting the names of the *Libertores* who had sworn the oath.

And suddenly raised his hand towards the Temple of Jupiter crouching on top of the Capitoline. Blazing in the morning sunlight. Like a funeral pyre of unimaginable size. Shouting, as though overcome with emotion at last, 'Jupiter, god of our ancestors, and all you other gods! For my own part I am prepared to defend or avenge Caesar according to my oath. But since it is the popular view that what we in the Senate have decided will be for the best, I swear to hold my hand! But I pray that it is for the best!' The senators behind the *Rostra* were the only ones to react to this mannered and clumsy outburst. Their anger was palpable. And in the face of the crowd's continuing refusal to take action, Antony was forced to change tack.

'Well, friends,' he said, his voice lower. Seeming to Artemidorus to have an undertone of defeat. 'We must think about the present. And the future. Not the past. We are poised on a knife-edge. We risk falling into yet another civil war. So.' He almost shrugged. 'Let us complete the funeral rights. Then simply take this body to the pyre. And let his spirit join the gods who are his brothers and his sisters now.' His voice broke on the last few words and he looked down. As though he was ashamed to let the people see that he was overcome.

Antony stopped talking. Dashed his hand down over his face. Clearly wiping away tears. Moved to one side. His shoulder touching the white cloth hanging from the point of the spear that stood by the box behind Caesar's ivory couch. The singers filed past the enraged, frustrated Fulvia and the wide-eyed Cyanea. Mounted the platform. Continued to sing their dirges. And then, while they did so, the actors came forward one by one. In ringing tones, they recited lines of elegiac poetry. By Archilochus of Paros and Pindarus, Quintus Ennius and Virgil. And speeches from tragic plays. By Sophocles and Euripdes. Gnaeus Navius and Lucius Accius.

At last, Antony stepped forward again. Taking the place of the final actor. Somehow it seemed to Artemidorus that his whole demeanour had changed. That the hesitation had gone. He had run out of patience with prevarication. He was finally committed to a course of action. Come what may. This was how Caesar had looked when he decided to cross the Rubicon, thought Artemidorus. His breath shortened and his hair stirred at the change. Antony looked up at the Temple of Jupiter once more. Then down at the crowd. It seemed to Artemidorus that the general met every pair of eyes there. As his booming voice recited a line from the tragic playwright Pacruvius' best-known and most popular play, *The Contest for the Arms of Achilles*. His intonation suddenly full of virile power.

'*And did I save these men,*' he bellowed. Voice echoing over the Forum. Like the thunder six nights since. Face streaming with tears. '*So that they could murder me?*'

Fulvia's cheeks went from red with rage to white with shock in a heartbeat. She staggered slightly. As though clubbed from behind. Cyanea held her steady. Artemidorus realised that Antony's dramatic words were some kind of signal. That the general had just committed himself to the course of action he most feared. To all-out war with the *Libertores*. And if the people still refused to move, then he would find himself fighting that war alone.

At Antony's signal, Antistius appeared briefly behind Caesar's couch. The mysterious box there opened. And it was as though the ghost of Caesar rose before their eyes. Women screamed. Some men too. The crowd staggered back. Then froze. As they realised what they were seeing.

Standing at the head of Caesar's couch was a life-sized model of his body. The wax model Antistius had told Artemidorus he would be making from Caesar's corpse. But, unlike the masks moulded from his face, this was not smooth and perfect. It showed in bright and graphic detail every wound inflicted by the murderers in the Senate five days ago. Painted on with medical precision. And, from the look of it, with thick dark blood from one of Spurinna's most sanguine sacrifices. Blood which ran almost black. Cascading down the pale but perfect model of the dead man. From the crown of his head. From his shoulders and arms. From his chest. From his cruelly disfigured face. From the great, gushing gash in his side.

Antony said nothing. He simply pulled the white rag hanging from the spear-point wide. Revealing it to be Caesar's bloodstained toga. The garment Antistius had carefully preserved at Artemidorus' suggestion. A stark white sheet. With more than a dozen dagger cuts, all red-rimmed and gaping. Like little mouths. All seeming to scream.

*

The crowd ignited like Greek fire. At last.

But all Artemidorus saw was Cyanea. Her face whiter than Fulvia's as she turned and began to run wildly away. But not from the crowd. Or from the *Rostra*. She was running, terrified, from that waxen figure which stood there still spouting black blood.

Then he was swept away himself. The senators ran for their lives. Calling no doubt for their *lictors*. And their litters. If they were doing so, no one could hear them over the howls of outrage that filled the forum and many of the nearby streets. The mourners, actors, and musicians fled. The torch-carriers dropped their flambeaus and disappeared. A couple of the soldiers caught them up and held them high. Still well ablaze. Suddenly the whole of the *Comitium* area behind the *Rostra* was empty. Then more citizens flooded into it. Taking the places of the fleeing senators. The crowd in the Forum surged forward. Artemidorus and Enobarbus went with it. They had no choice. And were lucky to keep their feet.

With the help of the soldiers, six of the largest men ran up to the shrine. Shouldered Caesar's couch. The wax model fell. Shattered. The purple and gold cloth fluttered to the ground, exposing the dead dictator's wounded face. The men carried the couch back towards the steps. The baying of the crowd grew louder still. As the *plebeian* pallbearers brought Caesar back down from the *Rostra*. Into the Forum. Escorted by the soldiers who worshipped him. To the citizens who loved him. There was an instant of quiet. Artemidorus looked for Antony. He was nowhere to be seen. Fulvia, Promus and the house slaves had all vanished as well.

'The Capitoline,' someone shouted. 'Take him to the Temple of Jupiter!' With Ferrata and his men forming a kind

322

of honour guard, Caesar was borne across the Forum and into the mouth of the *Vicus Juagarius*. Artemidorus and Enobarbus went with them. Only to find the path and the steps up to the temple blocked. The temple priests had put up with a lot recently. The *Libertores* all but desecrating the holy space for which they were responsible. The gladiators guarding them. The comings and goings of their friends. And those who were called to listen to their speeches. They were not about to see the most sacred space in the city turned into a funeral pyre. They took swift action to forestall the citizens. They might not be soldiers. But they understood well enough how to close a narrow pathway and an even narrower set of steps.

Thwarted, the men bearing the couch turned once more.

'Take him to the *Campus Martius*!' shouted another voice. 'To the pyre there.'

'No!' shouted others. 'That's where the legionaries are. Back to the Forum!'

The whole of the crowd seemed to take up this cry and they surged back. With one intention. With one mind, thought Artemidorus. Almost with one body. When they got into the Forum once more there was no more hesitation. They placed Caesar's couch outside the open doors of the *Domus*, then went to work. The five triumphal Caesars all joined in as well. Now distinguished by the golden robes they were wearing. Their wax masks long gone.

Men and women alike were tearing apart the shops and stalls round the edge of the square. Chairs, stools and benches from the public areas in the old basilica along the south side. Wooden scaffolding from the as yet unnamed, half-built basilica beside it. In whose flooded foundations Priscus and the boy still lay undiscovered. Still more wood from the shops and law courts in the new basilica to the north. Artemidorus was certain he recognised tables and stools from the *taberna* where he had bought Ferrata breakfast this morning. There was even some bedding from the brothel next door. Well used and in urgent need of a wash. Greasy and easily flammable, thought the spy. All of it piled increasingly high before the *Rostra* with its empty shrine. Its empty box. And its shattered, blood-spattered wax mannequin. Even as he watched, the box and the shrine were smashed to kindling so that they could join the increasingly impressive pyre.

It took surprisingly little time. Astonishingly quickly, the pyre was erected. Dry kindling of cloth, bedding and splinters shoved into the side of it. Caesar laid reverently on the top. Then the two soldiers holding the blazing flambeaus thrust them into the wooden sides and in a heartbeat it was all alight. The crowd gathered round the flaming pyre. Looking in simple awe at what they had done. Like men awakening from a nightmare. Or a bout of madness. Many still sobbing. Men and women alike. The flames licked up through the hillock of wood and cloth. Reaching hungrily for the ivory couch and the corpse resting on top of it. Like the Temple of Jove sitting unscathed on the crest of the Capitoline.

Then one of the triumphal actors tore off the cloth of gold robe he was wearing and threw it into the fire. It writhed among the flames as though it was alive. Melting and vanishing. Instantly it seemed that everyone else there was emulating him. The other triumphal costumes joined the first. The triumphal decorations that had adorned them. The soldiers joined in. They had no legionary identification marks. But many of them were wearing personal decorations. For bravery. Long service. Badges of rank. First one and then another pulled these free and threw them into the flames. Lucky amulets. Neck chains. Women stripped off their rings. Necklaces. Bangles. Earrings. Pulled out silver and gold combs. Belts with gilded links. Ornate buckles from girdles and shoes. Buttons cast in precious metal. All of it went into the pyre. The crowd members at the back jostling forward to add their precious possessions to the fiery sacrifice. Sacrificers by the hundred. Sacrifices by the thousand. As the flames roared higher. And higher still. Wood hissing, splitting and sparking angrily. As the smoke boiled upwards, covering the sky like a mourning shroud. As the heat of the blaze drove the crowd further and further back. As Caesar finally disappeared into the heart of the inferno.

And, watching it all, Artemidorus was suddenly pulled back in his mind to the night before the Ides. When he still believed he had a chance of stopping all of this. Running through the stormy darkness with Puella. Guided by the lightning that turned the roadway at their feet into a river of gold. For there was another river running out of the bottom of the pyre. Pumped out like blood from a wound as the structure began to collapse at its centre and settle. Trickling dazzlingly across the stones of the Forum. Only this time the stream of molten metal was not an illusion. This time the river of gold running down into the gutter was real.

*

The spy had no idea who first tore a blazing stick out of the fire, yelling, Almost inarticulate with rage and grief. But making his message clear enough. The echoes of his voice scarcely seemed to have died before there were a dozen more like him. Waving their burning torches and shouting. Not just citizens either, he noted. Several soldiers joined the mob in their quest for revenge. And as they ran past him, one stopped. A familiar pair of eyes regarded him from between tight-tied cheek flaps. Red-rimmed. Not quite sane. And a familiar voice said, 'Septem. As agreed, I think I should warn you that I'm planning to roast a senator or two!' And he was gone.

'Ferrata!' Artemidorus called after him. But he was too late. Like most of the rest of the hate-filled mob, he had vanished. Heading for the *Carinae* and the senatorial villas beyond it on the Esquiline. Leaving only a small number of weeping people and a few old soldiers round the pyre. And a range of wreckage, armour and weaponry on the ground. Helmets. Shields. The spear that had held Caesar's toga. Artemidorus jerked himself out of his stasis. Went across to the front of the *Rostra*. Walking carefully clear of Caesar's smouldering pyre. Picked up the spear. The toga was gone. As was the purple and gold cloth which had covered the body. Maybe as a sacrifice into the fire. Maybe as a relic, bound for someone's household shrine. Caesar was, after all, a god now.

Beside the spear lay the shattered, half melted figure Antistius had cast from the corpse. And, beside that, a legionary *scutum* shield. Covered in red leather. With a sharp metal boss at its middle. A design like four bolts of lightning joining the boss to the corners. Edged all round with iron. The centurion picked up the shield as well. Hefted it thoughtfully, assessing its weight and solidity. It was heavier than it looked, he thought. Stood it on the ground. It curved around his feet and covered him up to his belt.

He exchanged a look with Enobarbus who was walking across the littered forum towards him. A look that bordered on bewilderment. That they should be here like this. Able to stand still. Amidst all this danger. Destruction. Emotion. It seemed incredible. Something that happened on the battlefield once in a while. To the victors at the end of a hard-fought engagement. As though they were in the still, calm centre of some terrible storm. Which was still raving madly all around them.

But then events overtook them once again. Two events almost simultaneously in fact.

Marcus Aemilius Lepidus led the first *centuria* of the VIIth Legion into the Forum at a full run. Obviously yet another part of Antony's carefully planned power play. Which seemed in all respects to be going very well indeed.

And Promus burst out of the mouth of the *Argiletum* roadway nearby, shouting, 'Septem! Septem come quickly!'

Without thinking, still in the grip of that dream-like moment, Artemidorus slung the shield over his shoulder and ran towards Antony's servant. He hardly even realised that he still had the spear in his hand. He was dimly aware of Enobarbus following close behind. But all his attention was focused on Promus.

'What?' he asked as he came closer.

'Cyanea! They've taken her!'

He knew the truth at once. But still he asked, 'Gladiators?'

'Led by one wielding a club. She should not have run off alone. A kind of madness seemed to overtake her. They snatched her off the street. I saw it happening. But could do nothing…'

'Don't worry. I know where they have taken her.' He swung round to face Enobarbus. 'Minucius Basilus' villa.' He said.

326

'I'll go straight there. Can you borrow a squad of men from my *centuria*? Quintus will pick the best. Follow as fast as you can.'

'Are you sure you don't want to wait until we've organised a squad to back you up?'

'No. It's either a trap for me. Or some amusement for Basilus as they threatened. Or both. But whichever, they'll have to work fast. Basilus is one of the senators Ferrata and his friends want to roast. He won't want to stay in the city for any longer than he has to. Even for the pleasure of seeing us die as painfully as possible.'

As he spoke, Artemidorus was on the move again. Running past Promus into the *Argelitum*. Following it round, through one smaller forum after another. Past the edge of the *Subura* towards the *Clivus Pullius*. Antony's villa and the Temple of Tellus. And beyond that, the roadways that led past Spurinna's more modest dwelling. And on up into the exclusive, expensive, patrician sections of the Esquiline. Where Minucius Basilus lived.

As he ran, memories of his adventures of the last few days kept flashing into his mind. The forum where he and Puella saw Cassius dare the gods to strike him down. The corner where Cestus and the panther met. The scaffolding where Telos had been crucified.

The memories were distracting. Dangerously so. For he was by no means running alone through a peaceful city. There was madness in the air. Gangs of men and women ran screaming from one place to another. Appearing out of side streets and disappearing into others. Sometimes warning of their approach with shouts and screams. Sometimes running silently. Like hunting wolves. Most of them armed. Many of them carrying flaming torches as they searched for any *Libertores* unwise enough to be out of their barricaded villas.

But the fact that he was obviously a soldier went some way to protecting Artemidorus as he ran through the mayhem. Fortunately so. For the unrest was spreading rapidly. And brutally. It was the worst he had ever seen within the Servian walls. Worse than those half organised by Antony's friend

Clodius Pulcher. Worse than that organised by Fulvia on Pulcher's death. Worse than those he'd heard tell of which happened during Sulla's times and before. When the Gracci brothers had been lynched in the Forum. And those in which Saturninus and Glaucia had been stoned to death with tiles torn from their roofs. The year Caesar was born.

Worse even than those he had experienced in Alexandria. Where the riots had been so bad they had nearly destroyed Cleopatra, Caesar and the four thousand legionaries trapped there with him.

By the time he was running past Antony's barricaded door, he had decided to treat the city as though it was a battlefield. He took the spear in his left hand and pulled his *gladius* free of its sheath on his right hip.

Which was how he was armed when he came upon the next of the day's horrors.

*

It started with Spurinna's slave Kyros. The normally sensible and level-headed lad came racing out of the side street leading to one of the smaller forums. He was looking over his shoulder and careered straight into the spy. Who had no chance to slow down or avoid him. He bounced off and fell flat on his back. The shock of the collision seemed to calm him. The look of horror on his face faded a little. But still lurked in the depth of his wide eyes. 'Septem,' he said. 'Did you see it?'

'What is there to see?' demanded Artemidorus. Impatient to be away. But unwilling to move until he found out what had frightened the boy so badly. And see him safe. 'Why are you out on the streets and what have you seen?'

'They tore him apart!' gabbled Kyros. 'The master sent me with a message to Lord Antony. The auguries are bad and getting worse. He should take care. We all should take care. I was on my way back when I saw the crowd attacking someone. Just ripping him to pieces! I wouldn't have thought it possible! That they could do it. That they would want to do it!'

'Who? Ripped who to pieces? What are you talking about?'

'He said he'd dreamed last night he dined with Caesar.' Said Kyros, his voice full of wonder. 'That he wasn't well. That he felt feverish. But came out anyway.'

'Who did this? Who said this? Kyros. Who are you talking about?'

'Him…' said the boy. Pointing. 'Them…'

Artemidorus turned. A group of men and women came pouring out of the street Kyros had just emerged from. They were blood-spattered. Wildly excited. Drunk with death and destruction. Almost lunatic. Artemidorus was put in mind of the Bacchantes who tore the poet Orpheus to pieces in the legend. For it was clear that the terrified boy had spoken nothing but the truth.

In the middle of the blood-soaked mob was a man holding a spear aloft. Flourishing it like a trophy. And on the point of the spear was impaled the head of a man.

'He said his name was Cinna,' said Kyros. 'Someone asked his name. He said it was Cinna. And they tore him to pieces. Just like that.'

It was difficult to identify the owner of the head from the horrified expression on the battered, bloody face. Difficult. But not impossible.

'But that's not *Cornelius* Cinna. It's not the Cinna who spoke against Caesar and joined the *Libertores*,' Artemidorus said, his voice filled with shock and wonder. And growing horror. 'That's Helvius Cinna. The poet. *Helvius* Cinna. He's Tribune of the Plebs…'

'I know,' whispered Kyros. 'He told them. But they just didn't care…'

The pair of them watched the grim parade as it went down the hill towards the forum. Laughing and shouting. As though they had won a great victory. As though they were in a triumph.

'Has Spurinna barricaded his doors?' asked Artemidorus as he sheathed his *gladius* and stooped to help the boy to his feet. 'I'm worried about him and Puella with all this madness about. Especially if his auguries are right.'

'Yes. He barricaded his door as I went out with the message. But he'll let me back in,' said Kyros. He gave a choking laugh. 'And I wouldn't worry about Puella. The master's taken a great liking to her. He's talking about buying her from Lord Brutus and keeping her for himself.'

'If Brutus has any sense, he and his family will be heading out of the city as quickly as they can – if they haven't left already. As things are, I don't think he'll be too worried about one female slave. Not in the meantime at least.' Artemidorus remembered all too clearly the look in Ferrata's eyes as he went off to 'roast a senator or two.' Brutus and Cassius would be at the top of Ferrata's list. And not just his list, either. The brothers-in-law and leaders of the *Libertores* would be at the top of everybody's list. For the sake of their families, he hoped that they had both barricaded their doors securely.

Accompanying the shaken boy to Spurinna's villa did not take Artemidorus far out of his way. Or cost him much more time. Even so, he redoubled his pace after seeing Kyros let safely in through the improvised fortifications around the augur's door. The wooden scaffolding that Telos had been crucified against was all gone. More weapons for the rioters, he thought grimly. More fuel for their torches. He really hoped that Enobarbus and Quintus were closing up behind him with a squad of hard-bitten legionaries. And that Lepidus and the VIIth were restoring some kind of order to the streets. But the wolfish howls that echoed from the roads and forums all around him made him doubt that order would be restored easily. Or quickly.

Without breaking his stride, he pulled his *gladius* out again.

*

As Artemidorus neared Basilus' villa, he began to slow. The whole area was quiet. Which in itself seemed a little sinister. Given the chaos in the rest of the city. And matters grew more sinister still as he came to the front of the vicious senator's home. For the door was not barricaded. Or protected in any way. On the contrary, it stood wide open. As though inviting entry. He knew he should hesitate. Check the lie of the land. Wait for Enobarbus, Quintus and the squad from the VIIth.

But instead of doing any of these eminently sensible things, he simply walked straight in.

It was a trap, of course. He knew that. Just as the last time he had entered this place had been a trap. But he calculated that trapping and dealing with him would distract Syrus – and Basilus if he was there – from hurting Cyanea. And if he lasted long enough, then Enobarbus could rescue her. Even if it was too late to rescue him. It suddenly entered his mind that he should have asked them to bring Antistius with them. For there might well be need of a good physician. Or at the very least, someone adept at making death masks.

The doors opened inwards and the instant he stepped through them into the *osticum* entry hall he swung round. But there was no one waiting behind them to slam the trap shut. So he turned again and walked through into the *atrium*. The open space, and what he could see of the rooms around it, showed signs of hasty departure. Boxes and trunks stood open. Clothing hung out of them. Scrolls were scattered on the *tablinum* office floor. So Basilus, his family and slaves had seemingly run for it already. To one of his villas in the country, perhaps. He'd heard the senator owned a palatial property down in Pompeii. Where the rich and sybaritic liked to spend their time in luxurious idleness.

This thought took him through the open *tablinum* office area. Which gave him his first clear view of the *peristyle* garden. With its whipping post in place of a fountain. And his first sight of Cyanea who was tied with her back to the post.

Naked.

As soon as he saw her he dived to the right, going down on one knee. Dropping his *gladius*. Relying on the *scutum* shield to cover his left side for the moment. Grounding the haft of the *pilum* spear. Hard against the side of his sandal's thick sole. So that the gladiator running silently out of the open *alae* wing hoping the spy would be distracted by the woman's nudity and vulnerability, received a death blow. Instead of delivering one. Unable to stop or turn away when he saw the deadly danger at the last moment. The spear point went into his belly just above his pubic bone and drove up into his heart. His dead weight came onto the haft. The metal tip tore out of his back just above his shoulders. Where the spine joined the neck.

As he crashed sideways onto the floor, Artemidorus let go of the spear and turned. Pulling the shield further onto his left arm. Reaching for the *gladius* with his right hand. But Syrus had been content to risk only one man. A man armed with an *acinaces* single-edged sword. Which the dead gladiator had been holding blunt edge down. Using it as a club. Not as a sword. With orders to stun, therefore. Not kill. Which meant Syrus was waiting to do the job himself. But how many others did he have with him? And would there be more traps?

Unlikely, thought Artemidorus. Traps like that depended on surprise. And it would be impossible to surprise him now. 'I hope you appreciate that,' he said to the dead man as he stood up. 'That was the spear which held Caesar's toga at his funeral. It's almost sacred. Though I don't suppose that will be much help where you're going.'

He locked his gaze on Cyanea's wide and terrified eyes as he fell into his fighting stance and moved forward. *Scutum* protecting his body. *Gladius* held low. Ready for the upward killing stroke. The one Antistius had said killed Caesar. Step by step he moved through the open *tablinum* towards the *peristyle*. And each step revealed more of the garden beside and behind Cyanea and the whipping post. As he moved, he tried to remember how many men had been with Cestus when the panther took him. Eight? Were the gladiators in a unit based on the army's *contubernium*, like Enobarbus' team of spies? If so, there were only four left. For Cestus was gone. The hard-to-kill Priscus and the boy. The corpse with the *acinaces* single-edged sword on the floor just behind him.

That might explain the trap which the dead man had tried to spring. Syrus getting a lot less confident now. For he and his men were clearly associated with the *Libertores*. Like Albinus' men. None of whom, suspected Artemidorus, were going to survive Caesar's funeral games. Syrus and his men must know they must be badly at risk now. Not only that, but their paymaster had vanished.

These thoughts took Artemidorus through the *tablinum* and out into the garden. Where he stopped. Stopped moving. Stopped thinking. There was no more time for speculation. No need for it. The area of grass in the middle of the *peristyle* was larger than usual in such gardens. Where a pool would have filled its centre there was nothing. Just more grass. The whipping post stood at the far end. No doubt to give Basilus or his slave master more room for a run-up before the lash landed. But here and now, it would serve very well as a battlefield for two combatants, he thought. And as he did so, Syrus stepped out onto the grass with three men at his back. Forming a wedge of muscular flesh between the spy and his lover. And a wall of armour. Syrus' companions looked to Artemidorus to be a *Thraex*. Whose armour was based on Thracian design, with a small round shield called a *parmula*. A helmet crested with a gryphon. With a face mask like the Samnite's helmet had. And a curved Thracian sword. A more heavily armed *hoplomachus* in quilted armour. With greaves protecting his shins. A *gladius*. A spear. And a *provocator* with body armour similar to Artemidorus' own. A *gladius*. And a *pugio* dagger. Syrus himself was free of armour. Wearing only a tunic. With a simple belt and sheath for a dagger. Carrying only his massive Syrian club. Like the god Hercules without his lion skin. 'You are so predictable,' he said mockingly. 'To be caught in the same trap twice…'

'You couldn't hold us last time. You won't be able to hold us this time. Especially as you'll be dead.'

'So you say,' mocked the gladiator. 'Well, who dies first? You or your *canicula* bitch?'

'If you want to play with her you'll have to kill me first.'

'Good point,' said Syrus. 'And, as ever, we are well ahead of you on that. So. That's decided then. You die first…'

*

Artemidorus stepped further onto the grass of the garden, falling a little lower into his stance. Knees bent. Shield up to his eyes. Armoured body filling the curve behind it. Very aware that he didn't have a helmet on. He tightened his grip on the *gladius*.

'… but this is hardly an equal contest,' Syrus continued. 'And I know you're a fair-minded man. Who wouldn't want to take advantage…' He stepped back. Lowered his club. Pulled the dagger from his belt and rested the point of it against Cyanea's throat. Exactly where an artery pulsed. Its beat racing to the dictates of her terror. The threat was immediate enough to make Artemidorus stop where he was. *Hurry, Enobarbus*, he thought. *Get Quintus and my men here!*

Syrus stood with his knife at Cyanea's throat. His three companions each removed some element of their armour. Strapping or tying it onto Syrus instead. Something they had clearly practised in the past. In a matter of moments, he was protected by the *provocator's* body armour. The *hoplomachus'* greaves. The *Thraex's* round *parmula* shield and gryphon-crested helmet. The gryphon thought Artemidorus inconsequentially. Companion to the terrifying goddess Nemesis. Goddess of Retribution. Also called *Adrasteia*, The Inescapable.

The dagger Syrus held at Cyanea's throat was replaced by the *provocator's*. The Syrian picked up his club as he sheathed his own dagger and stepped forward. 'Now,' he said, his voice muffled by the iron mask that covered his face. 'That's better. I might even simply cripple you and let you lie in agony. Watching us take the woman. Before you finally die. I would enjoy that. Let us begin.'

Artemidorus attacked at once, running forward over the grass. Relieved to feel that the ground was firm and not too slippery. The grass was short. And the storms had made little impression on the hard earth beneath it. If he had expected to surprise his opponent he was disappointed. Syrus threw his left arm wide. As though disdaining to use the small round *parmula* shield on his forearm. As though inviting Artemidorus closer still. As though offering his armoured torso to the sword. But the gesture was only to balance him for the in-swing of his massive club. Which hit the top corner of Artemidorus' shield with a force that almost tore it from his grasp. Bouncing up to skim over the top of his head. Close enough to stir his hair.

He would have pushed on in for the kill. But the power of the stroke knocked him sideways. He lost his footing. Went down on one knee. Lowered his sword point slightly. Left arm numb and shoulder painful from keeping hold of the shield.

Syrus charged forward at once, club high. Artemidorus just had time to raise the shield before another massive blow crashed down onto it. With such force that the spy was beaten further back still. Surprised that the shield did not shatter into splinters around him. But the power of the blow put Syrus off balance too. He began to topple forward. Artemidorus forced himself back up. The solid *scutum* ground against the smaller *parmula*. And the full weight of Syrus bearing down on it.

Syrus aimed a half-hearted blow over the top of the spy's shield. The club smacked into the backplate of his armour. Knocked the wind out of him. He stabbed upward with his *gladius* in retaliation. Missed Syrus' thigh. But only by a hair. Syrus reared back. Artemidorus stood erect. Also stepped back. Fell into his fighting stance again. Shoulder throbbing. Shield arm feeling dead and useless. Chest burning for want of breath.

Then he immediately attacked. For the third time. There was no alternative in any case. Syrus was oozing confidence now. Tossing the club expertly from one hand to the other. Dancing backwards, sure-footed on the hard ground. Allowing his arms to go wider and wider as he juggled with the massive weapon. Showing off to his appreciative audience. Laughing as they cheered him on. Artemidorus leaped forward. And Syrus struck again. But the club was in his left hand now. And his target was not the spy but his *gladius*. The club smashed into the sword blade, crushing it against the edge of the shield. Tearing it out of Artemidorus' fist to fly across the garden and land at Cyanea's feet. She screamed.

The blow did more than disarm Artemidorus. It knocked him to the ground. Stunned. Agonised, half convinced that his left arm was broken and his shoulder shattered, he fought to get his shield back in place. While he used his bruised right hand to push himself back up into a crouch. The shield held just above him.

Syrus' club thundered down onto it again. With such force that the shield slammed against his forehead. Transmitting to his skull some of the awesome power behind the blow. Lightning seemed to flicker behind his eyes. He could almost feel his brains slopping about like *cena* porridge in a bowl. There was wetness on his upper lip. He tasted iron. His nose was bleeding. Cyanea called out again. A scream of warning. Syrus was closing in for the kill. Or for the crippling.

Artemidorus reached his right hand round and pulled Brutus' lethal dagger from its sheath. He raised the shield slightly, as though trying vainly to protect his head from the inevitable. Beneath the lower iron-bound edge, he could see the grass. And on it, Syrus' feet in their *caligae* sandals as the gladiator came closer still. Overconfident. Trying to be sure that this stroke would be the last. Or the beginning of the end at least.

Artemidorus threw himself forward. Shield raised a little higher. Its edge crashed into the metal greaves on Syrus' shins. Doing no damage at all. But the dagger stabbed down unstoppably through the straps of the gladiator's right sandal. Through the arch of his instep. Through the sole. Deep into the ground. Until its crosspiece hit the flesh of Syrus' foot. Artemidorus released his grip on it. Reared back, taking firm hold of his shield. Dived forward. Drove the iron rim of its lower edge down with all his might. Across the sandalled toes beneath.

It was an old soldier's trick. A ruse of last resort. Syrus would hardly have felt the dagger pin his foot to the ground. So he didn't yet know he had lost after all. But the shield smashed onto his toes so hard they burst like grapes in a wine press. And he felt that. His scream of agony was the loudest sound the spy had heard today. But the action wasn't over yet. No sooner had Artemidorus destroyed the club man's toes than he drove the shield upwards again with all his might. His target was Syrus' face – even though it was masked with iron. But as fate would have it, the gladiator was still swinging his club down. Caught in the impetus dictated by the heavy weapon. So the sharp upper edge of the shield hit his wrists. There was a *snap*. The breaking of a dry branch. The sound a slingshot makes when it hits at close quarters. It was Syrus' right wrist shattering. In three heartbeats, hardly more, the gladiator had gone from confident winner to crippled loser.

And even though the club smacked into his backplate once again before spinning free, Artemidorus continued to push himself upward. Driving the boss of his shield into his opponent's belly. Syrus tried to step away. Still howling with agony. But he only managed to fall flat on his back. With his right foot anchored to the ground and his toes hanging half off. Artemidorus came fully upright, until he was towering over his adversary. He looked at the three stunned henchmen. Who stared back. Eyes wide. Almost as shocked as Cyanea at the sudden, total reversal.

He stooped, pulled the dagger out of the ground. And out of Syrus' foot. Leaned down. Slit the lace holding the helmet in place. Caught the gryphon crest and pulled it free. Now it was he who was Nemesis. And inescapable. 'Your choice,' he said. '*Gladius*. Club. Or one of the daggers that murdered Caesar. How do you want to die?'

But Syrus' answer was the last thing the spy expected. 'Wait,' said the defeated gladiator. His voice ragged with agony and defeat. 'There's something you ought to know.'

*

Artemidorus' eyes narrowed. 'Nothing you can say will save you,' he warned.

'I don't mind dying,' gasped Syrus. 'But I don't want to leave you in ignorance when I do.'

'Very well, then. What is it?'

'Your man Telos. He never said a thing. Cestus beat him to death with those spiked gloves of his. But he never said a word.'

'NO!' screamed Cyanea. 'Don't…'

'*He* never sang like a lark. In spite of the note we pinned to him. It was *her*. She was our little *alaude*. We didn't even have to touch her and she told us everything. Spurinna's predictions. Telos' lists. The tribune's plans for Caesar and Antony. Everything she knew.'

'No!' she screamed again. Artemidorus looked up. Saw at a glance the guilt in her lovely eyes.

'The information she gave us made all the difference.' Syrus persisted brutally. 'It let Lord Basilus choose the one conspirator you didn't suspect. Decimus Albinus. Brief him with exactly what to say. Knowing what you would have already said. Knowing how to make the difference. When it all turned on a word or two.'

Artemidorus straightened. Understanding all too well how Cyanea had managed to hide her guilt. Even in his bed. In his arms. Until she and Puella started washing Caesar's corpse. Then every wound must have been like a little red-lipped mouth accusing her. And the wax effigy. Running with blood. No wonder she had fled from that. Overcome with guilt and horror.

'Thank you for giving me that information,' said Artemidorus. As he leaned down. And cut Syrus' throat with Brutus' dagger.

Even as the last of Syrus' blood was spraying out of his neck. And the last of the light was draining out of his eyes. The sound of footsteps running through the house behind him made Artemidorus turn. He expected to see Enobarbus, Quintus and men from the VIIth. But no. It was Ferrata, still holding a blazing piece of wood. And men from the VIth. Still on the hunt.

'Roasted any senators yet?' asked Artemidorus.

Ferrata didn't seem to hear him. He was transfixed by the sight of Cyanea.

Artemidorus repeated the question.

'No,' said Ferrata, his eyes still fixed on the naked woman. 'They'd barricaded themselves in. We couldn't get to them.'

'Well, you've got in here. This villa belongs to one of the ringleaders. If you want to set a fire that will burn out the *Libertores*, you couldn't choose a better place to start.'

'We might just do that,' said Ferrata. 'Who are these? Who's the corpse?'

'Right-hand man to the most dangerous of the murderers. I've just settled accounts with him.'

'And the woman?'

'You can have her if you want her,' said Artemidorus. 'Have all of them. The gladiators and the woman were all working for Brutus, Cassius, Albinus and Basilus. The woman especially. If anyone's to blame for Caesar's death, then she is.'

Wearily, he turned and began to walk back out of the villa.

She called his name. Her voice full of sorrow, longing and terror.

He did not look back.

A little way down the hill. Just before he reached Spurinna's barricaded door. He met Enobarbus, Quintus and the squad they were bringing to rescue him.

'Alone?' demanded Enobarbus. 'Where's Cyanea?'

Artemidorus looked back up the hill. To where Basilus' villa was already ablaze. Ferrata and his men already running on up the Esquiline, searching for more *Libertores* and their helpers to slaughter. More senators to roast.

'Dead,' he said. '*Canicula mortuus est*. The bitch is dead.'

EPILOGUE

What was left of the *contubernium* met in Antony's *tablinum* as the sun began to set on the day of Caesar's funeral. Enobarbus was unusually quiet. Weighed down by the knowledge of what Artemidorus had told him about Syrus' information and Cyanea's guilt. Information they agreed should be kept to themselves. For now at least. As it could change nothing.

Spurinna on the other hand was elated. Ebullient. He had brought Puella with him and could hardly keep his eyes off her. Antistius looked exhausted after everything he had done within the last few days. Almost as exhausted as Antony their general. Who was – just – too proud to sag against Fulvia's shoulder. A shoulder not quite as square as the old Legionary Quintus'. Though given the thickness of his armour – the best that money could buy – his was a great deal less inviting than hers.

'Lepidus is still out there with the Seventh trying to restore order,' said Antony.

'The fact that he's taking so long to do it proves just how well your plan worked,' observed Artemidorus.

'In the end,' said Fulvia.

'In the end,' agreed the spy.

'But now we have to plan for the future,' said Antony. 'For tomorrow, next week, next month and next year.'

'You and Lepidus can hold Rome for now,' said Enobarbus.

'While you wait to see what Caesar's adopted heir Octavian will do,' added Artemidorus.

'He's nineteen!' snapped Fulvia. 'Only just into his *toga virilis*. And sickly into the bargain. He will do what Antony tells him to do!'

'I have no doubt of it,' said Enobarbus placatingly.

Artemidorus wondered whether he was the only one to pick up a tone in the tribune's answer that made it seem that he had a lot of doubts about it.

'The gods have not yet given their opinion of the present situation or any guidance toward the future,' said Spurinna.

'I can tell you about the immediate future,' said Artemidorus. 'Any *Libertore* still in Rome will be gone by tomorrow. Brutus and Cassius were lucky to survive today. Basilus' villa is ashes by now, though he was not in it when it burned. They'll all be gone as soon as they get the chance. That goes for their supporters. I'm certain Cicero is on his way to his nearest country villa. And if Cinna isn't on his way out of the city, he's mad. After what happened to the poet. Just because he had a similar name.'

'Casca's been in contact,' said Antony. 'That's the elder brother Publius Casca. He says he didn't actually hurt Caesar at all. Though he struck first, he missed. Got Caesar's stylus through his arm instead. Technically not one of the murderers, therefore.'

'That's his defence is it?' asked Artemidorus with an exhausted chuckle. 'He'll have to get Cicero back to argue that for him!'

There was a short silence. Promus entered. '*Cena* will be served when you are ready,' he said.

'Let it wait!' growled Antony. And Promus disappeared.

'He'll still want it perfect, whenever he gets round to eating it,' Fulvia informed them all.

'We have business to finish here!' snapped Antony.

Fulvia was uncharacteristically quiescent.

'Whatever Lepidus and… and *Octavian*…' he shrugged dismissively as he named Caesar's heir, '… decide. There is still work for the rest of you to do. All of the *Libertores* are still alive. All of their supporters and apologists are still alive. That is a situation I wish to put right. However long it takes.

'But as you have seen already, a man in my position cannot always follow the shortest route. The surest way. It may be that I will have to come to accommodations. Agreements. With these people. They are not without friends. Influence.

341

Power. But no matter what I may have to do to keep the peace. Or to win the battle. Your mission will never vary.

'You are my dogs of war. My secret wolf pack. It is your duty. No matter what. To hunt down and kill every one of them. Take any other men you want. That Ferrata and his friends from the Sixth, for instance. But every *Libertore*. Every hanger-on. Every man who had a hand in Caesar's death or the aftermath.

'You will track them. You will find them. You will kill them.

'Every single one of them!'

ACKNOWLEDGEMENTS

With thanks to those who helped with research and advice, including (briefly but crucially) Tom Holland and Linsey Davis; Richard Foreman. Nick Slater, the Classics Department of The Judd School Tonbridge, especially Ben Gregson who tracked down Cicero's whereabouts on The Ides for me. And to the Tunbridge Wells Writers, especially Peppy Scott, Dave Smith, Justin Richardson, Michael Benenson and Glyn Harper.

Made in the USA
Monee, IL
18 May 2020

31407500R00203